MIDNIGHT IN NASHVILLE
SONGWRITERS SERIES BOOK TWO

ALI SPOONER

MIDNIGHT IN NASHVILLE
SONGWRITERS SERIES BOOK TWO

ALI SPOONER

Affinity
RAINBOW
PUBLICATIONS

Midnight in Nashville
Songwriters Series Book Two
© 2022 by Ali Spooner

Affinity E-Book Press NZ LTD.
Canterbury, New Zealand

Edition 1st

ISBN: 978-1-99-004999-6 (paperback)
ISBN: 978-1-99-004996-5 (EPUB)
ISBN: 978-1-99-004997-2 (PDF)
ISBN: 978-1-99-004998-9 (KINDLE)

Editor: Angela Koenig
Proof Editor: Alexis Smith
Cover Design: Irish Dragon Designs
Production Design: Affinity Publication Services

ACKNOWLEDGMENTS

I would like to thank my fans for following my stories and providing great feedback and encouragement. Writing wouldn't be so much fun without you. I appreciate the frequent reminders to work on the next book in your favorite series and promise to get back to them soon. Thanks to Affinity, Irish Dragon, for the cover art and the great team of editors, readers, and publishers who continue to help me grow as a writer.

TABLE OF CONTENTS

CHAPTER ONE

"That was much better Cedra, but let's run through it one more time," Bud Roberts called out from the production booth. Cedra Tyler and the rest of the Bentleys band had been in the studio for their first day of recording for four grueling hours. They had managed to nail down one track and were almost to the point of finishing another.

Cedra nodded to Bud. "What do I need to improve?"

"Take the range up just a bit when you hit the harmony this time. After this track, we will take a lunch break," Bud promised. "You all have done very well today."

"Thanks, Bud," Juliet replied as she took her seat beside Cedra. "I think we're all ready for a break," she said to Cedra with a wink.

"Bud told us this morning in orientation this wouldn't be easy, but I like the sound of the first track. I will nail this one so that we can have a break," Cedra replied. "Ready, boys?"

Stone, Keith, and Wayne all nodded.

"One, two, three, four," Cedra called out and began playing.

Bud's voice rang through the studio when she sang the last chord. "That's it. That's the one I was waiting on. Good job, guys."

"Hallelujah," Keith cried out. "My kidneys are about to explode."

Bud grinned. "Lunch is set up in the break room. I'll see you there."

Cedra placed her guitar in the stand and stretched her arms above her head. "This has been a great first day, don't you think?"

Juliet smiled. "My fingertips aren't bleeding yet, so I consider this a win. Seriously, it's not as difficult as I thought it would be. We've managed to cut two of our original four tracks already."

Stone smiled. "I can't wait to hear what they sound like; they sounded great from in here."

"Maybe Bud will play them for us after lunch," Wayne said. "Let's go. I'm starving."

Juliet looked at Wayne. "You're beginning to sound a lot like Keith."

Wayne smiled at Juliet. "Ma's bacon and French toast are long gone. It seems like days ago since we had breakfast."

†

Bud and Carrie were already seated around the table when they entered the break room. Cedra hadn't seen their agent in the studio.

"I didn't know you were here. Good afternoon, by the way."

"Carrie has been here for the last two hours," Bud replied. "I wouldn't let her into the production booth, so she's been watching from here." Bud picked up a remote and turned on a large monitor.

"You all sounded great," Carrie said.

"They have done well so far today. Are you all up for a few more hours? I want to shoot for one more track," Bud told them.

"We are good until seven tonight," Keith replied as he returned from the restroom.

"I don't think it will take that long, but that's good to know. How about we take a run at 'Backwoods Boogie' after everyone gets refueled?" Bud asked.

"Oh, heck yeah. That song always gets us reenergized," Wayne answered.

Cedra placed a turkey sandwich on her plate and picked up a bag of chips. She walked to the table and sat beside Carrie. "Are you eating?"

"I've been nibbling for the last half hour." Carrie smiled.

"Do you want water or something else?" Juliet asked Cedra from the drink area.

"Some water would be great. Thanks, Juliet," Cedra answered.

When everyone was settled around the table, Bud spoke. "I am very impressed by your work ethic today. I've worked you pretty hard, and there hasn't been one complaint from any of you."

"We are all excited to be here, and we appreciate everything you are doing for us," Juliet said.

Bud smiled at her. "Eat up then, and I want to share the first two tracks with you. We have them nailed down, but I want you all to agree that the sound is what we are looking for."

Carrie stood and walked over to a cabinet and took out seven pairs of headphones, placing one in front of each of them. "These will block out any external noise and give you the pure sound of what we recorded," Bud explained.

"Eat up, guys, I can't wait to hear this," Cedra replied.

All heads turned to Keith. "I'm eating as fast as I can without choking," Keith mumbled between bites.

"Be thankful there are no cookies or sweets, or we could be here for a while," Cedra informed Bud.

"Those will be available after the next track," Bud assured them. "We will break again around four and see how everyone feels. I don't want to wear you out on day one, but damn, you all are doing great."

"We all agreed to work as long as the sound was good, or you tell us it's time to quit," Juliet told him.

Bud looked at Carrie. "I already love working with this group."

"I told you so." Carrie smiled at Bud. "They are hard workers and dedicated to being successful."

Bud nodded his head and looked around at the smiling faces. "I have an excellent feeling about you all. I believe you're going to do well in Nashville."

"Thanks for all your hard work, Bud," Cedra replied.

"You all are making it easy for me. All I have to do is sit back and listen. Are you ready to hear what we've created so far?"

"Heck yeah," Keith said.

Bud pushed a button on the remote, and their first track started playing. He paused after the song ended and smiled at Juliet and Cedra. "What do you think?"

Cedra was the first to answer. "I am shocked by how great it sounds."

Juliet nodded. "I knew it was good, but this is amazing. Every note sounds so pure."

Bud chuckled. "Big Machine has spared no expense in purchasing the best equipment possible. Are you ready for track two?"

"Bring it on," Stone replied with excitement.

The duet with Cedra and Stone was the best version of the song. Their voices blended perfectly, and Cedra smiled as she saw tears pooling in Juliet's eyes.

"I believe that was just the sound it needed," Cedra told Bud.

Bud nodded to Cedra. "I'll admit to a dilemma. Carrie asked me to recommend a song for your first release, and it will be hard to decide between that one and 'Six Strings' and we haven't even recorded it yet."

"All he's heard so far is the recording I made on my iPhone Saturday night," Carrie replied. "Even when he heard that version, Bud told me, 'We have to record that song.'"

"Yes, I did. We could work on that next if you want or wait until you are fresh tomorrow," Bud suggested.

"Let's stick with 'Backwoods' for now, and if that goes smoothly, maybe we can take a run at 'Six Strings' today while still energized," Juliet suggested.

"That works for me. I have no problem cutting four tracks today as long as you all are feeling good," Bud replied.

"We have waited all our lives for this opportunity," Juliet answered. "We're all good."

"I love it," Bud declared with a chuckle. He looked at Carrie. "Thank you for bringing them to me."

Carrie stood and began picking up the headphones. "I knew you wouldn't be disappointed."

Mark came rushing into the breakroom. "Hello," he spoke to everyone. "I just finished listening to the first two tracks. Damn, they sound good."

"We have worked hard this morning, and we hope to have one to two more done today," Bud told him.

"Would you mind if I stayed to watch for a bit?" Mark asked.

"You can join Carrie in here," Bud replied. "You're too much of a distraction in my sound booth," Bud added with a soft laugh. "I will turn the video on so you can watch."

"That works for me. You all do sound great," Mark told them.

"We have been pleased so far," Juliet remarked.

"I'm going to head back to the booth, but take your time and come back to the studio when you're ready," Bud told them and left the room.

"So, what do you think about Bud?" Mark asked.

"He's a genius and so much fun to work with," Cedra replied.

Keith held up his hands. "No bloody fingertips yet."

"He will work you hard as long as he sees effort in you," Mark told them. "I believe he's enjoying working with you all. I haven't seen him smile like that in ages."

"We hope to keep him smiling then," Cedra told him. "I need to hit the ladies' room, and I'll be ready if y'all are."

"That's a good idea," Juliet agreed, and stood to leave the room with Cedra.

†

Cedra locked the door behind them and took Juliet in her arms for a kiss. "I've been wanting to do that for hours."

"I have, too," Juliet admitted. "How do you think things are going so far?"

7

"Better than I thought possible. I like the way we sounded on those two cuts. Bud, Mark, and Carrie seem pleased as well."

"Yeah, they do. I hope we can do two more today. I think we've performed 'Backwoods' enough that we've got it down pat," Juliet said.

"I think so, too. Let's hurry and get back out there," Cedra suggested. "One last kiss, though, to hold me until later."

Juliet kissed Cedra, and after they used the facilities, they returned to the studio.

†

It took two tries to get the sound Bud wanted for "Backwoods." It was hard to tell who was more excited to take a run at "Six Strings." "Do you need a break?" he asked from the sound booth.

"No, we're good to go," Juliet answered.

"I'm ready when you are," Bud said.

"Let's do this," Cedra called out, and they began playing. Cedra looked into the booth halfway through the song to find Bud smiling and his head bobbing along with the music.

When the song ended, Bud's voice came over the speaker. "That was a good first run, but let's do another. A bit heavier on the banjo and bass this time, boys."

Wayne and Keith nodded. "Heck yeah," Keith replied.

"Just don't go crazy with it," Juliet teased.

"I'm ready when you are," Bud replied.

Juliet looked at Cedra and nodded. "One, two, three, four," Cedra called out, and began playing.

"Meet me in the break room in five," Bud said. "Something's missing, and I want to let you hear it for yourself."

"Let's hit the ladies' room," Juliet told Cedra.

Juliet turned to Cedra. "What do you think it is that's missing?"

Cedra's face scrunched up in thought. "The only thing we've done differently is the bass guitar. Why don't we ditch it for this one and go back to Stone's fiddle?"

"That's what I thought, too. The bass isn't suitable for this song," Juliet answered. "Let's see what the boys come up with."

Keith couldn't resist a cookie as he entered the room. He grabbed two and took a seat at the table.

"You are such a sweet hound," Cedra teased.

Bud joined them and played "Backwoods" first. "I think we're good on this one. That's a fun song, by the way. Something is not clicking on 'Six Strings,' but I can't put my finger on it." Bud frowned.

"We have an idea but want to hear the recording and see what the boys come up with," Cedra told them.

They listened to the track, and Keith was the first to answer. "As much as I loved playing it, the bass just doesn't fit that song."

Juliet nodded with a smile. "That was our conclusion too. The bass was the only thing we did differently. Let's drop it and go back to Stone's fiddle."

"Yes, that's precisely what it needs," Bud answered. "I was hoping you would come up with the same solution."

"We passed our test then?" Cedra teased Bud.

Bud nodded. "Yes, ma'am, you did. I need to make sure that I stay on the same page with the artists when suggesting changes. No one knows your sound better than you."

"Can we take another run or two at it today?" Juliet asked.

"I'm certainly up for it if y'all are," Bud answered.

"Let's do this," Juliet replied.

They huddled up in the studio before they began playing. "I know we've all worked hard today, but let's finish the day with our best," Cedra replied. "I want there to be no doubt in Bud's mind that 'Six Strings' is our debut single."

The band picked up their instruments, and when Bud nodded, they began to play.

Cedra closed her eyes for a second and envisioned being on Ma's porch. Her lead-off stanza was terrific, and she opened her eyes to watch each of her band mates perform their parts. The harmony in the chorus was perfect, and when they stopped playing, they all looked at the sound booth for Bud's reaction.

"That is it!" Bud cried out with excitement. "Come listen."

Carrie and Mark were back in the break room when they entered. "That was the best yet," Mark said.

Bud walked into the room and picked up the remote. He looked at Mark and Carrie. "We have our debut single." He pushed the button, and they all listened carefully.

Juliet smiled broadly. "That's the best we've ever done on that song."

"I agree," Cedra replied.

"How long will it take to burn fifty copies?" Mark asked.

"I'll have one of the assistants do them tomorrow," Bud replied.

"We will start shooting them out to radio stations on Monday, then," Mark informed them. "That's too good to wait for the entire album."

"Hell yes." Cedra high-fived Juliet.

"You all have had a heck of a great day," Bud praised. "Why don't we call it done? Are we on for tomorrow?"

"Same time, same place," Cedra answered.

"We should be able to finish two or three more tracks tomorrow. My goal is to get halfway through," Bud replied. "I think you're going to take off like a rocket, and I don't want fans to have to wait long for the album."

"What studio time is available to us next week?" Juliet asked.

"Any time you are ready," Mark said.

"We'll compare work schedules tonight and let you know tomorrow," Cedra replied. "Two or three more sessions to complete the album?" she asked Bud.

"Definitely by three."

Carrie looked at Juliet. "I know you've had photo shoots and have begun working on the cover art. Will you bring in your files tomorrow, and we can have our artist review and take over from there?"

"Consider it done," Juliet answered. "Will you need full lyrics for each of the tracks?"

"Yes, as well as the writer's name."

"That should be easy enough."

"Oh, before I forget." Mark pulled an envelope out of his briefcase. "Your advances and apparel allowance. We split everything five ways on the apparel. Have fun shopping. Go easy on the Wrangler goods. I think you will receive plenty of their products when you go on your first tour."

"Thank you so much." Juliet looked at her friends. "Let's load up and head home."

"Great first day, guys. I'll see you tomorrow," Bud called to them.

"Goodnight," Cedra answered and followed the rest back to the studio.

†

"I am so excited about today." Cedra entwined her fingers with Juliet's on the ride home. "We had an incredibly productive day."

"Yeah, we did. I was amazed we got four tracks cut. Bud was easier to work for than I expected. He's a really nice guy."

"I was expecting someone much more aggressive, but he treated us with respect and allowed us input. I've heard horror stories about some producers having *carte blanche* and taking all the controls away from the artists," Cedra replied. "I was happy to find he was the complete opposite."

"That was a huge relief, and I think he genuinely enjoyed working with us today."

"What's not to love about working with us? We gave it everything we could, and I think he appreciated our effort."

Juliet lifted Cedra's hand to her lips. "That sounded just like something I would say." She kissed her hand.

"I think you're a good influence on me," Cedra replied.

Juliet chuckled. "I hate to sound like Keith, but I hope Ma has something cooked for dinner. I'm hungry."

"You know she'll have a spread ready for us," Cedra replied. "My sandwich is long gone, too."

"After dinner, do you want to help me collect the lyrics for the album cover?" Juliet asked. "I've got a few of them typed up already. I don't have Stone's, though."

"We can ask him to type up his three tracks and email them to you while we work on the rest," Cedra suggested.

"That sounds like a plan." Juliet turned into the drive.

The boys had already arrived and were piling out of Keith's truck. They waited for Cedra and Juliet on the porch before entering the house.

"I guess this would be a good time to pass out checks."

"I agree. I think everyone is anxious to have the first checks in their hands. It's so exciting," Cedra said.

Juliet parked and pulled the envelope out and handed it to Cedra. "Would you do the honors?"

"I'd love to," Cedra replied. "How about a payday?" she asked as they stepped onto the porch.

"Hell yeah," Wayne yelled.

Cedra began sorting through the checks and handed each of them an advance check and apparel allowance check. "Thanks." Keith kissed her cheek when she offered him the pair.

"The first of many, I hope." Cedra left hers in the envelope.

"Amen," Juliet replied. "You want me to take yours upstairs as I go?"

"Yes, please. I need to take a picture to send to Dad."

"That's a great idea," Stone agreed. "I'll be right back."

"Don't be too long," Ma called from the front door. "Dinner will be on the table in ten minutes."

"Yes, Ma," Stone replied and jogged over to his truck.

"I hope y'all had a great first day in the studio," Ma said as they filed into the house.

"We did, Ma. We got four tracks cut," Wayne answered. "We got our first checks, too." He showed her the checks.

"That's a fine day all around," Ma agreed with a proud smile.

"The best part is that we've recorded and decided on 'Six Strings' to be our debut single. Bud is burning the copies tomorrow. Mark and Carrie will begin sending them out Monday. We could be on the radio soon, Ma," Juliet reported.

"I can't wait to hear it," Ma said.

"We were blown away with the sound," Cedra replied. "The quality of the studio equipment made a huge difference."

"Is that your fried chicken I smell?" Wayne asked.

"Yes, it is," Ma responded.

"That was my first meal in my new home," Cedra replied. "It's still one of my favorites."

"We also have a big bowl of fried okra, rice, and chicken gravy, green beans, corn, and biscuits," Ma informed them.

"That sounds perfect, Ma. Thank you for another great meal and cooking some of our favorites." Cedra leaned down and kissed Ma's cheek. "You are so good to us."

"You all make it easy on me. I cook it, and you eat it with never a complaint," Ma answered.

"There's never anything to complain about," Juliet replied as she returned to the kitchen. "What can we do to help?"

"You can pour drinks and help me get dishes set on the table," Ma replied.

"No problem." Juliet walked to the counter and began filling glasses with tea. "Oh, dear Lord, pecan pie for dessert? I have died and gone to heaven."

Ma's chuckles filled the kitchen. "You are all so incredibly good for my ego."

Stone rushed in just as everyone was taking their seats. "Oh, my goodness. This meal looks and smells terrific."

"Have a seat and let's get to eating," Ma said. "I think we need to bless the good lord for this meal and the success of the Bentleys," Ma stated. She reached for Keith's and Cedra's hands and then blessed the meal for them.

"Thank you, for everything, Ma. We wouldn't be here without you," Juliet told her as she speared a piece of chicken when Wayne passed it around the table.

Ma shook her head. "I wouldn't be here, and as proud as I am if it weren't for the five of you. I could never have selected a better family."

"This is so delicious, Ma," Cedra praised.

"I'm glad you are enjoying it," Ma replied. "What's the next step for y'all?"

Juliet passed the bowl of okra back to Cedra with a smile. "To finish the other eight tracks for the album and finalize the cover art. Cedra, Stone, and I need to copy the song lyrics tonight. Once Carrie and Mark begin distributing the debut track, we hope to get some airtime and maybe an interview or two."

"I wonder how they would feel if we continued to play live at Wild Bill's or the Iron Horse?" Keith asked.

"That would be a question for Carrie tomorrow," Juliet answered. "I think it could go either way, but they may want us to limit free performances until they can start gigging us."

"This is the first time since I moved out of my parent's home that I didn't have to worry about money," Wayne said.

"Just don't go crazy with it. It can go away just as fast as we make it," Juliet replied. "I'll feel more confident once we have regular checks rolling in or consistent gigs."

"I'm sending the majority of mine home." Stone smiled. "Sarah will spend it more wisely than me." He grinned.

"I finally have enough to open a checking account." Keith laughed.

"I think we will all enjoy going to the bank next week," Cedra answered. "Okra, anyone?" Cedra held up the bowl.

"Go for it, sweetie," Ma told Cedra.

"I don't mind if I do," Cedra replied and scraped the last of the fried delicacy onto her plate. "So damned good."

"Is there anything you need around here, Ma?" Wayne asked. "A bigger freezer or anything?"

"If I did, I wouldn't use your hard-earned money, but thank you for the offering. You deserve to spend that on you or your family," Ma replied.

"I've got you now, Ma," Wayne teased. "You have told us many times you are claiming us as family, so you are considered family. A chest freezer or upright?"

"An upright we could fill with cookies and milk, so we'd never run out," Keith suggested.

"They do have a point. We could fill it with vegetables from the Farmers Market for the winter," Juliet replied.

"I don't have room for it," Ma pointed out.

"Nonsense, it will fit right by the backdoor," Wayne said. "You just need to tell us if you want white or white," he added with a grin. "I don't think they come in any other color."

"You don't have to do anything," Ma answered.

"Please just let us have this one little win?" Keith pleaded. "Wayne and I will split it."

"Cedra and I will take you to the Farmers Market to buy the vegetables you want to freeze," Juliet replied.

"I guess that leaves me gallons of milk and a couple of cases of cookie dough," Stone joined in on the fun.

"I guess it's white then, boys," Ma replied.

"Yes!" Keith answered. "We can get it Monday and get it cooling down."

"That reminds me. What is everyone's work schedule next week? We need to reserve more time in the studio," Juliet reminded them.

"I'm off Tuesday and Wednesday," Cedra replied.

"Wednesday and Thursday for me," Stone answered.

"When do you guys work Wednesday?" Juliet asked.

"I'm off," Keith said.

"I go in at eight," Wayne answered.

"Do we want to try for as many hours on Wednesday as we can? If we have another good day tomorrow, maybe one more full day will be enough," Juliet stated.

"If not, we can do some late afternoons when Cedra and Stone get off work," Keith suggested.

"That works for me," Cedra replied.

18

Juliet turned to Stone. "Can you type up the lyrics for the three songs of yours we are using and email them to me tonight? Cedra and I will do the rest."

"Sure, that won't take long at all," Stone agreed.

Keith smiled at Ma. "I'll clear the table and load the dishes if you start serving pie."

"We can all pitch in, Ma. We won't let Keith destroy the dishes," Cedra teased. "You can supervise him putting away the leftovers."

Wayne chuckled. "That won't take long at all. There's not much left to store."

"You can start a pot of coffee," Ma told Wayne.

"What can I do, Ma?" Stone asked.

"You can empty the garbage can and put in a new liner."

"Easy enough," Stone answered. "I'll wait on the dishes to be emptied first."

"What do you all want for breakfast?" Ma asked. "I assume you're going in at nine again?"

"How about biscuits and gravy? Your gravy was off the chain tonight, Ma," Wayne praised.

"I'll make a fresh batch of biscuits in the morning if that's good for everyone," Ma stated.

"I'd never turn your cooking down, Ma," Stone responded.

"That's easy enough then," Ma said. "Keith, will you bring me a pie, a knife, forks, and some fine china?"

"You bet I will, Ma," Keith answered and went to work.

Wayne worked on the coffee pot while Stone carried plates to the kitchen counter for Cedra and Juliet. "I knew my serving skills would come in handy," Stone teased as he balanced a large stack of dishes.

†

Juliet sat on the bed with her laptop as Cedra sat at her desk. "I'll start from the bottom and work up if you want to start with the first tracks," Juliet offered.

"This shouldn't take us long at all," Cedra replied. "Especially with three of us working together."

"Did you take a picture of your checks to send to your dad?" Juliet asked.

"Thank you for reminding me," Cedra replied. She quickly snapped a photo and sent it to her dad. "I bet my phone will ring within five minutes."

"Probably less," Juliet replied. "I wish my family was as supportive as your dad."

Cedra's head turned to look at Juliet. She was about to comment when her phone rang. "Hey, Dad," she answered and put the phone on speaker.

"Hey, Baby Girl. That's impressive money for day one." He chuckled. "Is Juliet with you?"

"Yes, she is."

"Hey, Dad," Juliet called out from the bed.

"Hey, Juliet. So, which one of you can I borrow from?" Hank teased.

"Either one or both," Juliet replied. "What do you need?"

Hank chuckled. "Nothing, sweetie, I am just teasing. You all should be very proud. I know I am. What's next?"

"Another day in the studio tomorrow and then one to two more next week to hopefully finish the tracks for the album. Bud, our producer, has already selected 'Six Strings' as our debut single. Mark and Carrie will begin distributing them to the media Monday."

"Wow. Things are moving quickly," Hank said.

"Yeah, Daddy, they are."

"I'd better start keeping the radio on twenty-four seven then," he teased.

"If we get a heads up, I'll let you know," Cedra promised.

"I'm so proud of y'all. I know your mother has to be smiling," he told her.

Cedra could hear the heartache in his voice. "I know she is. I feel her with me all the time," Cedra told him. "Thank you for encouraging me to follow my dreams."

"This is only the beginning, Baby Girl. There is so much coming your way. I can feel it in my bones."

"I sure hope so, Daddy. I can't wait for you to come up in a few weeks. We will have a jam session for you when you're here."

"I'm looking forward to that. I bet I will hear you on the radio before that."

"I pray you're right."

"I won't keep you tonight. I know you've got stuff to prepare for tomorrow. I wanted y'all to know how proud I am for you."

"Thanks, Daddy. I'll call you soon. Hopefully, with more good news. Goodnight."

"Goodnight, ladies. Love you both."

"Love you too, Dad," Cedra and Juliet answered.

Cedra turned to look at Juliet and saw tears in her eyes. "What's wrong, baby?"

"I wish my dad would talk to me like that," Juliet answered.

"You never talk much about them. Do you talk to your family often?" Cedra asked.

"No, but it's my fault. The last time I talked to Dad, he was so negative, I went off on him. That was months ago."

"Maybe it's time to reach out to him again?" Cedra suggested.

"Not until we have a song on the radio. I don't want to jinx anything." She wiped a tear from her eyes.

"I don't think you can jinx us, but I will support your decision. Does your dad know anything about the band?"

"Nope, nothing at all."

"Would you mind if I make a suggestion?" Cedra asked.

"Not at all, sweetie."

"Why don't you get a copy of the single tomorrow and send it to him? I was thinking of asking for a copy for Dad and Ma."

Juliet smiled. "That's a good idea. Thank you."

"I know Daddy has enough love for two, but I believe family is important, and you should try to keep a relationship with them," Cedra replied.

"I'll send them a CD, and we'll see where it goes from there," Juliet promised.

Cedra leaned over and kissed her. "I love you."

Juliet smiled. "I know you do, and if your love is all I have, it's enough to carry me through."

"More people than me love you," Cedra replied. "Just keep me at the top of your list."

"Always," Juliet said. Her phone pinged with an email from Stone. "Stone's done with his project. I guess we'd better get busy."

"Yes, boss." Cedra smiled at turned back to her laptop. She emailed the first four tracks to Juliet, who saved them on her jump drive an hour later.

"I'm almost done, too. Do you want to go back down for another slice of pie?" Juliet asked.

"That does sound good. Coffee? I can go get a pot started while you finish," Cedra suggested.

Juliet nodded. "That works for me. I'll see you in a few."

Cedra leaned down to kiss her. "Don't be too long."

"I won't. Hopefully, the boys left some pie." Juliet smiled.

"Good point. If not, I'll bake us some cookies."

"That works, too," Juliet replied.

†

Cedra walked downstairs and the lights were on in the kitchen. Ma and the boys were sitting around the table. "Is there any pie left?" she asked Keith.

"Why are you asking me?" Keith smiled.

"Because you are the biggest sweet tooth in the house," Cedra said as she looked at the coffee pot. "Will you drink some coffee, Ma?"

"I could do another cup," Ma replied. "The pie is in the fridge. Do you want me to heat some for you?"

"I'll get it, Ma. Juliet is coming down as soon as she finishes the last of the lyrics."

"I got the coffee," Wayne offered.

"What have y'all been up to?" Cedra asked.

"Just dreaming," Keith answered. "We've been planning our first tour."

"Where are we going?" Cedra asked.

"We thought it would be cool to play the college towns in the south. Most of the larger schools have country venues in town that would help grow our younger fan base," Keith explained.

"That's not a bad idea. Is this something that is done regularly with new artists?" Cedra asked.

"I think it's a possibility until the music festivals start in the spring," Wayne answered as he filled the coffee pot.

"Maybe we should pick Carrie's brain about it tomorrow to see what her plans are for us," Cedra replied. She cut two pieces of pie and placed them in the microwave.

Juliet arrived just as Cedra removed the pie. "That was good timing," she joked as she entered the kitchen.

"Coffee will be up in a minute," Wayne replied.

"The boys have been planning our first tour of college towns," Cedra told her as she brought the pie to the table.

"Not a bad idea," Juliet agreed as she picked up her fork. "Towns like Athens, Gainesville, Knoxville, Baton Rouge, and Lexington have some awesome country venues." She cut a bite of pie. "We could travel on Fridays, do a show Friday night, Saturday, and be home on Sunday. You may have to drop down to working four days a week."

"I don't think that would be a problem for any of us," Keith answered. "The winter months can be slow at the theater."

"I could bartend part time too," Wayne replied.

"Lisa Marie asked if I would consider some part-time work at the café," Ma said. "Maybe I could fill in on the days when y'all are on the road."

"That would be good. You're an early riser, and you wouldn't have us to look after," Juliet teased.

"Working at the café would be cake compared to tending to us." Keith chuckled.

"You all aren't bad," Ma replied. "It's quite a comfort having you around."

Cedra finished her pie and sipped on her coffee. "I know Lisa Marie would benefit from your help. You wouldn't have to worry about cooking but one meal. She'll feed you well for breakfast and lunch."

"This is sounding better by the minute." Ma smiled at Cedra. "I think I could handle two or three days a week."

"I'm sure you could, Ma," Cedra replied. "It would get you out more too."

"That's an added benefit I hadn't considered."

"Thanks for the pie. I reckon we all need to get some rest. Tomorrow will be another long day," Cedra stated.

"I hope it's as productive as this one was," Wayne said. "Goodnight, ladies."

"Goodnight, boys," Ma said.

"Do you two have any recommendations for dinner tomorrow night?" Ma asked Cedra and Juliet.

"How about a taco night? We haven't done one of those in ages," Juliet replied.

"With an ice cream sundae selection for dessert?" Ma asked.

"That works for me," Cedra agreed. "Do we need to pick up anything from the store?"

"Naw, I'll go shopping after y'all head to the studio tomorrow," Ma replied. "It'll give me something to do."

"Why don't you invite Patsy over, too, for some company and dinner? I'll drive her home," Juliet replied.

"That's not a bad idea. Maybe we can sip on a margarita while we cook." Ma chuckled.

"There ya go. I can't do the liquor, but I'll have a beer with you when we get home," Juliet promised.

"Have a great night and get some sleep. I'll see you for breakfast."

"You too, Ma. Goodnight." Juliet reached for Cedra's hand, and they climbed the stairs.

†

Cedra and Juliet stretched out on the bed as reflections from a candle flame danced on the ceiling. "Today was a great day," Cedra replied.

"Yes, it was. I wasn't expecting it to be so productive," Juliet admitted.

Cedra turned toward Juliet. "Will you do something with me Monday when we get home from work?"

"Sure. What do you want to do?"

"I want to go shopping for some boots. I've never had a nice pair before. I know you have a collection, so you could guide me on what to buy."

"I love going boot shopping. If I didn't have six pairs already, I'd buy more," Juliet answered. "I know just the spot to take you."

"Thanks," Cedra replied and snuggled into Juliet.

"We sounded good today, didn't we?" Juliet asked.

Cedra frowned. "I think everyone was surprised. It won't be disappointing to fans if we don't sound so perfect when we perform live, will it?"

"No, not at all. We sound good when we go live. Fans realize the acoustics and studio environment enhance the quality."

"When we start performing gigs, will we still do some cover songs?"

Juliet's smile grew. "We will mix some in, but I think we will need to play mostly songs from *Six Strings*. Maybe some others as we develop them to prepare fans for our next album."

Cedra laughed softly. "We haven't finished cutting our first album yet, and you are already planning a second."

"Of course, I am. You have so many songs already written we could be busy for months in the studio, even after you offer some to other artists."

"I love that you have that much confidence in me," Cedra replied.

"You have such a beautiful talent for writing tremendous lyrics," Juliet replied. "I fully believe once Carrie and Mark get their hands on the lyrics in your songbooks, they will go wild promoting them."

"I hope the words never leave me," Cedra said.

"Just write from your heart and the music you want to hear created and don't try to conform to a template. Too many artists fail to write new tunes, and their music has the same sound with different words. That's so bland and lacks imagination."

"I have to agree with you there. Even if the first song was successful, it could be ruined by diluting it with different lyrics."

"Exactly my point. You take a winning song and don't create beyond that. I don't want us to ever do that. With the skills you and Stone have, I don't think we are in fear of running out of good material anytime soon."

Cedra rolled over and blew out the candle. "We won't. If anything, my writing has dramatically increased since we met. Lyrics just seem to pour from my head onto paper."

"It must be love," Juliet replied and kissed Cedra.

"It's definitely love. Goodnight, sweetie."

"Goodnight, my songwriting wonder."

Cedra laughed and snuggled into Juliet's warmth.

CHAPTER TWO

"Great as ever, Ma," Juliet said as she kissed her cheek and headed upstairs to brush her teeth.

"Do you mind if I take a mug of coffee to go?" Cedra asked. "It will empty the pot."

"Go ahead. I think I've had enough already," Ma replied. "Go brush up, and I'll fix it for you."

"Thanks, Ma." Cedra followed Juliet upstairs and nearly got run over by Wayne and Keith rushing down. "Slow your roll before you kill someone," Cedra teased.

"Sorry, Cedra. We're just a wee bit excited," Wayne called out as they passed.

"Go ahead and load our instruments then, and we'll meet you at the studio."

"On it," Keith answered as they rushed out the door.

"What's all the commotion?" Juliet asked as she stepped outside their bedroom door.

"Wayne and Keith are a bit excited about today and went rushing out of here with their hair on fire," Cedra teased. "Let me brush my teeth, and I'll be right down."

"See you in a few then," Juliet replied and kissed her. "You smell good."

"Thanks, baby. I'll be right there. You're driving this morning, right?"

"Yes, I am. Why?"

"Ma is fixing me a travel mug of coffee to go." Cedra smiled. "You can drive while I enjoy."

"That's cool. Love you."

"Love you, too."

Cedra walked into the bathroom and picked up her toothbrush. When she looked into the mirror, she smiled. Juliet had left a post-it-note on the surface with a heart and a message that read, 'Juliet loves Cedra.'

Cedra brushed her teeth and met Juliet in the kitchen. "Thanks for the sweet note."

"You're mighty welcome." Juliet handed her the mug of coffee. "Are you ready to roll?"

"Yes, I am. We'll see you tonight, Ma. Have a good day."

"You, too. I hope it's another productive one."

"Me, too," Cedra called back to her.

†

They were halfway to the studio listening to the radio when Cedra cried out. "Listen to that."

"What? It's Blake's 'Ol' Red.' We've heard it a million times."

"The harmonica in it," Cedra replied. "We could cover this, and you could play your harmonica."

"Wayne would love that. He could sing this song in his sleep," Juliet teased.

"There are so many good songs we could cover to get an audience involved," Cedra replied.

"We should begin a list, starting with that one," Juliet told her. "Six to ten should be plenty. We already have several we cover pretty well."

"That should be easy. Maybe we should start the list and let the boys come up with the rest," Cedra suggested. She flipped open her songbook and started making a list.

Juliet pulled into the lot at the studio, and Cedra snapped her book shut. "How many did you get?"

"Four, counting 'Ol' Red,' Sam Hunt's 'House Party,' 'Country Girl Shake it for Me,' by Luke Bryan, and 'Body Like a Backroad,' also by Sam Hunt."

"Should I be worried about Sam Hunt?" Juliet asked.

"He's one heck of a songwriter as well as performer," Cedra commented. "I like Thomas Rhett, too."

"Why not 'Craving You,' then? I think you and Stone could do that well."

"Good one," Cedra agreed and opened the book to add it. "You know, if we were to tour college towns, we might need to tailor our cover songs to match the crowds."

"That's a good point. What music crowds like in Athens may not be the same in Baton Rouge," Juliet agreed. "Are you ready to make some music?"

"Yes, love, I am. After a stop to the bathroom to lose some coffee," Cedra added with a laugh.

Juliet smiled. "I'll meet you in the studio."

†

Juliet walked into the studio, where the guys set up the instruments. Keith looked up at her and frowned. "Where's Cedra?"

"What? She didn't ride with you?" Juliet replied.

"Well, no, she didn't. Did you leave her at home?"

"No, silly, she's in the bathroom." Juliet started laughing.

"That was so not right."

"Do you honestly believe she would leave her, bro? They are practically joined at the hip," Wayne teased. He punched Keith in the arm playfully.

They were still laughing when Cedra entered. "What? Do I have a trail of toilet paper or something?" she asked.

"Sorry, Cedra, Juliet had Keith thinking we left you at home when she came in without you," Wayne shared.

"That was mean," she scolded Juliet.

"I know, but he set himself up so well, I just couldn't resist." Juliet looked at Keith. "I'm sorry, man." Juliet burst into giggles again.

"Let me know when you kids are ready to get to work," Cedra replied.

"You took the words right out of my mouth," Bud announced from the booth.

Keith and Juliet snapped to attention at the sound of Bud's voice. "Sorry, Bud," Juliet apologized.

"No need to be sorry. You got Keith good, but it's time to get serious," Bud replied. "If we're going to beat the Ten-Year-Town curse, we need to get busy."

"Ten-year town?" Cedra asked.

"It takes the majority of new talent ten years to be successful in Nashville," Bud explained. "That's why so many good artists throw in the towel so soon. We hope to fast-track you guys, but you need to recognize that even then, it could take several years for you to reach the top. Nothing but heartache happens overnight in this town."

"Got it. Thanks for explaining that, Bud."

Bud smiled and nodded to her from the booth. "Let's get to it then."

It took two runs at her mother's song for Cedra to get it right. "That's beautiful," Bud called from the booth. "Great job. Do y'all need a break?"

None of them did, so they decided to keep working. "Let's try for one more track," Bud suggested.

The next song was primarily Juliet on vocals, and Cedra thought she had nailed it well after the second run.

"Are you good for one more run at it, Juliet? A little bit slower on the second verse this time," Bud directed.

"Got it," Juliet answered.

Cedra found herself watching Juliet as she played, and when Juliet opened her eyes, she smiled at Cedra as she sang the song. They maintained contact through the rest of the song.

"That's the one. Meet me in the break room in five," Bud said.

Carrie was exiting the restroom as Juliet and Cedra entered. "Great job, ladies." She walked to the sink to wash her hands and left.

"Ah, that's a relief," Cedra replied.

Juliet listened for the flush to hide her laughter. She flushed and met Cedra at the sink. "No more travel mug for you," Juliet teased Cedra. She leaned over to kiss her as she reached for a paper towel.

"It normally doesn't run through me so quickly," Cedra answered. "I'd guess it was high octane stuff the way the guys were buzzing through the house this morning."

"No more grocery shopping for them then," Juliet joked.

"Let's go listen to our work this morning," Cedra suggested.

"Right behind you. Uh-hmm, love the way you walk," Juliet teased.

"Come on, silly woman." Cedra chuckled.

†

"Great work, guys," Bud said. "Ladies, you were exceptional this morning. Let's take a listen."

After listening to both tracks, Carrie nodded. "Very nice. You're halfway to an album."

"We were having a debate at home about what's next once we finish. Someone mentioned a college town tour. Is that something that may be possible for us?" Juliet asked.

"That's always a possibility, but we will have to see what Mark thinks about the idea. We may be too late in the year to schedule those venues," Carrie answered. "Let's see how the first single is received in the media before we make those plans. If it goes well, getting you booked will be easy. It wouldn't hurt to start putting some sets together regardless of the venue. It can't hurt to be prepared."

"What mixture of cover songs should we plan on?" Cedra asked.

"Depending on the length of the sets, you are given anywhere from three to five. You need to focus on your songs as much as possible," Carrie answered.

Juliet placed a plate with a sandwich and fruit in front of Cedra with a water bottle.

"Thanks, Juliet."

"Did you compare work schedules for this week so we can schedule more studio time?" Bud asked.

"Wednesday, you can have us all day. If we need more time after that, any afternoon after three," Cedra reported.

36

"Let's plan on starting at eight on Wednesday then. If everything goes well, we may not need but possibly one more session," Bud suggested. "As quickly as this morning's tracks went, we may get three in this afternoon."

"Let's eat up so we can get back to it," Juliet said.

†

They were getting into the tracks of Stone's songs, and the band hadn't played through them as many times as the other tracks, so Cedra was worried the afternoon would be less productive than the morning session. Her fears gained life after the first song.

Bud was frowning when the song ended. "I have to ask, what's different about this song? The energy just isn't there."

Cedra was the first to speak. "The next three are songs we haven't played as often as the rest of the tracks."

"That would explain it," Bud replied. "Do any of you have a problem with waiting on these three until Wednesday? Allow yourselves to play through them several more times to become more familiar. The sound is tentative and not snappy."

Cedra looked around, and everyone nodded. Stone seemed a bit embarrassed that his song wasn't up to par. "That sounds great. We'll concentrate on those for Wednesday and have them down by then," Cedra replied to Bud.

"Let's move on then," Bud instructed. "Play me something you know."

"Ouch," Cedra whispered to Juliet.

Juliet smiled. "It's okay. We aren't as well prepared for Stone's songs, and it showed. We'll get there."

"Sorry, guys," Stone apologized.

"Stop right there," Juliet warned. "They are good songs. We just need to play them more. Starting tonight."

"Let's hit it," Wayne said.

The next song went smoothly and only took three runs to get it perfect. The second run would have been fine until Keith dropped his pick, and they had to start over.

"Take a quick break," Bud called from the booth.

"Sorry for being a bonehead," Keith said.

"I'm glad it was you and not me," Juliet teased. "It was just a matter of time before we messed up a song. The tracks were rolling too smoothly."

"She's absolutely right," Bud agreed. "Don't think we will ever cut an album without a few speed bumps, so shake it off, take a break, get some fresh air, and we'll get one more track in today and call it a night. Y'all have played hard the last two days."

"Come on, guys, let's step outside," Juliet said.

They walked outside, and Juliet sat on the hood of her car beside Cedra. "No more I'm sorry. We need to get back to having fun and not be so stressed about being perfect. We've got this."

Cedra looked at Keith and Stone. "Juliet is absolutely right. We've got seven tracks cut in less than two days. I bet that's pretty rare, especially for Bud. He knows what he wants and won't settle for mediocre. We should be thankful for that. We will know we have the best album possible when we get done."

Juliet grinned. "We go back inside in a few minutes and kick ass on this last song, and then we go home and practice Stone's tracks. In hindsight, we should have thought of that on our own. Maybe our confidence got a bit ahead of us."

Wayne shuffled his feet. "It was definitely a reality check."

Keith bounced back to his usual cheerful self. "Nobody said it would be easy. I've got my pick drop out of the way, so I can relax," he joked.

"If it makes you feel any better, I was a nanosecond away from sneezing," Cedra said. "I'm glad you dropped it before I sneezed. It scared the sneeze right away."

Keith broke out laughing. "You're kidding, right?"

"No, I'm dead serious," Cedra replied.

Juliet was relieved to see everyone smiling again. "Are we ready to blow Bud's socks off?"

Wayne gave her a high five. "Yeah, let's do it. We can listen to this afternoon's tracks and go home. If dinner's not ready, we can jam for a bit."

"Or afterward if dinner is ready," Juliet said. "There are still several cold beers in the fridge, and it may loosen us up a bit if we all have one."

"Let's roll," Stone said.

†

The band killed the next song, and Bud smiled at them when they finished. "Remind me to send you outside more often. That was great. Let's listen to it and decide if we need another run at it. I don't think we do, though."

"Good job, guys," Juliet praised. "Let's go take a listen, and we can pack up for the day."

They all agreed the two cuts were good and decided to call it a night. "I'm sorry if I sounded a bit short earlier, but the song wasn't up to what I expected from you."

"No worries, Bud, they will be great by Wednesday," Juliet told him.

"We can be finished with the final four tracks on Wednesday, and I can start putting the album together for us to review," Bud replied. "Don't sweat it if we don't finish Wednesday. We will use whatever time we need to roll out your best. You've all done really well so far. Get some rest, some practice, and I'll see you bright and early Wednesday."

"Thanks, Bud," Cedra said and led them back into the studio. "Two-thirds of the way done, guys. Who would have thought this two weeks ago?"

"Not me, that's for sure." Keith shook his head.

"Me either," Wayne added.

"Nope. I thought it would be months or years ahead of us," Stone joined in.

"Well, here we are. So close. We just need to sharpen up the last four tracks, and we're good." Juliet opened her case and saw the thumb drive lying there. "I knew there was something I was forgetting. I wonder if Carrie is still in the building?" She took the thumb drive out. "I'll be right back."

"I'll meet you at the car," Cedra said.

†

Juliet nodded and left the studio in search of Carrie. When she opened the break room door, Carrie and Bud were there. "They did good but weren't totally prepared on a couple tracks," she heard Bud say.

"Sorry to interrupt, but I forgot to give you this," Juliet said as she handed the thumb drive to Carrie.

"Thanks," Carrie replied and took the media from Juliet.

"We will be completely ready for Wednesday," Juliet told Bud. "We let our confidence get in the way, and that won't happen again."

Bud smiled. "I'm still impressed with the effort and progress you all have made. As long as you keep that level, we will be good to go on the album."

"Thanks. Have a good night." Juliet turned and left the room.

†

Juliet slipped in behind the wheel. "I am glad that is over with," she said to Cedra.

"Not as much success as yesterday, but we still made progress," Cedra replied. "We'd be foolish to believe everything would be smooth sailing. I thought we would have sounded better on Stone's tracks, though."

Juliet nodded. "We will get there, but we need to make sure he doesn't get down on himself, or the others get disappointed. It's all a growing process."

"Yep. We just need to buckle down and get better performing the last four tracks. That shouldn't be too difficult for us. Stone's lyrics are solid, and the music is good. We just need the practice." Cedra reached for Juliet's hand. "I'm happy we've made it this far."

"Me too. Let's go home, eat, and get back to work," Juliet replied.

†

Wayne and Keith were arranging their instruments on the front porch when they pulled up to the house. Stone was walking toward them with his guitar case.

Juliet and Cedra emerged from the car, and Wayne called to them. "Ma says it will be at least a half-hour before dinner is ready."

"Why don't you grab us a cold one then," Cedra suggested.

"That sounds good to me. Come on, I'll help ya," Stone said as he set his case down.

Cedra and Juliet sat in the wooden swing. Juliet draped an arm around Cedra. "It's good to be home."

"Today wasn't a total train wreck," Keith said.

"No, it wasn't. We still have a lot to be proud of," Cedra replied.

"Lots of work to do, too." Keith nodded. "Nothing we can't handle."

"That's right." Juliet smiled. She took two beers from Wayne. "Thanks, bro."

"My pleasure, sis." Wayne grinned.

"Where do we need to start tonight?" Stone asked.

"You pick, and we'll start with that song," Keith suggested.

"Let's go with number seven then. I think that's the hardest of my three to play," Stone replied.

"That sounds good to me, but let's just chill until we get something to eat. Let go of the music for a bit," Juliet suggested. She looked at Wayne. "How were Ma and Patsy doing in there?"

"I think they have a little buzz going." Wayne chuckled.

"That should be fun to witness." Keith grinned. "I have never seen Ma buzzed."

"Me either, but they were giggling like teenagers when we walked in for the beer," Wayne replied.

"No telling what those two were talking about," Cedra said.

Juliet twisted off the top and held her bottle up. "Here's to being two-thirds of the way done. Cheers, my friends."

"Cheers," they all answered and tapped the necks of their bottles together.

When they finished the beer, Wayne looked at Juliet sheepishly. "Should we go check on them?"

"It did get quiet," Keith teased.

"Go ahead. You're closest to the door," Juliet suggested.

Wayne collected the empty bottles and headed inside. When he returned moments later, he was smiling. "Ma said to come in. It's time to eat."

The group walked into the kitchen, where Ma and Patsy had placed bowls on the table. "Welcome home," Ma said. "I hope you had a good day."

Juliet noticed the rosy cheeks Ma was sporting. She couldn't hold back a chuckle. "We did, but apparently, you two had a better one."

Patsy snickered. "We did have a great afternoon. We decided to have piña coladas, and they sure were tasty."

"How many?" Juliet asked.

"A few," Ma answered. "Don't worry, the food will still be edible."

"It smells fantastic, ladies," Keith said.

"Let's eat then," Ma replied.

Juliet and Cedra poured tea while everyone started making tacos and burritos.

"Juliet, hon, will you get the hot sauce from the fridge?"

"Sure, Ma," Juliet replied. "Do we need anything else?"

"The sour cream," Wayne said.

"Got it," Juliet said and passed it to Wayne.

"These are really good, Ma," Cedra said as she took a second bite.

"Easy to make, too," Ma said. "It's supposed to get cold this week, so I thought I'd make a pot of chicken and dumplings or chili."

"Or both," Keith said. "It's supposed to be cold through the weekend."

"Yes, or both." Ma smiled.

†

Stone drove Patsy home with Cedra following. She asked Juliet to stay behind so she and Stone could have a conversation on the way back. After seeing Patsy safely inside, Stone jogged back to Cedra's truck.

"What's up? I have a feeling you wanted to talk to me in private."

"I just wanted to make sure your head is in a good place. You seemed down this afternoon."

Stone shrugged. "I'd be lying if I didn't admit to being disappointed that my tracks didn't get cut today."

Cedra smiled at him. "You can't take it personally. We have played my songs so many times we could do it in our sleep. We just need to get that comfortable with your tracks."

"I guess it was just a blow to my ego."

Cedra cocked her head at him. "I can understand that. We pour everything we have into our songs, but I promise we will get there and be ready to cut your tracks Wednesday."

"I know we will. I've just got to put my big boy britches on and use it as motivation for doing better."

"We all need to do that. I think we got a bit ahead of ourselves and weren't as prepared as we should have been for today." Cedra smiled and put the truck in reverse. "Let's go home and get some practice in before we have to head off for bed."

"Four will come early," Stone replied.

"Yes, it will. After we get home tomorrow, Juliet and I will hit the bank and do some boot shopping. Do you want to go?"

"Ask me again tomorrow."

"No problem," Cedra replied and drove home.

†

"Soon, we will have to start taking these jam sessions inside," Ma said as Stone and Cedra returned. "It's starting to get cold at night."

"Yeah, it is," Juliet agreed. "We don't have much time tonight, so let's try to gut it out." She grinned. "These three are up with the chickens again in the morning."

"I don't know how y'all do it," Keith said. "I am not a morning person, especially that early."

"I like it," Cedra said. "Everything is quiet and still in the house."

She and Stone took their seats. "Are we ready to get cranking?"

"Let's do it," Juliet said.

†

They were able to run through each of the last four tracks three times before Ma yawned. "I'm going to call it a night," she announced. "I'll see you two for coffee," she told Stone and Cedra.

"Goodnight," Cedra replied. "Rest well."

"I'm sure I will," Ma answered. "Goodnight, everyone."

"We should wrap it up for the night, too," Juliet said. "I think we made good progress, but it wouldn't hurt for us to play through them again tomorrow night or Tuesday."

"I don't see a problem with that," Stone replied.

Cedra was happy to see him smiling again. "I think we've all gotten more comfortable with the tunes."

"They sounded damn good," Wayne added.

"Tomorrow night then?" Keith asked. "We have a few hours before we head to work."

"Cedra and I are doing some shopping, but we'll be back for dinner."

Keith looked at Juliet. "What are you going shopping for?"

Juliet smiled at Cedra. "Bama girl needs some boots," she teased.

Keith nodded. "Ah, good luck. I was hoping for another pair of Ariats soon myself."

"You want to go with us?" Cedra asked.

"We won't be back for dinner if I do. I'm like a kid in a candy store when it comes to boots. We'd be there all night."

Keith chuckled. "I'll wait and go this weekend when I can take my time."

"I hear ya, bro," Wayne said and gave him a high five. "I think the three of us boys should go together."

"I'll give the store a forewarning then," Juliet teased as she placed her guitar in the case.

"Probably not a bad idea," Stone said. "I'm as bad as Keith. I want to try everything on."

Cedra looked at Juliet. "Remind me to never go shopping with the divas."

"Consider it done." Juliet laughed softly.

"I'll see you in a few hours," Cedra told Stone. "We'll see the rest of you later in the day."

"Goodnight, ladies," Wayne said. "Sleep well."

†

They stored their instruments, and Cedra slipped into a nightshirt. "My bank account will be glad for this deposit tomorrow," she said as Juliet walked into the room.

"I hear ya. Mine was starting to echo a bit."

"I'm thinking of going ahead and paying Ma up for the next four months," Cedra said as she stretched out on the bed.

"That's not a bad idea. I think it would show Ma our commitment to continue to live here in the future. I'll suggest it to the boys tomorrow too."

Cedra patted the bed. "I'll take care of Stone. He may not be able to if he's sending most of his home."

"Yeah, he's got a whole different perspective than the rest of us," Juliet agreed as she stretched out beside Cedra. "Did you feel good about how we sounded tonight?"

"I think we were all more comfortable with the music and lyrics after tonight's session. I think it was a good lesson for all of us to be better prepared."

Juliet laughed. "It was definitely a reality check. Overall, I think Bud, Carrie, and Mark are pleased with our progress."

"I do, too, and if we work hard, that will continue. How do you think the single will be accepted by the media?"

"Coming from Big Machine, I think, will make a big difference. More so than coming from the artist," Juliet replied. "Big money talks."

"I can't wait to hear it," Cedra said with a dreamy quality in her voice.

"It's just a matter of time."

"I know." Cedra cuddled with Juliet until she turned the light off.

†

As Linea pleasured her orally, Carrie's fingers were buried in her lover's blond hair. "Oh yes, Cedra," she called out without realizing as her climax ripped through her.

Linea didn't miss the error, though. She heard it quite plainly. "Who the fuck is Cedra?" she asked loudly as she climbed from the bed.

"What are you talking about?" Carrie asked.

"In your throes of passion, you called out her name instead of mine. Was Cedra who you thought you were with?"

Carrie ran her hand through her disheveled hair. "No. I'm so sorry. She's one of the band members we just signed. I haven't turned my brain off from the recording session yet today."

"The women you were gawking at in the restaurant the other night?" Linea growled.

"Yes, she was there with her lover."

Linea climbed off the bed and stormed into the bathroom while Carrie dressed.

"Hey, I'm sorry. It was an honest mistake," Carrie called from outside the door. "I'll talk to you later this week."

Linea stood in front of the mirror with tears streaming down her face. "Damn right, it was a mistake." She knew that Carrie wasn't interested in a long-term relationship with her, but calling out another woman's name was not something she would easily forgive. Obviously, something was going on between the two, and she vowed to remedy that situation.

CHAPTER THREE

"Have a great day," Ma said when she sent Cedra and Stone off with coffee the following morning.

"You too, Ma. We'll see you later. Keep your radio on," Cedra teased.

"You can bet I will," Ma assured her. "I'm baking pies for dessert tonight, so I can listen in all day."

"Sounds wonderful," Cedra said. "Let's roll."

†

They had just finished the breakfast rush and were sitting down to a meal when Teddy cried out from the kitchen. "Hey, listen. You guys are on the radio," he called out.

"Crank it up," Lisa Marie called back.

51

The DJ was just announcing a debut single by a brand-new band when Cedra heard the radio. "What station?"

She was about to text Juliet when her phone rang. "We are on the radio," Juliet screamed on the other end.

"We are listening, too, so be quiet," Cedra teased.

"What a great new sound," the DJ said after the song was played. "If you missed it listeners, that was 'Six Strings and a Dream,' the debut single and title track of the Bentleys' soon-to-be-released album. Welcome to Nashville."

"That's freaking awesome," Cedra could hear Keith say in the background.

"Damn, we sound good," Cedra told Juliet as she high-fived Stone.

The customers in the café broke out in applause. "That was great," someone called out.

"My thoughts exactly. I am so excited. Hopefully, that will be the first of many times we hear the song. We may have to start taking turns calling in to request they play it," Juliet teased.

"I don't think you'll have to worry about that," Lisa Marie replied. "It did sound fantastic."

"Thanks, Lisa Marie." Juliet smiled. "You've really helped us along."

"Nonsense. I made a killing the night you guys played here. I should be thanking you."

Cedra chuckled. "You have. Several times, boss."

"Maybe I can get you to sit in for another show before y'all hit the road," Lisa Marie replied.

"Just name it, and we'll be there," Juliet replied.

"If it's okay with Carrie," Cedra had to remind her. "Maybe we could do a short charity show or something they would be fine with."

"Let me bring it up to Carrie. That way, you guys aren't stuck in the middle of things," Lisa Marie suggested.

"That sounds like a perfectly devious plan to me," Juliet answered.

Cedra nodded. "That's good for me."

"Wednesday is your off day, so I'll ask her then," Lisa Marie said with a laugh.

"Good deal. Now get back to work so we can go shopping," Juliet teased Cedra.

"I'll see you soon. Keep listening." Cedra ended the call and turned to Stone. "It's official. We have made it to the radio."

"My heart is still racing," Stone replied. "I just sent Sarah a text, and she's excited, too."

"I don't think that feeling will ever get old for you," Lisa Marie said.

The door opened, and Carrie walked in to find them all smiling. "Am I missing something?" she asked.

"You're about five minutes too late. 'Six Strings' just got played on the radio," Cedra told her.

"That's fantastic news. I'm sure it will be the first of many times it gets played," Carrie replied. "Congratulations."

"Thank you for helping us make it happen," Cedra said.

"That road goes both ways. If things go as planned, you're going to make a lot of money for Big Machine in the future."

"I hope you're right. What can I get you? The usual?" Cedra asked.

"Hell, no, I'm going to celebrate with a bacon cheeseburger and onion rings." Carrie smiled.

"That's the spirit." Cedra called out her order.

"Can you join me for a few?" Carrie asked.

"Sure, let me grab some tea for you, and I'll be right there," Cedra answered.

Cedra returned to the counter and poured two glasses of tea. "I'll be right back."

"Take your time. I can handle things until the rush starts," Stone said.

†

Cedra placed a glass of tea in front of Carrie and took a seat across from her.

"Thanks. I just wanted to check on how everyone was doing after yesterday's session. I know the afternoon wasn't as smooth as you hoped it would be."

"It was a good lesson for all of us, and we practiced hard last night. We will be ready for Wednesday's studio session," Cedra promised.

Carrie smiled. "I have no doubt. Bud is super excited to work with you all. He sees a lot of potential in you, and that's not common for him with brand new artists."

"He's been a joy to work with," Cedra stated.

"He can also be a bear if he doesn't think you put enough effort into the songs," Carrie warned. "I think you saw a tip of that yesterday."

"We will do our best to prevent seeing any more. We realize we have to work even harder to make the best music we can. We took for granted that we were prepared to cut all the tracks, and we weren't. That won't happen again."

"Order up," Teddy called from the kitchen.

"I'll be right back with your food." Cedra returned to the kitchen. She poured a container of honey mustard and put it on the plate.

Carrie smiled when she saw the container. "Thanks for remembering the honey mustard."

"That's what good servers do." Cedra smiled.

"Speaking of which. How long do you plan to continue to work here?"

"Until we find out exactly where we are going as a band. We may drop down to part-time when we begin getting some gigs," Cedra told her.

"Hopefully, that won't be too long. I've been thinking about what y'all mentioned about the college towns for weekend gigs, and I think that may be a possibility. Let's see what this week brings with 'Six Strings' being released to the media. If it stirs up the interest we hope, then small gigs will be an easy sell."

"That sounds great," Cedra replied.

The door opened, and a large group came inside, followed by another couple. "It looks like things are heating up in here too. Thanks for spending a few minutes with me."

"My pleasure. I'll check back on you in a few minutes for your dessert order."

"You are so evil," Carrie said and then laughed. "Buttermilk if you have it."

†

Linea followed Carrie's car as she left the office and circled the block while Carrie parked. She pulled into the back of the parking lot and watched the door until she saw Carrie exit the café wearing a smile. She waited until Carrie left and then stepped out of her car. "Let's just see why you're so special," Linea spoke aloud. She walked into the café and was greeted by a handsome young man who seated her and provided a menu. "What may I get you to drink to start while you review the menu?"

"Sweet tea is fine," she murmured as she watched the other server, a female, move from table to table.

The door opened behind her, and a large man walked in. "Guess what I just heard on the radio, Cedra?"

"Do tell, Rob," Cedra teased.

"I just heard a beautiful song by a brand-new band called the Bentleys. Damn, y'all sounded good."

"Thanks, Rob. We actually heard it earlier. It did sound good," Cedra replied.

"One of your songs?" another customer asked.

"The lyrics, yes, but I had lots of help with the music," Cedra told him. "Coffee or tea, Rob?"

"Some sweet tea, please, ma'am," Rob answered.

Linea hid her glare behind the menu. *She's so sickly sweet, but the men just eat it up. I guess Carrie does, too.*

When the server returned with her drink, he asked, "Have you decided on lunch?"

"I'll take a cheeseburger. Well done with the works and fries. Bacon included, please." She managed a weak smile as her eyes tracked Cedra's movement. *Not much to look at. A bit on the skinny side and no boobs. What does she see in her?*

"I'll be back with your order soon," Stone told her.

"That's fine. Thanks!"

"So, what's the next step?" Rob asked.

"Carrie said if the single is well-received this week, maybe some weekend gigs, but it's too early to tell."

When Linea heard the woman talk so casually about Carrie, it made her anger rise.

"Carrie's the best in the business, but I hear she can be hard to work with," Rob said.

"She's been nothing short of a sweetheart," Cedra replied with a smile.

Linea nearly kicked her chair over when she stood up abruptly and walked toward the restroom sign. Her hands gripped the sink tightly as she mocked Cedra. "She's been nothing short of a sweetheart," she growled at the image staring back at her in the mirror. Her usually bright blue eyes were bloodshot with rivers of red from the tears she had shed after Carrie left. "I'll have to come up with a plan for you. I can't have you taking Carrie from me." Linea washed her hands and returned to her table, turning the heads of several male customers as she swayed her hips seductively.

"Who is that?" one of them asked Stone.

"No clue. I've never seen her before," Stone answered.

"You'd remember that." The man snickered. "She's freaking hot."

"Calm down, Roscoe, or I'll have to put you in the walk-in cooler to cool down," Lisa Marie said.

"Can't hurt a man to look." He chuckled.

"I bet you wouldn't say that around Wanda," his buddy said.

"Hell no. Wanda would bash my head in." Roscoe laughed.

"Order up," Teddy called from the kitchen. Stone picked up the order and carried it to the blond customer's table. "Is there anything else I can get you?"

"I'm good, thanks," Linea answered. She bit into the burger and moaned. *At least the food is good.*

Stone refilled her glass. "Any dessert today?"

"No, thanks. Just a check," Linea answered. She glanced at the clock. *I bet other servers will be coming in soon.*

†

Rob finished his meal and headed toward the counter. "Thanks for a great meal, Cedra. Have a great night. See you tomorrow?"

"You will. Hopefully breaking in some new boots. We're going shopping today," Cedra replied.

"Better bring some comfy shoes just in case. Breaking in boots can take some time," Rob suggested.

"Thanks, Rob. Advice taken. Maybe I'll break them in a bit first." Cedra smiled.

"Good idea. See ya." He handed her a five-dollar tip.

Cedra started wiping down tables while waiting for the next customer to enter. Stone was cashing out a customer at the register when Teddy yelled from the kitchen.

"Here it is again." He turned up the volume.

"Is that someone you know?" Linea asked.

"It's the debut song for the band that Cedra and I are in," Stone said proudly as he nodded his head toward Cedra.

"Congratulations," Linea replied. "Good luck." She handed Stone a five for a tip.

"Thanks. Appreciate your business." Stone smiled.

"The food and the service were great. I'll definitely be back," Linea told him. The door swung open, and two women came in. "You're replacements?" Linea asked.

"They come in to start their shifts for the lunch crowd. Cedra and I finish up around 2:30," Stone answered.

"Have a great rest of your day," Linea said, storing that information in her brain.

"Thanks, you too," Stone replied.

Linea exited the building and walked to her car. She climbed in behind the wheel and decided the wait until Cedra left for the day. She would wait to see which vehicle was Cedra's and then head home to devise her plan. Cedra was not going to get her woman.

†

"Twice in one shift, that's good," Lisa Marie told Cedra.

"What's that?"

"Hearing you on the radio," Lisa Marie said.

Cedra smiled. "Yeah, that's pretty awesome. I know the local stations were getting copies of the single today from Big Machine. I think they planned to send electronic copies out across the country to some of the bigger media outlets."

"You sound like such a professional already," Lisa Marie teased.

"Ha! I just pay attention to everything Mark and Carrie tell us."

"That's a good habit to get into," Lisa Marie advised.

Cedra nodded. "I hope to learn everything I can from them."

"One thing about it, you'd be learning from the best. It can't hurt to be informed about the business aspect and the performance." Lisa Marie smiled. "I hear Carrie can be tough."

Cedra tucked her order pad in her pocket. "I have no doubt about that. I hope to stay on her good side."

"I don't see why you wouldn't." Lisa Marie smiled. "Do you two want some lunch before you head out? It doesn't look like we'll be swamped."

"I can always eat," Stone replied. "Do you want something, Cedra?"

"I'll take a grilled cheese and some fries," she answered as she greeted the next guest.

"Let Vanessa or Jennifer get them," Lisa Marie said. "Jennifer's running short on money again," she said with a shake of her head.

"She's still young. Hopefully, she'll learn to budget better," Cedra said.

"Or party less," Lisa Marie said with a frown.

"That too," Cedra said as she poured tea for herself and Stone. "Want some?"

"Why not?" Lisa Marie answered.

"What have you heard about the new super flu lately?" Cedra asked as she sat beside Lisa Marie.

"It's now being called Corona virus and is supposed to be wicked," Lisa Marie said. She frowned. "I'm not sure how it's going to affect business yet. We may be forced to shut down the dining room and offer take-out only."

"People still have to eat. Whatever comes, we'll work through it." Cedra smiled.

"I wish I could feel your confidence," Lisa Marie replied. "I've never had to shut down before."

Cedra put a comforting hand on her boss's shoulder. "We'll figure it out if it happens."

Lisa Marie nodded. "I've been trying to imagine some changes that could keep us going."

"Like what?" Cedra asked.

"If we have to close to take out only, we could station someone at the door to monitor traffic and take orders electronically to send to Teddy in the kitchen. Someone to seat customers waiting for orders within the distance requirements, someone on the register and maybe a second cook to keep things moving quickly."

"See, you're already thinking progressively. Can you stock up on take-out containers and plastic utensils? You seem to be getting a good supply of masks, gloves, and cleaners," Cedra noted.

"We'll need to disinfect tables and chairs every time someone leaves," Lisa Marie said. "I think we would shut down after lunch. I can bring Vanessa and Jennifer in mid-morning to keep everyone bringing home a check."

"You have been planning," Cedra said. "That's good."

Stone walked over with their food, and the conversation ended.

"Boot shopping, huh?" Lisa Marie asked.

"Yeah. Juliet thinks I need boots for performances. I guess I'll have to retire my loafers." Cedra smiled.

"If you're going to be a country band, they are gonna expect boots and ball caps," Lisa Marie teased.

"That's where I draw the line. No cap or cowboy hat for me."

"I'll get a nice Stetson," Stone chimed in. "I know Wayne and Keith are planning for an upgrade from ball caps too."

"It'll seem funny not seeing Keith in that John Deere cap," Cedra replied.

"You'll adjust," Lisa Marie promised. "Eat up, and the two of you can take off for the day."

"Thanks, boss," Stone said.

"Maybe we can start shopping early and get back in time to jam some before dinner," Cedra suggested. "We sounded better last night."

"But extra practice won't hurt us."

"Right. Eat up, big boy, so we can roll," Cedra teased.

Stone smiled. "You might want to call ahead and warn Juliet we are coming home early."

"Good point." Cedra pulled her phone out to text Juliet.

†

"See you tomorrow, boss," Cedra said as she and Stone headed for the door.

"Have fun shopping," Lisa Marie called back.

"We will."

Stone opened the door and they walked to Cedra's truck. "I may catch a quick nap while you ladies are gone. Or maybe get some lyrics uploaded to the laptop. That would probably be a better use of my time," Stone said.

"Have you tried creating lyrics using the software yet?" Cedra asked.

"I played with it a bit, but not near enough," he answered.

"Juliet is just about caught up entering my songbooks. Do you want her to start working on yours next?"

"That would be great. I'm sure Juliet types faster than me." Stone demonstrated his hunt and peck skills on the dash.

"Yeah, probably a good idea for Juliet to work on them then," Cedra said with a soft laugh. "Let's go home."

†

Linea watched Cedra and Stone emerge from the café. She was surprised when they both got into the same truck. "No matter," she said. She waited until they pulled from the lot, started her car, and headed home. "If subtle hints don't work, I'll take it up a notch," she spoke to herself.

†

"Are you sure you don't want to go shopping with us today?" Cedra asked Stone as they arrived home.

"Naw, we'll make it boys' day out this weekend, but thanks for asking. I can't wait to see what you come home with. I need some Christmas ideas for Sarah and Destiny."

"That's very sweet. I'll keep my eyes open for little girl stuff. Any ideas on sizes?"

"No clue. Whatever a two-year-old wears."

64

"Um, Stone sweetie, it doesn't work like that. Ask Sarah for clothing and shoe sizes, and I'll help you shop."

"I guess I need help, huh?"

"Yes, you do, but I'll be happy to assist," Cedra said as she turned off the truck.

†

Ma and Juliet were in the kitchen when they entered the house. "We've heard the song four times already today," Juliet said.

"That's incredible," Cedra replied. "We only heard it twice."

"Once was probably on your drive home."

"We were talking, and I didn't think to turn the radio on," Cedra admitted.

"That's okay. At least we know we're getting some serious airtime. Do you want to shower before we go shopping?"

Cedra nodded. "I won't be too long."

"Okay, I'll wait for you down here. Don't forget your checks to deposit," Juliet reminded her.

"Thanks, I would have forgotten. What would I do without you?"

"Let's not find out." Juliet smiled. She leaned down and kissed Cedra. "Go, and hurry back."

"Someone's excited to go shopping," Stone teased. "Do you need help with anything, Ma?"

"No, I've got everything under control. The dumplings are cooking, and the pies are in the oven."

"Would you mind if I bring my laptop over and use the table for a bit?"

"No, I'd love the company," Ma answered.

Stone looked at Juliet. "Cedra said you might help enter the songs from my songbook."

"I'd be more than happy to," Juliet replied. "Is that what you're going to work on while we're gone?"

"Yes, I need the practice." He grinned.

"Leave the laptop and your songbook, and I can work on those during the day."

"Thanks," Stone said and left the kitchen.

"That was nice of you to offer to help," Ma praised.

"It's either that or find some work to do, and I'd rather focus on our music right now," Juliet replied.

"That makes sense. Will y'all be back in time for dinner at five?"

"We should be, but if not, go ahead without us, and we'll eat when we get home. I don't foresee a problem since Cedra got home from work early."

"Have fun shopping. I'll keep the food warm for you," Ma told her.

"Thanks, Ma. Do you need anything from town?" Juliet asked.

"Not that I can think of, but thanks for asking. I may need your help next week with shopping for Thanksgiving dinner and meals when Cedra's dad is here."

"Just let me know when." Juliet smiled. "My schedule is open."

"I think I'll put the boys to work collecting more pecans for a couple of pies," Ma commented.

"That sounds great to me. Maybe I can get a caramel cake, and we can make brownies and cookies. You know the boys will love that," Juliet replied.

Stone returned to the table. "Are you going to be here for Thanksgiving?" Juliet asked.

"Yeah, I told Sarah I'll ask for time off at Christmas to come home."

"Could they come up?" Ma asked.

"Sarah needs to stay close since Dad's not back to 100% yet. I feel bad about not being there to help, but they understand."

"Maybe soon you can fly home whenever you want," Juliet suggested.

"That would be great," Stone replied.

"I know you must miss them terribly."

"Yes, Ma, especially Destiny. She's growing up so fast," Stone said with a smile.

Ma returned his smile. "You blink, and the next thing you know, they are teenagers."

Stone nodded. "I don't want to miss all of that. Destiny has already decided she's a big girl and has toilet trained herself. She loves her Princess big girl panties."

"That's so cute," Juliet said. "Do you plan on having more?"

"Maybe one day, I would love to have a little boy."

"Every man's dream," Ma said. "Do you have brothers?"

"Just one, Thomas. He and his wife haven't started having kids yet. He's a year younger than me."

"Maybe if we get a college town gig, we can meet your family in Gainesville," Juliet suggested.

"That would be awesome," Stone replied.

Juliet heard footsteps and looked to see Cedra walking down the stairs. "That was quick."

"I told you I wouldn't take long. You ready?" Cedra asked.

"Just waiting on you, my dear, we will see y'all later."

"Be safe and have fun," Ma called to them. "Turn your radio on."

"Yes, Ma."

†

Cedra was amazed at the large selection of boots when they walked into the store. "I don't know where to begin," she told Juliet.

"Thank goodness you're with a professional," Juliet teased. "Let's start here."

Juliet began selecting a variety of boots for Cedra and brought them to her to slip on. After five or six selections, Cedra found a pair that felt right.

"These feel good," she told Juliet. "Like slipping into a warm pair of gloves."

"Walk around in them a bit," Juliet suggested. She was going through a stack of blue jeans as Cedra walked around the store. "Yeah, I like these."

"Okay, that has the brown covered, now we move on to black," Juliet told her.

"Black ones, too?" Cedra replied.

"Yes, you need some variety. Do you see anything in black that you like?"

"What about these?" Cedra asked as she held up a black Harley Davidson cowboy boot.

"Those are nice. Let's get your size to try on," Juliet replied.

"Oh, yeah," Cedra replied when she slipped her feet in the boots. "They are a little heavier than the Ariat's, but they feel just as comfy," Cedra said.

"You look fantastic in them," Juliet said with a smile. "Will you try these on?" She held up a small stack of blue jeans she had picked out.

"You obviously think I need more jeans." Cedra chuckled.

"I can't wait to see what you look like in the Cinch or Levi boot cuts. What you wear to work is acceptable for work and recording, but you need newer jeans for other activities, like interviews, and live performances."

"Are you getting some, too?" Cedra asked.

"I am. I promise I will learn how to iron them too," Juliet teased. "We have a look to maintain."

Cedra grinned. "Ma will be proud your fashion sense is finally kicking into gear."

"Since you picked out Harley boots, I think a matching shirt should go with them," Juliet said as she picked up a long-sleeved shirt. "The dressing room is through there." Juliet pointed to a door. "I'll wait for you out here." Juliet strolled through the aisles and searched a clearance rack, picking out a short-sleeve Ariat, and an Iron Horse T-shirt. She heard the door to the dressing area open, and when she looked up, her heart lodged in her throat. Juliet swallowed hard.

"Damn, turn around, girl," she said and twirled her hand. "The Cinch jeans are perfect for you."

Cedra smiled at Juliet's praise. "They do fit good, don't they?"

"Oh, hell yes," Juliet agreed. "Try the Levi's next. I don't think they can look any better."

Juliet picked out a black Harley belt and a plain brown one to add to the stack for Cedra. When Cedra stepped out to model the Levi's, Juliet smiled. "They look good, but not like the Cinch jeans."

"Get them, or no?" Cedra asked.

"Get three Cinch and two Levi's," Juliet suggested.

Cedra nodded and walked back to change. When she returned, Juliet handed her the two boot boxes, and she picked up the jeans and belts. When they reached the checkout, Juliet split off from Cedra.

"What are you doing?" Cedra asked.

"I'm buying these for you," Juliet answered. "Don't even think of arguing with me."

Cedra paid for her purchases and waited for Juliet. "Thank you."

"You're welcome. I like shopping with you." Juliet smiled. "Are we ready to go home?"

"I think so," Cedra replied.

†

"Welcome back," Ma said as they carried their bags inside. "Did you have fun shopping?"

"We certainly did," Juliet said. "You should see Cedra in her Cinch jeans, Ma. She looks terrific."

"I think you're a bit biased," Cedra said.

"There's only one way to find out," Stone said.

Juliet smiled at Stone. "Fashion show," they said in unison.

"Do we have time, Ma?" Cedra asked.

"We certainly do, so go."

"Boots and belt, too," Juliet said. "She looks fantastic in them."

Cedra climbed the stairs with the bags to her room to change. The receipt from Juliet's purchase slipped onto her bed as she pulled the jeans out, and she was shocked by the amount. "Good lord," she whispered as she put the receipt on her desk. She undressed and pulled the Harley shirt and a pair of the Cinch jeans over her hips. She slipped on the Harley belt and black boots. Cedra looked in the mirror and ran a brush through her hair, then started for the stairs. She was halfway down when Wayne and Keith walked through the front door.

"Brr, it's getting cold out there," Keith said. "Holy hell," he cried out when he saw Cedra.

"Woohoo, where'd that sexy woman come from?" Wayne called as Keith whistled.

"I rest my case," Juliet said from the kitchen.

"You look like a proper country singer," Ma said. "Y'all did well."

"Juliet picked everything out."

"Damn, if you'll make me look that sexy, I'll take you shopping with me," Keith said.

"You know I love to shop. The store had some good stuff on clearance today too. I almost bought a long-sleeved John Deere shirt for you, but I wasn't sure of the size."

"I wear a medium for future reference," Keith teased. "Are those Cinch jeans?"

"Yes, they are," Cedra said and turned around.

"I am definitely getting Sarah some of those for Christmas," Stone replied.

"They have them in Destiny's size, too," Juliet said. "I checked."

"Thank you," Stone said. "I'll have to get the exact sizes for them when I talk to her tonight."

"Find out shoe sizes, too. They've got some cute girl's boots," Cedra said.

"Stone, if you'll shut down the computer, Juliet can set the table while Cedra changes clothes, and we'll be ready to eat."

"I'll help," Keith offered.

"Are we ready for drinks too, Ma?" Wayne asked.

"Yes, you can go ahead and pour," Ma answered as she began dipping out the chicken and dumplings.

†

"Are we jamming in the living room tonight?" Wayne asked.

"If you have time." Juliet nodded.

"We've got a good hour before we have to head to work," Keith said.

"Grab the instruments. Cedra and I will help Ma in the kitchen," Juliet told him.

"Go. I've got this. We can have coffee and pie after you've practiced."

"Now we're singing my tune," Keith said and ran upstairs.

"I figured that would get you motivated," Ma called out behind him.

"I'll get ours if you want to get the coffee pot set up," Cedra told Juliet

"Deal." Juliet kissed her as they passed in the dining room.

†

Ma listened from the kitchen as they played, and when they finished a song Ma called out to them, "That sounded great. Call it a night and come get some pie."

"You don't have to ask me twice," Keith said. "Milk, boys?" he asked on the way to the kitchen.

"Sure," Wayne and Stone answered.

"Coffee with us, Ma?" Cedra asked.

"I'm ahead of you. Grab your mugs and bring them to the table." Ma had already cut the pies and plated slices for everyone.

"Tonight, sounded even better than last night," Wayne pointed out.

"We just needed the extra practice," Stone replied. "Damn, this is good, Ma."

"How cool was it to hear our song on the radio today?" Juliet asked.

"I think we heard it four times," Wayne said. "We sounded legit."

"It will be interesting to hear the feedback from Carrie and Mark on Wednesday," Keith said.

"I'll pick Carrie's brain tomorrow," Cedra said. "I'm almost positive she'll be in for lunch."

"Hopefully, she will give you some information," Juliet replied.

"Aw crap. I just realized I hadn't shared my conversation with Carrie with you all yet," Cedra said.

"You're holding out on us?" Keith teased. "Spill it."

"She came in for lunch right after 'Six Strings' played. I joined her for a few minutes, and she told me that they had discussed our idea of some college town gigs. She said a lot would hinge on how well the song was received this week."

"That would be freaking awesome," Wayne replied.

"It would help us grow a young crowd fan base for sure," Juliet suggested. "The younger generation isn't as hardcore about the evolution of today's country music."

"That's true. They don't mind a li'l hip hop in their mountaintop," Keith joked.

"That's one way of putting it," Cedra replied. "I'm not sure we are a hip hop type, though."

"Not on our own, but there have been many collaborations recently that have proven successful," Wayne reported. "We need to be successful before we start branching out like that."

"I think we have a unique sound of our own," Cedra said.

Ma chimed into the conversation. "I agree with Cedra. Stick to what you know and do well before you start chasing rabbits."

Juliet grinned at Ma. "That's certainly one way of putting it. We can all understand chasing rabbits."

"I'm from the country, and I like it that way," Stone sang, bringing a round of laughter to the table. "I hate to leave the good company, but my boots are dragging tonight. I'll see you all tomorrow. Is it okay to leave my stuff here, Ma?"

"Of course, it is, Stone. Have a good night, and we'll see you in the morning."

"Yes, ma'am, you will. Goodnight, everyone," Stone said and left the house.

"I hope he stays warm out there," Juliet said.

"We talked about that today, and I told him he could sleep in the spare bedroom downstairs when it started getting really cold," Ma reported. "He assured me he was fine for now but appreciated the offer. I'm positive we will have colder weather heading our way."

"There's little doubt of that," Juliet agreed.

"We need to get rolling too," Wayne said to Keith, who was finishing his second slice of pie. "I'm going to brush my teeth and get the truck warming while you finish stuffing your face."

"Let me have your keys, and I'll get your truck started for you," Juliet offered.

Wayne dug his keys from his pocket. "Thanks. I'll be back down in a minute."

Cedra rinsed the plates and put them in the dishwasher as Ma prepared the coffee pot for the morning. Juliet returned, rubbing her hands together.

"It's getting colder at night already."

"I turned the heat on today," Ma said. "Everyone should be toasty warm tonight."

Cedra waited for the boys to leave before pulling an envelope out of her pocket and handing it to Ma.

"What's this?" Ma asked.

"Juliet and I decided we wanted to go ahead and pay our rent for the next few months," Cedra told her.

"You don't need to do that," Ma said.

"We wanted to do it. That way, if you run short on anything, you've got a bit of padding," Juliet said as she placed an arm around Cedra.

"Thank you. I'll take it to the bank tomorrow," Ma replied. "You really didn't have to do this."

"We know, but we wanted to," Cedra repeated.

Ma walked to the front door and locked it behind her to hide the tears forming in her eyes. "Are you two coming upstairs?"

"Right behind ya, Ma," Juliet answered.

"Sweet dreams, my sweet girls," Ma called down when she reached the top of the stairs. "I'll see you in the morning."

"Goodnight, Ma," Cedra replied.

†

"For a second, I thought Ma was going to cry."

Cedra nodded. "I did, too. I think she was genuinely grateful for the advanced rent payments. I never hear her complain, but I know to house and feed the lot of us can't be cheap."

"I want to talk to the boys about pitching in to buy the groceries for the Thanksgiving feast I know Ma will plan."

"That's the least we can do."

They dressed for bed, and Juliet took Cedra in her arms. "You looked incredible today."

"You have a great sense of style," Cedra praised. "I'm glad you went with me today."

"It was my pleasure. Now I'd like to show you a bit of different pleasure," Juliet said in a sultry voice.

"I do love the sound of that." Cedra climbed onto the bed.

Juliet's hand slipped beneath Cedra's nightshirt as her teeth nibbled the soft skin on her neck. Cedra's nipples were rock hard as Juliet's lips closed around her ear lobe. "Your body seems super sensitive tonight," Juliet whispered.

"I've wanted you ever since I got home today."

"I missed you, too. The first time you walked out of the dressing room wearing the new jeans, I got a lump in my throat. You looked so damn good."

"I had this brief flash of you following me into the dressing room and us making love in the tiny room," Cedra admitted. "The way you looked at me made my panties more than a bit moist."

"Now there's a fantasy we may have to explore on our next shopping trip." Juliet laughed softly against Cedra's skin as her hand moved lower. "I love the fact that you can read my looks, and your body reacts."

"Just being near you and listening to your voice turns me on," Cedra said. "You've already got me soaking wet."

Juliet was surprised that Cedra wasn't wearing anything beneath her shirt. Cedra opened her legs as Juliet's hand moved further south. Juliet's fingers traced the outside of Cedra's lower lips and felt her shiver. "I don't believe you're cold." Juliet chuckled.

"Hardly," Cedra answered. "I feel like a volcano with lava flowing out of me."

"I can feel that fire burning inside you," Juliet replied as two fingers slipped into Cedra. "Hot and silky," she breathed into Cedra's ear. Her thumb stroked across Cedra's swollen clit. "I'm going to have my lips wrapped around this soon." The tip of her tongue traced the outer edge of Cedra's ear.

Cedra moaned. "Is it soon yet?"

"It can be." Juliet gently removed her fingers and positioned her body between Cedra's legs. She placed Cedra's thighs over her shoulders, spreading them wide. Juliet's fingers opened Cedra's lips as she used the tip of her tongue to tease her lover. "You taste so good."

Juliet's warm breath on her sensitive skin had Cedra grabbing the bed sheets as she lifted her hips toward Juliet's exploring tongue. "I want to come with you, baby."

"Yes, Juliet," Cedra groaned.

"Trust me?"

"Of course, I do."

"Will you try something with me?"

Cedra nodded. "If it will allow us to come together, hell yes."

"I promise you it will feel great for both of us. I'll be right back."

Juliet walked to her room and returned with the sex toy she had bought earlier. She climbed onto the bed and showed the object to Cedra. "One end for each of us, and the vibration is remote controlled." She placed a small egg-shaped object in Cedra's hand. "Squeeze to control to go at a speed that feels good to you. What you feel, I'll feel."

Cedra nodded.

"You willing to give this a try?"

"Yes, I am."

Juliet slipped the shorter end G-spot stimulator inside her wetness. "Damn, that feels good even without vibration, but turn it on."

Cedra squeezed the remote, and Juliet's face lit up in a smile. "You are going to love this." Juliet leaned forward and placed the toy's tip inside Cedra's center. She rested on her elbows as the toy slipped deeper inside Cedra. "Okay, so far?"

Cedra nodded her head.

Juliet's tongue traced Cedra's lips, then parted them for a kiss as she began slowly rocking her hips into Cedra. The vibration on her G-spot was heavenly. "How does that feel?"

"Feels incredible. Is it good for you?"

"Every movement of my hips presses the vibrator against my G- spot."

"More?" Cedra asked as she held up the remote.

"As much as you want." Juliet waited until Cedra increased the speed. "Hell yeah," she groaned and covered Cedra's mouth with a heated kiss.

Their hips rocked together as they both received pleasure from the sex toy. "I'm not sure how much more I can take."

"Me too," Cedra said. "Come with me, baby."

Juliet thrust into Cedra as her climax coursed through her, and she felt Cedra's body shaking beneath her. Juliet stopped her motion and looked into Cedra's face. "Oh, my goodness," she said between gasps for breath.

"That was freaking intense," Cedra said. Her hand squeezed the remote, and it raised the vibration up to the max level. "Oh, crap," Cedra said. "How do you turn it off?"

Juliet smiled, took the remote, and pressed the button to stop the vibration. The toy was still buried inside them. "No pain?"

Cedra shook her head. "Not at all, but I want to use that with you."

"I'll be back in a minute." Juliet eased the toy from Cedra's wetness and then walked to the bathroom to clean the toy.

When she returned, Cedra was lying on her side. Juliet climbed in beside her. "Ready?"

Cedra nodded and positioned herself between Juliet's legs. She slipped the toy into her body. "This feels so strange but good," she said.

"Wait, it gets better." Juliet turned the vibration on.

"Holy shit," Cedra said. "That does feel good. You ready?"

"Oh, yeah. Make me come for you, Cedra," Juliet purred.

The sultry need in Juliet's voice sent a new wave of wetness through Cedra. She leaned into Juliet, and the tip of the toy slid easily inside, adding pressure against her G-spot as they moved. Cedra positioned her hands along Juliet's sides as their hips joined, and they moved together. Juliet's hands covered Cedra's breasts, teasing her nipples between her thumb and forefinger. Cedra closed her eyes, focusing on her hips moving with Juliet's as the intensity of the vibrations grew. Their second orgasm took more time but was as pleasurable as the first when it arrived. Cedra collapsed onto Juliet's chest as the toy continued to hum away inside them. "Damn, that felt great."

Juliet smiled at Cedra. "Yes, it did. I'm glad you enjoyed that. I worried that it might scare you."

"I trust you completely. I know you wouldn't do anything to hurt me," Cedra answered. "But."

"But what?" Juliet frowned.

"If you don't turn that off, neither of us is going to get any sleep tonight," Cedra teased.

Juliet grinned and turned the toy's vibrator off. Cedra carefully removed the toy and placed it on the bed beside them. "Will you clean and store while I relieve my bladder?"

"Sure thing," Juliet answered and left the bed, reaching back to help Cedra up. She was at the sink, cleaning the toy when Cedra called from the bathroom.

"It's broke," she said.

"What's broken?" Juliet asked.

"My body. I can't pee," Cedra replied with a worried voice.

Juliet walked into the bathroom and knelt in front of her. "Relax. You are trying too hard."

"I'm not broken?" Cedra asked with genuine concern.

"It's not uncommon that it's challenging to urinate after intense orgasms. Your body is still sensitive. Just close your eyes and rest, and when you feel your muscles relax, try again."

Cedra nodded her head, and Juliet returned to the sink to brush her teeth. She smiled when she heard the toilet flush, and Cedra walked over to the sink. "Mission accomplished?"

"Yes," Cedra answered with a blush. "That was a bit scary. I've never had that happen before."

Juliet kissed her sweetly. "It's perfectly normal."

"That was intense." Cedra grinned.

"For me, too. Let me see if I'm broke."

"Go ahead and make fun of me," Cedra said with a pout.

"Never, darling. I need to see for myself," Juliet answered. A moment later, she called out, "All good."

Juliet blew out the candle and joined Cedra in the bed. "We are going to need a new candle soon." She chuckled as she pulled the covers over them.

"I'll pick some up this week," Cedra replied.

"Or we can pick them out together."

"That works too. I love you."

"I love you too," Juliet answered. "You make my life complete."

"I never knew what was missing until I met you," Cedra told her.

Juliet brushed the hair from Cedra's face. "That sounds like a country song if ever I heard one."

"I'll work on that." Cedra laughed softly. "Soon."

"With everything going on, you haven't had a lot of time to write, have you?"

"Not really, but the lyrics are still bouncing around in my head. I'll take some time to write them down soon. Maybe after tomorrow night's final jam session."

"At least you won't have to be up before the sun on Wednesday," Juliet replied.

"We all need to be well-rested, though," Cedra said. "We need to give Bud something to be proud to produce."

"I have no doubt we will."

†

Cedra fell asleep listening to Juliet's strong heartbeat and dreamed about their future. She crept from the bed and climbed into the shower when she woke the following day. Cedra was surprised when the draft from the shower curtain opening allowed cool air inside. She smiled when she felt Juliet's arms encircle her waist. "What are you doing awake so early?"

"I'm starting to enjoy early mornings with you," Juliet replied as she took a washcloth and washed Cedra's back.

"Who woulda thunk it?" Cedra teased. "Miss Late Riser up before the sun without an army to pull her from the bed."

"No army is needed when I can get this close to you," Juliet said and turned Cedra around for a passionate kiss. "Good morning, my love."

"Good morning. That was a romantic thing to say. I'm almost tempted to be late for work."

"This is your last day before two days off. Well, sort of. At least you won't have to be up so early."

"What plans do you have for the day?" Cedra asked.

"Ma and I are going to hit the Farmers Market to see what produce is left. Wayne and Keith are bringing her new freezer out this morning to set it up to start cooling. If all goes well, Ma and I will be freezing some veggies."

"That sounds incredibly domestic for you," Cedra teased.

"Ma says I'm a work in progress." Juliet smiled. "When you go back to work Friday, Ma and I are planning to do the holiday shopping."

"How much do you need from each of us?" Cedra asked.

"The boys have given me fifty dollars each. I think once you and I ante up, we will have plenty to shop with."

"I will give you seventy-five since my dad will be here," Cedra told her.

"If there's money left, we'll just add it to the Christmas week meals. Do you think your dad will come back?"

Cedra nodded. "I hope so. I've never spent a Christmas without him."

"We'll just have to make sure he has such a good time that Hank will want to come back."

Cedra smiled. "I think Stone plans to go home for Christmas, so it will be hard for both of us to be off at the same time. I think he really needs to see his family."

"I don't know how he handles it." Juliet smiled. "It would drive me crazy to be away from you."

Cedra kissed Juliet. "You say the sweetest things sometimes. I'm going to step out while you finish bathing. Love you."

"Ditto. I'll see you before you head downstairs."

†

Cedra was tying her shoes when Juliet stepped into the room covered by a robe. "Will you be a few minutes downstairs before you have to leave?" she asked Cedra.

"Yes, I believe so. It's going to take some time to thaw out my truck this morning."

Juliet glanced out of the window. "Damn, it does look cold. Do you have a jacket to wear?"

"Yes, I have a light one. It's not leather-jacket or down-jacket cold yet." Cedra pulled a light windbreaker from her closet.

"Oh, no, that won't do at all. Hang on, I'll be right back."

Cedra slipped her keys in her pocket as Juliet returned, carrying a denim jacket lined with Sherpa cotton. "This will keep you warm." Juliet held the coat open for Cedra to slide her arms into and pulled it up over her shoulders. "That looks like it fits well."

Cedra looked up at her and smiled. "It does. Thank you. I won't need it once I get to work, so I'll take it off and keep it safe."

"No problem. It's actually gotten a little snug on me, but it seems to fit you perfectly, so why not keep it?"

"It is warm," Cedra replied. "Can I buy you one to replace it?"

Juliet nodded. "Next time we go shopping, we'll look. I've got several coats I can wear in the meantime."

Cedra finished buttoning the jacket. "I'm going to start my truck. See you in the kitchen in a few?"

"Yes, ma'am, you will," Juliet replied. She straightened the collar on the jacket and kissed Cedra. "It looks good on you."

"Thanks. It sure feels good."

"I'll be right back, Ma. I'm going to start my truck to get her warming," Cedra called out as she bounced down the stairs.

"That's not a bad idea. It's frigid out this morning."

Cedra passed Stone in the doorway. "I'll be right back."

"You want me to go start her?" Stone asked.

"Naw, get some coffee in you. It won't take me long."

She climbed in behind the wheel and started the engine. As she leaned forward, her face was near the jacket lining, and she could smell Juliet's cologne in the fabric. "That's an added plus," Cedra spoke to herself. She buried her nose in the scent. After waiting a few minutes, she turned the heater and defroster to full heat before leaving the truck. Her breath formed a vapor in front of her as she walked back to the porch. "Damn, it's cold."

Juliet, Stone, and Ma were seated around the kitchen table.

Ma pointed to a plate of tasty-looking pastries. "I know you don't normally eat breakfast this early, but I made a pan of cinnamon rolls since it was so cold outside."

"I can't say no to those," Cedra said and picked up a pastry. She bit into it and moaned. "These are fantastic, Ma. Thank you."

"I was thinking about making some sticky buns tomorrow using some of the pecans. Y'all can eat them on the way to the studio after a full breakfast," Ma said.

"I may have to return those new jeans for a larger size," Cedra complained.

"No way. We'll just have to work the calories off ya," Juliet teased. "If it warms up today, we can harvest the rest of the pecans. I'm sure there are not many left."

"I'll gladly buy some at the Farmers Market if you'll keep making pies," Stone offered.

"We already have them on our list this morning," Ma answered. "Since you're up and dressed, we can get an early start on the shopping if you want? The boys can finish off the cinnamon rolls if they wake up before we get back."

"That's fine with me," Juliet replied. "We can catch the farmers as they first arrive and get first picks."

"It will be nice to have some home-grown vegetables in the freezer for this winter," Ma stated with a sparkle in her eyes. "They are so much better tasting than the store-bought kind."

"Maybe we can have some fresh vegetables and fried pork chops for dinner tonight," Juliet suggested.

"That does sound good," Ma agreed.

The clock chimed in the hallway. "I guess we need to get moving. Thanks for the goodies, Ma. Y'all have fun today." Cedra kissed Juliet and then followed Stone out the door.

"Be careful and stay warm," Ma called after them.

"Yes, ma'am," Stone answered and swung the door open for Cedra.

†

As they climbed into her truck, Cedra looked over at Stone. "Are you warm out there in the camper?"

"It got a bit cold last night, but I kicked the heat on, and all was good. Ma said I could use the small room downstairs anytime I needed to, so I may take her up on that if it continues to get colder." Stone smiled as he held his hands in front of the vent to warm his hands.

"I think we both need to invest in some gloves," Cedra said with a grin. "Neither one of us is used to this cold weather."

"We typically get a few days of cold weather, but they don't last for long, and we're back in the seventies," Stone replied.

Cedra nodded as she turned the windshield wipers on. "About the same in South Alabama. Maybe just a bit colder, but nothing like this so early in the year."

"Thank goodness your heater works well," Stone said as Cedra backed out of the spot.

"We'll be toasty in no time."

†

Lisa Marie was coming out of the office when Cedra and Stone entered. Cedra noted the look of worry on Lisa Marie's face. "Is everything okay?" she asked.

"I don't know. I have to attend a meeting of the downtown food merchants this morning to talk about revisions to how we operate moving forward with this virus explosion."

"We can handle everything here. I hope the meeting turns out better than you hope," Cedra added to cheer her up.

"Let's grab some coffee and think through this process," Lisa Marie suggested.

"I'll bring the coffee," Stone offered.

"Ask Teddy to join us too," Lisa Marie requested.

When the four of them were around the table, Lisa Marie brought them up to date on how the virus, what they were now calling Corona virus, would affect local businesses. "Best case scenario is we close down the dining room and do takeout orders only," she stated. "I believe we can make this work with some modifications."

"Like what?" Teddy asked. "I can't afford to be out of work."

"None of us can, but I believe that if we shut down at two after the lunch crowd, we will still be able to keep everyone in a whole paycheck. I'll pull Vanessa and Jennifer in to help with the new process."

"What can we do to help?" Cedra asked.

Lisa Marie looked at Teddy. "Who would be your choice of assistants in the kitchen? We need to double up to keep the flow high to limit everyone's exposure."

"Damn, that sounds like something from a horror movie," Teddy said.

"It sure does, man," Stone said.

"As grumpy as she can be, Vanessa has helped me in the kitchen and would probably be the most familiar with the equipment and processes," Teddy answered.

"Good. That was what I was thinking too," Lisa Marie said. "Stone and I can take care of the coffee orders, call ahead orders, and cash outs while Cedra greets and takes orders which she'll send electronically to the kitchen. I'm having a screen installed for you this morning, Teddy." She looked at Cedra. "I have an iPad already loaded with the menu and ordering software. If the screen gets installed today, I'd like to try it out to see if we need to work through glitches."

"That sounds like a good process," Teddy replied.

"Jennifer will be in charge of seating the waiting customers and delivering orders. We will have strict protocols to follow for social distancing and sanitizing areas, so we'll need to shut down several tables in the dining room."

"How do you think the customers are going to react to that?" Stone asked.

"I'm sure they won't be pleased, but that may be our only option," Lisa Marie said. "They will only be allowed to enter the café if they are wearing a mask. If they refuse, they will have to wait outside for their orders."

"Would you mind a suggestion?" Stone asked.

"No, go ahead," Lisa Marie said.

"Swap Jennifer and me to allow me to work the seating. I'll be closer if anyone gets rowdy and can handle it better," he suggested. "I don't anticipate any of our regulars having an issue, but we don't know how the additional stress is going to affect people."

"That's a great point and excellent suggestion. Thank you, Stone."

"What's the worst-case scenario?" Teddy asked.

Lisa Marie sighed. "That we are closed down completely, but I hope it won't come to that if business owners work together to comply with the city's mandates."

"Me, too," Teddy said. "Will we be eligible for unemployment if we have to shut down?"

"Yes, you will, and I have a week's salary available for each of you to tide you over until the benefits kick into effect," Lisa Marie answered.

"That is very considerate of you," Cedra said. "What time is the meeting?"

"At eight. I've asked Vanessa and Jennifer to come in at twelve to meet to plan after the lunch rush once we know more. Is that okay with everyone?"

"Yes, ma'am," Stone replied.

Teddy and Cedra nodded in agreement.

"Keep your fingers crossed everything goes well. We are fully stocked in masks and food handling gloves. We might need to begin wearing them for protection, depending on what we are told this morning."

"We have customers outside," Stone said. "Are we ready to open?"

"Go ahead and let them inside, Stone. Please remember to wash hands or use the hand sanitizers often," she told them.

†

"It's more crowded than I would have thought at this time of the morning," Juliet said as she parked her car.

"I think people are getting a bit spooked by this Corona virus that's rapidly increasing," Ma said. "I'm afraid people will start to hoard food and other items in a panic."

"Are there items we need to stock up on? Besides food," Juliet asked.

"Probably some paper products like toilet paper. I keep a decent stock of cleaning supplies."

"Should I text the boys to pick up some toilet paper? We can get some, too, before we go home."

"That's not a bad idea," Ma suggested. "They can pick some up at the store where they are getting the freezer."

Juliet nodded and sent Wayne a text. He responded with a thumbs up within seconds. "All set. Let's go see what we can find. Two carts?"

"It would be great if we could fill them both."

Juliet nodded as they entered the Farmers Market.

"That's a relief," Ma said as she looked at the aisles filled with fresh vegetables. "Get four of those small baskets of crooked neck squash. Have you ever had acorn squash?"

"I don't think so."

"Get three then." Ma picked out bundles of greens and made a beeline to the refrigerated section of the vendor's stall. Inside were all kinds of peas and beans already shelled. "All we'll need to do to these is blanch them and bag them for the freezer," Ma told Juliet. She picked out six bags of each type and placed them in her cart. "We'd better get out of this section before we go broke," Ma teased and paid the vendor.

"It looks like many of the stalls have items pre-shelled or shucked."

"It keeps them from going bad if they don't sell quickly," Ma informed her.

"That makes sense. There's still white corn on the cob that's been shucked, and some cut from the cob."

"Let's grab a bunch of that. Corn goes with everything," Ma said.

"Anything else from this vendor?"

Ma chuckled and pointed to the bottom of the cooler. "You'd better take care of your gal," she teased.

Juliet bent down to see bags of okra. She began pulling containers out and stopped at six. "I can't be greedy. There's got to be others out there that love it as much as Cedra." There was a massive mound of sweet potatoes. "These store well in the cool, don't they, Ma?"

"Yes, and they are packed full of vitamins. Fill us up a bag," Ma said.

"I've got bags already filled," the woman behind the counter said. "Five or ten pounds?"

"Give us two ten pounders," Juliet answered and paid the woman for the goods.

Ma and Juliet searched the aisles for bargains and came out with five pounds of shelled pecans and two bushels of apples. "Those will make excellent pies and goodies," Ma said. "The cooked apples freeze well too."

Juliet picked up a large bag of shelled walnuts and held them up to Ma. "Brownies?"

At the next stall, Juliet turned to Ma. "I know we came primarily for veggies, but what about some of those ham steaks for your freezer and a frozen ham for Thanksgiving?"

"Not a bad idea. We need some ham hocks for the greens and beans, too," Ma replied. She picked up a large head of cabbage. "How about some coleslaw to go with dinner tonight?"

"Sounds terrific to me," Juliet agreed. "Can we freeze blueberries and strawberries?"

"Yes, we can. We need to stop for some freezer bags on the way home." Ma picked up another basket of strawberries. "Let's see if they have an angel food cake in the bakery section."

"You realize how dangerous it is to take me into that section, right?" Juliet grinned.

"I'll buy you some cookies or one of those big pretzels to keep you occupied," Ma teased. "You can munch while I get baked goods and some cheeses for a snack tray before Thanksgiving. Hopefully, I can keep the boys out of it." Ma chuckled.

"Should I go back to the meat section and pick up some slices?"

"No, we have time for that yet. We can pick that up early next week. It would be too tempting for a midnight snack." They pushed their carts inside to the air filled with heavenly aromas. "What's it going to be? A pretzel or cookies?"

"A pretzel," Juliet said, "with some of that beer cheese."

Ma grinned and ordered the pretzel. "Wait here, and I'll be back."

†

Ma went straight for the angel food cakes and picked out two. She spotted a caramel cake on her way to the cashier and smiled. That was always a crowd favorite. "Will you also box up that caramel cake?" Ma asked when she made it to checkout.

"Just one?" the lady teased.

"Do you have more I'll take another if you have one."

"Two it is then," the lady responded. "I'll be right back with them."

Ma paid and made her way back to where she had left Juliet, but she was nowhere in sight. Ma started down an aisle toward the cheese selection, where she heard Juliet talking with the vendor.

"Yes, I'd love a sample of that."

"Are you grazing?" Ma asked cheerfully.

"No, I've bought several types. You've got to try this smoked cheddar with me," Juliet said.

"What have you gotten so far?"

"The cheddar, some gouda, and pepper jack. I think a pound of each should work, don't you?" Juliet answered as she received her change. The vendor handed Ma a slice of the smoked cheddar.

"That is delicious," Ma said. "We better get out of here before we're bankrupt."

"I see you bought more than an angel food cake," Juliet teased.

Ma shrugged. "They had their cakes on special, so I bought two caramel cakes. I know they won't go to waste."

"You're right. We better leave now."

They stopped off at a store for the freezer bags, and they both picked up a large package of toilet paper. "We should probably pick up a pack every time we come out," Ma said. "It may become a rare commodity soon."

"I noticed the bleach section was nearly empty as well." Juliet smiled. "I hope we can steer clear of that virus."

"We have to be smart when we venture out. Make sure we eat and drink well and get plenty of rest." Ma picked up three packs of surgical masks and dropped them in the cart. "I've got some cloth and elastic at the house. I think I will sew some fabric masks for us."

"They would probably be more comfortable and reusable after washing," Juliet said. "I can't sew a button on, but if you can show me what you need, I can cut the fabric and elastic."

"You have a deal. It will be critical for Cedra and the boys who are still working in public to be protected."

Juliet's face went white. "I hadn't thought about that."

"We'll be okay, as long as we play things smart," Ma said. "Protecting ourselves protects us all."

"I hope to be as smart as you when I grow up."

"There's hope for you yet," Ma teased.

†

Wayne and Keith were fussing in the backroom installing the new freezer when Juliet and Ma arrived home. "How damn difficult can it be to unpack this danged thing?" Keith fussed.

"They wrapped it well for transport, bro. We've almost got it," Wayne said.

"You boys need help?" Juliet teased. "You unwrap and plug it in," she instructed.

"We know that, but I swear they've taped up every piece they possibly could," Keith groaned and pulled off another piece of tape. "Every time I think we've got it all, we find something else taped."

"Take a break for a few and come to help Ma and I unload. I promise it will be worth the effort, and if you need me to finish here, I will."

"No way this is going to beat us," Wayne said, "but we'll come help unload."

The four of them had the car unloaded in no time.

"Is that what I think it is in the boxes?" Keith asked with sudden glee.

Juliet grinned. "Ma got a great deal on caramel cakes and bought two. Chill your jets, though. We're having strawberry shortcake tonight."

"That works for me, too," Keith said. "Come on, Wayne, let's finish this monster."

Juliet looked at all the goods they had purchased. "Where do we start, Ma?"

"You can start by taking this toilet paper and the masks upstairs. Just place them on my bed for now. Put one of the packs of toilet paper in your bathroom."

"Got it."

Ma looked at the crowded table. "I'll start sorting through the vegetables while you're gone."

†

Cedra looked up when Lisa Marie returned from her meeting. The worried look was still on her face. Cedra was between customers, so she approached her boss. "How'd it go?"

"Just as we expected. Take out only, starting on Monday." Lisa Marie frowned. "I'll create and post a notice on the front door to notify our customers tomorrow morning. I had an idea, but I'm going to need help from you and Stone."

"Just let us know what you need, and we'll do everything we can."

"Thank you so much. I think I need some coffee. Are you two about ready for breakfast?"

"I think it's a good time. Stone's customer is about done. I'll place our orders. Do you want something?" Cedra asked.

"Not right now. I've got to get a few things from my truck."

"Do you need help?"

"No, I've got this."

Cedra placed their breakfast orders and asked Teddy to join them for a break. Stone cashed out his customer and joined them at the counter. "How'd it go?" he asked Lisa Marie as Teddy brought out their breakfast.

"Just as we expected. We have to reduce to take out only orders starting Monday. I want us to begin masking immediately. This is more serious than anyone thought." She passed out masks to them. "I know you two are off tomorrow and Thursday, but can I get your help Thursday?"

"Of course, you can. What do you want us to do?" Stone asked.

"I need help with a project. I've ordered some clear tarps that I would like you to hang on the poles lining the sidewalk to protect our customers from the wind and cold while they wait. I plan to line the entire front and make one line for call ahead order pick up and the other for walk-up orders."

"That's a good idea and hopefully will help us from getting bottlenecked at the front door and encourage customers to call in their orders," Cedra said.

"We also need to measure six-foot lengths and encourage customers to maintain the appropriate distance. We'll use spray paint until I can get some stickers ordered," Lisa Marie said. "If you two can handle that project, I'd be grateful."

"We can handle that and recruit Keith and Wayne to help," Stone suggested. "Do you have a ladder?"

"Yes, in the stockroom. I'll pick up zip ties to secure the tarps later today," Lisa Marie replied.

"We can handle that with ease," Cedra said. "What else can we help with?"

"I know it's not supposed to start until Monday, but maybe we can go ahead while we have some muscle and move some of the tables into the stockroom." Lisa Marie had tears in her eyes.

"We can wait until Sunday morning to do that if you want?" Stone said. "Wayne, Keith, and I can do that quickly, and it won't interfere with customer flow."

Lisa Marie nodded. Cedra reached out and placed her hand on Lisa Marie's shoulder. "We'll get through this." She looked at Teddy. "Is there anything we need to do in the kitchen?"

"Just make sure we have plenty of Styrofoam take-out containers. It probably wouldn't be a bad idea to order some plastic bags too," Teddy said. "Jennifer can double-check the orders and bag them for delivery. What about some drink caddies, too?"

"I'll get them ordered today," Lisa Marie said. "Great plan, Teddy."

"Thanks, boss." He smiled. "What about Tom?"

"We'll need him to clean tables between customers and make sure the bathrooms stay stocked," Lisa Marie said. "He'll be back tomorrow, so I'll bring him up to speed then." Lisa Marie sighed. "I'm going to be placing hand sanitizer stations throughout the café. We need to make sure we stay gloved up and sanitize as often as possible. I hate that we have to do this, but it's the only way to stay open right now. There will be pop-in inspections by the Health Department to ensure compliance. If not, they will close our doors until the mandates are lifted."

"That's severe," Stone said.

"This virus is already killing hundreds by the day and is only getting worse. We may have to look into a walk-up delivery if things get worse."

"That could be done easily," Stone said, and all heads turned to him.

"How so?" Lisa Marie asked.

Stone pointed to the side door they used to enter in the mornings. "You replace that door with a Dutch door. The top swings open while the bottom remains closed."

"That's a great idea." Lisa Marie smiled for the first time since they began planning. "I'll measure today and get one ordered."

"If you give me a tape measure, I'll do it for you," Stone offered. "The sooner you can order, the better. You might even consider a local merchant to custom build one as a faster resource."

"I'll try that avenue first. I'd like to keep our local resources as busy as possible. The impact will touch many industries."

"It's going to kill the bar scene," Teddy said.

"They have to comply with strict limits inside and even in outdoor areas that don't have good ventilation," Lisa Marie told them. "That upset a lot of bar owners this morning."

"I bet it did," Cedra said. "It's going to drastically impact their revenues."

The lunch customers started to arrive, and Lisa Marie headed to the office to make calls. When Jennifer and Vanessa came in, Cedra sent them to the office as instructed.

"What's with the masks?" Vanessa asked.

"Lisa Marie will fill you in on what's going on," Cedra said.

Carrie arrived for lunch and stopped in her tracks when she saw Cedra and Stone were wearing masks. "I take it the meeting didn't go well this morning," she said.

Cedra shook her head. "Things will be tough for a while, but we'll pull through. Starting Monday, we have to close down the dining room and only offer take-out or call-ahead orders. We'll also close at two."

"Damn. I bet the bars were hit hard, too."

"Minimal capacity. If they don't have outdoor seating, it will really cut into their business."

"This is getting serious quickly, isn't it?" Carrie asked.

"Worse than anyone expected or prepared for. How will it affect the studio?"

"Minimally, at least at first. The studios are isolated, so distancing isn't going to be a problem. The common areas will have to be monitored closely. It shouldn't limit your availability if that's worrying you. You'll get plenty of time to record. It will have impacts on live performances, though."

"At least we can continue to write and record. I hate that it will delay playing any gigs," Cedra said. "Your usual?" she asked.

"Yes, please."

Cedra placed the order with Teddy. "I know that one by heart now," Teddy joked.

"Yeah, she's pretty consistent."

Stone walked up with an order. "Are you okay?"

"Kinda bummed. Carrie says we will still be able to record, but live performances won't occur for a while."

"That gives us plenty of time to record more music and get better performing together before we hit the road. Maybe we can do some videos."

"Maybe so," Cedra replied and made rounds with a tea pitcher while she waited for Carrie's order.

†

"You're doing great," Ma praised Juliet as she filled bags with blanched peas and beans. "We're making good progress this morning."

"I'm surprised how easy this is."

"There's not much to it, but it can be time-consuming. Getting a lot of these already shelled really helped speed up the process." Ma turned off a burner to let a pot of beans cool. "How about some grilled cheese sandwiches and soup for lunch?"

"That sounds good to me. Do we have tomato soup?"

"We do indeed. Will you check on the boys and see if that's good for them?"

"Yes, ma'am. I'll be right back." She walked into the back room and found Keith and Wayne sitting on the floor beside the new freezer. "You got her up and running?"

"Finally, we just need to clean up our mess, but she's running and starting to cool," Wayne said.

Juliet smiled. "Good job. Ma wants to know if grilled cheese sandwiches and tomato soup are okay with y'all for lunch?"

"That sounds great. I'm starved," Keith replied.

"We'll take care of this mess and pick up pecans until you call us in for lunch," Wayne said.

"Bundle up. It's still cold out there," Juliet warned.

Wayne laughed. "Will do."

†

"Thanks for all your help and suggestions today," Lisa Marie told Cedra and Stone at the end of their shift. "I was able to order the Dutch door. If the owner can install it by Sunday, we may change our setup to serve the coffee and call-in orders through there. He seemed appreciative of the business, so that was a good call, Stone."

"That would be great," Cedra replied. "We can set up a table and coffee pot for Jennifer there."

"I can run food orders over to her, too," Stone said. "We'll make it work."

"Yes, we will," Lisa Marie said with a smile. "Good luck at the studio tomorrow, and I'll see y'all Thursday. I won't keep you a minute longer than necessary."

Cedra smiled. "That's no problem. Just make a list of anything else that needs to get done, and we'll take care of it for you."

"I am blessed to have such a great team," Lisa Marie said.

"We will survive this," Cedra promised. "See you Thursday." Cedra slipped Juliet's coat on and smiled at the scent of her cologne. It was a very comforting smell after a long shift.

"Let's go home and see what help Ma needs," Stone said.

"Why don't you give them a call to see if there's anything she needs while we're in town," Cedra suggested as they walked to her truck.

"Sure will." Stone pulled out his phone.

"What on earth?" Cedra said as they approached the truck. Underneath her windshield wiper, there was a small envelope. She picked it up and opened it as Stone climbed inside and called Ma. Cedra leaned against the door as she read the note.

She's mine, and I will not tolerate you trying to take her from me. Stop now, or there will be worse consequences.
"What the hell?" Cedra was confused by the cryptic message. She slipped the note into her pocket and looked around the parking lot before entering the truck.

"Everything okay?" Stone asked.

"Yes, I'm fine," Cedra replied and cranked the truck. "Six Strings" was playing on the radio. *What a perfect diversion*. She felt her insides quivering from the strange message. "Great timing," she said to Stone as she put the truck in gear, and they sang along.

"Ma said they didn't need anything but to pick up toilet paper if we stop anywhere."

"If I stop at the store, will you run in and pick up a jumbo pack and some milk? We always seem to run out of milk," Cedra said.

"I sure will."

Cedra drove to a nearby store and dropped Stone at the door. "I'm going to snag that parking place," she said and pointed to an empty spot.

"I won't be gone long. Do you want a drink or something?"

"I could use a Mountain Dew."

"You got it."

"Do you need some money?"

"No, I've got this covered, but thanks."

Cedra maneuvered the truck into the parking spot and turned it off. She pulled the envelope from her pocket and read over the note again and still couldn't make any sense of the warning. Was the person talking about Juliet? Could it be Viper? Cedra was no closer to solving the mystery when Stone returned. She quickly stuffed the note back in her pocket. "That was quick."

"Good thing we arrived when we did. This was the last pack of toilet paper in the store," Stone reported.

"I guess whenever we see some, we'd better pick it up."

"I got two gallons of milk. At least that's not running short yet. Here's a cold Mountain Dew for you." Stone handed her the drink.

Cedra opened the drink and took a long sip. "Man, that's good. Thank you." She was reaching to start the truck when her phone rang.

"Guess what I just heard?" her dad asked when she answered.

"What, Daddy?" she queried with a wink to Stone.

"I heard y'all on the radio, and y'all sounded great," Hank said. "The DJ was excited to play the song and highlight you as the local talent. I bet he gets several more requests to play the song. I think I'll call in a couple times per day to ask for it to play."

"That can't hurt, Daddy."

"Okay, I won't keep you. I just wanted to say I heard my baby on the radio. I'm proud of you and love you. Call me later."

"I will, Daddy. I love you, too. Bye for now."

"He was excited. It's great to hear it's being played outside of Nashville."

"Yes, it is," Cedra replied and started home.

†

"Wow," Juliet said when they took the last batch of corn to the new freezer. "We did good today," she said to Ma.

"Yes, we did. We can have vegetables for a while now. We still need to buy fresh when we can to preserve these for the future, but we are in good shape. Thanks for all of your help today, and thank you both for the new freezer," Ma told Keith and Wayne.

"Do you think we should stock up on some meats as well?" Wayne asked. "The news reports are predicting some shortages if meat processing plants get shut down."

"That's probably not a bad idea. Can we send out two groups to shop after Cedra and Stone come home?" Juliet asked.

"Why don't we let them come home and rest while we shop?" Wayne suggested.

"We can do that. I'll send Cedra a text," Juliet said. "They are probably on their way."

"They are. I just got a call from Stone twenty minutes ago and told him to get some toilet paper," Ma said. "They should be pulling up any time now."

The door opened a few seconds later, and the group broke out laughing.

"Did we miss something?" Cedra asked.

"We were just about to leave to go meat shopping when Ma said you would be home soon. You two can stay and rest or go with us," Juliet replied.

"I'm not tired," Cedra answered.

"Me either, and it will go faster if we all shop," Stone added.

"Why don't you go with the boys and bring them up to date on the café, and I'll go with Ma and Juliet?" Cedra suggested.

"That sounds ominous." Juliet scowled.

"Ma, why don't you give the boys instruction on what to get while I run upstairs for some money," Cedra suggested. "I've got a card to the wholesale club if we want to go there," she added.

Cedra started for the stairs as Ma began writing a list for the boys. "I don't want us to feel panicked, but I want us to be prepared."

"Let me get you some money," Cedra heard Ma say when she returned.

"No, Ma, we've got this," Keith said. "We need to help fill our bellies."

"Okay then, let's shop. I'll cook dinner as soon as we get back." Ma looked at Cedra. "We need to put large storage bags on our list for the wholesale club. We used a bunch today for the vegetables."

"What about milk?" Juliet asked.

"Stone got two gallons, but it can't hurt to have a few more," Cedra answered.

"We can take my truck," Wayne suggested as they left the house.

"Mine's already warmed up, too, and it will hold more than your car," Cedra told Juliet.

"Mission carnivore underway then," Keith joked.

†

Carrie's phone pinged with a text. *Dinner at my place tonight? I have a special present for you.*

Carrie smiled. *See you around six.*

Perfect, Linea answered.

"I'm going to give you the ride of your life," Linea spoke to herself. She tucked a bag under her arm and walked to her car.

†

"We need to add some starches to our list," Ma said from the back seat of Cedra's truck. "Rice, different kinds of pasta, and flour. If nothing else, I can keep us in rice and gravy."

"We should be able to get big bags of rice and flour at the wholesale club. They usually have bulk boxes of macaroni and cheese and quick-fix dinners," Cedra informed them.

"Let's all grab a cart when we arrive. You and Juliet grab the starches while I start the meats," Ma suggested.

"That sounds good," Juliet answered. "How about tea bags and sugar, too, Ma?"

"Coffee and creamer as well. We can get some extra loaves of bread to put in the freezer, too," Ma added.

"We'll see you in a few," Cedra called out as they went in separate directions. "You get the coffee and tea stuff, and I'll go for starches."

"I'm on it," Juliet replied.

Cedra loaded three large bags of rice into her cart and two large bundles of macaroni and cheese, flour, and pasta salad meals. She also added multiple large cans of chicken

112

and tuna. When she reached the end of her aisle, she saw Juliet heading her way.

Juliet grinned when Cedra reviewed her cart. "I grabbed several family-sized boxes of cereal and pop tarts. They will make for an easy meal or snack."

"Good deal. Let's see how Ma is making out," Cedra suggested. "Hey, grab a couple gallons of milk as you pass by and some of the butter too."

"What about eggs?" Juliet asked.

"Go ahead and get a couple twin packs."

Ma was just ahead, looking at the meat selections. She had filled her cart half full already. Cedra waited for Juliet to return. "I'll take your cart if you go back for several packs of gallon freezer bags. We forgot those."

"No problem," Juliet said.

Ma looked up when Cedra approached. "Where's Juliet?"

"We forgot the freezer bags, so she went back for them," Cedra explained.

Ma nodded. "Grab a couple of those twin packs of pot roasts. The bigger, the better."

Cedra picked out three packs and placed them in her cart. "What about these pork chops?"

"Yes, a couple of those as well. I got several large pork shoulders we can grill or cook in the oven and six whole chickens. They are cheaper than packs that have been cut and taste just as good."

"I know how to cut them up. I did it all the time at home."

Juliet returned, carrying two large containers of gallon-sized bags and a six-pack of brownie mix. She placed them in her cart. Cedra smiled at her lover. "Go back to the cooler section and grab a dozen packages of the cookies too. I know they will get eaten."

"Do you like calf's liver?" Ma asked.

"As long as I don't have to smell it cooking," Juliet replied.

"Grab a bag of sweet onions when you go for cookies. They are almost giving the liver away. It's a great source of iron and easy to cook."

"What about bacon and sausage?" Cedra asked.

"They were on the boys' list, but it doesn't hurt to check their prices," Ma said.

"That's not a bad price on the thick-sliced bacon, and that five-pound sausage roll can be divided. We can make patties or just leave it rolled and patty it before we cook it."

"I can make patties," Juliet said.

"Get two rolls then," Ma said. "Then we need to get out of here."

Cedra smiled and led them to the checkout. Juliet nearly passed out at the total.

"We got a lot of meals for that money. We shouldn't have any problems eating for the next couple of months," Ma said.

"You haven't done much grocery shopping, have you?" Cedra teased.

"That would be a big no," Juliet answered. "I'll grab some boxes to put the meats in, and we can slide them into the bed of the truck."

"It's a good thing you came in today," the cashier said. "Tomorrow, they are going to start placing limits on meats and other items."

"That's good to know. Thank you," Cedra replied as she paid for the goods. "Stay safe," she told the worker.

"You, too," the woman answered.

"Damn, should we go back and look for masks?" Cedra asked.

"We've got a few packs of disposable ones already. Juliet is going to help me make some cloth one's," Ma added.

"What? Did I hear you correctly?" Cedra teased.

"I'm going to cut the fabric from a pattern," Juliet clarified.

"That's still being helpful." Cedra smiled. She closed the tailgate on her truck. "We did get a lot."

"We won't be going hungry," Ma said. "Let's get home so I can start dinner while you two begin packaging this meat for the freezer."

Keith saw them pull up. He, Wayne, and Stone rushed out to carry the boxes inside. "Y'all did much better than we did," Stone said. "A lot of the meat had already been bought out."

"Let's get busy storing this, and then we can have dinner. Cedra, I'm putting you in charge of storage."

"You got it, Ma," Cedra answered. "Keith, you can start on the easy stuff. Milk, cookies, and bread. The packages of bacon can go in the freezer."

"Do you want me to go ahead and start making sausage patties?" Juliet asked.

"That would be great. Wayne, can you store the rice and flour in the pantry, then help Juliet make sausage patties?"

"What can I do?" Stone asked.

Cedra pointed to the table. "Eggs and butter in the fridge, then you can split the packs of beef roasts and put them in freezer bags to go in the new freezer."

Ma had veggies cooking in crock pots all afternoon and coleslaw chilling in the fridge. She needed to boil the corn and fry the okra and pork chops. "Do we want some cornbread with dinner?" Ma asked.

"That would be great, Ma," Cedra answered. "Do you need me to mix some up for you?"

"No, you continue on the meats. I'll get it in the oven and start frying," Ma said. "Stone, pull us out another stick of butter, please."

"You got it."

Cedra began cutting up the chicken, and as she rinsed it, Keith held a bag open for her to slide it into.

Ma looked at Cedra. "Leave two of the chickens whole and I'll have some baked chicken tomorrow night when y'all get home with more veggies."

"That works for me. Is the liver packaged good for you, Ma?" Cedra asked.

"Yes, it can go straight into the freezer. Do you boys like fried liver?"

"Sure do, Ma. I can't say I'm a fan of the smell while it's cooking, though," Keith said.

"We'll find something else for you and Juliet to do while I'm cooking it then. Have either of you heard anything about your work situations yet?" Ma asked.

"We have a staff meeting Thursday at four," Wayne answered.

"No word from the Ryman yet." Keith shrugged.

"Speaking of Thursday, I need to ask for your help at the café for a few hours," Cedra said.

"I've already asked, and they've agreed to help," Stone told Cedra.

"Thanks, Stone."

"What am I missing?" Juliet asked.

"We're putting up some tarps along the sidewalk to shelter our customers while they wait. You can help, too," Cedra said. "We've got to mark the sidewalk in six-foot increments with spray paint. I think you and I can handle that."

"That sounds like a plan." Juliet smiled.

After the meats and other goods were stored, Cedra looked at Ma. "What else can we help with?"

"It will be another half an hour before dinner is ready. One of you can cut up some of the strawberries for dessert.

I'd like to get some pies frozen and ready to be baked. Could someone peel and slice some of those apples?"

"If Juliet can handle the strawberries, the boys and I can handle the apples," Wayne answered. "How many do you want prepared?"

"As many as you can get done before dinner," Ma replied. "I'll cook them tomorrow and then fill the pie shells Thursday while you all are at the café."

"Do we have room to pre-cook some pecan pies, too, Ma?" Cedra asked.

"I think we can manage one or two," Ma answered. "Once we take that monster turkey out to thaw, we should have room for several."

Keith chuckled. "You said to get a big one, Ma."

Ma smiled at him. "You did a perfect job of picking our turkey."

"I was thinking about getting one of those honey hams," Wayne said.

"Don't," Cedra replied. "Dad is bringing one. He'll be here Tuesday. Hopefully, we can stay out of it for a few days."

Juliet placed the strawberries on the table. "We picked up one at the Farmers Market, too. I don't think any of us will go hungry."

Ma looked at Cedra. "Will you grab a notepad and pen, and we can decide on a menu for next week?"

"Sure, Ma." Cedra retrieved the items and took a seat at the table. "Starting when?"

"Let's start on Sunday. French toast for breakfast?" Ma suggested.

"With some of that bacon?" Wayne asked.

"That will work," Ma answered.

They worked through the menu until Thanksgiving Day. Cedra looked at Ma. "We already know ham and turkey are on the menu. What else would you like?"

"Dressing for sure. How about a sweet potato casserole, mashed potatoes, gravy, green beans, and corn?" Ma looked around the table. "Deviled eggs, macaroni salad, and pies. Will that work for everyone?"

"Heck, yeah," Keith said. "Cranberry sauce, too? I love it on leftover turkey sandwiches."

Ma looked around the table. "That's not a problem. Have I left off anyone's favorite dish?"

"Can I make a squash casserole with some of the squash we put up today?" Cedra asked.

"Oh, yes. That sounds good." Ma smiled at Juliet. "I'm putting you in charge of the pre-meal snacks."

"Simple enough even for me," Juliet said.

Wayne smiled at Ma. "What can we help with, Ma?"

Ma pointed at Stone. "Peeling potatoes and slicing them." She looked at Wayne. "Boiling eggs and making deviled eggs." She saw his eyes grow wide. "Don't worry, I'll talk you through them."

Wayne relaxed. "Thank goodness."

Ma smiled at Keith. "Snapping green beans and shucking the corn. You can also be my gopher in the kitchen and keep the trash cleared."

Keith nodded. "I can do that."

"I imagine Cedra will be my right hand in the kitchen. So, you can help keep her father entertained while we cook."

Cedra smiled. "He offered to smoke the turkey if you didn't plan to cook it in the oven."

"That's not a bad idea. Keith, you could be Hank's assistant, too. That would free up the oven considerably. Everyone okay with that?"

"We could plan on some fresh rolls, too," Cedra suggested.

"Tell your dad, we'd love to take him up on his offer, then," Ma answered.

Cedra chuckled. "He would drive us nuts in the kitchen wanting to help, so getting him outside would be a good thing."

"I'll clean up the grill and get it set up near the back porch. We can get out of the wind back there," Keith said.

"Speaking of cleaning up, you all can clear the table and set it. Dinner will be ready in five. Y'all did well on the apples," Ma added. "Are you going to play a bit after we eat?"

"It wouldn't hurt us at all," Cedra replied.

"Let's do it then, but after dessert," Keith said.

"That was a given." Juliet smiled at him.

†

"That was another great meal, Ma," Wayne said as he pushed back his plate.

"We all had a productive day," Ma replied. "I'm going to put these apple slices away, but I'll be listening."

"You sure you don't need help?" Cedra asked.

"I'm good. Y'all get out of my kitchen," Ma teased.

"You heard the lady, boys. Let's move," Juliet said.

Cedra sat where she could see Ma in the kitchen, and she smiled at the bounce in Ma's step to the music they were playing. They ran through each of the songs twice before calling it a night.

†

"If I have a light breakfast ready by seven, will that give you enough time to get to the studio?" Ma asked.

"I would think so, Ma," Juliet replied.

"I'm going to make a couple plates of sticky rolls then with some of those pecan bits," Ma said. "It should be enough sugar to get y'all up and running."

"That sounds delicious, Ma," Wayne added.

Stone shuffled his feet. "I think I'll sleep in here tonight, if that's okay, Ma."

"I put clean sheets on the bed already," Ma answered. "Go get your clothes for tomorrow, and you can use my shower in the morning while I cook."

"Yes, ma'am." He smiled and left the house.

"That makes me feel better. It's going to be cold for the next few days," Ma said.

"If he needs to stay inside longer, Dad can have my room," Juliet replied.

"We may need to do that," Ma said. "This weather is so danged unpredictable these days. I'd rather have him inside than freezing out there when we have options."

"I agree," Cedra said. "You ready to head up to bed?"

"Yes, ma'am. I'm tired, but we did get a lot done today," Juliet said.

Cedra nodded. "We did. I feel good about the food stores we have now. We'll see y'all at seven. Goodnight, all."

"I'll get Stone all set and be right behind ya," Ma said. "I'm tired too."

†

Juliet followed Cedra upstairs into their rooms. Cedra pulled the envelope from the jacket pocket and hung it in her closet. "Is everything okay with you?" Juliet asked. "You've been surprisingly quiet today."

Cedra sat on the bed and handed the envelope to Juliet. "This was underneath my wipers when we got off work today."

Juliet took the envelope and sat beside Cedra as she read the note. "What the fuck?"

"That's what I said. What do you think it means?"

"I don't know what to make of it."

"Do you think it could be Viper?"

Juliet considered her response for several seconds. "I don't think so. I don't see her going to this much effort, to be honest. Do you think it's warning you away from me?"

Cedra shrugged. "Who else could it be? You're the only one I'm involved with? I can't think of anyone else."

"What do you think we should do?" Juliet asked.

"Nothing for now. Hopefully, it was not meant for me. Stone rides with me, so I'm not alone. Let's wait and see if anything else occurs."

"Does Stone or Lisa Marie know about this?" Juliet held up the note.

Cedra stuffed the note back into the envelope. "No. Stone saw it but didn't pry. Our song was playing on the radio, which distracted him. I didn't go back inside to talk to Lisa Marie."

"I think you should let both of them know to be on high alert, just in case something else odd happens."

"Lisa Marie already has enough stress on her."

"Then tell Stone," Juliet insisted.

Cedra nodded. "I'll tell Stone before we go back to work."

"I can follow you to work and keep an eye on the truck while you're working," Juliet said.

"I don't want you freezing out there. I think it's just a case of mistaken identity." Cedra regretted telling Juliet.

"You've got to promise me that you'll tell me if anything else happens," Juliet said.

"I will."

†

Linea refilled Carrie's wine glass for the third time and straddled her lap. "I hope you had enough to eat."

"I did. It was an excellent meal. Thank you."

"I felt like I needed to apologize after your last trip over here. I also bought something I think you'll enjoy," Linea said and handed Carrie a gift-wrapped box.

"What's this?"

"Open it and find out for yourself."

Carrie opened the box and frowned in confusion. "I thought you said you'd never do that with anyone."

"You're not just anyone. Bring your wine, and let's go give it a try."

Linea took the box containing a leather harness and a dildo into her bedroom. She quickly removed Carrie's clothing and secured the harness around her waist. "You look damn sexy," she purred. She handed Carrie a tube of lubricant as she removed the tiny amount of clothing she had on. Carrie sat her wine glass on the bedside table and began coating the toy's shaft with the lubricant.

Linea climbed onto the bed but remained on her hands and knees. "I want you to do me doggie style," she told Carrie. "Make me scream your name."

"You are a naughty girl," Carrie said. The wine had an unusual effect on her, but the temptation Linea was offering was too good to pass up.

"I'm dripping wet already. Fuck me, Carrie. Make me your bitch," Linea implored, her voice gruff with desire.

Carrie slipped the toy's head into Linea's entrance, and it slid in deeply with little effort. *This ain't her first rodeo, but if it's a wild ride she wants, I'll sure give her one.*

Carrie took Linea in various positions until she was exhausted and could barely raise her hips for Linea to remove the harness and toss it to the floor. The next thing she knew, it was five in the morning, and she snuck from the bed and carried her clothes into the living room to dress. Carrie made it home in time to shower and prepare for work. She'd work from the studio instead of the office, so the ride to work would be much shorter than usual. Her legs were sore as Carrie slipped into her shoes. She smiled as she strode out to her car for some breakfast. Carrie was starving after burning so many calories during the fuck fest with Linea.

CHAPTER FOUR

When they arrived at the studio the following day, Carrie and Bud were waiting for them. Cedra was surprised to see Carrie at the beginning of their session. "Is everything okay?" she asked Carrie.

"Yes, of course. I just wanted to be here to give you something on your first break."

"That's not for a few hours yet."

Carrie shrugged. "I didn't have anything scheduled this morning."

"What she's failing to tell you is all the excitement she's received over the debut," Bud said. "We've had numerous calls wanting more information on the Bentleys since the song first hit the airwaves. Congratulations. It's been well received by the media, and not just in Nashville."

"My dad said he's heard it several times in south Alabama," Cedra said.

"It's made it to Florida, too," Stone added. "Sarah called me this morning to say she's heard the song."

"Satellite radio has picked up on its popularity, too," Carrie told them.

"That can't hurt. Those stations broadcast across the nation," Bud added. "Are y'all ready to get back to work?"

"Yes, sir." Juliet grinned.

"Let's go." Bud pointed to the studio. "Get warmed up, and let me know when you're ready."

"Let's nail this first song off the bat to show Bud we've been working hard," Juliet encouraged as they unpacked their instruments. "Just like we did them last night."

"Hell yeah," Wayne hollered.

Bud smiled and nodded his head as they ran through the first song. "That was good, but let's run through it one more time and compare the two," he suggested.

When they finished the next run, he smiled and told them to meet him in the break room.

They filtered in and found a seat. "Put your headphones on and tell me which you like better."

Carrie rushed into the room and put a set over her ears. She smiled when the songs came to an end.

"Which did you like better?" Bud asked the group.

"Without a doubt, the second one," Stone said.

"I agree," Cedra and Juliet answered.

"I think we're all in agreement," Wayne answered.

Carrie nodded. "The second track was a lot richer sounding."

"Are you going to put them immediately back to work, or can I have them for ten minutes?"

"You may not," Bud replied. "I need them focused. You will just have to wait until we get another track cut."

"Get back to work then," Carrie instructed.

"I need to hit the bathroom, and I'll be right there," Cedra said. "Don't start without me."

"You goof. You're lead on this song, so we can't," Keith teased.

"I know." Cedra stuck her tongue out at him. "I'll hurry."

"Hell yes," Bud said after the last note sounded. "For someone who thinks she's not a good vocalist, you and Juliet sounded good together."

"Will you believe it from Bud?" Stone teased. "We've been telling you how good you sound all along."

Juliet looked at Cedra. "We did sound great on that song."

"Okay, come to the break room for a listen before Carrie blows a fuse," Bud joked. "She's got presents for y'all."

"Presents? New Ford trucks for all of us, I hope," Wayne joked.

"Keep dreaming, bro," Keith replied. "One day, we'll be able to buy whatever truck we want."

"Yeah, we will," Juliet agreed. "Let's go."

Carrie was beaming when they walked into the room. "Finally. I got a call from the head of promotions for Wrangler on Monday after he heard 'Six Strings' asking for your coat sizes. He said he was sure you'd be playing on one of their sponsored tours soon, so he wanted to get you outfitted. Just in time for the weather to turn cold, too." Carrie opened a large box and handed Juliet and Cedra hip-length Sherpa-lined coats. The boy's cuts were more traditional waist-length.

"These are beautiful," Juliet declared. "Thank you." She slipped the coat on, and it fit perfectly.

"I took a guess at the sizes, but I think I did pretty well," Carrie replied.

"Perfect," Stone uttered. "This will be warmer than anything I have."

"These aren't cheap either," Wayne stated.

Carrie shook her head. "No, they aren't. If your music continues to improve, I think it's safe to say you will receive many gifts from future sponsors."

"Any updates on there being any live performances anytime soon?" Cedra asked.

"Not yet. I've got an idea I want to run past Mark before I bring it up to you all, but I think it may be a viable option."

"Let's take a listen to this track, and then y'all can decide to continue or break for lunch," Bud suggested.

Cedra's head bobbed along to the tune she was singing. "I like it," she stated.

"I don't," Keith said, and all heads swiveled toward him. He quickly raised his hands. "I'm just teasing." He grinned. "It was perfect, Cedra."

"Just for that, you can wait outside for the pizza delivery," Carrie told him. "Everything is paid for, including the tip. I hope you like pizza. I can't do another cold sandwich."

"Pizza is perfect," Wayne answered.

"I'll be right back," Cedra announced.

"Me, too," Juliet said. She followed Cedra to the restroom. "You knocked that one out of the park, Baby Girl," she told Cedra. "Are you feeling, okay?"

"Yeah, the coffee is just going straight through this morning," Cedra answered as she headed into a stall. An Indigo Girls tune began playing, and Cedra started to sing along.

Juliet picked up on the harmony as she entered a stall, and they didn't hear the door open behind them.

†

Carrie walked into the bathroom to wash her hands. She smiled when she heard them singing to the tune. They harmonized perfectly together and an idea began to form. Neither of them exited until the song ended. Carrie heard two toilets flush and started clapping when they emerged from the stalls. "That sounded great. Have you ever covered any of their music?"

Cedra laughed. "No, that was a first. I used to wear their tunes out when I was in high school."

"They were popular in Athens, so I got to see them live a few times," Juliet said. "I had a huge crush on Emily for at least a year."

"Those two know all about writing to harmonize. Emily and Amy have the perfect voices to blend together," Cedra replied.

Carrie laughed. "You two sounded great even if you were sitting in toilet stalls. Do you know the music?"

"Yeah, I think so," Juliet said.

"I could play that one in my sleep," Cedra admitted.

Carrie's face was beaming with a smile. "I want the two of you to record it for Mark and me while we're waiting for lunch. Are you good with that?"

"Sure, just the two of us?" Cedra asked.

"Will the boys know the music?" Carrie asked.

"Only one way to find out," Juliet said and tossed a paper towel in the trash.

When they walked into the room, Wayne and Bud were the only one's present. Keith and Stone had gone to the front lobby to wait for pizza.

"Wayne, do you know the music for the 'Power of Two?'" Juliet asked.

"The Indigo Girls? Heck yeah, I do," he answered.

"Come with us then." Carrie motioned toward the studio. She waited until they left the room. "You've got to hear this," she told Bud.

"I'm all ears. I'll even let you in the sound booth."

When they were set with their guitars, Bud nodded from the booth. "Whenever you're ready." He turned on the recording and closed his eyes.

Juliet and Cedra repeated the song they had just sung in the bathroom. The music sounded purer as they smiled between verses, looking at each other. Wayne's head moved to the beat as he watched his friends nail the song.

"They were singing this along to the piped-in music in the bathroom just now," Carrie explained to Bud.

"These two harmonize perfectly together," Bud said. "You can feel the connection between them."

"I want to run something past Mark. I'll explain it to you in a second. Tell them to meet us in the break room."

"That was great, ladies. We'll meet you in the break room to give it a listen," Bud said.

Carrie looked at Bud. "With this stupid virus, we won't be able to get them out much to promote them until it gets under control. I'd like to pitch to Mark to use the Big Machine streaming program for half an hour to highlight them several times a week."

Bud nodded. "They could perform a mixture of covers, like that one, and mix in some original music. I like the idea, and I bet he will also."

"Their talent can't be allowed to fall through the cracks," Carrie said. "If you agree, I'll talk to him after lunch."

Bud nodded. "I'm totally on board. We'll be set to pick out more songs they can cover that well. They have enough original music we haven't even touched yet to keep us going for a while."

†

When Cedra, Juliet, and Wayne entered the room, Stone and Keith were spreading out pizza boxes and paper plates at the table. "We wondered where everyone had gone," Keith said.

Juliet looked at Cedra and broke out laughing.

"What's so funny?" he asked, confused by their laughter.

"Carrie caught us singing to the piped-in music in the bathroom and wanted us to play the song for her," Cedra answered.

"What song?" Stone asked.

"'Power of Two' by the Indigo Girls," Juliet said.

"I bet y'all nailed that," Stone replied.

"We're about to find out," Wayne pronounced as the door opened and Bud and Carrie stepped inside.

"Let's take a listen before we start eating," Carrie suggested.

They put their headphones on and listened to the song.

Keith's eyes lit with excitement. "That was fantastic. You two are perfect together."

Stone nodded. "I agree. You couldn't ask for better harmony."

"I have to agree with their assessments," Bud said. "That sounds terrific." He looked at Carrie. "Do you have other songs picked out that you'd like to cover?"

"Only about fifty," Stone declared. "We've been adding to it for weeks. I don't know why we didn't add that song to the list."

"Add it now and any others you feel passionate about," Carrie instructed.

"Do they need to be strictly country?" Keith asked. "We talked about picking songs from artists located around college towns. The B-52's and REM were huge in Athens, and Tom Petty is a Florida grad."

"We've also chosen Sam Hunt and Thomas Rhett songs," Stone added.

"Not at all. It can show the wide range of talent you have," Carrie answered. "I love your idea of picking college town favorites. Kenny Chesney's not the only Tennessee fan, and Chris Young went to school in Murfreesboro."

"You could have some fun with that," Bud replied. "Okay, eat up so we can knock out the last two tracks today. I'd like to meet back sometime this weekend to listen to the entire album if possible."

"Will Sunday after three be good for you?" Juliet asked. She looked at Cedra and Stone. "You two work Sunday, right?"

"Yes, at least for now," Stone answered.

"That will be perfect," Bud stated.

†

When the group returned to the studio, Carrie left searching for Mark. She found him in the boardroom, already listening to the three tracks. When he looked up and saw Carrie, he smiled. "They are a diamond in the rough. That cover song was amazing."

"I heard them singing it in the restroom during a break and asked them to sing it for Bud." Carrie sat beside him. "I want to run something past you."

"Go ahead. You seem excited about something. You've been batting a thousand with the Bentleys so far."

"I don't want them to get lost in the weeds or fall through the cracks with whatever this virus is going to bring. I'd like to propose a program on Big Machine Streaming called the Bentley Break to run for a half hour several times a week. I think you can see they can cover well, and we'll mix some of their original tracks in to keep them in listeners' ears until things get back to normal, and we can start setting up tours again."

Mark listened intently to Carrie's plan. "I only have one issue with your plan."

Carrie's forehead wrinkled in a frown. "What is it?"

"I don't think several times is enough. I think it needs to be a part of the daily schedule, at least in the beginning to see if they will catch on fire."

"Daily? Oh, hell yeah. We've got work to do," Carrie said.

"Why don't you try something a little different, too, since this is such a new platform?"

Carrie waited for Mark to continue.

Mark continued, "Plan on four songs per session. Have one or more of them introduce the song and tell a bit about it if it's original or why they chose the song if it's a cover?"

Carrie smiled. "I like it. Listeners can begin to meet the band."

"They are all so passionate about the music they play. I think that passion will become contagious or addictive to the listeners," Mark explained.

"You're a genius, Mark," Carrie said as she stood to leave. "Will we be able to start in January?"

"Sooner, if they get more studio time during this pandemic," Mark replied. "I can see bars, restaurants, and other venues being shut down if things don't drastically improve. We could be the only income they have coming in, and we have to give the music fans the best we can during these challenging times."

"That sounds great. We're meeting Sunday at 3:30 to listen to the final run of the album. Will you be there?"

"I wouldn't miss it for the world," Mark replied. "Congratulations, Carrie. You picked a winner with these kids."

"Thanks, Mark. I think so too."

"Go make some music."

Carrie left the board room so high that her feet barely touched the floor.

†

"That second run was much better. Are you ready to push through, or do you need a break?" Bud asked.

Juliet looked around the group and found everyone smiling. "Let's push through, Bud." She turned back to Keith and Wayne. "The last one's on y'all. Make us proud," she teased.

Wayne smiled at Juliet. "Got it. You ready, bro?"

Keith nodded. "Let's do it."

Cedra, Juliet, and Stone played the background music while Wayne and Keith performed the lyrics.

After the second run, Bud's voice rang in the studio. "That was the best you two have done yet," Bud said. "Let's run it one more time. This time, Wayne, tone the harmony down a notch. You're overpowering Keith a bit."

"You got it, Bud," Wayne answered with a smile.

The next performance was perfect, and Bud called it. "It's a wrap. Let's go take a listen."

Carrie was already in the room waiting for them. Her excitement was palpable as she paced the room.

Bud looked at her. "Come sit down and listen with us. You can share your news after we're done."

"Spoilsport," Carrie teased but took her seat.

Juliet picked up water for herself and Cedra and sat beside her love.

"I think we've got the final tracks finished," Bud said. "Let me know what you think?" He played both tracks and looked around the table at the excited faces. "Are we good to go?"

Cedra was the first to answer. "Yes, I think we are. What's the next step?"

"I'll spend the next few days fine-tuning the quality to edit out any glitches and engineering the final tracks for the album. I'll have the final product ready for Sunday afternoon. Once we're all in agreement, we start mass production of physical CDs and upload the electronic copies to the digital markets."

"Is either of the markets producing better these days?" Stone asked.

"It's still about fifty-fifty. Us old folks still like to have an actual CD to hold onto, but the younger crowd is almost exclusively digital," Bud explained. "Any other questions?"

"No, I think we're good," Juliet said.

Bud looked at Carrie. "The floor is yours."

"Thanks, Bud. Congratulations on cutting the final tracks for your debut album. I met with Mark while you recorded this afternoon, and I want to run a plan past you."

"Go for it," Keith said.

"Big Machine has recently begun a streaming service. It's still in the infant stage, but I want to schedule a thirty-minute time slot for what I'd call a *Bentley Break*." Carrie looked at the excited faces around the table. "Each session would consist of four tracks. A mixture of your original music and cover tunes. Before each song, one or more of you would explain the creation of the original music or the selection of the cover tunes to the listeners so they can begin to learn who you are." She smiled at Cedra and Juliet. "We love the passion you have talking about your music, and we feel that it will become addictive to your fans."

"Four songs, seven days a week. That's twenty-eight songs," Wayne quickly added. "We've only got the original twelve recorded."

"That's right. We have a lot of work to do," Bud informed them. "Once you have a couple of weeks recorded, I think we could re-run those sessions to ensure all listeners have an opportunity to hear those tracks."

"What's the mix of cover to the original music?" Stone asked.

"That's negotiable," Carrie answered. "Any thoughts?"

"We may need to be fifty-fifty until we can get more original tracks developed," Juliet suggested.

"I think that's a good plan for starters, then move to seventy-five percent original," Carrie answered. "All of it will be driven by the amount of time y'all can spend in the studio."

"Could you be prepared to record two more covers by Sunday?" Bud asked.

Juliet looked at Bud. "Hell yes."

"Our work schedules will be changing next week. Stone and I may be working seven days a week, but we'll be done by two," Cedra said.

"We still don't know about our work situations yet," Wayne added, "but we work nights predominantly anyhow."

"We have Thanksgiving next week, too, so the studio will be closed Thursday and Friday," Bud replied.

"That gives us Monday through Wednesday," Keith expressed.

"I've got a suggestion," Carrie injected. "Work on covers that don't require Stone and Cedra next week, and we can record them while they are working. They can join us after work to cut more tracks. How does that sound?"

Juliet looked at Cedra. "Would you be okay with that?"

"It does make good sense to get a jump on the covers," Cedra replied. "Stone?"

"I agree a hundred percent. It makes great business sense. I know we can select songs that will be perfect for them."

Bud smiled. "It also gives us a look at more original music for a second album."

"I do love the way you think, Bud," Carrie said. "I'll run the idea past Felecia, the producer of the streaming service, and get us set to go. I'll ask her to drop in to meet y'all at five on Sunday. That should give us plenty of time to review the album."

"Is there a chance she will nix the proposal?" Wayne asked.

"Not a snowball's chance in hell," Bud said. "She was looking for some unique ideas to produce the other day. This should be right up her alley."

"Does this mean that live performances will be pushed out a while?" Juliet asked.

Carrie nodded. "At least until we find out what's going on with this virus. This will keep the Bentleys in the public's ears until they can meet you in person."

"Another plus to doing this is that you could be in higher demand for better tours by already being a known entity," Bud added.

"You've all taken good care of us so far. I don't see any reason to not trust your judgment on this," Cedra replied.

"Good. So go make us some good music," Carrie directed. "I'll see you all Sunday."

"Thanks, Carrie," Juliet answered. "Y'all ready to go home?"

"Let's get busy," Wayne stated.

The group picked up their new coats and left the studio.

CHAPTER FIVE

Cedra smiled at Juliet. "I wasn't expecting any of that to happen. Were you?"

"Only that we would finish the tracks for the album today," Juliet answered. "I had no idea Carrie had come into the bathroom."

"Me either, but look what it's spiraled into. There are several of their songs I'd like to cover with you."

"'Watershed,' for sure. 'Least Complicated' and maybe 'Galileo.'" Cedra smiled. "I think we would sound good on those."

"We'll need the rest of the band for those, for drums and additional guitars," Juliet said. "I'll download them tonight."

"How about 'Free Fallin,' and 'I Won't Back Down' by Tom Petty?"

"You better start writing these down," Juliet teased as she drove. "Sam Hunt. 'Body Like a Back Road' and 'House Party,' 'Kinfolks' too."

Cedra laughed. "Thomas Rhett. 'T-Shirt,' 'Look What God Gave Her,' and 'Craving You.'" Cedra jotted down notes. "Kenny?"

"'No Shoes, No Shirt, No Problem,' and 'I Go Back.'"

"Oh, how about 'Burning House' by Cam?"

"I could so rock that with you," Juliet answered. "I don't think covers will be a problem for us."

"The Chicks. 'Wide Open Space' and 'Landslide.' 'Sin Wagon' would feature fiddle and banjo," Cedra replied. "We have to do some Eric Church for the boys."

"You know this is turning out to be more fun than I ever dreamed it could be. Much better than being a solo artist."

Cedra smiled. "I'm glad to hear that. I was worried that you might regret making the decision to join the group."

"I would have been a damned fool if I did. Every day with you just keeps getting better."

"I agree, and I hope we can say that six months down the road."

"Or six years."

Juliet pulled into the drive and parked. "I can't wait to share all the good news with Ma."

"Me too. I do have one request, though," Cedra replied.

"What's that?"

"That you wear my new coat until it smells like you. Or else I'll keep wearing this one. I love to turn my head and catch your scent."

Juliet stopped and just looked into Cedra's eyes for several long seconds. "I will gladly do that for you. No one has ever loved me the way you do. The things you sometimes say take my breath away. You make being a romantic seem so effortless."

"I only say the things I feel are true about you and about us."

"We better get inside before you make me start ugly crying," Juliet warned.

Cedra nodded when she saw the tears in her lover's eyes.

The boys pulled up beside them and bailed out of the truck. "Come on, slowpokes," Keith teased. He raced them all to the door.

†

Ma heard the stampede coming through the front door and turned to see five excited young faces smiling at her. They were all holding nice denim jackets.

"What's got you all so riled up?" Ma asked.

"New coats, courtesy of Wrangler for starters," Wayne said, and held up his new coat. "Wrangler is so impressed with our debut single they wanted to send us a gift to prepare us for future tours they will sponsor."

"We also got some terrific news. Oh, and we finished the last tracks for the album," Juliet said.

"Have a seat and tell me all about it. We've still got a few minutes before dinner is ready." Ma picked up her cup of coffee and joined them at the table. "Lay it on me."

"There's probably not much of a chance of our going out on tour soon because of this virus," Cedra said.

"Well, that's not good news or surprising."

"No, but what Carrie and Bud have planned for us is very exciting," Juliet stated. "Big Machine has begun a streaming service, and Carrie has convinced Mark to give us a daily thirty-minute spot called the *Bentley Break*."

"What?"

Cedra smiled. "A thirty-minute show to play four recorded tracks and to introduce those tracks to the listeners. We will start with two of our original songs and two covers until we can get some other tracks recorded."

Juliet stepped into tag-team Cedra. "We will record our introduction to each song with the motivation behind the music or the reason we chose a particular cover, to give the listeners a concept of who we are until they can meet us in person through live performances."

"That is brilliant," Ma agreed.

"Juliet, Wayne, and Keith will do some recording of cover tunes during the mornings that don't require Stone and me. We will join them as soon as possible once we get off work at the café," Cedra continued.

"You all are going to be very busy. I am so happy and proud of you."

"This also presents us with a chance to work on tracks for a second album," Wayne added.

"That sounds very promising. What are y'all going to do tonight?"

"I think we need to start getting serious about cover songs," Cedra replied. "Juliet and I started a list on the way home."

"That sounds doable, and we can choose two to record Sunday," Wayne said.

"We have an appointment to review the final album at 3:30 on Sunday, Ma. Would you go with us?" Keith asked.

"I'd love to," Ma said.

"Bud wants to record two more covers afterward. You could stay for that, and maybe we can grab some dinner before coming home," Cedra suggested.

Ma smiled at Cedra. "That sounds great. We'll need to mask up for that, but we have plenty of disposables. If Juliet helps me on Friday, I'll sew us some cloth masks."

"You got it, Ma," Juliet replied.

"Y'all start working on your lists while I finish dinner. It won't be much longer."

"Y'all go ahead and move into the living room, and I'll set the table and join you," Cedra said and handed Juliet her songbook.

As the group left the kitchen, Ma turned to look at Cedra. "Is everything okay?"

"Yes, things couldn't be better, Ma. Unless this virus would die off quickly. I think we're all very excited about the *Bentley Break* idea."

"That makes perfect sense. If a shutdown happens, you can get more studio time in. It may be a blessing you got your advances when you did," Ma added. "Unemployment benefits only cover part of your salary, and it takes a couple of weeks normally to get them started. If there's a massive shutdown, it may take much longer."

"I think it would affect Wayne, Stone, and me the worst since we also count tips into our earnings. Keith should be okay since he's straight salary."

Ma smiled. "One thing for certain. We won't starve with all the food we've collected."

Cedra walked to get the dishes. "I think if we're smart, we will navigate through a shutdown just fine. Instead of taking two vehicles to the studio, we will all cram into one of the trucks and save gas.

"I can't think of anything else we'll need except the usual groceries. Milk, bread, eggs, and the like. Maybe we should have invested in a cow." Ma chuckled at her comment as she checked on the chickens.

"Dang, those smell delicious."

"If we don't finish both of them tonight, I'll make some chicken salad for sandwiches tomorrow."

"Lisa Marie will probably insist on feeding us tomorrow for helping out, but you know food never goes to waste around here." Cedra had the table set and glasses out for drinks. "Give me a holler if you need any help."

"I will," Ma assured her. "Thanks for setting the table."

"Anytime," Cedra replied and left the room. She walked into the living room. "Did you finish the list?"

"Yeah, right," Wayne said. "We've added a bunch to it, though."

"I think we've narrowed the covers for Sunday down to three," Juliet said. "Two of the Chicks' songs and one from Sam Hunt."

"Which ones?" Cedra asked.

"'House Party,' 'Landslide,' and 'Wide Open Spaces.'"

Cedra clapped. "Those will be fun. We can start working on those tomorrow if you'll print out the lyrics and music for us."

"I'll get right on it after dinner while the rest of you continue working on our list."

"I think I'll let the boys do that while I go back through my songbook to look for other original tunes we can begin working on," Cedra said.

"That works, too," Stone offered. "I'll look at mine later and pick out a few as well. I think I have several that Juliet and the boys can perform without us."

They went through a list of Eric Church songs and picked out a few. Keith talked about Little Big Town and Florida Georgia songs until Ma called them to dinner. "Hold those thoughts," Wayne said. "I'm starved."

"That's usually my line," Keith teased as they walked to the kitchen.

"That smell is heavenly, Ma," Juliet said as she began pouring tea.

When they finished eating, Cedra looked at Ma. "No chicken salad tomorrow." She chuckled.

"No, but I can always make some later. I'm glad everyone got full bellies."

"Did I mess up eating seconds?" Wayne asked.

Ma shook her head. "Not at all. I mentioned to Cedra I would use any leftovers to make chicken salad for sandwiches tomorrow, but we have plenty of other options."

Stone swallowed. "Lisa Marie will probably stuff us with cheeseburgers when we get done, anyhow."

"That's exactly what Cedra said. If you get hungry before dinner, I'm sure we can find something to hold you over." Ma sipped her coffee. "I was thinking of a pot of spaghetti, salad, and garlic toast for tomorrow night."

"Sounds perfect, Ma. With the other half of the caramel cake we'll devour tonight?" Juliet asked.

Ma nodded in agreement. "That works. Biscuits and gravy in the morning? It's supposed to be cold again."

"Wayne and I'll help Ma clean the kitchen if y'all want to keep looking at songs," Keith offered.

"That works for me," Cedra replied.

"I'll go print out those songs," Juliet added.

Stone smiled. "Little Big Town, here we come."

†

"Oh, this would be perfect for all of us," Cedra announced.

"Which one?" Keith asked from the kitchen.

"'Wine, Beer, Whiskey.'"

"Heck yeah. Easy to play, and the lyrics are simple, too," Wayne said.

"I get the captain verse," Cedra claimed. "We can sing individual verses or do it with everyone to sound more like their version."

"I'll take Tito." Keith laughed.

"Jack, for me," Stone said.

Cedra looked at Wayne. "That leaves the wine, the beer and whiskey verses for you and Juliet, and we'll all do the chorus," Cedra said.

"What am I missing out on down there?" Juliet called downstairs.

"'Wine, Beer, Whiskey,'" Keith called back.

"That'll be fun to play. Print it out?"

"Yes, please," Cedra replied.

"I don't think I've heard that one," Ma said.

"Play it on your phone, please, Cedra," Keith requested.

"Here you go, Ma." Cedra hit play.

"Oh, that would be fun to sing," Ma replied.

"Should we do that instead of Sam Hunt? That's one we can do without Cedra and Stone," Keith noted.

"I'm fine with that," Cedra agreed. "Whoa, wait. We don't have a horn player. There's a bit of trumpet in that song."

"We can call Bud and see if he knows someone?" Wayne suggested. "I'd almost bet they've got someone on standby. Or someone he can record later and dub into the track."

"I hadn't thought of that," Keith answered.

"I can get that covered," Juliet told them as she bounced down the stairs. "I've got a friend who plays everything." She chuckled. "I'll get him to meet us Sunday, and he can sharpen up on the song. I think we need to sing it all as a group, though. Just my two cents."

"Ya know it takes out the party song feel if it's done individually," Ma stated.

All heads turned back to Ma. "That's exactly why we need you to help us," Cedra said. "We hadn't thought of that aspect."

Juliet sat beside Cedra and sent a text. Her phone pinged seconds later. "Tony says hell yeah. He'll see us Sunday."

Ma settled into her chair. "Dessert in a half hour?"

"Perfect," Juliet replied.

"What other songs are you considering?" Ma asked.

"'Wide Open Spaces' by the Chicks," Cedra answered.

"Play it for me, please, Cedra."

Ma smiled as the song came to an end. "The Dixie Chicks?"

"Yes, but they are just the Chicks now," Juliet said. "They dropped the name Dixie to be more politically correct. Doesn't affect the greatness of their music, though."

"Not at all. The Chicks all have great voices," Ma agreed.

"We have our two songs for Sunday then?" Juliet asked.

Heads bobbed around the living room. "Sounds like it." Cedra grinned.

"What else?" Ma asked.

Keith began reading off a list of songs they had put together.

"You'll mix some of your original music with these, right?"

"Yes, Ma. Fifty-fifty at first until we can get some other tracks recorded," Juliet replied.

Ma noticed Keith kept looking at his watch. "I think Keith is ready for dessert. The coffee is brewed. Go pour your milk, boys, and I'll cut the cake."

"Now we're talking," Keith exclaimed.

"What time do you need to be at the café in the morning?" Ma asked.

Cedra looked at Ma. "I told Lisa Marie we'd be there around eight-thirty."

"Breakfast at seven then?"

"That will work. Is there anything I can help with?" Juliet asked.

"Nope. That's a simple breakfast. Will you load your dishes in the dishwasher and run it when you get done? I'm going to call it a night."

"We will, Ma. Thanks for another great dinner," Cedra replied.

Stone walked to the garbage can. "I'll take the garbage out, too."

"Thanks. I'll see y'all in the morning."

†

Cedra rinsed the dishes and handed them to Juliet to place in the dishwasher.

"What do you think will happen for y'all at work tomorrow?" Juliet asked Wayne and Keith.

"As long as the Ryman stays open, I think I'm okay. I'm far enough away from the crowds I'll stay safe. I'll be wearing a mask, too," Keith answered. "They may have to go to reduced capacity to keep the doors open."

"Probably so," Cedra agreed.

They looked at Wayne. "I've got no clue. It doesn't sound good for the bar business. Hopefully, we'll be able to operate with limited capacity. If not, then who knows."

"I think it's a blessing we got the advance. We may be living on that for a while," Juliet said.

"It makes efforts to market in any way we can more important too," Cedra stated. "The *Bentley Break* and anything else we can come up with will help get our name and our music out there."

153

"No matter what happens, we will make it through as long as we work together," Juliet answered. "We may not be working for an immediate paycheck, but the effort we make now will pay off in the future."

Cedra turned the machine on to wash the dishes. "I'm heading up. See you guys in the morning."

"Goodnight. We can knock out the work at the café quickly tomorrow and come back to get some practice in," Wayne said.

†

Juliet followed Cedra upstairs. "I'm glad to hear that everyone is trying hard to stay positive," she told Cedra as she began undressing.

"There's so much unknown to us at this point. It's scary. What you said about us working together was so spot on. I think we all needed to hear that."

"It's truer now than ever."

"Are we conserving water in the morning?"

"Absolutely." Juliet grinned.

"Good, we can sleep an extra thirty minutes then." Cedra set the alarm.

Juliet wrapped an arm around her when Cedra stretched out. "I'm so happy we can cover some tunes together. I think it's hilarious Carrie caught us singing in the bathroom."

"That was funny, now that we think of it. That's the kind of creativity we will have to demonstrate moving forward.

We also need to be open to trying different things, even if it stretches our comfort zones a bit."

"I'm always up for new and different," Juliet said and wiggled her eyebrows.

"You are so incorrigible," Cedra teased.

"That's why you love me, right?"

"Maybe." Cedra kissed Juliet before turning off the lamp.

CHAPTER SIX

"That looks great, guys," Lisa Marie stated as she looked at the sidewalk lined with clear tarps. "That should work really well. Are you getting hungry yet?"

"We're always hungry," Keith joked.

"Okay, I'll get some burgers and fries ordered if that's good for y'all?"

"That sounds perfect," Stone answered.

Lisa Marie followed the yellow spray paint marks to the end of the building and around the corner. She found Cedra and Juliet marking the last spot. "I'm going to get burgers started. Are you two about finished?"

"That's our last mark," Cedra replied.

"Bring it on in then and get washed up. Lunch will be ready soon. Oh, our door will be installed on Saturday," Lisa Marie said.

"That's great news," Cedra answered. "That will make things so much easier and keep things moving." She smiled at Lisa Marie. "We got this, boss."

"Yes. I'm feeling very hopeful," Lisa Marie replied.

"We'll be inside in just a minute. We'll check on the boys to see if they need any help," Juliet said.

"They are just about done too," Lisa Marie told them. "The windbreak looks great."

"What kind of response have you gotten from customers?" Cedra asked.

"A few grumbles, but for the most part, people are appreciative that we're trying to remain open. People still need to eat and drink coffee."

"We've got a great customer base. I was thinking one other thing this morning as we worked."

"What's that?" Lisa Marie asked.

"People may opt to order online instead of waiting for a landline to free up. Do you think we can get that added to the website?"

"For once, I'm one step ahead of you. An order option will go live Saturday, too." Lisa Marie smiled at Cedra. "We'll just need to remember to check the order line once payment is made. We should get an email to the kitchen and counter to make us aware of the order." She shrugged. "I guess it's time for us to enter the twenty-first century of technology."

†

Lisa Marie and Stone served the burgers and fries. "I'll grab a tea pitcher and join y'all if that's okay."

"Like you have to ask," Cedra answered.

Wayne's phone pinged for a text. "Well, that solves that riddle. I'm effectively laid off."

"I'm sorry to hear that, Wayne," Stone replied.

"I could use another hand here," Lisa Marie suggested. "Jennifer has decided to stay at home after today."

"Heck yeah," Wayne declared. "What can I do?"

"I need someone to take phone and internet orders. In between, you can help with deliveries. Can you handle that?"

"Yes, ma'am. Just show me what I need to do, and I'm on it," Wayne told her.

"Come in with Cedra and Stone tomorrow, and we'll get started on working this new system." Lisa Marie looked around the table. "Does anyone need anything?"

"I think we're good," Juliet answered.

Cedra smiled at Wayne. "As one door closes, another opens."

"Amen to that, sister," Wayne said and held his glass up to Cedra.

Keith swallowed and looked at Juliet. "I guess it's down to just you and me for some morning cover sessions."

"We can do a few, and if it doesn't work out well, we just wait to come in with everyone else," Juliet replied.

"I'm sure Ma wouldn't mind some help around the house. We can do the shopping and anything else she needs to limit her exposure," Keith added.

"That's very true," Cedra replied. "She may even consent to give you both some cooking lessons."

"I'm not sure we should expose Ma to that," Juliet declared with a laugh.

Keith grinned. "Maybe some baking lessons. Cookies, brownies, and a cake. Those shouldn't be too difficult."

"Don't forget we have the last of the pecans to harvest, too," Juliet reminded him. "Maybe tomorrow?"

Keith had filled his mouth with fries, so he nodded his response until he swallowed. "Sounds good."

"You can slow down, you know. If we run out of fries, I'll go get more," Stone teased him.

"These are just so danged good," Keith replied.

"I'll get Teddy to drop another big order," Stone told them.

"What do you need?" Lisa Marie asked as Stone approached.

"More fries for the endless pit of Keith," Stone answered.

Lisa Marie handed Stone the tea pitcher and her glass. "Take these, and I'll get Teddy to cook more."

"Yes, ma'am," Stone said and returned to the table.

Cedra lowered her voice. "Save room for dessert, everyone. There's buttermilk pie in the case today."

"I've never had that. Is it good?" Wayne asked.

"It's to die for," Cedra declared, "and fairly easy to make."

"We could add that to our list of lessons from Ma," Juliet teased as she elbow-bumped Keith.

†

Lisa Marie was on her way to the table with a platter of fries when the door opened, and Carrie walked inside.

"I think I'll just follow you," she told Lisa Marie. When she saw where Lisa Marie was headed, she laughed. "Mind if I join you?"

"The more, the merrier." Keith got up to pull another chair to the table.

"Thanks, Keith."

"Do you know what you want to eat?" Lisa Marie asked.

"Is there any hamburger left?" Carrie teased.

"I'm sure Teddy can round up another. Fries?"

"Why not?"

"Honey mustard on the side," Cedra said.

"Got it," Lisa Marie replied and headed back to the kitchen.

"What's got you all in here today?" Carrie asked.

Cedra took a drink. "Lisa Marie asked for some help getting ready for the change next week. The boys put up the clear tarps while Juliet and I marked off the social distancing prompts."

"They've been a huge help, too," Lisa Marie said. "I've also added to my staff." She nodded to Wayne.

Wayne shrugged. "I got laid off one minute and hired at the Redbird the next. Not too bad for a Thursday morning."

160

"Why don't we just move the recording sessions to the afternoons entirely then? Bud likes working later in the day. Maybe from three to eight?"

"I thought y'all had wrapped up the album," Lisa Marie said with a puzzled look.

"Oh snap, we forgot to tell her the good news," Cedra replied.

Carrie grinned. "You eat, and I'll fill her in on the *Bentley Break* idea."

Lisa Marie listened to Carrie's explanation. "That's a fantastic idea. If y'all need off before two, we can make it happen," she offered.

"No, ma'am. We need every bit of business we can get for the café," Cedra replied. "We will have plenty of time to record after work. Will we continue to stay open seven days a week?"

"No, I think we will close on Mondays, to give us all a break," Lisa Marie answered.

"We'll do whatever you need us to do," Stone offered.

"Ma and I can even help out if needed," Juliet said.

"Y'all don't know how much I appreciate all your hard work and dedication."

Cedra noticed the tears in Lisa Marie's eyes. "You gave us all a chance when we needed it most, and it's time for us to do the same for you."

"Order up," Teddy called out from the kitchen.

"I'll be right back," Lisa Marie said.

"That is very kind of all of you to help Lisa Marie out," Carrie told them.

"She's like family to us, and that's what families do," Stone answered.

"Given the recent changes, do you want to get some time in the studio before Sunday?" Carrie asked. "I'm sure Bud would meet Friday and Saturday if you want to try some covers."

Juliet saw the smiles grow on her friends' faces. "I think that's a big yes. I'll need to see if I can get Tony on Friday night."

"Who is that?" Carrie asked.

"He's a horn player. We want to cover 'Wine, Beer, Whiskey,'" Juliet replied. "None of us can play the trumpet."

"That's fine. If you need other instruments in the future, just let Bud know, and he can arrange them for you."

"Should I cancel with Tony then?" Juliet asked.

"Heavens no, we may get a new horn man out of it," Carrie said.

Juliet smiled. "Cool. Can I share that with Tony?"

"By all means. There is no telling how scarce musicians may become during this pandemic."

Lisa Marie delivered Carrie's food. "Did I hear someone wanted buttermilk pie?"

"Yes, ma'am, you did," Wayne answered.

"Just be sure to hold me back a slice, please, Lisa Marie," Carrie teased. "I've seen how these boys eat."

"I've got you covered and a pie to take home to Ma as well for loaning you guys out to me today."

"Awesome," Keith said as he raised his fork. "All set."

"I'll be right back," Lisa Marie replied.

Stone refilled their tea glasses and went for another pitcher. "Thanks for everything, boss," he said and carried small plates to the table for Lisa Marie.

†

Carrie's phone pinged with a text. *Dinner out tonight? It may be our last chance to eat out for a while.*

That's fine. Eating lunch with Cedra and the others. I'll call later to confirm.

Dessert at my place.

Sounds great.

"Cedra. Cedra, Cedra. I'm sick of hearing her name. That's all she ever wants to talk about anymore," Linea growled as she slammed her phone into the couch.

†

They devoured the pie and stacked the dishes in a pile. Stone carried them back to the kitchen.

"We need to head home and get busy practicing," Juliet said. "Thanks for the great lunch."

"I appreciate all your hard work today. Hang on and let me box up a pie," Lisa Marie said. She grinned at Cedra,

Stone, and Wayne when she returned to the table. "I'll see you three bright and early."

"Yes, ma'am, you will," Stone said. "If we don't see you tomorrow, will we see you Friday at the studio?" he asked Carrie.

Carrie nodded. "I wouldn't miss it. I'm excited to hear the covers you've selected."

†

Wayne carried the pie inside and handed it to Ma. "I got laid off and hired in five minutes." He grinned.

"What?"

"I got laid off from the bar, and Lisa Marie hired me on the spot to take phone and internet orders. I start tomorrow."

"That's fantastic news," Ma told him. "I'm sorry, and congratulations."

"It's all good. We've decided we'll hit the studio in the afternoons after work to record, and Keith and Juliet will help you out here with shopping and stuff."

"Oh, and some baking lessons," Juliet said.

"Really?" Ma asked. "You two cooking?"

"Well, at least baking," Keith replied. "We thought that may be less stressful for you."

"I bet I can teach y'all how to cook a few meals," Ma replied. "Without burning down the house."

"That sounds great. What are you cooking that smells so wonderful?" Wayne asked.

"Pork roast and some of those sweet potatoes."

164

"I hope there will be leftovers for sandwiches tomorrow night," Keith replied.

"That's the plan," Ma said. "With chips, slaw, and potato salad. I can add some baked beans as well."

"Now we're talking," Wayne exclaimed. "Go easy on the roast tonight, boys."

"You've got more caramel cake and now a buttermilk pie to eat, too," Cedra teased.

"Our first baking lesson will be brownies tomorrow," Ma told Keith and Juliet.

"After we harvest the rest of the pecans," Juliet reminded Keith. "That shouldn't take us long. I don't think there are many left to harvest. We bought some from the Farmers Market, though."

"Let's get set up and play until dinner is ready. Did you remember to text Tony about tomorrow night?" Cedra asked Juliet.

"Nope, but I'll do it now. Thanks for the reminder."

†

They practiced covers until Ma called them to dinner. "Y'all were sounding great in there."

Juliet smiled. "I think we've settled on those four covers to start. If we get two to three done tomorrow night that would be great. The fourth would be amazing."

Wayne grinned. "I think if we all play our best, we can make amazing things happen."

"I agree," Cedra replied as she began pouring tea.

Juliet's phone pinged with a text. "Tony says he'll meet us at Big Machine. He's all set to play and excited to possibly get more work at the studio."

"I hope that works for him," Keith said. "Maybe we can find other covers to give him more work."

"I think that would be a good request to make of him and see what he comes up with," Juliet suggested.

"You're going to the studio right after work tomorrow?" Ma asked.

"Yes, but we should be home shortly after eight. Is that okay, Ma?"

"That will be fine for leftover sandwiches. It's going to make long days for the three of y'all," Ma stated to Cedra, Stone, and Wayne.

"I know it may seem like work, but when we play, it's so much fun the time passes quickly," Cedra said. "We would be jamming together here, so at least in the studio, we're cutting tracks."

Ma nodded. "Now that you put it that way, it doesn't seem as bad. Just don't run your batteries too low."

"Point taken," Juliet agreed. "Ma's right. We need to bust it hard for a few days and then take some time off to recharge."

"Well, next week, we'll have at least Thursday and Friday off for Thanksgiving. The café will be closed, so we'll have two days to rest and go at it again," Stone pointed out. "I don't know about you, but I've got some new lyrics running around my head," he told Cedra.

"Maybe you can get some writing done. I'll be spending as much time with Dad as possible while he's here. Sunday, will come all too soon."

"I bet he would enjoy going with you to the studio after work on Wednesday or Saturday," Ma said.

"Or both," Juliet added.

"Probably, knowing Dad. He was a musician when he fell in love with my mom," Cedra told them. "He let go of his dreams when she got pregnant with me."

"It may make him feel good to see how well his Baby Girl is doing in making sure his dream lives on," Juliet injected.

"Whoa, it's getting mushy in here," Keith teased.

"Shut up, Keith," Wayne and Stone said simultaneously. They broke out laughing and high fived each other.

†

"One more run through?" Juliet asked. "Then you early risers need to get to bed."

"Yeah, I think we can handle that. Someone may have to drag me out of bed in the morning," Wayne said. "I'm not used to being up that time of day."

"You'll get used to it," Ma assured him. "It's a quiet and peaceful time. I'll have a cup of coffee ready for you when you come down."

"Let's do it then," Wayne called out.

†

When they closed up their instrument cases, Ma smiled at Wayne. "Do I need to knock on your door in the morning?"

"Yes, please, Ma, until I acclimate to the time," Wayne answered.

"You're a better man than me, bro. I don't think I could get up at that time of day," Keith teased.

"Tell me something I don't already know," Wayne said and punched Keith's arm.

"Goodnight, everyone," Ma replied as she headed for the stairs.

"Goodnight, Ma," Juliet answered. "Do you want Keith and me to bring the instruments tomorrow?"

"Yeah, that would be great," Cedra replied.

"Consider it done. Everything will fit in my back seat," Keith assured them.

"Let's call it a night then," Wayne suggested.

CHAPTER SEVEN

"This is an ungodly hour to be awake," Wayne complained as he stumbled into the kitchen.

"You'll adapt." Stone chuckled.

Ma handed him a travel mug of coffee. "Here, this will help."

"Thanks, Ma. Are we ready?" Wayne asked.

"We need to give the truck another minute or two to warm up. The windshield is iced over," Cedra said.

Wayne took a sip of the strong coffee. "That's perfect, Ma."

"Strong to give you a jumpstart to the morning." Ma smiled.

Cedra looked out the window. "I can see through the windshield now. "You ready, buttercup?" she teased Wayne.

"I'll take the back seat. Maybe I can get five more minutes." Wayne grinned.

"Have a great day. I'll see you all tonight," Ma called out.

"Thanks, Ma, enjoy your cooking lessons," Cedra said.

"It should be interesting." Ma smiled.

†

The morning passed quickly, and Wayne mastered the art of phone and internet orders. Wayne and Lisa Marie practiced internet orders for an hour, but he and Teddy both promptly caught on to the process. Cedra began processing table orders with the iPad to give her some experience for the coming change.

"How are the electronic orders going?" Lisa Marie asked her during a lull.

"They are fine, except for one thing," Cedra replied to Stone and Lisa Marie.

"What's that?" Lisa Marie asked.

"I don't have any place to scribble down lyrics when they come to my head without an order pad," Cedra replied with a smile.

"I'll make sure you both have access to a notepad and pen," Lisa Marie promised once she stopped laughing.

"That was a good one," Stone said. "You had me going, too."

"How is Wayne the wonder boy doing?" Cedra asked.

"Now that he's fully caffeinated, he's caught on well," Lisa Marie praised.

Wayne smiled. "Thanks, boss. I'll eventually get used to being awake at this insane time of the day."

Still smiling, Lisa Marie said, "I know you will, so I'm not worried. I'll be sure to keep an extra pot of jet fuel full for you." She looked at Cedra. "Do y'all want to get some breakfast in now?"

"That would be great," Cedra replied. "I'll circle around with a coffee pot and tea pitcher while you order for us."

"I can help with that," Wayne replied and grabbed a coffee pot.

†

By the end of the shift, Wayne groaned, "Man, my feet are killing me, and I didn't do a third of the walking y'all did."

"Once we go live with the internet and phone orders, you won't have as much walking to do," Cedra replied.

"I certainly have a new perspective on what you two experience every day. Much respect, too," Wayne said. "It's much different from serving drinks all night."

"I'm not sure I could do that," Cedra replied. "Are you guys excited to do some recording?"

"Sure am," Stone replied.

"Let's clock out and hit the road," Cedra suggested.

When they walked outside to her truck, Stone looked at Cedra. "Houston, we have a problem."

Cedra stopped walking. "What?"

"You have an extremely low tire," Stone replied.

"What? These are practically new tires," Cedra exclaimed.

Stone walked over to the rear passenger tire and frowned. He stood up and looked around quickly but did not see anyone in sight.

Cedra saw the look on his face. "What's wrong?"

"Someone intentionally let the air out of this tire. The dumbass left the cap sitting on the ground. Whoever it was must have been scared off."

"Why would someone do something like that?" Wayne asked.

"Who knows," Stone replied. "I think Lisa Marie has an air tank in the storage room. Let me go back inside to get it."

†

Lisa Marie frowned when she saw the look on Stone's face. "What's wrong?"

"Someone let the air out of one of Cedra's tires. Can we borrow your air tank?"

"Sure, you can. You think it was deliberate?" Lisa Marie asked.

Stone growled, "Yes, the dumbass left the cap on the ground."

Teddy cleared his throat. "I didn't think anything was odd, but there was a blond woman near Cedra's truck earlier. I'm sorry I didn't mention it earlier."

"You couldn't have known someone was up to no good, Teddy. Was she anyone you recognized? A regular?" Lisa Marie asked.

Teddy shook his head. "No one I remember seeing before. She was beautiful, so I would have remembered."

"If you see her again, will you let me know?"

"Sure thing, boss," Teddy answered and resumed cooking.

Stone retrieved the tank. "I'll bring this right back."

"Thanks. Please tell Cedra I'm sorry."

"It's not your fault, but thank you," Stone replied.

†

Lisa Marie waited until Stone returned the tank and left before walking into her office. She dialed a security company and ordered two security lights and cameras to be installed. "It's a damn shame our world has come to this," she growled as she hung up the phone.

†

Carrie met them at the door. "We were beginning to worry about y'all. Is everything okay?"

"We had a bit of a hiccup," Stone said. "Someone decided to let the air out of Cedra's tire."

"They what?" Juliet yelled as she walked up and heard Stone's comment.

173

"Teddy, the cook, said he saw an attractive blond by her truck, but that doesn't mean anything," Stone said.

"How do you know it was intentional instead of a slow leak?" Carrie asked.

"Because the dumbass left the cap sitting on the ground," Stone replied.

"First, a note, and now this?" Juliet growled.

"Note? What note?" Stone asked.

"Oh, shit. I'm sorry, Cedra," Juliet said when she realized what she blurted out.

Cedra sighed. "There was a note left on my windshield the other day. It was a bit of a warning to stay away from 'her,' whoever 'she' is," Cedra answered.

"What? Why didn't you say anything?" Stone asked.

"I didn't think there was much to it," Cedra said. "Maybe just mistaken identity or something. Now, I realize that's probably not the case."

"An attractive blond. Well, that rules out Viper," Juliet said. "Did Teddy recognize the woman?"

"No, he didn't, so she isn't a regular," Stone replied.

Carrie frowned. "Do you think you need to call the police?"

Cedra shook her head. "All they could do was make a report. We have no evidence against the blond woman or anyone else."

"I guess that's true," Carrie answered. "Is there anything we can do? Hire a private detective or security?"

"I have two strong, capable men riding with me every day," Cedra replied.

"That's fine, but do any of you have a concealed carry permit and protection?" Carrie asked.

Cedra nodded. "I do. But I hadn't seen a need to carry until now."

Everyone looked at Cedra in surprise. "Really?" Wayne said.

"Dad made me get one before coming to Nashville."

"I'd suggest you start carrying then," Carrie said. "Just as a precaution in case anything else happens. Hopefully, the fear of being caught was enough to scare them away."

"If they are smart enough to recognize that," Juliet said as she reached for Cedra's hand. "Are you okay?"

"Heck yeah. I'm ready to make some music."

"Bud's waiting on us, and he's excited to see what we have for him, so let's give him a show," Juliet replied. "He doesn't know what we're covering yet."

"Did Tony make it?" Stone asked.

"He sure did," Juliet said. "I thought we'd lead off with that just like we planned."

†

Carrie walked into the break room and turned on the video to watch the group perform. The news of a potential stalker for Cedra was very upsetting to her, and she found it hard to focus on the music. An attractive blond. Surely, Linea would fit the bill, but would she do something so

175

devious? She was considering the likelihood when Bud's voice came over the speaker.

"Don't tell them I said it, but that sounded as good as the original. Great job, guys. Let's do one more cover and take a break."

"Give us five minutes, please," Juliet said. Then she turned to Tony, who was putting away his horn. "You were fantastic. Bud and Carrie both have your contact. Don't be surprised if you get a call soon."

Cedra smiled. "Could you do something else?"

"Sure, what can I help with?" Tony smiled.

"Find some more covers with horns so we can give you more exposure. That was an awesome performance," Cedra replied.

"I'd be glad to do that. I'll get back to you soon. Thanks for the opportunity." Tony snapped his case shut, and fist-bumped the guys on his way from the studio.

"'Wide Open Spaces,' next?" Juliet asked.

"Yeah, let's go for it." Cedra smiled.

†

Bud waited for them to finish. "Let's take one more run at that one. It's missing something."

"Any idea what?" Juliet asked.

"Not sure yet, but let's record one more and give them a listen," Bud replied.

"Let it rip," Juliet said.

176

Cedra could feel the energy in the band during the song, and she knew that the harmonies were much more robust. She glanced a look at Bud, and he was smiling in the recording booth.

"That was much better. Let's give those songs a listen. I'll meet you in the break room in five."

"Thank goodness. I thought my kidneys would burst," Keith said as he rushed out of the studio.

Juliet laughed at his antics. "That's not a bad idea, though," she said to Cedra.

"I'm right behind you."

Once they reached the privacy of the restroom, Juliet turned and kissed Cedra. "How are you?"

"I'm okay," Cedra replied. "I'm happy we've gotten those two tracks cut."

"That's not what I meant. The tire situation," Juliet said as she cocked her head.

"It was a bit disconcerting at the time, but I'm trying not to dwell on it. I will start carrying, though, just as a precaution."

Juliet smiled. "My pistol-packing mama." She sighed. "No idea who it could be?"

"No freaking clue," Cedra answered as she headed toward a stall. "I don't remember any blond-haired women except Viper, and I don't think she'd make that much effort to warn me away from you."

"Do you really think it's about me?" Juliet asked. "I have no ties with anyone that I know of that would act like this."

"Who else could it be? You are the only woman in my life."

"That, my love, is the sixty-four-million-dollar question. I know it's after the fact, but next time anything odd happens, we need to involve the police."

Cedra flushed. "I will. I just pray nothing else happens."

"Well, there is one good thing about the change of routines at the café. There will be many sets of eyeballs milling around outside waiting on orders. Hopefully, that would be enough to deter any further shenanigans."

"I hope so. This virus is enough drama to deal with."

†

"I think those two are good," Bud said after they listened to both songs.

"I really liked the first one," Carrie agreed. "It was hard not to sing along, and well, you've heard my voice, Bud."

"If y'all put all that energy into the rest of the covers as you have today, we'll be in great shape," Bud replied. "I want us to do something a bit differently tomorrow night."

Cedra raised an eyebrow. "What's that, Bud?"

"I want to spend the time recording some of the song introductions and give your singing voices a break. I want you all to select at least one song and write an introduction to it for the show. Your inspiration for writing the songs or choosing the song as a cover." Bud lifted his hand. "Keith, before something comes out of your mouth, I am pretty aware that Cedra and Stone wrote the original songs, but you could talk to them about why they wrote what they did. They can help you produce an intro that will be wonderful."

"How did you know I was going to say something?" Keith chuckled.

"I could hear that intake of breath that told me you were about to ask something silly," Bud teased.

"Aw, now that's cruel," Keith said and grabbed his heart.

"But true, bro. You know that's exactly what you were about to say," Wayne replied.

"Yeah, yeah," Keith admitted.

"Do we have time for one more cover?" Stone asked. "We want to take advantage of this extra time."

Bud looked at the clock. "Let's take a run or two at it. What's next?"

"Sam Hunt's 'House Party.'"

"This should be good." Bud smiled. "Let's do it."

†

They recorded three cover tunes and arrived home by seven. "Y'all are earlier than expected," Ma said when they walked in. "Did everything go okay?"

"It was great. We recorded three covers," Juliet answered.

"That's good. Why is everyone so glum-looking?"

179

"Bud gave us a non-singing project, and everyone is a bit nervous, except for Cedra and Stone," Wayne replied.

"What on earth?" Ma asked.

"We have to begin recording introductions to the songs for the show," Juliet disclosed

"Stone and I will help you," Cedra promised. "You can each do one of the new covers, and we'll work on the rest."

"We should be able to knock them out easily," Stone assured them.

"You both are writers, and you know exactly what to say," Wayne complained.

"We all need to quit over thinking this," Juliet said. "We know exactly why we chose the songs that we did. We just need to put that down into words that make it interesting."

"I can help y'all with that," Ma offered.

"You would do that for us, Ma?" Keith asked.

"I'd love to help. Since Stone and Cedra have the most work to do, why don't we let them get started, and the three of y'all can help me with warming up dinner?"

"I'm going to head out to the truck. I'll give Sarah a call and start writing," Stone told them.

"I'll be upstairs in my room," Cedra replied.

"We'll call you when dinner is ready," Ma told them. "Let's get busy."

†

Cedra walked upstairs, removed a waist pack from her drawer, and checked that her pistol was loaded. She hated to resort to carrying a weapon, but she would not allow herself or her friends to be injured. "Hopefully, this won't be a long-term thing," she told herself as she sat down to begin writing her introductions. They proved to be an easy process for her since she was behind the passion for writing the majority of the original songs on the album, and she had four drafted by the time Juliet came upstairs to get her for dinner.

"How's it going?" Juliet asked.

"Good. I have four drafted and four to go," Cedra answered.

"Damn. I wish I could write as easily as you. It feels like pulling teeth for every word I write."

"We will have to work on that," Cedra replied as she stood and pulled Juliet in for a kiss. "I know you can do it."

"I was thinking we should write an introduction for the band for the first segment as well. What do you think?"

"I think that would be an excellent idea. We can work off of the bios we created for the album cover. You can help me with that after we write your cover song intro if you'd like," Cedra suggested. "It won't hurt us to have one drafted for Felecia if she likes the idea."

"Do you think she'll be there during the recording of our introductions?"

"If I was the producer for the show, I would want to be there."

Juliet nodded. "We'd better go if you want anything to eat tonight." She reached for Cedra's hand.

†

Juliet returned upstairs with Cedra to work on her introduction for the "Power of Two." "Should I mention how the song came about in a bathroom stall?"

"I think that would be hilarious. And the truth. If we hadn't been singing it when Carrie entered, we might have never covered the song."

"I think we would have eventually made it around to the Indigo Girls. They have such beautiful music."

"Shoot me a copy of the bios we used before you start drafting away, please. I'll start working on the band intro."

"You got it," Juliet replied and turned on her laptop. "I've also got 'Wide Open Spaces' to draft."

"See what you can do with it, and we'll tackle it together. By the way, I forgot to tell you how good the pie was. You did a great job."

"Thanks. If I had been with Ma five years ago, I could probably cook something other than pop tarts. My mom didn't have the patience or desire to teach me, and Ma has plenty of both."

"She's a great person and friend to us."

"How are you going to address the inspiration behind the 'Wedding Song?'"

"With complete honesty. I am not ashamed to admit I fell in love with you. Is that okay with you?"

"We should probably get Carrie's position on that first. Nashville is slowly becoming more progressive, but I don't want it to harm the band's chance of success," Juliet replied.

"Do you think it could?"

"In this crazy world, anything is possible."

CHAPTER EIGHT

"Good morning, guys," Lisa Marie said when they walked into the café.

"Is it really possible for someone to be that chipper this early in the morning?" Wayne groaned.

"Get used to it. Lisa Marie is always smiling first thing," Cedra replied.

"It's always nice to wake up to a new day," Lisa Marie said. "While I have all three of you in a captive audience, I want to discuss something. Stone told me about your tire yesterday, and I suspect that's not the first odd thing that's happened."

Cedra slowly nodded her head. "I had a note left on my windshield earlier also, but I didn't want to make a big deal out of it."

"Well, it's a big deal to me. I don't know if you noticed, but there is a new light outside the side entrance and the front door. I thought it was time I upgraded the lighting, and both units house security cameras that cover a wide scope of the property. The side camera will cover the parking lot, so don't change where you park."

"I'm sorry you had to go to that expense," Cedra said.

"It's not your fault someone is playing games, but I don't want y'all constantly looking over your shoulders either."

"Hopefully, whoever the asshat is got scared at the thought of being caught and won't try anything else," Stone replied.

"I notice you wearing a pack. Is that what I think it is?" Lisa Marie asked Cedra.

"Yes, I wanted to ask your permission this morning to carry. I'm licensed and trained to use it for protection."

"I don't have a problem at all with that, and I'm glad you have two strong men commuting with you as well. I won't schedule you without one or both of them."

Cedra forced a smile. "I was fine before either of them started working here," she reminded Lisa Marie.

"Times have changed. People will do all sorts of strange things when they are under stress. I actually don't mind that someone on staff is armed and trained." Lisa Marie looked at Wayne and Stone. "No offense, boys, but I'm happy she has additional protection."

"No offense at all. I'm comforted knowing Cedra has it, too," Wayne stated. "I know Cedra will take it out only as a last resort. I'd probably shoot myself in the foot."

"Or worse," Stone teased.

Lisa Marie smiled. "We all need to keep our eyes open for strange behavior, and I'm counting on all three of you to be completely honest if something weird happens. I won't hesitate a heartbeat to close this place down if any of y'all are in danger. Understood?"

"Let's pray it doesn't come to that," Cedra said.

"The police will be called, too, if anyone tries another stunt. Teddy is not always the sharpest tool in the box, but I've put an additional screen in the kitchen. If he sees the blond woman he saw near your truck, he is to notify me immediately."

"Crank up your iPads, and I'll pour some coffee," Stone offered.

Lisa Marie smiled and handed Cedra her apron. "This will conceal your package from any prying eyes."

Cedra smiled and tied it around her waist. "I feel almost normal now."

"How did your recording session go yesterday?" Lisa Marie asked.

"Great. We cut three covers before Bud and Carrie gave us another assignment," Wayne replied.

"What now?" Lisa Marie cocked an eyebrow.

"We have to write introductions for the songs that will be played on the *Bentley Break* show. Easy for these two since they are writers already, but Juliet, Keith, and I struggled on the covers, even with Ma's help."

"I think y'all did pretty well," Cedra replied. "If it makes ya feel better, I didn't finish my last two tracks."

"Well crap, that still means you wrote six introductions," Wayne exclaimed. "I struggled with one."

"Seven," Cedra stated. "I wrote one introducing us as a band. We need to do that so listeners know who is talking. I used the bios we created for the album cover. Juliet and I added to them."

"Show off," Stone teased with a wink. "I finished my four."

"I'm sure they will all turn out fine," Lisa Marie declared. "The sooner you get them done, the faster you can get back to the music." She smiled. "As an added plus, it's making the non-writers of the group learn to be more creative. Did you think about that?"

"No, but that makes perfect sense, to make us get out of our comfort zones. It's much easier to hide behind an instrument." Wayne grinned.

"You know, that gives me an idea," Cedra exclaimed.

"Oh Lord," Stone replied.

"I think everyone should write one song for the next album," Cedra replied.

"You do want it to sell, right?" Wayne teased.

"Of course. We can work together to draft the lyrics, but I think the idea should be original. That way, you understand the motivation behind the song."

187

"That's actually a good idea," Lisa Marie imparted.

"I like it. I know we can make it work," Stone agreed.

"You've obviously never seen my attempt at writing. I couldn't fill up a post-it-note," Wayne groaned.

"You haven't had two of Nashville's best and brightest working with you before," Stone replied with a wink to Cedra.

"Yeah, what he said." Cedra broke out laughing.

"I hate to break up our party, but we have folks at the door," Wayne informed them.

"Well go let them in," Lisa Marie said.

†

Lisa Marie walked them to the door at the end of the shift. "I'll see you tomorrow. Take it easy on these guys today," she told Cedra.

"I'll do my best."

Stone and Wayne gave the truck a once over as they approached. Stone looked at Wayne and nodded. Wayne pulled the door open for Cedra.

Keith and Juliet were waiting for them in the parking lot. "Why didn't you go inside?" Cedra asked.

"We wanted to practice a bit more before we go inside and embarrass ourselves," Keith said.

"Come on. We're all going to do fine," Cedra teased them out of Keith's truck.

"It feels odd walking in here without instruments," Wayne said.

Juliet chuckled. "That's what feels so different."

"Come along. The sooner we get done, the faster we can get to playing," Cedra reminded them.

Five barstools and microphones were set up when they walked into the studio. They looked up to find Bud and a raven-haired woman sitting side by side.

"That's odd," Juliet said.

"What is?" Bud asked.

"You never let anyone in your sound booth, not even Carrie."

Bud broke out laughing. "Felecia actually understands what to do inside one of these," he answered.

"Hello, everyone. I'm Felecia, the Big Machine Streaming program producer, as Bud said. I wanted to sit in with you today to hear your introductions and maybe provide a bit of guidance." She smiled from the booth. "Bud has given me a preview of your album, and I'm genuinely impressed. I'm looking forward to showing you off to the listeners."

Bud introduced the band to Felecia. "Where are we starting today?"

"We wondered if we needed to introduce ourselves as a band first before we get into the songs?" Cedra asked. "We took our basic bios from the album cover we made and doctored them up a bit."

"Let's give it a shot," Bud said.

Juliet took a seat in the middle with Cedra on her right and Stone to her left. Wayne was next to Stone, and Keith sat next to Cedra.

"My name is Juliet Tucker, and I'm the lead vocals for the Bentleys. I've been asked to give some background on the band," Juliet started. She told how they all came to live at Ma's and the inspiration behind selecting the name. Each of them took turns introducing themselves until Wayne wrapped up the introductions.

"May I ask a few questions?" Felecia asked.

"We're all yours," Cedra said.

"I'm curious, Juliet, you seemed to have a rising solo career, so why did you decide to join the band?"

Juliet smiled up at her. "Singing solo was fine in the beginning, but when Cedra arrived, and the four of us finally came together in one place and started jamming together on Ma's front porch, I knew we were meant to be a group. When Stone joined us, adding a second songwriter, we completely gelled, and I wouldn't have it any other way."

"Cedra and Stone wrote the entire first album? Is that correct?"

"Eight of the twelve tracks are exclusively Cedra's. Three are mine, and one is a collaboration," Stone answered.

"That's very impressive. Cedra, how would you describe the experience of writing your first album?"

"Writing comes as naturally to me as breathing. On days when I can't write at least one line, I feel a tightness in my chest like I'm struggling to breathe."

"That's deep and a rather poetic answer. No wonder your songs are so full of emotion," Felecia said. "Bud brags that you have hundreds of songs written. Is that true?"

Cedra laughed softly. "A bit of an exaggeration, but I've been writing for this opportunity for years."

"Why now? What took you so long to arrive?" Felecia asked.

Juliet placed her hand on her shoulder. "I'm okay," Cedra assured her.

"My mother had a stroke shortly after my high school graduation, and I spent the next few years providing care for her and my dad until she passed away. I would sit up for hours at night, writing and singing to her when the pain was so intense, she couldn't sleep."

Juliet looked into the sound booth and saw Felecia wiping tears from her cheeks.

"I'm sorry to hear that. I know it wasn't easy losing someone so young," Felecia said.

"She and my dad made me promise that one day I would pursue my dream of becoming a songwriter in Nashville. I've kept my promise."

Felecia smiled at her. "From what I've heard so far, I know they would both be extremely proud of what you have accomplished, and you've just begun."

"Thank you."

"I really like what y'all have done to introduce yourselves, and I'd like to use the recording and maybe the title song for your first show. Cedra, I will gladly edit out any of the information that you feel is too personal if you'd like."

"That's okay. I think it explains who I am very well," Cedra replied with a smile.

"I'd have to agree a hundred percent," Felecia said. "Thank you for sharing that. Do you all mind if I ask other questions during your song introductions?"

"I don't think we'd have any problems with that," Juliet answered.

Bud spoke into the studio. "Why don't we take a ten-minute break, and we can get started on the intros?"

"Sounds good. Is Carrie here?" Cedra asked.

"Yes, she's been listening in the break room," Bud answered.

"Thanks." She looked at Juliet. "Do you want to chat with Carrie and me, or do you want me to ask her about the 'Wedding Song?'"

"I'll be right there with you," Juliet said.

Stone stepped up next to them. "If you're going to ask her about saying about who you really wrote the song for, we'd like to be there for support. We want you to be honest. Love is love, and it doesn't matter who it was written for," Stone replied.

"Damned right," Keith said.

Felecia had stood prepared to exit when she realized Bud had left the studio sound on, and she heard the exchange between them. "Bud, you've got a diamond in the rough if this is truly who they are," she said.

"They are inseparable. Worse than any siblings I've ever known." He chuckled. "Come on, you will probably need to weigh in on this question."

Carrie looked up when the group entered the break room. "Hey, guys. It sounds like things are going great in there."

"So far, so good, but we have a question for you before we move on," Cedra replied.

Bud and Felecia entered the room. "I hope you don't mind us weighing in on this," Bud answered.

"Of course not, Bud," Cedra replied. "I wrote what you call the 'Wedding Song' for Juliet. When I introduce the song and my motivation for writing it, I want to be honest with listeners and let them know I wrote it for her and for us," Cedra blurted out in one breath. "I'm proud of who we are and how much love we have for one another."

"She has our complete support," Stone added, "but we wanted your thoughts."

Felecia cleared her throat. "I realize I'm the newcomer to this group, but from what I just witnessed amongst you all, you need to tell the truth. It's evident to anyone who spends five minutes with you to know how much you all love one another. The words you have written for Juliet fit any two people who are lucky enough to find their person to share a life with. Ultimately, it's Carrie's decision, but you have my full support."

"Thank you, Felecia," Cedra said.

Carrie raised her hands in surrender. "How can I argue with that? It has the potential to backfire on you for the listeners who are not tolerant of different lifestyles. Still, it also shows the courage and pride you all demonstrate for who you are individually and as a group."

Cedra looked at Bud, who simply shrugged. "I've loved you all since I met you."

Cedra had to grin. "Bud, are you going soft on us?" she teased.

"Hell no," he growled and then smiled. "Hit the restroom, and let's get back to work."

✝

Carrie waited for them to leave before turning to Bud and Felecia. "Do you think this is a smart move?"

"I think it's going to be epic," Felecia said. "The song speaks for itself, and I dare anyone to sing it and not feel the love between those two."

Bud nodded. "If there's a handful of listeners who change the channel, then who really gives a damn. Their music is good, and that's all they should be judged on."

"I should probably run this past Mark," Carrie said.

"There's no need. I heard every word, and I agree with your decision. Let the music speak for them."

Carrie was careful to mute the audio feed. "Damn, I forget he can hear anything in this room when we're recording," Carrie said, then laughed. She pressed the button and waited for the recordings to resume.

†

"That went smoother than I thought it would," Juliet admitted in the restroom.

"I know. I was prepared to have to argue at least a little."

"Don't sound disappointed. I'm sure we'll have some battles to fight in the future." Juliet kissed her. "You ready?"

"Almost." Cedra stood on her tiptoes and kissed Juliet again. "Now, I'm ready."

"I love you."

"I know." Cedra pulled the door open. "I love you too."

†

"Let's start with 'Six Strings,'" Bud said. "Felecia wants to introduce that first and one cover, so pick your poison on the cover."

"That's a no-brainer. Keith is going to pass out if he has to wait much longer," Juliet teased.

"Do you need to go first, Keith?" Bud asked.

"No, I'll wait until Cedra finishes," Keith answered.

"So, Cedra. Tell us about the title track to the debut album *Six Strings and a Dream*," Felecia said.

Cedra's voice was pure and confident as she spoke about writing the perfect country song. "I wanted to write something that every artist that ever rolled into Nashville could relate to. One that gave a bit of perspective to who each of us is and the dreams we chase in the Music City."

"You wrote this song for the members of the band?" Felecia asked.

"I used this song to describe our road to success, not just for the five of us, but the thousands that came before us."

"I can easily see some big names scrambling to cover this song. How would that feel?" Felecia asked.

"It would make me proud to learn that other artists relate to the song, and if it's a big name, that gives me hope that we will be there one day."

"That's a perfect answer. Thank you. I know it's received great reviews so far. How did you all feel the first time you heard it played on the radio?"

Juliet was the first to answer. "It's seemed surreal to most of us. I was with Wayne and Keith when we first heard it, and we were all like, damn, we sound good."

Stone nodded. "Cedra and I were working at the Redbird when we first heard it. There were still customers in the building who stopped what they were doing to listen with us. It was a proud moment for sure."

†

Keith was next to introduce "Wine, Beer, Whiskey" as a cover song, and he recited his thoughts perfectly and answered Felecia's questions with ease.

Juliet had everyone rolling with laughter as she relayed the story of Carrie overhearing them singing "Power of Two" in the bathroom. "I have to admit, that's one of the most original inspirations behind a cover tune I've ever heard," Felecia said as she wiped away tears of laughter.

Everyone had a turn at introducing their prepared song, and Bud asked, "Are you up for one more?"

"Yes, I'd like to do the 'Wedding Song,'" Cedra answered.

"Hit it then, kiddo."

Cedra left everyone speechless at the introduction she had written about the song written to describe her love for Juliet. When she finished, Felecia smiled. "After listening to you and watching you interact, there is no doubt regarding the depth of love you have for one another. It doesn't matter who it was written for. What matters is the love you have so beautifully wrapped in the lyrics. Thank you for writing this song."

"Thank you for helping us share it with listeners," Cedra replied.

"I think that's a wrap for tonight. You guys did very well," Bud told them. "We're still on to approve the album tomorrow at 3:30, and then if you want to record a few more covers, we will have time."

"I'll be back here Monday if you want to work on more intros," Felecia stated.

"That sounds great. I think we all understand better what type of information you're looking for," Juliet answered.

"I'll still be asking questions," Felecia replied. "I want to draw out every bit of information it takes for the country music world to fall in love with the Bentleys, like I have today."

"Thank you for allowing us the opportunity," Cedra said.

Felecia shook her head. "I should be thanking you. I think the *Bentley Break* is going to be a huge success, so keep writing."

Cedra looked at Stone. "We will. We have so much left to write."

"I love the sound of that," Felecia declared.

†

"I'll see you tomorrow," Bud said. "Relax the rest of the night, and we'll get back to it tomorrow."

"Let's go home," Juliet told the group.

"I hope Ma has something good cooked. I'm starved," Keith exclaimed.

"So, what else is new?" Cedra laughed and draped her arm across his shoulders.

†

When Tuesday arrived, Cedra paced the floor of the café, excited for her dad to arrive later in the day. The group had decided to work on some cover recordings without Cedra and allow her to greet her dad when he arrived. She had protested at first, but she eventually saw the logic to their suggestion. The café had been busy, and the time was passing quickly.

As Cedra took orders, Stone was busy filling the call-in orders through the Dutch door. "May I help you?" he asked as an attractive blond approached.

"I'm here to pick up an order for Carrie Brooks," the woman said.

"I'll be right back," Stone answered and walked to the kitchen window to call for Carrie's order.

Teddy glanced over at the screen, expecting to see Carrie. "That's her. That's fucking her," he called out.

Lisa Marie had heard the excitement and the F-bomb coming from the kitchen and walked back to investigate. "What's going on?"

Teddy pointed to the screen. "That's her. That's the woman I saw by Cedra's truck."

Stone looked at Lisa Marie. "She's picking up Carrie Brooks' lunch order. I think I remember serving her weeks ago, but I can't be sure."

"Okay, fill the order and let me think through this. Don't say anything to Cedra," Lisa Marie warned them.

"Yes, boss." Stone smiled and carried the order across the café. "Here you go, Miss. Tell Carrie I said hello," Stone requested.

"I sure will, Stone. She talks about y'all constantly," she answered and spun away on her heels.

"So much for getting her name, but she knew mine." Then he remembered he was also wearing a nametag. "Don't get ahead of yourself," he muttered as he waited for the next customer.

Lisa Marie looked at Wayne. "Can you handle things for a few?"

"Sure, boss. It's starting to slow down a bit," Wayne replied.

"I'll be back in a few." Lisa Marie poured a glass of tea and headed to her office. She pulled up the security feed on her desktop and froze the image of the woman. "Who are you, and what games are you playing?" She stared at the frozen image for several minutes? "What should I do? If she's picking up Carrie's lunch, Carrie obviously knows who it is. That's as good as any place to start." Lisa Marie took a sip of tea and looked up Carrie's number in her contacts. "Here we go." She pushed a button to send a call to Carrie.

"Carrie Brooks," Carrie said when she answered the phone.

"Hey, Carrie, it's Lisa Marie from the Redbird."

"My credit card wasn't declined, was it?" Carrie joked.

"No, nothing like that, but I have something to ask you that may seem rather odd."

"What is it? Is everyone okay?"

"Yes, everyone is good. I need to ask who the woman was that picked up your lunch order today."

Carrie was quiet for a second, then she spoke to someone in the office. "Can you give me a minute?" Carrie took a deep breath. "Her name is Linea. We've used her in several music videos, and we're friends. Sort of," Carrie added. "Why do you ask? Did she do something inappropriate when she picked up the order?"

"Nothing like that, but can you come to see me today after three?" Lisa Marie asked.

"I have to go out to the studio. Would it be possible to do two?"

"Yes, I can send Cedra home early. Her dad comes in today."

"I have to ask. Is everything okay with Cedra?"

"To be honest, I'm not sure. That's why we need to talk."

"I'll see you in an hour."

"Thanks, Carrie, I know this seems odd, but it's important."

"I know it is if you're worried. No problem."

†

Carrie ended the call. "What the fuck?" She tried to imagine what could have set Lisa Marie off with just picking up a to-go order. "I guess I'll know soon enough." She stood and walked across the room and motioned Linea back into the office. "Sorry, I had to take that call."

"No problem, baby. I hope everything is okay," Linea answered. "Are you ready to enjoy this nice salad?"

"Yes. Thanks for picking it up for us," Carrie said.

"No problem. I ate lunch there several weeks ago, and it was delicious," Linea answered.

†

Lisa Marie returned to the counter and then walked over while Stone delivered an order.

"Hey, boss."

"Hey. I'm curious about something. You said the blond woman was in here for lunch before. Do you remember when? Could it have been the day Cedra found the note?"

Stone's face turned into a frown. "I don't remember the exact date, but yeah, it was probably close to that time. What are you thinking?"

"Hell, I don't know, Stone. I'm just trying to put the pieces to this puzzle together. I'm going to send Cedra home at two today so she can go wear out Ma's floor with her pacing." Lisa Marie smiled.

"She is a bit excited for him to get here. Especially since the weatherman said we had a chance of snow later tonight."

"Really?"

"Yeah, some weird-ass winter storm swinging down from Canada," Stone replied. "Will you at least keep me informed if there's something I can do to help?"

Lisa Marie crossed her heart. "You will be my first call."

"Thanks, boss." Stone's smile returned.

†

Lisa Marie walked over to Cedra. "Last order for you."

"What?"

"I want you and the boys to have a nice lunch, and you're off the clock at two to get ready for your dad's arrival.

202

You've already worn a groove in my floor today," she teased. "Cheeseburgers and fries?"

"Sounds great. Thanks."

"I'll get Teddy working on some lunch for y'all," Lisa Marie said.

†

Stone's mind was churning, and he realized that the blond had been in the café that day because it was the same day 'Six Strings' came out. Cedra had failed to answer him about the note when their song came on the radio to distract them. Stone caught Lisa Marie's attention and waved her over. "I've been thinking. She was here the same day."

"How did you remember that?"

"Because it was the same day 'Six Strings' first came on the radio. When she tucked the note in her pocket after reading it, she deflected my question about it when she turned the truck on, and the song was playing. I forgot all about the note and never asked her about it again."

"You're amazing," Lisa Marie said. "Bacon cheeseburgers will be ready soon, so come over after you handle this delivery." She pointed to the approaching customer. "Thanks, Stone."

†

Lisa Marie felt a puzzle piece slide into place as she walked back toward the kitchen. "Burgers up," Teddy called out.

"Hand over your iPad and head to the counter peacefully," Lisa Marie teased Cedra.

"Yes, boss."

Lisa Marie took the iPad and sat at the counter facing the front door to watch for customers. "Eat up. You've earned those today."

†

After Cedra left for the day, Lisa Marie huddled with Wayne and Stone. "Carrie is coming in to meet with me in a few minutes. Can y'all handle the clean-up?"

"Sure thing, boss. We've been trying to clean as we go," Wayne said. "Everything okay?"

"Yes, we're just discussing a few things." She looked up when she noticed movement at the door. "Thanks, guys." Lisa Marie walked over to the door to let Carrie inside and led her to the office.

"I'll see y'all at three," Carrie said as she passed Wayne and Stone.

"Yes, ma'am, you will," Wayne said after swallowing the last bite of his burger.

"Damn, bacon cheeseburgers. I should have ordered one of those today," Carrie said.

"There's always tomorrow." Stone smiled.

"Yes, there is," Carrie agreed.

†

Lisa Marie pointed to a chair in her office. "Thanks for coming to see me on such short notice."

"I sense it's something urgent. What's going on?"

Lisa Marie turned her computer monitor toward Carrie to display the image on the screen.

Carrie nodded. "Yes, that's Linea." Carrie frowned. "When did you get a security system?"

"After the second incident targeted at Cedra. Are you aware of the threatening note and the air being let out of her tire?"

"I had no clue about the note until the tire incident made them late arriving at the studio. What's going on?" Carrie asked.

"Several things. They may be coincidences, but honestly, I don't believe in them."

"You've got my attention," Carrie replied.

"After the tire incident, Teddy, our cook, had gone out to drop some trash in the dumpster. When he looked up, he saw an attractive blond near Cedra's truck who walked away quickly, but he didn't think anything of it until we learned her tire had been flattened."

"Okay, I'm following so far. I think." Carrie smiled.

"Teddy said he'd never remembered seeing her before but said if he saw her again, he'd recognize her. I installed a security monitor in the kitchen, and when she came to pick up your lunch order, he nearly had a heart attack when he recognized the woman from the parking lot."

Carrie was about to speak when Lisa Marie raised her hand. "Wait. There's more. The same woman came in earlier, and Stone waited on her at lunch. That was the same day the note was placed on Cedra's truck."

"How could he remember that?" Carrie asked. "It's been weeks."

"Because it was the same day 'Six Strings' was played on the radio. Cedra deflected his questions about the note when she cranked her truck, and it was playing on the radio."

"Linea did tell me today after our call that she came in for lunch a while back," Carrie said. "What are you implying here?"

"You mentioned that you and Linea were friends. I have to ask, does that carry over into the bedroom?" Lisa Marie asked with a cringe.

Carrie's face turned a deeper red. "I consider us friends with benefits, but nothing serious, and I have made that clear to Linea." Carrie gasped as she finally caught up with Lisa Marie's train of thought. "Do you think Linea is harassing Cedra?"

"It's all circumstantial, but the 'her' referred to in the note could easily be you if Linea thinks Cedra is stealing you away from her. Her being on the property when those two events occurred is just uncanny."

"Oh my God." Carrie covered her mouth with her hands.

"What?" Lisa Marie asked, even more, worried than before.

"I made a mistake and called out the wrong name in a sensitive moment. I had worked with Cedra and the band all day, and in the throes of passion, I called out her name instead of Linea."

"That would flip my switch."

"That may have triggered something, and she complains they are all I talk about." Carrie looked utterly unsettled. "How do we address this?"

"I can only see two options. You talk with Linea, and we see if this foolishness ends or we go to the authorities." Lisa Marie frowned. "I doubt either of them needs the negative attention a police investigation could present."

"It could ruin careers. Especially Linea's."

"Cedra doesn't know any of this, but she's concerned for the safety of the band more than her own personal well-being. She's licensed to carry concealed and is armed to protect those she loves. I would hate to think of what would happen if she was backed into a corner and forced to protect them."

"I wouldn't want to even think of that as a possibility," Carrie replied. "Do you have any solutions to recommend?"

"Only one that I think holds any merit, but you might not like it," Lisa Marie replied.

"I'm game for anything at this point," Carrie said.

"She obviously is not a mentally stable person if she would stalk someone over what you have described as a fake relationship. It sounds like she's more into creating that possibility of a relationship with you if her perceived competition is out of the picture." Lisa Marie let that sink in for a few long seconds. "Going to the police is not a top option because of the negative publicity for all involved and those innocently involved. The rumor mill thrives on juicy stuff like this even if Cedra has done nothing wrong."

"Which she hasn't," Carrie agreed. "This is my problem to solve."

Lisa Marie nodded. "You could demand she seeks assistance from a mental health perspective, but I doubt Linea sees anything wrong with what she's done to protect what she believes is hers. That could very likely backfire on you, too."

"I hope you have another idea up your sleeve," Carrie said, almost in tears.

"Do you have any contacts in California who may be looking for a model or actress?"

"I could call in some favors."

"What I would do is confront Linea and let her know that not only do you know about the threatening note and letting air out of Cedra's tires, but others do as well, and we are prepared to file malicious trespassing charges against her that would ruin her career. You can bend the truth a bit and say there is video evidence to attest to this and that she would go to jail. You could offer her a choice of a way out if she agrees to go to California immediately to pursue an acting or modeling career while she still has the chance."

"With the stipulation that she never returns to Nashville, or restraining orders will be issued?" Carrie added.

"That could work. How long would it take to make the arrangements?"

"Other than clothes, some personal items, and her car, I don't think she has much," Carrie answered. "I can make calls tonight."

"Cedra's dad is coming to town for Thanksgiving, so she won't be working here again until Sunday when we reopen," Lisa Marie said. "I doubt she knows where Cedra lives, or would she confront her openly around so many others? Could you have her packed up and on her way by Saturday?"

"All I can do is try. The decision of where Linea wants to take this should be black and white, but I can't make her go."

"Then I'd suggest you put on your best game face and convince Linea it's the only option for her." Lisa Marie scowled. "Otherwise, it won't end well."

"I've got some calls to make. I'll keep you posted. Thanks for your help, Lisa Marie. I can't tell you how much I appreciate it."

"I won't lie, Carrie. I'm doing this mainly for Cedra. I will not sit by and watch anyone ruin her dream through no fault of her own. You're a grown woman who made some wrong choices, and now it's up to you to fix the problems they have caused." Lisa Marie saw Carrie recoil from her statement.

"I guess I deserve that. I promise I will make this right. I agree Cedra has worked too hard to have that taken from her by my stupidity," Carrie answered.

"We all make mistakes, but you've got to fix this one before someone gets hurt," Lisa Marie replied.

Carrie stood to leave. "I will."

Wayne and Stone were nowhere in sight when Lisa Marie walked Carrie to the door. She locked it behind her and walked back to her office. She opened a drawer in her desk, pulled out a metal flask, and took a drink. "Thanks, Jack. I needed that." She looked at the security camera and saw Carrie sitting in her car.

†

"Fuck, fuck, fuck." Carrie pounded her hands against the steering wheel. "I've gotten into a fine mess this time," she screamed at herself. Carrie took several deep breaths and wiped tears from her face before starting her car and leaving the lot.

CHAPTER NINE

"Hey, Bud. Would you mind if I didn't attend today's session? I've had some things come up I need to take care of," Carrie spoke to Bud.

"No problem at all. We'll crank out as many covers as we can today before the holiday break. I've sent out a ton of CDs, but we can discuss that later."

"Thanks, Bud. I'll be in touch."

"Sounds good. Take care and Happy Thanksgiving if we don't talk tomorrow."

"You too, Bud. We have a lot to be thankful for this year." Carrie tried to remain calm.

"Yes, we do, and next year is looking good, too. See ya."

†

Carrie pulled into the garage at her condo and closed the door behind her. She needed a stiff drink to steel her nerves as she made her plans and poured three fingers of scotch as soon as she stepped into her living room. The burn from the liquid felt like fire traveling down her throat to her belly. She pulled out her address book and started scanning down the pages until she found the right one to start. Brenda Walton was a music video producer in LA that she had helped set up in the field, so she figured Brenda owed her a big favor. She wouldn't go into much detail, but hopefully, Brenda would give Linea a chance for a break, and Linea would be bright enough to recognize the opportunity. She took another drink and punched in the number.

"Hey, Bren. This is Carrie Brooks," she announced when the phone was answered.

"Hey, Carrie. It's been a long time. What's up, girlfriend?"

"Working my tail off and trying to survive this danged virus going around," Carrie replied. "I was hoping I could ask a favor."

"Sure, if there's something I can do."

"Are you still producing music videos?"

"We stay so busy I don't know if I'm coming or going." Brenda laughed.

"That's excellent news. Do you need a drop-dead gorgeous blond for some work? She has experience in several videos for some top performers here. She wants to break into Hollywood, and I was hoping you'd keep her in some work while she tries to get into screen acting."

"I can always use beautiful women if they aren't into drugs or booze and will show up reliably."

"Linea is as consistent as clockwork and performs well in front of a camera. Doesn't do drugs, smoke, and rarely drinks anything beyond an occasional glass of wine. Says it's bad for her complexion."

"She sounds pretty ideal. Send her my way, and I'll give her some work."

"Thanks, Brenda. You're a lifesaver. I'll email you her photo and contact information. If all works out as planned, she can be in LA next week."

"Not a problem. I appreciate you sending me some talent. I hope the next time you're out this way, we can get together for a drink."

"I'll even buy the first few rounds. Talk soon."

"Bye, Carrie."

"That part went too smooth. I wish the rest would work out that well."

†

Dinner at six? Linea sent a text.

Sounds good. See you then.

Carrie drained her glass and walked into her bedroom. She showered, dressed in jeans and a sweater, then relaxed in her recliner until it was time to go to dinner.

Her heart raced in her chest, and her head pounded as she stepped out of the car to walk toward Linea's apartment. Carrie took a deep breath and pressed the doorbell.

Linea swung the door open and sighed. "You look and smell delicious," she said as she looked at Carrie from head to toe.

"Thanks. Do you have some Tylenol? I've got a headache." Carrie walked past Linea into the apartment.

"Let me go get some from the bathroom," Linea replied. "Pour yourself a drink, and I'll be right back."

Carrie walked into the kitchen and poured a glass of ice water to wash down the pills.

Linea returned and handed Carrie the pills. "Tough day?"

"It was a bit hectic," Carrie answered honestly.

"Why don't you go relax on the couch while I finish dinner? It won't take long. I'm making spaghetti," Linea announced.

"It smells wonderful." She swallowed the pills and walked into the living room.

"Stretch out, and if you fall asleep, I'll wake you when it's time to eat."

She's being so sugary sweet. It makes it hard to believe she could be so unbalanced. Carrie stretched out on the couch.

"Do you want to watch some television or listen to some music?" Linea asked.

"Nope, just some peace and quiet."

†

Carrie pushed her plate away and took another drink of tea. "That was a great meal. Thank you."

"I'm glad you enjoyed it, and I hope you'll stick around for dessert," Linea purred.

Carrie sighed. "We need to have a serious conversation."

"Can't it wait just a little bit longer?"

"No. Quite frankly, it can't," Carrie said a bit too harshly.

"What has gotten your panties all in a wad?" Linea chuckled.

"I learned some disturbing news today, and we need to talk through some solutions."

"What on earth could be so bad?"

"You have been identified as someone stalking Cedra," Carrie said bluntly. She observed Linea's face as she spoke. "You're on video leaving a threatening note and letting the air out of her tires. Both are severe criminal acts since they were committed on private property, and you could serve jail time for those. What were you thinking, Linea?"

Linea shrugged. "I wasn't going to sit by idly and watch her steal you away from me."

"Cedra has no interest in me. She has a woman she's in love with. We just have a professional relationship."

"She's all you ever talk about anymore."

Carrie looked into Linea's eyes. "You knew right from the start, that I'm not romantically interested in you or anyone else. I think I made that perfectly clear."

"I think you would have come around to love me as much as I love you if that hussy hadn't arrived on the scene," Linea growled.

"Linea, Cedra isn't a hussy and is very sweet and totally uninterested in anyone but her Juliet," Carrie explained.

"I just thought I could convince her to leave you alone."

"She is and has not ever done anything to or with me that wasn't associated with her band's music. It's strictly a business partnership."

"I don't believe that for one second. You eat lunch with Cedra every day," Linea spat out.

"I eat lunch at the café because it's the closest with the best food to my office," Carrie said. "I ate lunch there all the time before Cedra even hit town. Have you been following me to find out what I'm doing?" Carrie felt her anger growing.

"Just for a little while. I wanted to see what Cedra had that I didn't. She's really not much to look at."

"You've taken things too far and I don't want to see you go to jail. It would ruin your chances of ever working in the industry again," Carrie warned.

"Do you really think that would happen? You have some power in this town after all, don't you?" Linea challenged.

"Not with the police, I don't. I've come up with a solution that you need to hear before making a rash decision. Are you willing to listen?"

Linea huffed. "Do I have any choice?"

"No, Linea, you've pissed your choices away. I have a friend in LA that produces music videos, and she's willing to give you some work if you can get there next week."

"That's pretty short notice. LA, huh. Do you think I could get some movie roles?"

"Your chance of doing that here is nil. You have to be there to be seen."

"If I decide to stay?"

"Restraining orders will be issued and charges pressed for criminal trespass," Carrie replied.

"Well, fuck. It sounds like I'm screwed."

"If you decide to stay or come back to Nashville, the restraining orders will remain in place."

"That sneaky little bitch is playing hardball." Linea's eyes narrowed.

"Cedra doesn't know anything about this yet. She did nothing to cause you to behave like that," Carrie replied hastily.

"So, you are quick to defend her and not me?" Linea pouted.

"Not after what I saw on video today. I'm doing whatever I can to keep you from going to prison. This is an entertainment town, for God's sake, Linea. They take stalking laws very seriously."

"How will I get to LA? I have little money, and while I don't have much, I can't fit it all in my car."

"Tomorrow, I will rent and pick up a small moving truck with a car hauler attachment and loan you the money to get set up in LA. You can pay me back once you hit the big time."

"Well, at least I'm month to month on my lease. I was hoping to convince you to let me move in with you. That should be easy to settle," Linea said. "Why tomorrow? Are you in that big of a hurry to be rid of me?"

"It will take several days for you to drive across the country for one thing. Second, there is a time limit for you to be out of town before charges are pressed," Carrie replied.

"That's ballsy. It must be that bitchy café owner pressing this. I should just torch that place down." Linea laughed.

Carrie wasn't sure if Linea was serious or not. "That wouldn't be a smart thing for you to ever voice again," Carrie warned.

Linea tossed up her hands. "I was just joking. It's not every day you get railroaded out of town like some cheesy western movie."

"Do you really not understand that you brought this on yourself?"

"I was driven to it out of my love for you," Linea replied. "Can we at least have one more romp in the bedroom for old time's sake?"

"I can't even think about that. I've got things I have to get done to help you out of this mess. I wish you would never have done any of this, Linea."

"Water under the bridge. I can't undo anything, so I need to go become a rich and famous movie star."

Carrie smiled. "You could do that if you apply yourself. You have the talent. All you need is the drive." Carrie stood to leave. "Will you need boxes?"

"I can get those in the morning. I mostly have clothes. No furniture or anything."

"I'll pick up the truck and be here by eleven then. If we can get you packed and the truck loaded, you can head out Thursday. That will give you several days to drive."

"On Thanksgiving? That's so cruel," Linea complained.

"Look at the bright side. You'll miss a lot of the holiday traffic."

"Yeah, right," Linea groaned.

"I'll see you in the morning." Carrie forced a smile and left the apartment.

†

Carrie drove two blocks away and pulled over. Her insides were shaking, and she was glad to be out of Linea's sight. Carrie was worried about the comment about burning down the café and determined to prevent any more foolishness. Her stomach churned with nausea and she opened her door to rid her stomach of its contents. She wiped her mouth with a napkin and picked up her phone and dialed the head of security for Big Machine.

When the phone was answered, she said, "Felix, it's Carrie Brooks. I need your best man for two to three days starting within the hour. Yes, I'm aware it's Thanksgiving, but I'll pay whatever is necessary. Thanks, I'll look forward to his call."

†

Carrie put her car in gear and drove home to make phone calls. She had reserved a one-way mini-truck with a car carrier and ordered a taxi to drop her off tomorrow to pick it up. "I'll worry about getting home tomorrow after everything is packed and loaded." Carrie got up and fixed a drink while she waited on David Bartle to call. He had done some security work before for her, and he was good at what he did. She was sipping on her drink fifteen minutes later when he called.

"Thanks for getting back to me so quickly, but this is very urgent. I'm going to text you a photograph and an address of a woman I need you to keep a very close eye on and then follow her out of the state of Tennessee on Thursday." David was smart enough to not ask questions. "One more thing, if she leaves her apartment and heads anywhere near the Redbird café, you do whatever you feel is necessary to keep her out of mischief."

"I understand completely," David replied. "I'm headed to my truck now and will be gone as soon as I get the address."

"Thanks, David. Send me your bill, and I'll take care of any expenses."

†

"Yes, Ms. Brooks. I'll take care of this for you." David hung up the phone and looked over at his boyfriend, Marco. "We've got a job to do, so pack a few things for a three-day trip. We can at least enjoy ourselves in Memphis when this is done."

"I do love Memphis," Marco said and stood to head to their bedroom.

"I'm going to send you an address and a photo by text in just a bit. We have explicit orders I will fill you in on later. See you soon." David leaned down to kiss his lover. "Dress warmly. It's going to be cold."

"Are you going to be okay tonight?" Marco asked.

David nodded. "I'll stop and fill a cooler with some caffeine and a bag of snacks. Bring some coffee with you in the morning. Love you."

"Love you more." Marco smiled.

Carrie's text came through as soon as he climbed into his truck. He responded and then entered the address into his GPS.

†

Carrie willed her body to relax. She knew that David, his lover and business partner Marco, would do a great job and keep Linea out of trouble until she was out of the state. Carrie sent Brenda an email with the particulars on Linea. She prayed that Linea would see this as an opportunity to make something of herself and forget about returning to Nashville once she got a taste of LA. Then Carrie printed out the most direct route to LA and placed it in an envelope with Brenda's contact information. Carrie made a list of things she needed to do in the morning before picking up the truck. She decided to purchase a pre-paid credit card at the bank for fuel for the moving truck, food, and hotel rooms. Carrie briefly considered giving Linea cash to get set up in LA but decided against it and would send a cashier's check that would have to be cashed or deposited at a bank. Linea could close out her own account for cash. As Carrie stared at her list, she realized how costly a mistake her involvement with Linea had become. "It would be much worse if she stayed. I could lose everything because I couldn't control my libido. Better to pay the piper now and pray that will be the last of her."

Carrie picked up her phone and dialed David's number. "I guess I need to explain what's going on," she said.

"It would be better to know exactly what I'm dealing with. Is she dangerous?"

"I don't think so, David, but I can't be sure anymore. Linea started out as an actress in some of our music videos, and she's been a fuck buddy with no strings attached for about a year. Or so I thought. She has recently begun stalking and causing mischief to a young woman with whom she believes I'm in a relationship with, but I'm not. She's been given the ultimatum of moving to LA to start fresh or stay and have charges filed against her. Linea threatened to burn down the Redbird Café where this young woman works, which makes me uneasy. I don't think she would normally do anything that serious, but she's unsettled enough to stalk someone totally innocent."

"It's best that you acted like you did to have her monitored until she's safely out of the state then. Marco and I will make sure she doesn't do anything stupid."

"Thank you, David. I can't believe I've been this stupid. Something like this could ruin my reputation and career," Carrie told him. "Once you see her cross the river in Memphis, I hope you and Marco will stay and have some fun at my expense. I'm sorry to have ruined your holiday."

"Marco was ecstatic about spending a night or two in Memphis. We'll go easy on the expense account. I've been in those shoes before with someone not as stable as I thought they were."

"Thanks, David. Call me if you have any questions. I plan to pick up a moving truck and help her get loaded tomorrow morning for a Thursday morning departure. Maybe we'll get lucky, and she'll leave once the truck and her car are loaded."

"No problem. Marco and I don't have any assignments until after the holiday anyhow. I guess I will see you tomorrow. Don't strain anything." David chuckled.

"She mostly has clothing and a few personal items. The apartment came furnished. She'll get boxes in the morning and contact the complex. She was already on a month-to-month basis."

"Was she planning to move?"

"She was hoping I'd ask her to move in with me," Carrie answered.

David sighed. "I hope this one will be out of your life forever soon."

"Me too, David."

"Get some rest. I have everything under control here."

"Thanks, David. Goodnight."

A glimpse of the clock revealed it was almost midnight. Carrie stripped out of her clothes and headed to bed. She knew she could sleep well as long as David was on the job.

†

"You fucking bitch," Linea growled as she began pulling clothes from her closet and piled them on the couch. She wouldn't even bother taking them off the hangers. "I'll get a couple of big boxes, and maybe that spineless Carrie will pull something in her rush to get me out of town. Wouldn't that be fitting?" Linea slammed another set of clothes on the couch. She walked to the refrigerator and pulled out a bottle of wine. "I might as well finish this off."

†

David watched the shadows of the woman inside as she stormed through the apartment. "Hopefully, she'll settle down in a bit." Not long after he arrived, he had placed a sensor on her car door to alert him if Linea left the apartment, just in case he dozed off. He pulled a bottle of a highly caffeinated drink from the drink cooler and a bag of chips. "Maybe this will help until Marco arrives to replace me." The mention of Marco's name brought a smile to his face. Maybe one day Carrie would find her Marco and settle down and quit hooking up with the psycho women who seemed drawn to her like a flame. This one had by far been the most serious, so maybe Carrie would learn to keep her legs closed. He chuckled at the thought. "Probably not, but at least it keeps me busy and well paid."

CHAPTER TEN

"I am so happy you are here, Dad," Cedra said as she placed a slice of pie in front of him.

"Me too. It's so good to see you happy and to meet your friends. If Ma cooks like this all the time, I might not go home," he teased.

"All the time," Juliet said.

Ma blushed. "You are more than welcome to join us anytime, Hank."

"Careful, I just might take you up on that."

"I thought we could have some brisket for dinner tomorrow night. We will have a couple days of turkey to look forward to after that."

"That sounds delicious, Ma," Juliet said. "Our treat, though. Cedra and I plan to take Hank on a tour of Nashville, and we can pick it up in time for dinner."

"That sounds great," Stone said and offered to contribute.

Juliet looked at him and the boys. "We've got this." She looked at Wayne and Stone. "Since you're working today, bring us something sweet from the café for dessert."

"We can surely do that," Wayne said. "Do you need anything from the store, Ma? I figured we'd buy a few more gallons of milk."

"I think we're good, but I'll call before you get off if there is anything we need."

"What's the plan for Thursday?" Keith asked.

"You and the boys are going to help Hank smoke our turkey, and stay out of my kitchen," Ma answered. "The girls and I will take care of everything in here. I'll make biscuits and gravy for breakfast while y'all get the smoker going and get the turkey cooking."

"Would you mind if we set up a television in the backroom to watch some football and finish off the keg while we're cooking?" Wayne asked.

"As long as you don't burn the bird," Ma said.

"There's not that much beer left. I hate to waste it, but the keg is due back for the deposit soon," Wayne replied.

"I was also going to add, don't let it ruin your appetites, but then I remembered who I was talking to," Ma teased.

"We will be more than ready to eat when it's ready, Ma," Keith promised. "I've been dreaming about a turkey leg all day."

"When do y'all have to go back to work?" Hank asked.

"The café is closed after tomorrow until Sunday morning," Cedra replied. She looked at Keith. "The Ryman is closed until Monday. We've got some studio time Saturday. We hoped you'd join us."

"I'd be tickled to join y'all. Will I get to hear you play before then?" Hank asked.

"Most definitely. We've got more covers and some new songs to practice. Maybe between lunch and turkey sandwiches Thursday and some on Friday."

"That sounds perfect." Hank smiled.

Juliet looked at Ma. "Do you need us for anything tonight, Ma?"

Ma shook her head. "No, I was planning to start some chopping. Do y'all want to play tonight?"

Juliet looked around at the smiling faces. "Yeah, I think we do. We can set up in the living room since it's cold out."

Hank turned to Ma. "Would you mind if I helped you chop veggies? We can still listen to the music."

"That would be great, and I would enjoy the company. You don't have to chop if you just want to relax," Ma added.

Hank smiled. "That was a long drive, and I need to feel like I've done something besides ride today."

"Sounds like someone else I know." Ma shot a wink to Cedra.

"The apple didn't fall far from the tree, Ma," Cedra joked.

"Y'all go get set up, and once Hank finishes his pie, we can start chopping."

Cedra kissed her dad on the cheek. "Love you, Dad."

"I love you too, Baby Girl."

"Where do we want to start?" Juliet asked. "More covers?"

"How about 'Body Like a Backroad' and then 'Pontoon?' We can get back to some original tunes if we pick up on those quickly," Stone suggested.

"That sounds like as good a plan as any," Keith replied.

"Okay, guys, y'all have 'Back Road' and then we'll all do 'Pontoon,'" Juliet said. "Who wants the first shot at the lead?"

"I think it should be Stone and Wayne," Keith suggested.

Stone chuckled and looked at Juliet. "I think you should take a crack at it as well. I can so see you singing this song live."

"Give it your best shot then, and I'll go last and show you how it's done," Juliet teased.

"Do they always interact this well?" Hank asked Ma.

Ma nodded. "They genuinely do. I've never seen five young people that can work the magic they do with music and have so much fun while performing."

"That's refreshing to hear. Any bets on which one will sing it best?"

"It could end in a tie between Stone and Juliet," Ma answered. "They both have tremendous vocal talent, but none of them lack the ability."

"While playing, or no?" Stone asked.

"You choose, bro," Wayne said.

"Let's all sing without playing then to keep it even," Stone suggested.

"That works for me," Juliet replied.

"Me, too," Wayne agreed.

"You're up, Stone," Keith said. "Let's hit it."

Ma watched Hank's face, as Stone began singing. She reached over and laid his knife down. "You might want to stop while they play. You may need those fingers later," she teased.

Hank nodded and listened to Stone's version of the song. "Wow, that was good," he said, then picked up the knife to start chopping again.

"I have to agree that was pretty good," Wayne said. "It will be hard to beat that, but I'll give it my best."

Wayne started singing, and Cedra nodded to the music. She turned her head for a glimpse of her dad's face to find him smiling broadly.

Wayne finished and shook his head. "Stone's voice is so much richer than mine."

All heads turned toward Juliet. "Are you ready?" Keith asked.

Juliet sat her guitar beside her. "Ready when you are." She waited for the music to begin and then started on the lyrics.

Hank looked at Ma in surprise. "I wasn't expecting that voice to come out of Juliet."

"She can belt them just as well, if not better than the boys."

"So, I see," Hank replied.

Juliet began moving her hands through the air like a curvy road as the band members started to smile. When she finished, she shot a wink to Cedra.

"All three were good, but I think it's a toss-up between Stone and Juliet," Wayne admitted. "What did the two of y'all think?" he asked Ma and Hank.

"They were all good, but I think Juliet's performance was the best," Ma said.

"I concur." Hank nodded.

"Why don't you both record and see which version Bud likes best?" Ma suggested.

"That's a good idea, Ma. As usual," Cedra said.

"Y'all ready to launch the 'Pontoon?'" Wayne teased.

"All set." Juliet hung her guitar over her shoulder.

†

Hank found himself dancing in his chair as they sang. "They are outstanding," he whispered to Ma.

"Wait until you hear the next one," Ma told him. "Cedra is singing one of her songs next."

Hank filled his face with a proud smile. "I can't wait. It seems like ages since I've heard her sing."

"She is amazing. She won't admit it, but she's growing into her singing voice," Ma said. "Fantastic," Ma called to them. "Hank and I were about to jump up and cut a rug."

Cedra laughed. "Go ahead anytime you get ready."

"You next, Cedra?" Stone asked.

Cedra nodded and took a deep breath. She started strumming her guitar and hummed for several seconds before singing. Her voice was strong and pure as she ran through the lyrics.

Juliet glanced at Hank and found him wiping a tear from his cheek. She smiled at him and nodded.

"I told you," Ma said.

"Perfect," Hank said. "I wouldn't change a thing."

"I agree," Stone replied. "That was really good."

"Let's run through your song, and then, if y'all are up to it, I'd like to try 'Landslide,'" Juliet said.

"I'll go get my banjo," Wayne said.

"Would you mind jumping in for an extra guitar?" Stone asked Keith.

"Sure, I'll jump in where I can."

Stone nodded. "I'll play through the music once. It's pretty basic."

Keith listened as Stone played and nodded. "I think I've got it," he told Stone.

"Okay, here we go."

Hank voluntarily placed his knife on the table and listened to Stone's song. He looked at Ma. "It needs something in the music."

Wayne came bouncing downstairs with his banjo. Ma and Hank looked at each other and nodded. "That's it, isn't it?" Ma asked.

"I think so," Hank answered.

When Stone finished, Ma chimed in. "Can we make a suggestion?"

"Sure, Ma," Stone said.

Ma smiled. "Add Wayne's banjo. The lyrics are beautiful, but the music is missing something, and I think that will be the perfect addition."

"You game?" Stone asked.

"Yes. It will warm me up for 'Landslide.'" Wayne laughed. "I'll need your notepad with the music. Unlike Wonder Boy Keith, I can't play it after hearing it once," Wayne teased.

Stone passed Wayne the notepad and let him read through it for several minutes. "Okay, I'm ready," Wayne announced.

Stone opened the song, and when Wayne added the banjo to the two guitars, it sounded much better. When they stopped playing, they all turned to Ma.

"That was great," Ma said.

"It did sound better," Juliet added.

"I agree," Stone replied. "Do you want us to play while the two of you sing?" he asked Juliet.

Juliet looked at Cedra, who nodded.

"Sounds good. Ready when you are," Juliet said. She sang the first verse, and then Cedra joined in for the rest of the song.

"I like that version better than the Fleetwood Mac one," Hank said when they finished. "Dixie Chicks?"

233

"Yeah, but they just go by The Chicks now," Cedra told him.

"That sounded really good." Hank smiled.

Juliet started laughing and pointed at the table. "Did you intend to chop that whole bag of onions?" she asked Ma.

Ma looked at the large bowl of onions on the table and the empty bag of onions. "No, but I'm sure they won't go to waste. I'll cook some in hash browns for breakfast tomorrow and Friday," she answered.

"I think we'll pack up here and help you clean the kitchen, Ma," Cedra said. "Tomorrow is going to be an early day for Stone and Wayne."

"I'm almost used to getting up that early," Wayne joked.

"Don't worry about the kitchen. Hank and I were pretty neat. I'll store that mound of chopped onions and get the dishwasher going while you get Hank settled in upstairs."

"I'll take the garbage out for you, Ma," Stone said.

"Thanks. You move a lot faster in this cold than I do."

"Goodnight then, Ma. We'll see you in the morning," Juliet said as she led Cedra and Hank upstairs.

"I'll see you for coffee and breakfast," Ma called to them.

"Does she get up early?" Hank asked when they got to the rooms.

"She wakes up to see us off to work in the morning and sends us out the door with coffee before she plans breakfast for whoever is at home," Cedra replied. "She's generally up around four."

"Good, so I'll have someone to drink coffee with." Hank smiled.

"Several pots." Juliet grinned. She grabbed her phone charger and walked into Cedra's room.

"If you need anything, just holler," Cedra said. "Goodnight, Dad." She stepped over to him and kissed his cheek. "I am so happy you're here."

"Me too, Baby Girl. I've missed you, and it's been great meeting all your friends." He nodded toward her room. "Especially Juliet. I see why you love her so much. I'm glad you two are happy together, and I am so proud of all of you. You sound fantastic."

"Thanks. See you in the morning." Cedra pulled the door closed behind her.

†

"Finally," David said when Linea settled in for the night and began turning off lights. "I was beginning to wonder if you'd ever go to bed." He looked at his watch and saw that it was almost two. Marco would arrive about five to take over the surveillance. "Not a moment too soon," David said and took another drink.

†

Marco tapped on his window several hours later, startling David from his nap. David nodded for Marco to climb into the passenger seat and cranked his truck.

235

"Good morning, Sunshine." David took the large cup of coffee from Marco. "Man, do I need this."

"Hey, sweetie. Did you have a quiet night?"

"Yeah, I did. I placed an open-door sensor on Linea's car and decided to take a nap after she finally went to bed."

"Do you want me to retrieve it, so you can go home and sleep in a bed for a while?"

"That sounds heavenly. I'm getting too old to sleep in a truck," David teased.

"You're not old. It doesn't help that you're so tall, though. Me? I fit just about anywhere." Marco leaned over and kissed David. "Go get some sleep, and I'll let you know if anything changes."

David yawned. "She's supposed to go out after boxes this morning. Carrie should arrive with the truck sometime after ten, so hopefully, it will be a quiet shift. She made an offhanded threat against the Redbird Café, so if she comes anywhere close to it, don't let her do anything stupid."

"Got it," Marco said. "I'll see you this afternoon. Love you."

"Love you, too," David replied and watched Marco as he deftly removed the sensor from the car and returned to his truck parked behind David's.

David pulled out of the complex and drove quickly through the quiet Nashville streets to their condo.

†

Cedra smiled when she heard the quiet sounds of her dad in the bathroom. She was tempted to get up for coffee with Hank and Ma, but the warm body snuggled into her felt too good to move. "We'll get up in a little bit," Juliet promised when she felt Cedra's movement.

"That's good. You can sleep in a bit longer if you want."

"Nope. I plan to enjoy every minute with you and Hank that I can. Unless you want some alone time with him."

"No. You are an important part of me. I want you around as much as possible."

†

"Good morning, Ma," Hank said as he stepped into the kitchen.

"Good morning, Hank. I hope you slept well. There's fresh coffee in the pot. I already have the mugs poured for Wayne and Stone."

"Slept like a rock." Hank poured a cup. "Do you want me to go ahead and put another pot on?"

Ma shook her head. "I'll get it in just a minute. I wanted to wash some of these potatoes to make some hash browns this morning to go with breakfast."

"Do you need them peeled?"

"No, I thought I'd leave the skins on for the vitamins and use a grater to cut them thin."

"I can do that for you," Hank offered.

"You just enjoy the coffee and keep me company. The boys will be here in a minute."

"I'm here, Ma," Wayne said. "I'm going to start my truck, and I'll be back. Good morning, Hank."

"Morning, Wayne," Hank replied as Stone walked down the hall. "Morning, Stone."

"Good morning, you two. It looks like we'll have another sunny, cold day in Nashville," Stone said as he picked up a mug. "Thanks, Ma." He sat next to Hank. "Is there any particular dessert you want us to bring home?"

"Since this will be the last day open, you can probably bring a variety of what Lisa Marie has left," Ma said. "We could have a smorgasbord of desserts. I lay claim to the buttermilk pie if there's only one slice left."

"I'll let you know the status of desserts. If they are running low, do you want us to pick up some buttermilk and sugar or see what the store has in the bakery?"

"If the café's wiped out, pick up a gallon of buttermilk and a five-pound bag of sugar, and I'll make some."

"Deal," Stone said as Wayne walked back inside.

"Brrr, it's cold out." Wayne picked up his mug. "That feels good on my hands."

"Do you two not have gloves?" Ma asked.

"Somewhere," Wayne replied.

Ma shook her head. "I think you need to be finding them. Can't have you losing fingers to frostbite. It's hard to play the guitar without fingers," Ma teased.

"I'll see if I can dig them out tonight," Wayne said.

She looked at Stone.

"I need to buy a pair, Ma. It doesn't get cold like this in Florida," he said. "I'll get a pair after Thanksgiving," Stone promised. He stood and pulled on his coat. "Thank goodness Wrangler sent us these nice coats."

"Are we ready to roll?" Wayne asked.

"We'll see you all later," Stone replied and nodded to Wayne.

"Be careful and stay warm," Ma called after them. She poured a fresh cup of coffee. "Are you ready for a refill?" she asked Hank.

"Yes, ma'am, I am," Hank replied and offered her his cup.

Ma sat a bowl of potatoes on the table and grated them for breakfast. She was nearly finished when Cedra and Juliet came down the stairs.

Juliet poured their coffee as Cedra looked at the pile of potatoes. "Stone and Wayne went to work, right?"

"Yes, but he who eats a lot is still with us," Ma said with a chuckle. "I expect the smell of cooking bacon will bring him from his unconscious state."

"Does he really eat that much? He's not that big," Hank said.

"Just don't get caught between Keith and anything sweet," Cedra teased. "Do you want me to start the bacon, Ma?"

"No, I've got this. You visit with your dad. Do y'all want eggs or pancakes?"

"I'll scramble some eggs, and Juliet can make the toast if you do the bacon and hash browns."

"That sounds like a deal too good to pass," Ma answered. "Enjoy your coffee while I get the bacon started."

"Yes, ma'am," Cedra answered.

"I'm going to take a shower and get dressed for the day," Juliet said. "I'll be back to make the toast and set the table before you finish cooking." She leaned down to softly kiss Cedra.

"Dress warmly. It's cold out," Ma said.

†

Keith arrived when Juliet headed back downstairs. "Something smells good," he said with a groggy-sounding voice.

"It sure does. Too bad you missed it," Juliet said.

"What?" Keith's eyes shot open wide as he picked up speed.

"Gotcha." Juliet laughed. "You can pour the drinks," she said.

"Dad's already set the table, so get to making some toast," Cedra told Juliet.

"I'm on it, boss," Juliet teased.

"What condiments do we need?" Keith asked.

"Butter is already out. Jelly, and ketchup for hash browns. I can't think of anything else," Ma answered.

"May I have some of your onions and shredded cheese, Ma?" Cedra asked.

Ma passed the containers to Cedra. "Knock yourself out," Ma replied.

Cedra added the onions to cook before pouring the whipped eggs into the mixture, and then when they were almost done, she shook on some of the shredded cheese. "Are we ready to serve?" she asked Ma.

"Just waiting on you," Ma replied and carried a bowl of hash browns to the table after handing Juliet the bacon. Ma looked at Hank. "A word of advice. Take all the bacon you want before passing the plate to Keith."

"Advice noted," Hank said and took several strips of bacon. Cedra handed Juliet the bowl of eggs. "Scoop me a spoonful if you would, please." She returned to the sink and washed her hands. "Does anyone need more coffee while I'm up?"

"I'll take some more," Hank said.

"Me, too," Ma replied.

Cedra looked at Juliet. She shook her head and swallowed. "I'm switching over to juice."

†

"That was an incredible breakfast, ladies," Hank said. "If I may be excused, I'll go shower and get dressed."

"Take your time, Dad, we've got all day," Cedra replied.

"I hope we'll do some walking. I think I need to burn some of those calories I just consumed."

"I don't think you have to worry about calories," Cedra teased.

241

Hank walked upstairs, and Keith looked at Ma. "Is there anything you need me to do, Ma?"

"I'll holler up to you if I think of something," she replied. "Going back to bed?"

"No. You won't believe this, but there's a song rolling around in my brain. I need to see if I can write it out." Keith grinned.

"That's great news, Keith," Cedra replied.

"Don't get too excited," Keith warned. "It may be total crap."

"Or, it may be terrific," Ma told him. "Only time will tell."

"Let's get these dishes washed up, and Ma can relax today. Do you want to go with us? You know Nashville better than any of us," Cedra said.

"If you don't mind, I'm going to stay in where it's nice and warm. These old bones don't do well in the cold. I'll cook some lunch for Keith and me and just kickback. Maybe listen to a hot new CD that was given to me."

"That reminds me. I need to give Dad a copy," Cedra said.

"Dump that coffee filter, and I'll take out the trash," Juliet said.

"You're already showered and clean, so let me take it."

"I won't argue with that," Juliet replied as she stored the condiments. "Is there anything special you want with the brisket tonight, Ma?"

"Some of those baked beans. Do you want me to boil some corn?"

"That would be great. Just thinking about it makes my mouth water."

†

Juliet navigated for Cedra as they toured Nashville. "Do you think we need to go ahead and call in our order for three o'clock?" Juliet asked.

Cedra nodded. "That's probably not a bad idea. You never know how businesses are being impacted by this dang virus. Is it bad at home, Dad?"

"From what I hear on the news, it's getting bad everywhere, honey," Hank replied.

"Are you well-stocked for food and supplies?"

"Yes. My garden produced well this year, and I've got enough cat food to last for six months." Hank chuckled.

"Masks and toilet paper?" Juliet asked.

"Plenty of TP and a few masks. I don't go out very often, but I do wear a mask when I have to go."

"That's good to hear," Cedra said. "I worry about you."

"No need to worry, Baby Girl. I take good care of myself. I promise. I want to be around when the Bentleys fill that stadium." Hank grinned as he pointed to Nissan Stadium.

"That may be a while yet."

"That's what I'm counting on." Hank chuckled. "Will local stations be able to pick up the *Bentley Break* shows?"

"That's only on the internet right now. Do you still have WiFi in the house?"

"No, I let it go when you moved out. I can get it again, though." Hank smiled.

"Wait, you have a smartphone. Do you have internet with that?" Juliet asked.

Hank shrugged. "I'm not real sure. The phone's smarter than me."

"Let me see your phone for a minute." Juliet took the phone from Hank and scrolled through to find he did have an internet connection. She downloaded the Big Machine streaming application for him and hit play. "You're all set. I'll show you how to use it later, and we'll let you know what time slot we get. You should be able to listen to us then."

"That's fantastic. Thanks, Juliet."

"You're welcome. We've got to keep our number one fan happy," Juliet replied.

Cedra looked in the rearview mirror and saw the grin on her dad's face. "That's right, we do." She looked over at Juliet. "Get to ordering us some food, woman," she teased. "I'm going to run by the café so Dad can meet Lisa Marie. It should be fairly calm right now."

"Yes, I'd like to meet her," Hank said. "It sounds like she's been really good to you."

"She has, Dad. She's been a great friend and boss."

"All set, but we have to pick up by two-thirty," Juliet said. "Closing early, due to staff shortage."

"I get that. We still have time for a quick visit?"

"Yes, we do," Juliet said.

†

Marco followed Linea as she left the apartment and drove to a liquor store for boxes. She filled her car, went to a nearby gas station, and bought gas. He was relieved that Linea didn't fill up a container, but that relief faded quickly when her car slowed in front of the Redbird.

"Just keep going," he said, then ducked into a parking slip when she hit her brakes and stopped directly in front of the café. Luckily there was no one in sight, and she drove past the building and turned right, heading back toward her apartment. Marco was glad to see the moving truck backed into a spot and Carrie sitting behind the wheel.

"One step closer," he said and pulled through the parking lot until he found a good vantage spot.

†

Carrie stepped out of the truck and helped Linea carry the empty boxes into the apartment. "I called the office this morning and told them I was vacating today. I left your number as a contact in case there were any incidentals."

"That's fine," Carrie answered and picked up a dress and started to take it off the hanger.

"Don't bother taking them off the hangers. Just stick them in a box and move to the next," Linea growled.

245

"What made you decide to leave today?" Carrie asked, genuinely curious but glad for the news.

"No reason to spend another night in this town. If I'm lucky, I'll make it through Memphis before dark. The sooner, the better."

"Fair enough." Carrie continued until she had a box full and taped closed. "I'll be right back." She picked up the box, carried it out to the truck, and placed it in the back. "Shit. I don't have Marco's number," she said from inside the truck. She texted David about Linea leaving today and prayed he wasn't sleeping. Carrie was walking back into the apartment when he answered.

Got it. Be there within an hour. Will leave Marco's truck for you to get back home and pick it up when we hit town if that's okay.

Perfect. Thanks again, David.

†

When they had carried out the last box, Carrie pulled the truck across the lot so Linea could position it on the car hauler. Once it was secured, they walked back inside.

"They said to leave the keys on the counter," Linea said.

Carrie pulled out an envelope and handed it to Linea. "Inside is a map, a prepaid credit card for gas, hotels, and food. There's also a cashier's check to help get you set up in LA."

"I guess this is it then. I know you think what I did was wrong, but I did it for us."

"Linea, there is no 'us,' and never will be. I hope you will use this break as an opportunity to start fresh and find a good life in LA." Carrie pulled her into a hug and gave her a chaste kiss. "Good luck, and I'll be watching for you on the big screen."

Linea nodded through her tears. "How are you getting home?"

"I've already called a taxi. Be safe and take care of yourself." Carrie was walking toward the door with Linea following her.

"I wish you could kiss all this goodbye and come with me," Linea said as they walked to the truck.

"My dreams are here," Carrie reminded her. She pulled the door open and closed it behind Linea. "Goodbye."

"Goodbye." Linea climbed in behind the wheel.

"Take it slow until you get used to pulling the car."

Linea nodded. "Thanks."

Carrie watched her pull out of the parking lot and let out a deep breath. She nodded to David and Marco as they drove past her and followed Linea onto the street. She waited until they were out of sight and then walked to Marco's truck. Carrie climbed inside and saw a flask with a post-it-note on the side. *Carrie, take a big swig* the message read. *Marco.*

Carrie twisted the top from the flask and took a long pull of the Jack Daniel's. "Thank you, Marco."

Carrie drove home, parked the truck, and switched immediately to her car. She called the café and ordered the bacon cheeseburger with onion rings to go. She was starving after skipping breakfast, and now that Linea was on her way out of her life, she felt like she could hold food down. Stone met her at the front door and turned to retrieve her order.

"Is Lisa Marie around?"

"Yeah, I'll let her know you're here."

Lisa Marie walked up to the door. "Hey, Carrie."

"Hey, I just wanted to tell you my problem is settled. Linea's on her way to LA and will be followed to the state line by some security staff to make sure she doesn't make a U-turn."

"That's excellent news. I hope Linea stays out west."

"She's got an excellent opportunity for a fresh start, so hopefully, she'll take advantage of that. If she returns, she's on her own."

"Let's both pray she doesn't, and she keeps her mouth shut," Lisa Marie said. "Not much she can do against us, but your reputation could still be tainted."

"I know all too well. I've done all I can for her. The rest is up to her."

"Here you go," Stone said and handed her a bag of food. "Enjoy."

"Thanks, Stone. I'll see y'all Saturday, right?"

Stone nodded. "Cedra's dad is coming with us so he can watch us record."

"It will be great to meet him. Thanks."

"See ya."

"That cheeseburger smelled good. Are you ready?" Lisa Marie asked.

"Heck yeah. I'll stick to the door if you'll put our orders in."

"You got it." Lisa Marie winked.

†

Stone filled two more orders while he waited on lunch. He looked up when he heard footsteps and smiled at three familiar faces. "Hey, guys," he said to Cedra, Hank, and Juliet.

"Hey, yourself. You been busy?" Cedra asked.

"Not for the last five minutes, so we have cheeseburgers on the way. Should I add a few more?"

"Not for me. We had a great breakfast. You hungry, Dad?" Juliet asked.

Hank smiled when she called him Dad. "No, I'm saving room for all this brisket you ordered."

"You just missed Carrie. She was here to pick up her burger a little while ago," Stone said. He handed each of them a mask and shrugged.

"We just wanted to stop in and introduce Dad to Lisa Marie," Cedra said as she put the mask on. "Is she around?"

"You looking for me?" Lisa Marie said as she carried plates of burgers out to a table.

"We are. I wanted Dad to meet you."

Lisa Marie sat the plates on the table and offered Hank an elbow bump. "So nice to meet you. Can I get y'all some drinks, dessert, cheeseburgers?"

"Some tea would be good," Juliet said.

"Sit tight, boss, I've got it," Wayne called out.

"Have you been giving Hank the grand tour?" Lisa Marie asked.

"We've been trying," Cedra answered. "We're picking up some brisket for dinner tonight if you want to join us."

Lisa Marie smiled. "I'm taking advantage of the café being closed to drive to Chattanooga to visit my sister and her family for Thanksgiving. I'll be back in time to open up Sunday morning. Will you still be here, Hank?"

"I'll be headed back south. I know my way now, so you can bet I'll be back."

"If you change your mind and have time for breakfast, we open early, and I'll treat you."

Hank shook his head. "I think I should be treating you for all you've done for my Baby Girl and her friends."

"They have done way more for me than I have them. You have done good raising this one," Lisa Marie said, placing a hand on Cedra's arm. "The rest of them are works in progress, but they're coming along." Lisa Marie laughed.

"I'll own that," Juliet said.

"Me, too," Stone agreed. "Two months ago, I would have spilled food or coffee over customers, but Cedra taught me well."

"Y'all enjoy the lunch and get good and full, so there will be more brisket for us," Cedra teased. "We need to head out. The restaurant is closing early now, too."

"Don't forget the milk and dessert," Juliet reminded them.

Lisa Marie laughed. "There are already two buttermilk pies boxed up. I'll send the other slices if you don't mind. I won't have to toss them that way."

"Keith will eat the heck out of them," Wayne said.

"That's what I figured. It was a pleasure to meet you, Hank. Don't be a stranger," Lisa Marie said.

"I won't. Nice to meet you too," Hank answered and stood with Cedra and Juliet.

"Later, boys," Juliet said.

"Happy Thanksgiving, boss," Cedra told Lisa Marie. "Drive safe."

"Y'all have a great one." Lisa Marie walked them to the door and locked it behind them.

†

Cedra was stopped at a red light. "How much farther to the BBQ?" Hank asked.

"About a mile, why?" Cedra asked.

"Can you drop me off at that boot shop and pick me up after you get the food?" he asked.

"Sure. Is there something you need, Dad?"

"Window shopping." He winked to Cedra.

She pulled into the lot, and he stepped out. "It shouldn't take more than twenty minutes or so."

"I'll be waiting right here," Hank said. After pulling his mask on, he watched them drive off then walked into the store.

"May I help you with something, sir?"

"Some warm gloves, please, young lady," Hank replied.

†

"What's your dad up to? Any ideas?" Juliet asked.

"Not a clue. There is no telling with Dad," Cedra replied as she pulled into a parking spot. "We made it with minutes to spare." She smiled. "Ready?"

"Oh, yeah. The smell of this place always gets my motor running," Juliet teased.

Cedra frowned. "I thought that's what I did?"

Juliet broke out laughing. "No, baby, you make my motor purr."

"Great answer. Come on."

They walked inside and saw bags of food on the counter. A young woman looked up at them. "I hope you don't mind, but we are closing, so we put some extra beans and some slaw in with your order. No charge, of course."

"That's perfect," Cedra answered. "Thank you."

"I know it will be enjoyed by y'all, and I hate to toss good food out," the woman replied.

"I promise a bite won't go to waste." Juliet smiled. "Thanks."

She picked up two of the bags and walked with Cedra outside. "I think there's more extra in here besides beans and slaw."

"I agree. Hang on a second, okay?" Cedra pulled one of the CDs out from the box behind her seat and took it back inside.

"We'd like to thank you for your generosity," Cedra said as she handed the CD to the woman.

She looked at the CD. "The Bentleys? Oh, hell yeah. I love 'Six Strings.' That's you?"

"That's who you've been feeding all this good food to. So, thank you from us to you."

"Oh my gosh. I can't believe this. Thank you. Is it okay to play in here?" the woman asked.

"Knock yourself out. I hope you enjoy the whole album and tell others about it."

"You can bet I will. I sing along with y'all whenever it comes on the radio."

"Thank you." Cedra turned to leave and stopped. "When we get a gig in town, I'll make sure you get some tickets."

The young woman put the CD against her chest. "That would be great. Happy Holidays."

"You, too." Cedra pulled the door open.

"I think you just made that young lady's day," Juliet said.

"I hope so. Let's go see what Dad's doing."

Hank was sitting on a bench outside the store, enjoying the sunshine when they pulled into the lot. He climbed inside with a bag. "Dear Lord, something is mouthwatering back here."

"It makes for a long ride home. Did you find what you needed?" Cedra asked.

"Yes, I sure did," Hank answered.

"Are you going to share with us or keep us guessing?" Cedra asked.

"Can't a feller buy some new underwear?" Hank asked.

Cedra looked at him in the rearview mirror. "I know that store doesn't carry underwear, but if you want to have a secret, that's fine with me."

"You'll find out soon enough," Hank teased.

†

They unloaded the bags of food when they got home, and Hank tucked his bag under his arm. They spread the food out on the table. "Did you order all of this?" Ma asked.

"Not at this quantity. The lady at the restaurant loaded us up since we were the last customer of the day," Juliet replied. She opened up the box with the baby back ribs. "Holy cow. She really loaded us up. A double order of ribs."

"She didn't slack on the brisket or beans either, and there have to be five loaves of garlic bread in here," Cedra replied.

Keith came flying down the stairs. "I knew I smelled BBQ."

"Wayne and Stone shouldn't be far behind us. They have plenty of desserts they are bringing home with gallons of milk," Juliet said. "You want us to go ahead and set the table, Ma?"

"Sure, I've already got the corn boiled and warming," she replied. "I think I'm going to have a cup of coffee. Hank, would you like some?"

"I sure would," he answered and placed his bag beside him on the table. Then he spotted the table in the foyer and put it there instead to have more room at the table.

Once everyone was seated around the table, he looked at Ma. "Can I have a minute before everyone gets their hands messy?"

"Sure can, Hank."

He walked to the table to retrieve his bag and began pulling out pairs of black leather, fur-lined gloves and handed a pair to each of the youngsters. "Now, you don't have to worry about frostbitten fingers." He smiled.

"You shouldn't have, Dad, but they are nice," Cedra said.

"Warm too," Wayne said as he wiggled his fingers. "Thank you, Hank."

"Yes, sir, thanks," came a chorus around the table.

"My pleasure. Can't have you not being able to play from lost fingers," Hank said and shot a wink at Ma.

"That's right. Hand them over, and I'll put them away, so you don't get them messy. I know you're going to be messy." Ma returned to her seat. "Let's eat."

†

After barely an hour on the road, Linea slowed down and took the exit in Jackson. "What's she doing? She can't need gas yet," Marco said.

"I don't know. Hopefully, Linea is just stopping for a rest break."

"Well, fuck," David growled when she turned on the signal to return east on I-40. "I knew it was too good to be true. We've got a few miles to the next exit, so let's make a plan."

Marco opened the glove box and pulled out a wallet. "It's time for Officer Bartlett to make a return."

"I do love the way you think," David replied. David was a reserve officer with the Tennessee Alcohol, Tobacco, and Firearms unit, so he still possessed a badge and dashboard blue light. He would hit Linea with the blue lights and pull her over. Hopefully, his performance would be enough to convince her to return to her route heading west. "Connect the light bar for me, please. Hand me the cuffs, too." David grinned. "Let me know when you're ready."

"All set."

"Activate the lights." David waited for Marco to flip the switch.

David sped up behind Linea and flashed his lights.

†

"What the hell?" Linea said when she saw the blue lights and the truck flashing lights at her. She turned on her signal and pulled onto the side of the road. She wasn't speeding or breaking any laws, so she was completely confused with what was going on. She looked in the side view mirror and watched a large man in dark glasses approach, tucking a set of handcuffs in his belt as he strolled toward the truck.

Another smaller man had his hand near his hip as he walked up from the passenger side.

†

David walked to the door and motioned for Linea to lower the window. "Linea Turner," he said.

"Yes, I'm Linea Turner. Is there a problem, officer? I wasn't speeding or breaking any laws."

David flashed his badge. "You have broken laws, ma'am. I have been assigned to ensure you leave the state and the U-turn you just made in Jackson leads me to believe you are heading back to Nashville in violation of your agreement."

"You're kidding me, right?" Linea growled.

"There is nothing humorous about stalking or criminal mischief, Ms. Turner. I am authorized to give you two options for this behavior," David replied. "You can take the upcoming exit and get back on I-40 heading West, or I can arrest you now, and we can have someone tow your vehicle to the local impound lot. The choice is yours. I'm inclined to take you into custody and take you back to Nashville, but that will bring hours of paperwork, and I'd like to spend a relaxing holiday with my family. But it really doesn't matter. What's your choice?"

"It's not like I have much choice."

David hid the smile threatening to form by adjusting his sunglasses. "Sure, you do, but you will end up in an orange jumpsuit, and I hardly think that's your color or style."

"Aren't you the comedian?" Linea scowled.

"I'm informing you this is your last opportunity at freedom. The next time I stop you, you will be arrested," David warned.

"Consider me heading west then," Linea said and rolled up her window. She turned on her blinker and pulled back onto the road as David returned to his truck.

He climbed inside and smiled at Marco. "Did you set the tracking device?"

"I sure did," Marco replied. "We can track her all the way to LA, and as long as it remains intact, we'll know if she gets within fifty miles of Nashville."

David smiled. "Let's hope she got the message this time. We can keep an eye on her for a couple of days to make sure she arrives in LA." He put the truck in gear and caught up with Linea as she exited the interstate. "Good girl."

"How far are we from Memphis?"

"A little over an hour. Are you going to nap?"

"I am." Marco reclined the seat.

"Enjoy your nap. I'll see our girl across the river and then find us a nice hotel, compliments of Carrie Brooks. How about the Peabody?"

"Oh, yes, I love those marching ducks."

David laughed at his lover and followed Linea back onto the interstate.

CHAPTER ELEVEN

Thanksgiving Day passed all too quickly. After filling their stomachs with delicious food, the guys retreated to the living room to watch football on the television. Ma, Cedra, and Juliet were in the kitchen preparing turkey slices for sandwiches later when Ma elbowed Cedra and nodded to the living room. Hank was sound asleep in the recliner.

"I think he's comfortable here, don't you?"

Cedra smiled. "Yeah, I'd say so. I think the turkey got the best of him."

"He was up pretty early, too, to get the smoker going and the bird cooking while the rest slept in a bit. If he'd relied on them, we'd still be waiting on dinner."

"Thank goodness he's an early riser," Juliet replied. "That meal was spectacular. One of the best I've ever had for Thanksgiving."

"Your family didn't celebrate like this?" Cedra asked.

Juliet laughed. "We were lucky to get a turkey, stove-top stuffing, and Kraft macaroni and cheese." She looked at Ma. "My mother wasn't as fluent in festive meals like you."

Ma had cut up small bits of turkey. "Have you ever had turkey croquettes?"

"No, never even heard of them," Juliet answered.

"I'll use that extra pan of dressing I made and these bits of turkey to make into patties, then brown them in butter in a frying pan tomorrow morning for breakfast. With some eggs and hash browns," she added.

"That sounds delicious," Cedra responded. "Do you still have onions chopped?"

"I think there's enough for hash browns. I'll grate the potatoes in the morning or put your dad to work if he's up early again," Ma stated. "I'm betting after his nap today he'll be up bright and early."

Juliet picked up a pie pan. "Only one piece left. Do you want to split it with me?"

"I don't," Cedra replied. "I can't eat another bite of anything right now."

"Ma?" Juliet asked.

Ma looked to see coffee still in the pot. She nodded. "Fix me a cup of coffee, too, while I put this turkey away."

"You got it," Juliet said. "You know, a nap doesn't sound like a bad idea."

"I was thinking the same thing. We can have some sandwiches later if anyone is hungry," Ma suggested.

"To me, that's the best part of the turkey. The sandwiches after the meal. With a slice of cranberry sauce, a bit of dressing, and mayo," Cedra replied.

When Ma and Juliet finished the pie, Cedra smiled. "Nap time?"

"Oh, yeah," Ma answered. "Sandwiches around seven?"

"That sounds good to me. Come on, let's go nap." Cedra took Juliet's hand. She looked into the living room and grinned. Stone and Wayne were asleep, and Keith looked like he was on his way.

"I'll take a comfy bed over a couch any day," Juliet said.

"Me, too."

✝

Later that evening, after finishing a stack of sandwiches, Ma looked around the table. "Thanks for a great Thanksgiving. I think we should all try to sleep in a bit tomorrow. I'll have breakfast ready at nine, and we can relax all day."

"That sounds wonderful. I just hope we can sleep in." Cedra laughed. "Some of us are used to getting up early."

"As full as my belly is right now, I don't think I'll have any problems," Stone said.

"Me either," Wayne replied.

"I never have a problem," Keith disclosed.

Hank shrugged. "I may be up by myself. Is there anything you need to be done for breakfast?"

"You can grate up about a dozen of those potatoes if you are determined to have something to do." Ma grinned.

"That's easy enough," Hank replied.

"Can you make some brownies tomorrow, Ma?" Keith asked.

"Nope," she answered. "But you and Juliet can," she teased.

"That's right. We know how to make brownies now," Juliet reminded him.

"I guess we know what we're doing tomorrow afternoon then," Keith said with a smile to Juliet.

"That works for me," Juliet replied. "Should we practice some tomorrow, or do y'all want the day off?"

Stone shook his head. "We had the day off today."

"I agree," Cedra replied. "We can get several tracks cut Saturday if we do the work to prepare." She looked at her dad. "Is there anything you want to do tomorrow?"

"Just spend time with you and your friends," Hank answered.

"I think we've got a plan then. Goodnight, everyone," Ma declared.

†

Cedra changed into her sleep clothes and looked at Juliet. "Would you mind if I sit up and write a bit?"

"Go right ahead. I know you haven't had much time to write lately. I'll just stretch out and watch you."

"Okay." Cedra opened her laptop.

"No songbook?" Juliet asked, surprised.

"I'm trying to get used to the laptop," Cedra answered.

Juliet turned on her side and tucked a pillow under her head to watch Cedra.

Cedra began making notes on a song she'd call "Broken Heart Syndrome" that had been running through her head all day. It would be a sad song, which surprised her. Life couldn't be more perfect for her, yet she felt compelled to write a song dealing with the loss of love. She heard the song in her head as she wrote line after line and went back to tweak what she had written. She glanced over at Juliet who had snuggled into her pillow, and was softly snoring. Cedra smiled, and her eyes returned to the lyrics growing on the screen. She read through them twice more and then saved her work. Cedra turned off the lamp and crawled into bed to snuggle into Juliet's warmth.

CHAPTER TWELVE

The Bentleys played for hours Friday afternoon, and when Ma called them for dinner, they packed their instruments away.

"What have you been working on in there, Ma?" Juliet asked.

"Turkey and dumplings with fresh biscuits. After today, I promise you won't have to look at turkey again until Christmas."

"I don't mind at all," Keith said. "We've had several great meals from that turkey. Those croquettes this morning were off the chain," he raved.

"I love your dumplings period, Ma, no matter what you cook with them," Stone added.

Ma smiled at him. "It was a toss-up between dumplings and rice. I figured the dumplings would suit the weather better. It's cold out."

"I think I heard the weatherman report that it would be back up in the fifties a couple of days next week," Wayne stated.

"That's crazy weather for ya," Keith grumbled.

Cedra finished her drink. "What time are we due at the studio in the morning?"

"Someone signed us up for eight," Wayne declared and nodded toward Juliet.

"Do you want me to move it back to nine?" Juliet asked.

Cedra shook her head. "No, it may be our entire last day together for a while. We need to make the most of it we can."

Hank looked at the group. "What will you be recording tomorrow?"

Cedra began pouring drinks. "More covers and more original work for the *Bentley Break* and the next album. I hope we'll get a report on how 'Six Strings' is doing. I know it's only been a few days, but I'm excited to see how it's selling."

"Will they release the whole album or a few songs at a time?" Hank asked.

Cedra stopped and looked at him. "I don't know. I would have assumed the album, but now that you mention it, they may release a song or two at a time. Hopefully, the whole CD is available in specific markets."

"I think the trend these days is to do a pre-release and make a limited number of songs available at one time," Juliet answered. "Listeners can hear the first few tunes and purchase the download of the album once it's released."

"I'm glad you know all this," Keith replied.

"I try to do my homework, but it will be a good question to ask Carrie tomorrow," Juliet replied.

Ma placed a platter of biscuits on the table then a large bowl of turkey and dumplings. "Dig in."

"Do you have some firewood I can chop or something to burn off all these calories?" Hank teased Ma.

"You know that's not a bad idea," Wayne said.

"Chopping firewood?" Keith scowled.

"No, but getting a load or two to stack on the back porch. With this weather, we may have some snow and ice. If that happens, we may lose power and heat. Ma's fireplace may be our source of heat for an extended period."

"I could get a couple extra tanks of propane, too," Stone offered. "In case we need to cook on the propane grill."

Ma nodded. "I'll call tomorrow and see if we can get some wood delivered. Y'all can stack it once the service dumps it."

"We can pick up some tanks on our way home tomorrow, too," Stone replied.

†

When they retired for the evening, Cedra turned on the laptop. "I want you to read something and give me your opinion on it."

"Sure," Juliet sat down and began reading the lyrics Cedra had written. She looked at Cedra with a frown. "Please tell me this isn't how you feel?"

Cedra covered her mouth with her hands. "Oh, gosh no, Juliet. I don't think I've ever been so happy, but these lyrics have been buzzing in my head for days."

"It's sad and gut-wrenching, but beautiful all at the same time if that makes sense. You can feel the heartache just reading through the lyrics. May I make a suggestion?"

"Sure, that's why I need your opinion."

"No strings for this one. Use the keyboard at the studio to record this song."

Cedra let the suggestion sink in. "That's a good idea, and I think you're right. It needs to be accompanied by soft music to set the tone."

"Exactly. Why don't we head into the studio early in the morning, and you can play it before the boys arrive?"

"That sounds good. I think I've got the music in my head. I'll need to print out the lyrics."

"I can print them for you tonight or in the morning."

"Wait until the morning. I'm sure Dad will be up at the crack of dawn." Cedra smiled. "His time here sure has flown by."

"That's usually the way things happen. Have you asked him about coming for Christmas?"

"No, not yet. I wanted to talk to Ma about it first."

"I don't think that's going to be a problem. Ma and Hank get along very well if you hadn't noticed." Juliet turned off the laptop and climbed into bed.

"Yeah, they do." Cedra smiled and reached up to turn off the light.

†

Juliet and Cedra showered then joined Ma and Hank downstairs the following morning. Juliet had texted Bud, who assured her that they could get into the studio early. "We need to change plans just a bit this morning, Ma," Juliet said. "Cedra and I need to get to the studio early this morning to test something out."

"Is everything okay?" Hank asked.

"Yes, just a new song that we want to try out on a keyboard," Cedra answered. "Do you want to ride in with the boys?"

"Sure, I can do that," Hank replied.

"I've got fresh biscuits and sausage patties. Will you take some so you'll have something on your stomachs?" Ma asked.

Cedra nodded. "It'll take a few minutes to thaw my truck out, so we can devour them and take some coffee with us."

"I'll pour some juice," Hank offered.

"I'll get the coffee if you make the biscuits, Ma," Juliet added.

"I'll be right back," Cedra said and pulled on her coat.

"Are you sure you don't mind riding with the boys?" Juliet asked Hank.

"Not at all. I can help Ma finish breakfast and drink a bit more coffee."

"Thanks."

"Jelly on your biscuits?" Ma asked.

"Yes, please," Juliet requested.

†

Bud met them at the front door of the studio. "What has gotten you two up and moving so early this morning?"

"A new song, Bud, but we don't have a keyboard. I really think it needs to be performed with one," Juliet replied as she grabbed their cases.

"That sounds intriguing."

Cedra smiled. "I've never performed it, and Juliet thinks it needs a keyboard instead of strings. We wanted to try it out before the others arrived."

"Let's do it then. I'll get the equipment ready while you set up."

Cedra nodded. She reached for Juliet's hand as they walked into the studio. She handed her guitar to Juliet and pulled off her gloves. "My gloves kept my hands nice and toasty," Cedra said with a smile.

"I know. Hank got the sizes perfect, too." Juliet opened Cedra's case and handed her the page of lyrics she had printed out.

"Thanks." Cedra placed the paper onto a stand. "I'm going to warm up just a bit," she told Bud.

Bud nodded from the booth. "Just let me know when you're ready."

Juliet sat close as Cedra took a seat in front of the keyboard and activated the power. The studio was silent as Cedra closed her eyes and waited for the music to arrive. Her fingers softly stroked the keys as the music for the new song came to life. It felt good to hear the beautiful sound, and she opened her eyes to find Juliet smiling.

"Is that how you imagine it to sound? It's beautiful," she said.

She nodded to Juliet and then looked at Bud. "I'm ready."

Bud nodded, pressed a switch, and put his headset on.

Cedra began playing the music and then started adding the lyrics.

The mixture of the music and the haunting lyrics being sung by Cedra brought gooseflesh to Juliet's arms, and she felt a shiver run through her. When the music stopped, she was speechless as she looked at Cedra.

"Will you try something?" Bud asked.

Cedra looked at him. "Sure."

"Bring Juliet over beside you and have her join you for the chorus," Bud suggested.

Cedra nodded and placed Juliet close enough to see the lyrics without accessing the keyboard. "Are you okay with this?"

Juliet nodded. "I'll give it a shot. Bud knows what he wants to hear."

"Are you ready?" Cedra asked.

"Yeah," Juliet said.

Cedra began playing, and when she arrived at the chorus, Juliet's rich voice joined hers. She smiled at her lover and how well they sounded together. When the song ended, they both turned to look at Bud. A smile lit his face. "Meet me in the break room for a listen."

"What did you think?" Juliet said.

Cedra laughed. "I think Bud's a genius. He always knows exactly what a song needs." She reached for Juliet's hand. "Let's go listen."

"What do you call this?" Bud asked when they walked into the room.

"'Broken Heart Syndrome,'" Cedra replied.

Bud nodded. "It's sad, but such a beautiful song, full of heartbreak and longing." He picked up the remote and played the recording of Cedra only; then, the second with Juliet joining her on the chorus. "Juliet adds another layer of sound to the chorus, but it also changes your voice." Bud chuckled. "What do you think?"

"I agree with your assessment. It sounds much better with Juliet."

"I've noticed that both your voices change when you sing together. Maybe it's excitement or the level of comfort you share, but the sound is noticeably different."

"Will you play the second run again, please?" Juliet requested.

Bud hit the remote and played the song again. Juliet smiled at Cedra. "He's right. We do sound better when we sing together."

"Solo was good, but together it's a much better song," Bud said. "Have the others heard it yet?"

"No, I just wrote it Thanksgiving night," Cedra replied. "I shared it with Juliet last night, and she suggested playing the keyboard instead of strings."

"That was an intelligent decision. The keyboard adds a layer of softness that a guitar can't mimic," Bud said. "Do you want to share it with them before we get started?"

"That's fine with me," Cedra said. "I hope you don't mind, but my dad is in town, and I invited him to come to listen today."

Bud smiled. "I look forward to shaking his hand."

Cedra smiled. "Will you play it one more time?"

"I'll play it as many times as you like. Did you hear something you want to change?"

"No, I just wanted to hear it again," Cedra replied.

"Would you mind a suggestion?"

"Not at all, Bud," Cedra said.

"Take a look at some Chris Stapleton covers. I know the two of you could kill some of his music with his wife, Morgan. 'Fire Away,' is the first to come to mind."

"I love that song," Juliet said. "Hell, I love just about anything he sings."

Bud looked at Cedra. "He started out as a songwriter, too."

"He's amazing. I hope I can have a sliver of his success as a writer."

"You will. I have no doubt of that, but I'm also glad you are expanding your vocals. You have a beautiful voice."

✝

The boys and Hank enjoyed a great breakfast and then hurried to get their instruments before heading out. "We'll see you tonight, Ma," Keith said then walked to the door.

"Enjoy your peace and quiet." Hank grinned and stepped outside.

"You can have shotgun," Keith called back over his shoulder.

Hank nodded and climbed inside the passenger seat of Wayne's truck.

"You've got it toasty in here, bro," Stone called from the backseat.

"I didn't want y'all to be cold." Wayne reached down and lowered the fan setting.

"I can't wait to hear what those two are up to this morning," Keith said.

"Something about a new song and needing access to a keyboard," Hank mentioned.

"That makes sense. I bet if Cedra played her cards right, she could get Carrie to buy her a keyboard," Stone said. "I think she's the only one who knows how to play one."

"I wouldn't mind one of those electronic drum pads either," Wayne replied.

"We have full access to whatever we need, so we don't need to go cramming Ma's home with a bunch of stuff," Keith replied.

"Yeah, you're right. I didn't think of it like that," Wayne answered.

"Keith's right. As long as you have access to the instruments you need, why go to the extra expense," Hank agreed.

"Did anyone think to ask Ma about dinner tonight? I don't know how long we will be recording today," Keith stated.

"Why don't you give her a call and see if it's okay if we bring home some pizza. Is that okay with you, Hank?" Wayne asked.

"That's perfectly fine with me," Hank answered.

"I'll give her a call then," Keith replied.

"It almost looks like it could snow." Wayne pointed to the sky. "Nothing forecast, but you never know."

"Ma's good with pizza. She said she'd make us some cookies tonight, too," Keith replied from the back seat.

"Now we are talking." Stone grinned.

†

Juliet, Cedra, and Bud met them inside the studio. Bud offered Hank his hand. "It's a pleasure to meet you. You have raised one talented young lady, sir."

Hank shook his hand. "I'm not always sure who raised who. She is incredibly talented, though, and I'm extremely proud of her and the rest of these youngsters."

Bud nodded. "Me too. They have such a fresh new sound. It's been a delight to work with them."

Keith was bouncing with excitement. "Hank told us you have a new song. Can we hear it?"

Cedra nodded. "Set your instruments up and meet us in the break room."

Hank slipped an arm around Cedra's shoulder. "Did it go as well as you hoped?"

"Even better, Dad. Bud suggested Juliet join me for the chorus, and it sounds great."

When everyone was around the table, Bud gave Cedra a nod. "Do you want to introduce the song?"

"It's called 'Broken Heart Syndrome.' A bit on the sad and longing side, but the lyrics have been buzzing in my head for days," she told them.

Bud pushed a button on the remote, and the music and video of them singing together played on the screen. Cedra shot a look at Bud when she saw the video. Bud smiled and gave her a wink.

Hank was the first to wipe at his eyes as the haunting tune tugged at his heart with Stone a close second.

When the music ended, Juliet looked at Bud. "You're sneaky. We had no idea you were recording the video, too."

"You never know, but I enter this as evidence of how well the two of you sing together," Bud replied.

"Every time I hear you sing, it only gets better," Hank said.

"Who would have thought this shy, young songwriter would blossom into such a great vocalist?" Juliet teased and raised her hand along with the rest of the band.

"She just needed to believe she could," Stone replied. "Well done, ladies."

"Are you all ready to get to work?" Bud asked. "I plan to get everything out of you I can today." He grinned.

The guys stood to return to the studio. Cedra looked at Hank. "You can sit and watch from here, Dad."

"No, he can come with me," Bud said.

"You hardly let anyone in the booth with you."

"He's hardly anyone, and I want to know more about you."

Cedra laughed. "Only the good stuff, Dad. Nothing embarrassing, please."

"Of course, Baby Girl." Hank stood to follow Bud.

†

It was comforting to see her dad in the booth with Bud. "You guys want to warm up for a few minutes?"

Stone nodded. "Do you want to start with a cover or an original?"

"Let's start with your new one, and then we can do a few more covers before lunch," Cedra suggested.

"Let me know when you're ready," Bud said.

†

Hank watched them as they warmed up.

"You really do have an amazing young woman," Bud said. "I've been impressed with her since the first time I heard one of her songs."

"She's worked hard and waited longer for this chance than what she should have, but I think that may have actually helped."

"I agree. Cedra's got a level of depth and emotion to her songs you don't usually see in someone so young. Life has been tough on her, but I think it's energized her creativity."

Hank nodded. "She's not had it easy, that's for sure, with her mom dying so young and then trying to piece me back together. It was hard trying to convince her to come here, but I'm glad she's finally chasing that dream."

"She's making it come true, for all of us. I thank you for that."

"I just gave her some genes. Cedra's done the hard work." Hank smiled.

"Damn nice genes." Bud chuckled.

†

"We're going to start off with one of Stone's songs," Juliet said from the studio.

Bud gave her a thumbs up and started recording as she placed the headphones on her head. He listened to the song as they played and turned to Hank. "Stone is a good writer, but his lyrics don't hold a candle to Cedra's," he praised. "You can feel the difference in emotion in his words."

They looked up at the booth waiting for Bud's reaction. "Cedra, would you mind adding keyboard?"

Cedra looked at Stone, who smiled back at her. "Let's give it a go."

They played through the song again, and Bud still felt like something was missing. "Juliet, will you sing with Stone this time?"

"Sure." Juliet nodded.

"She has an awesome voice," Hank said. "She's kind of like a female version of Chris Stapleton."

"Funny you should say that. I've asked her and Cedra to cover a few of his songs while we were waiting this morning. I can see them nailing 'Fire Away' and several others." Bud smiled.

"I can, too," Hank agreed.

"Much better," Bud said on the next take. "Do you want to try a cover next, and then we'll break?"

Cedra nodded. "'Pontoon?'"

"Oh yeah," Keith said.

"You're going to love this one," Hank said.

"That's a take. One more while you're on a roll?" Bud asked.

"Heck yeah. 'Landslide.' Grab that banjo, Wayne," Juliet said.

"This just keeps getting better," Hank told Bud.

Bud's dancing in his seat demonstrated his agreement with Hank's assessment. "Damn. I love these kids."

"Me, too." Hank chuckled.

"I almost hate to break, but you probably need one. I see Keith bouncing around in the back there," he teased.

"I'm outta here," Keith said and bolted for the door.

Laughter broke out in the studio as everyone followed Keith's exit.

"I do need something to drink," Cedra said. "That was fun."

"Yeah, it was," Juliet replied. "Bathroom break?"

Juliet held the door open and kissed Cedra as she stepped inside. "I think Hank's been having fun with Bud. Neither of them has stopped smiling and laughing since we started playing."

"I think Dad's had a great visit."

Juliet smiled. "Me, too. Do you think we can get one or two others before lunch?"

"I think so. What did you think of Bud's suggestion?"

"I can't believe we haven't thought of him before now. He's got some great songs."

†

Ali Spooner

When they walked into the break room, Hank and Bud were chatting with Carrie.

"It sounds like y'all have been incredibly busy already. I do have one complaint, though."

"What's that?"

"What's a girl got to do to get booth time with you?" Carrie teased.

"You're too chatty, and you mess with my buttons. Hank has been a joy to have beside me."

"It's been fun seeing how this all works," Hank replied. "Thanks for the opportunity."

Juliet grabbed bottles of water to pass around. When everyone was settled, Bud looked at Carrie. "Hold on tight."

Bud played all the songs they had recorded, starting with the new one from Cedra. Felecia came busting into the room. "You've cut four tracks already, and it's not even noon?"

"Not a bad morning, huh?" Bud asked.

"Felecia, this is my dad, Hank," Cedra said.

"Nice to meet you," she told Hank. "I'm sorry. I didn't mean to bust in, but damn, that sounded good."

"Thanks," Juliet said. "We've been working hard."

"I can tell. Those covers sounded great." She looked at Cedra. "If my mascara is running, it's your fault. That song was just, wow."

"I'm glad you enjoyed it." Cedra smiled.

"Can you believe she wrote that in one sitting?" Stone said.

280

"Yeah, but those lyrics have been in my head for days," Cedra added.

Felecia looked at Hank. "Did she inherit this talent from you?"

"I can't claim an ounce of that. I taught Cedra a few songs on a hand-me-down guitar, and after that, she just took off," Hank admitted.

"Don't let him fool you. Dad can play and sing."

"Could when I was young, but never been able to write lyrics like you," Hank corrected her. "She had to have gotten that from her mom or her grandpa. Cedra sure didn't get that from me."

"You all sounded fantastic," Felecia said. "I can't wait for the *Bentley Break* show to start."

"Are you still thinking after the first of the year?" Carrie asked.

Felecia nodded. "I know they will have plenty of music recorded before then, but I don't want them to get lost in the holiday season. I want to bring the Bentleys out as a band to watch out for in the new year."

"Do you have any reports on how 'Six Strings' is doing?" Juliet asked.

Carrie looked at Bud. "You didn't tell them?"

"Honestly, they were so excited when they arrived, I forgot, so go ahead."

Carrie was nearly breathless. "'Six Strings,' the single was number four of the most downloaded songs on Apple Music last week. Mark and I have been toying with the next single to release to spur the sales of the album we plan to release in two weeks."

"That was the next question. If the whole album would be released or a few singles first," Cedra said.

"Mark thinks two more singles. Any suggestions?" All heads turned to Bud. "Well, Bud?" Carrie asked.

"'Backwoods Boogie,' and the 'Wedding Song,'" he replied immediately. "I had another thought this morning. Can I show you something else? I don't know if it would fit into the show, but I thought it was pretty damn awesome."

"Let's see what you're talking about." Felecia took a seat next to Hank.

"They had no idea I was recording this, and I think that's what makes it so pure." Bud played the video of Cedra and Juliet singing together.

"I need that," Felecia said. "We normally just stream the music, but this is too good to not share."

Juliet laughed. "I think we just made our first music video, Cedra."

"The first of many, I hope," Carrie said.

"Let's get back to work until lunch arrives," Bud said. "I think I heard we have BBQ coming today."

†

Keith and Stone knocked out "Written in the Sand," and then Wayne recorded "Kinfolks" before Bud announced lunch was delivered.

They listened to the recordings while they ate. Juliet turned to Stone. "Do you have your fiddle?"

"I sure do. 'Devil Went Down to Georgia,' Keith?" Stone asked.

"Hell yeah."

"Two others and we're done for the day," Bud stated.

†

After listening to the final cuts, Bud looked around the room. "Tomorrow is a short day, so why don't we work on recording more intros. We are much further along on covers than I dreamed possible. Good work, guys."

"Will Felecia be here to ask questions?" Juliet asked.

"The answer to that is yes," Felecia's voice sounded over the intercom.

"Damn, I can't get used to y'all seeing and hearing everything," Juliet said. "Not even the bathroom is safe as long as Carrie is in the building."

Everyone laughed but Hank, who looked a bit lost. Cedra smiled at him. "Carrie walked into the bathroom when Juliet and I sang along with the Indigo Girls. She insisted we record it as one of our covers."

"Good thing I did. Look at what the two of you have blossomed into." Carrie chuckled.

"Okay, out of here for the night. We'll see you tomorrow." Bud turned to Hank. "It was a pleasure to meet you and I hope to see you again."

"You will. I want front row seats when the band plays at Nissan Stadium," Hank stated.

"You will have the best seats in the house. I guarantee you," Bud promised.

†

Cedra looked at Hank as they packed up their instruments. "Do you want to ride with the boys or us?"

"I'll ride with y'all," Hank answered. "It'll be less crowded with all the pizzas these boys are going to get."

"Y'all need money?" Cedra asked.

"Nope, we've got this," Keith said.

"See ya at the house then."

†

Juliet slipped into the back seat. "What did you think of today, Dad?"

"I had the time of my life," Hank replied. "You and Cedra sound amazing together. I get teary-eyed every time I hear you sing. Bud is pretty amazing, too. I think you've hooked up with some great people."

"Thanks, Dad," Cedra said. "I think we did too. Will you consider coming back for Christmas?"

"I would love to. Ma already asked me this morning." He grinned.

"Sneaky," Cedra replied. "I think everyone will be here except for Stone. He's going home for the holidays."

284

Hank looked at Cedra. "Do you think you can tolerate me for ten days? I planned to come up before Christmas and head home after New Year's."

"Heck yeah."

"I'll talk to my friend about checking on the kittens for me, but as long as they have food, water, and a clean pan, they could care less if someone is around."

"I bet they miss you. I know Elvis and Elvira love playing with you. I can't wait to meet them," Cedra told him.

"They can be hilarious. Maybe the two of you will come for a visit?" Hank suggested.

Cedra's fingers tapped on the steering wheel. "I think we could arrange that. We seem to be ahead of schedule on the new album and the music for the *Bentley Break*. It doesn't seem like there will be live shows anytime soon."

"I saw an interview with Chris Stapleton not long ago," Juliet said. "He wrote most of his *Traveler* album while he and Morgan were driving from Arizona to Nashville. Maybe I can drive, and you can write?"

"Or I can drive, and you can write."

"I might be able to write a verse between here and Monroeville."

"I think we could write together."

Hank chimed in. "With the connection the two of you have, I think you could write well together."

"Ha! He's never seen my lyrics." Juliet laughed.

Cedra looked at Hank. "They aren't nearly as bad as she makes them sound."

"I'm sure they aren't. Just like you were unsure of your singing voice, Juliet's unsure of her writing ability. Like anything else, it takes practice and effort."

†

"How'd things go today," Ma asked when they arrived.

"You should have seen them, Ma. They were incredible," Hank praised.

"We did have a great day. We got several tracks cut and even our first music video." Juliet chuckled.

"Where did that come from? I didn't know you had a video planned."

"We didn't. Bud had other ideas, and he recorded a video of Cedra and me singing her new song together. I have to admit, it turned out pretty awesome."

"Felecia was there today, too, and she told Bud she wanted to use it for the *Bentley Break* show. We would be her first streaming video," Cedra reported.

"That sounds amazing. What's the plan for tomorrow?"

"To record more intros, since it will be a short day with Cedra, Wayne, and Stone going back to work in the morning," Juliet answered.

"I may need to borrow your pry bar in the morning to get Wayne up and moving," Cedra teased.

"I'll make sure he's up." Ma turned to Hank. "Are you planning to head home tomorrow, too?"

"Yes, I'd like to get an early start."

286

"Don't forget Lisa Marie invited you to breakfast," Cedra reminded him.

"I guess I just need breakfast for Juliet and Keith then," Ma said. "You're still planning to come for Christmas, right?"

"Yes, ma'am, I'll be here." Hank smiled.

"The boys are coming down the drive. What does everyone want to drink?" Juliet asked.

Hank smiled at Juliet. "Tea is fine."

"Me, too," Ma answered.

"I think I'll have a soda," Cedra replied.

"That does sound good. Will you get the fine china out?" Juliet asked as she started pouring drinks.

†

"This has been the most incredible day," Juliet said as they snuggled together.

"Things just keep getting better and better. I keep wondering when we will hit a speed bump."

"If, and when it happens, we will handle whatever comes."

Cedra smiled. "I love your confidence."

"You make me feel like I rule the world."

"That's so sweet. Nice line, too."

"You'd better turn that writer brain off and get some sleep. Four comes early." Juliet kissed her goodnight.

"Goodnight. I love you," she said when she nuzzled Juliet's neck.

"Love you, too." Juliet wrapped her arm around Cedra's shoulder.

CHAPTER THIRTEEN

"I'll drive this morning so you can ride with your dad," Wayne told Cedra.

"Thanks, Wayne," Hank said.

"Have you already taken your bags out?" Stone asked.

"Yes, I've got the old girl running. It takes her a while to warm up," Hank replied. He turned to Ma. "Thanks for everything, but especially for taking good care of my Baby Girl."

Ma smiled and placed four travel mugs of coffee on the table. "It's been a pleasure meeting you, but I'm not sure who takes care of who around here. Cedra was great when I was sick a few weeks ago."

"Are you ready?" Hank asked Cedra.

Cedra pulled her jacket on. "I am now. See you tonight, Ma."

"Be safe and let us know when you make it home, Hank," Ma called after them.

"Yes, ma'am," Hank answered and slung his arm around Cedra. "It's been great seeing you and meeting everyone." He pulled the passenger door open for her. "Especially Juliet. I can see why you love her so much." He closed the door behind her.

Cedra smiled at him when he climbed behind the wheel. "Thanks, Dad. Your approval means the world to us."

"I'm thrilled she makes you so happy, and that's all that matters to me." Hank backed up and followed Wayne to the café.

†

"I am so glad you came for breakfast," Lisa Marie said when Hank entered the café. "Just let Cedra know what you'd like to eat, and I'll warm up your coffee."

"Bacon, eggs over easy, and toast?" Cedra asked.

"You know me too well," Hank said. "I guess you've cooked that for me a few hundred times."

"At least." Cedra smiled.

"Crank up that iPad, Wayne, and see if we have any early orders." Lisa Marie looked at Hank. "Let me guess. Apple juice?"

Hank returned her smile. "Yes, please."

"Just a couple of food orders, but several coffee orders," Wayne replied.

"Send the food orders to Teddy, and let me know how many coffees to get ready to pour."

"Six coffee orders so far."

Lisa Marie set out six large Styrofoam cups with lids on the counter. "Let me know when they arrive, and I'll pour them fresh."

"Three are outside already," Wayne teased.

"Stone, will you make up the sugar and creamer packets?" Lisa Marie asked.

"On it, boss," Stone replied and went to work.

†

Hank finished off his breakfast and pulled out his wallet.

"No, sir, this one's on the house," Lisa Marie said. "Do you want to walk out with your dad after I refill his coffee?"

Cedra nodded and grabbed her coat. "I miss you already," she said as they walked to his truck.

"It's been a great visit. I couldn't be happier to see your dreams coming true. I am very proud of all of you, but mainly you. My little girl has gone and grown up on me," Hank teased. He pulled her into a hug. "I love you, Baby Girl."

"I love you, too, Dad. Be safe, and let me know you've made it home, please."

"I'll text you, and you can give me a call tonight if you want."

"I sure will." Cedra closed the door behind him and waved as he drove away. She wiped her tears away and walked back inside.

"Are you okay?" Lisa Marie asked when she hung her coat on the back of a chair.

"Yes. I just hate to see Dad go."

"He'll be back," Lisa Marie said with a smile.

†

The business was hectic until just after noon, so Cedra didn't dwell on missing her dad. Juliet had sent her a text to say she loved her, but nothing from her dad yet. She thought he should be arriving home at any time, but it was too early to worry. Cedra would call Hank if she didn't hear from him before they got to the studio. She was finishing her salad when the phone pinged.

Made it home safely. Love you.

Cedra smiled. *Love you too. Glad you made it home. Miss you.*

I'll see you soon.

Juliet waited for her just inside the lobby of the studio. She smiled brightly when Cedra, Wayne, and Stone walked in. "I've missed you today. Having you with me all day has gotten me spoiled," she said and kissed Cedra softly.

"How sweet," Wayne teased. "I never thought I'd see the day Juliet Tucker went all mushy, but I do believe it has arrived."

"I do believe you may be right," Stone replied.

"Come on you goofballs. Let's get to work," Juliet said.

†

At six, Bud called for a wrap to end the day. "You all have had a wonderful week. Do you need a day off?"

"That probably wouldn't hurt to give us a night to work on more covers and a new song or two," Juliet answered.

"Keep your radios on tomorrow," Carrie prompted. "The 'Wedding Song' drops tomorrow."

"Yes," Juliet cried out with a fist bump.

"We'll see you Tuesday afternoon then," Bud replied. "Have some fun, and we'll get back to work."

"Thanks, Bud," Cedra said.

"I'm going to ride with the boys," Keith told Juliet.

Cedra and Juliet walked to her car. "That was a good session," Juliet remarked.

"Yes, it was."

"Are you in a hurry to get home?"

"Not really. Can we go to the bluffs?"

"Perfect." Juliet smiled as they left the studio lot.

†

Carrie's phone chimed with an email. She opened it to find a message with an attached invoice from David Bartle.

Your problem has safely landed in LA and shouldn't be returning anytime soon. We have installed a GPS tracker on her vehicle which will alert us if she comes within fifty miles

293

of Nashville as long as it remains active. Marco says thank you for a couple of glorious nights at the Peabody. He loves watching the ducks march off to bed. Let me know if further assistance is needed. David

Carrie typed a quick response of thanks and then closed up her office and headed home for a stiff drink and relaxation. She had been on pins and needles since Linea left town. "Finally." She breathed a sigh of relief. "No more stupid decisions."

†

Juliet and Cedra took a detour on the way home and went to the bluff overlooking Nashville. The skyline blazed with lights as a sky full of stars twinkled.

"It was great to meet your dad," Juliet said as she parked the car.

"The time passed all too quickly. I miss Dad already, and he barely made it home."

"He will be back for Christmas," Juliet teased. "He and Ma got along well, too."

"Yeah, they did." Cedra smiled. "Is it too cold to step out for a few minutes?"

"Not with our warm new coats."

"I need some fresh air."

They stepped out of the car, walked to the front, and leaned against the hood. Cedra breathed in deeply and let out a puff of steam. "This is much better. Thank you."

"My pleasure. You know I'll never turn down an offer to come here with you. I see this as our spot."

"I do too. That's one of the reasons I wanted to come here tonight. I want to talk to you about something."

Juliet had draped an arm over Cedra's shoulders. "Nothing bad, I hope."

"No. Not at all. At least I don't think so," Cedra teased.

"Spill it then. You've got me worried."

"I have been thinking about something for days now. I wanted your opinion on this idea."

"That sounds painless. My opinions are always free. What is it?"

"I want you to write the title track of our next album."

"You want what?" Juliet exclaimed.

Cedra smiled. "I want you to write the title track. I know you can do it. I've already come up with the name."

"Forget what I said about it sounding painless. I'm not a writer."

"You can be if you apply yourself. Do I need to remind you that you have two great songwriters to help you?"

"Writing comes as natural to you as breathing. It feels like I'm pulling my own teeth to write one line of decent lyrics," Juliet admitted.

"That's more the reason why you need to write this. To learn to believe you can," Cedra told her. "I will help, but I want it to be your song."

Juliet let out a deep breath. "What name did you have in mind?"

Cedra lifted her hand and pointed toward Nashville. "'Midnight in Nashville.' You, more than any of us, has experienced the feel of performing in a smoke-filled bar on Broadway."

Juliet nodded her head. "That's true, but that doesn't make a writer out of me."

"I believe I can. I didn't think I would ever feel comfortable singing, but you have taught me to believe and trust in my voice. I want you to trust in your ability to write."

"You must be a glutton for punishment," Juliet teased.

Cedra nodded. "Stubborn and perseverant for sure."

"You really think I can do this?"

"Nope. I know you can. You have the passion inside you, and that is what you need to put to music."

"Damn. That's not fair. Almost everything that comes out of your mouth is poetic," Juliet groaned. "All I can do is try."

"That's all I'm asking. Stone, and I have been talking, and he will start working with the guys. We want the next album to be from all of us."

"I'm perfectly content singing your songs."

"You do an excellent job of it, too, but I want you to experience singing one of your own. Is that asking too much?"

"You're going to help me, right?"

"I'll be right beside you, baby. Every step of the way."

Juliet turned to face her and pulled her in for a deep kiss. "You have yourself a deal."

"Yes," Cedra shouted and fist-pumped the air. "Think about the nights you have spent gigging or filling pickle jars in one of the honky-tonks. How did it feel to have the bright lights beating down on you? What were the environment and crowd like? Could you hear the buzz of the neon lights as you warmed up backstage?"

"Okay."

"Then how did it feel when you stored your guitar and stepped outside in the cool midnight air to take the road home? What did you think with the bills tucked in your pocket? Did the stars come out to greet you as you took the fresh night air into your lungs?"

Juliet pulled her close once more. "You've practically got the song written in your head. You don't need me to write it for you."

"Not for me. For us," Cedra corrected. "We haven't experienced it yet, but one day we will. Of that, I'm sure." She pointed out the stadium. "One day, we will fill Nissan Stadium with screaming fans, eager to hear us perform. That's our dream. Never forget."

"I don't think you'd let me."

"Damn straight, I won't. Are you ready to go home? I remember Keith saying something about Ma making cookies tonight after hamburgers for dinner."

"Oh, shit. We'd better hurry then if we hope there will be any left." Juliet nodded toward the car. "Let's roll."

†

"Can we work on the song tonight?" Juliet asked. "If I can get a plan started, maybe I can fill in some blanks tomorrow while you're at work."

"We can head upstairs after dinner if you'd like."

"Yeah, that would be good. Do you have something you're working on as well?"

"There's always something bouncing around in my head." Cedra laughed. "I'll call Dad, and we can get to work."

Juliet turned off her motor. "That sounds good to me. I don't know about you, but I'm hungry."

"Me, too. I'm so ready to sink my teeth into a burger," Cedra replied as she climbed out of the car.

†

"Finally," Keith called out from the dinner table. "We were about to send out a search party."

"Sorry, guys, we had to make a side trip. You didn't have to wait for us," Cedra replied.

"You know Ma won't let us start without y'all," Wayne stated.

"That's right. I've got to make sure there is food left to feed everyone," Ma teased as she placed a platter of bacon on the table.

"This looks and smells delicious, Ma," Juliet said as she hung their coats in the hall.

"Have a seat before Keith explodes. I've had to move the French fries out of his reach twice already," Ma teased.

"Dig in, boys." Juliet took her seat.

†

"That was a great meal, Ma," Cedra praised. "After we help you clean up, Juliet and I are going to do some writing."

Ma's eyebrow shot up. "I've got this. You two go get started. I'm making cookies later if y'all want to come down for some."

"I'll probably need a break by then," Juliet replied.

Ma nodded. "I'll send one of the guys up when they are ready."

†

"Do you want to use the laptop or your songbook?" Cedra asked.

"What are you using?"

Cedra smiled at Juliet. "My songbook for now, so use the laptop. It's already set up on my desk and ready to go." Cedra picked up her songbook and placed some pillows behind her as she leaned against the wall to write and watch Juliet.

Juliet typed in the song title. "That was easy enough." She laughed. "Now what?"

"Make some notes on four to five verses and come up with a chorus. They don't have to be lyrics yet, just notes that will hopefully lead you to lyrics."

"Notes. Got it."

299

†

Juliet started making notes, and Cedra smiled at the intense look on her face as she typed on the laptop. Juliet seemed excited and terrified to be writing a song, but Cedra would do all she could to make it the best possible.

†

Juliet started typing keywords on the screen: *Music City walk of fame, buzzing neon, smokey honky-tonks, pickle jars, bright lights, cold beer, and fresh air.* Then she added the emotional words: *cold sweat, shaking hands, inspiration, heart racing, blinding lights, ringing ears, pride, fear, and love.* She felt her head begin to bob as the music started coming to her.

†

Cedra sensed movement and looked up to see Juliet's body moving to the music running through her. She thought that was a great sign as she watched Juliet tapping the keys. Cedra scribbled the lyrics that had been traveling through her head all day. The group had already recorded three new tracks for the second album. If Juliet, Wayne, and Keith could add one each, they would be halfway through the tracks. She and Stone could easily pull out six more with what they had written, and new songs they had been developing.

†

Keith knocked on the door and stepped inside. "The cookies are ready," he told them.

"Perfect time for a break," Cedra replied and looked at Juliet. "You good to break?"

"Go ahead. I'll be right behind you. Pour me some milk, please." Juliet smiled.

"I will." Cedra kissed the top of her head when she climbed from the bed. "I'll do my best to save you some cookies."

Juliet looked up briefly. "I won't take long."

Cedra followed Keith downstairs.

"Juliet looked pretty intense," he said when he took his seat.

"I think she's beginning to feel her song. How are the two of y'all coming with yours?" Cedra walked to the refrigerator for milk.

"I wish I could say I was feeling it," Wayne groaned.

"They aren't doing too bad," Stone replied. "I think we'll take over the living room and try to write tonight, too."

Cedra sat the glasses of milk on the table. "That would leave six for you and me. I think we can pull some from the songs we've already written and maybe add one to two brand new ones." She looked at Keith. "You need a refill?"

"Yes, please," Keith answered.

"Me, too," Wayne responded and offered Cedra his glass.

"Stone?" Cedra asked.

"Naw, I'm good."

†

Cedra looked up when she heard Juliet's steps on the stairs. There was a glimmer of excitement in Juliet's eyes as she walked into the dining room. *Yeah, she's feeling it,* Cedra thought and passed Juliet the plate of cookies. "These are great as usual, Ma."

"Thanks. The boys said y'all were taking a break from the studio tomorrow. Any idea of what you'd like to eat?"

"Baked chicken, yellow rice, and broccoli."

Ma smiled. "That didn't take long. Anything else?"

"How about some baked sweet potatoes?" Wayne asked.

"And brownies," Keith added.

"Stone, is there anything you would like to add?" Ma asked.

"No, Ma. That sounds good to me."

Cedra noticed that Stone seemed disconnected today, and she hoped everything was good at home. Hopefully, it was just her imagination.

†

Juliet went straight back to the laptop when they returned upstairs. Cedra changed into a sleep shirt and

302

climbed back on the bed. "Does something seem off with Stone to you?"

Juliet turned to face her. "I was wondering the same thing. Do you think he's just homesick?"

"That could be it. It won't be long before he goes home for Christmas."

"That's true. Hopefully, Stone will come back."

Cedra's head shot up. "Do you think he won't?"

Juliet shrugged her shoulders. "I've got no clue. If he doesn't, we'll still move forward and give him writing credits."

"You don't think it will negatively impact the group?"

"You'll have to do the bulk of the writing, but you do that already," Juliet said. "Maybe the rest of us can do more writing to help out." Juliet shrugged. "We started out originally to be a band of four. I think we will continue to be successful with or without Stone." She turned to face Cedra. "I hope that didn't sound horrible. I've enjoyed him playing with us and writing songs, but they don't hold a candle to yours. I can see that on Bud's face."

"It's got to be hard being away from your wife and daughter. Then add this damn virus which only makes the worry worse."

Juliet turned back to the laptop. "Well, it doesn't look like we'll be going on the road anytime soon, so maybe a break at home is what he needs. He can still write, and if we choose to record his songs, we will. When the time comes to hit the road, and he's not back, we will need to make some decisions."

"A bridge we will cross when we need to." Cedra picked up her songbook and started reviewing her notes.

†

Cedra heard the clock downstairs chime eleven. "Damn, the time sure flies these days."

Juliet looked at the clock. "I had no clue it was that late. I'll wrap up here in just a few minutes."

Cedra placed her songbook on the desk. "No rush. I'm not going anywhere."

Juliet smiled at her, the excitement in her eyes from earlier. "I love you," she said and leaned down to kiss Cedra. "Did you set the alarm?"

"I did. Love you too." She snuggled under the covers.

†

Five minutes later, Juliet looked over to find Cedra fast asleep. Cedra looked like an angel as she slept and it took great effort to tear her eyes away. She was making good progress and decided to keep writing as long as the words still flowed. Juliet stopped typing and read the song that was growing on the screen. She felt the ache of the smile on her face, and when the clock chimed midnight, Juliet shut everything down and slipped in beside Cedra.

"You're cold," Cedra groaned. "Come here." She opened her arms to Juliet. "That's better already. Goodnight, babe."

"Goodnight, Baby Girl," Juliet replied and settled in. Her mind was still racing with excitement as she dreamed about the song she was creating.

CHAPTER FOURTEEN

"Someone was up late," Keith teased when Juliet came downstairs for coffee and breakfast.

"The words were flowing, so I didn't want to stop," Juliet answered. She looked out the window to see who drove and was delighted to see Cedra's truck still parked.

"What are you looking for?" Ma asked.

"I wanted to see who drove this morning," Juliet replied.

"Wayne was the first down, so he got his truck warmed up," Ma said. "Do you have plans for something?"

Juliet took a sip of coffee and nodded. "I thought I'd show Cedra the Music City Walk of Fame for some inspiration today. I don't think she's seen it yet."

"That sounds like a great idea. How is your song coming along?" Ma asked.

"Better than I thought it would," Juliet admitted. "How's your song coming?" she asked Keith.

"Slower than yours apparently." Keith smiled. "I've barely finished the first verse."

"I want to try to finish my rough draft today before I head into town," Juliet said.

"Show off," Keith teased. "Is Cedra helping you?"

"Nope, she's working on a song of her own," Juliet said and puffed out her chest. "She did give me some thoughts to ponder, and they've been a help, but the lyrics are all my creation."

Ma smiled at Juliet's excitement. "I made Keith some French toast. What do you want for breakfast?"

"Could I get a couple fried egg sandwiches?"

"Easy, peasy," Ma said.

"Since I'm going to town, is there anything you need?"

"Nope, I'm sending Keith to the store with a list," Ma answered.

"You'd better add milk and cookie dough to the list. You know Keith will come back with some," Juliet teased.

"Top of the list." Ma chuckled. Ma placed the first sandwich on the plate. "Start on that one while I cook the next."

"Thanks, Ma," Juliet replied and took a bite. "Damn, this is good."

"You're making me want one," Keith responded.

"Bring me your plate," Ma requested. "It's dangerous sending you to the store hungry."

Keith chuckled. "You got that right, Ma."

†

"I'll be upstairs if you need anything," Juliet told Ma.
"Good luck with your song." Ma smiled.
"Thanks." Juliet showered, dressed, and sent Cedra a text. *I'm picking you up after work.*
Everything okay?
Yes, something I want to show you. See you at three.
Okay. Love you.
Love you, too.

Juliet turned on the laptop and opened her song. She read through it two more times and tweaked a couple of words before sending it to the printer. Juliet folded the paper and stuck it in her pocket, then pulled out her guitar and started playing some music while reading through the lyrics on the screen.

†

At two, Juliet walked downstairs to find Ma in the kitchen. Keith hadn't made it back from the store yet. "Do you want something to eat before you head out?" Ma asked.

"No, I'm good, Ma. I'm saving room for tonight," Juliet answered as she pulled on her coat. "Do I need to hunt down Keith?"

"Naw, he'll show up directly." Ma chuckled.

"We'll see you in a bit then. We won't be long," Juliet promised.

"Be safe," Ma called after her.

Juliet climbed into her car just as her phone pinged.

Getting off as soon as you get here.

On my way, babe. I'll text you when I get there.

Be safe.

†

Juliet pulled into the parking lot and texted Cedra before pulling up to the side door. Seconds later, the door opened, and Cedra came strolling through.

"Hey, babe." Cedra leaned over to kiss Juliet as she put her belt on. "So, where are we headed?"

"To someplace I don't think you've seen yet. It's not far."

"Sounds good. Brr, it's cold." Cedra lifted her hands to the heater vent.

"Did you bring your gloves? Where we're going is outside."

"Yeah, I did."

Juliet smiled. "Put them on, then we're almost there."

Cedra pulled the gloves out of her pocket. "You weren't kidding about it being close. Have I been missing a gem all this time?"

"I think so." Juliet grinned. She turned on her signal and lucked into a parking place. "Holy cow." Juliet turned up the radio.

Turn on your radio, Wayne texted.

We hear it. Sounds great. Cedra replied.

"Wow, that sounded great. It's still hard to believe that's our music on the radio, sometimes," Juliet said.

Cedra reached over and pinched her. "It's real." She laughed.

They stepped out of the car, and Juliet reached for Cedra's hand.

Cedra looked up and saw a sign. "Nashville Music Garden," she read. "Oh my God, are you taking me to the Music City Walk of Fame?"

"Yes, have you seen it yet?"

Cedra shook her head. "On my to-do list, but I haven't made it. Until now." She looped her hand through Juliet's arm as they strolled through the park and read the stars engraved on the sidewalk. "Garth and Trisha. Tim and Faith," Cedra read. "It's great to see couples together."

"I guess they can't divorce if they are engraved in stone," Juliet teased. "There are so many great musicians and writers here. I love that it's not just country music, too."

"There are so many singers and groups that have made it big in Nashville that aren't country. Jimi Hendrix? Wow. Christian, pop, bluegrass, all rolled into one. We are truly among music royalty."

"That's what makes this place unique. We will be here one day. Maybe next to Lady A, Rascal Flatts or Keith Urban."

"That's a dream well worth chasing. Thank you for sharing this with me. I didn't realize it was so close."

Juliet pointed to a bench. "Do you mind sitting for a minute? I have something I want to share with you."

"Sure."

Juliet reached into her back pocket, pulled the paper out, and handed it to Cedra. "A rough draft of 'Midnight in Nashville.'"

"You finished it already?"

Juliet nodded. "The rough draft, yes. You may think it's total crap, and I need to start all over."

Cedra saw the anticipation in Juliet's face as she slowly opened the paper and began to read. She felt the smile grow on her face. Cedra looked up at Juliet. "I knew you could do this. Do you have music in mind?"

"I think so, but I'm not sold on it yet. So, its okay?"

Cedra looked up at her with tears in her eyes. "It's much more than okay. I can't wait to hear you sing it."

"You're not just saying that because you love me?"

"I do love you, but I wouldn't let you slide that easy. If it wasn't good, I'd tell you that. As gently as I could, of course, but, damn baby, I knew you could write like this. Fast, too, that's impressive."

"I have to admit, I channeled some energy from this place while I was writing. There's so much talent engraved in these stones."

"It doesn't matter where the inspiration comes from as long as it continues to flow." Cedra smiled up at her lover. "Are you ready to write more?"

The smile Juliet wore made Cedra's heart swell with pride. "Yes, I am. I've got this."

"Come then, let's go share this with the boys." Cedra jumped to her feet. "They are going to be surprised at how quickly you wrote this."

"No more so than me. You were right, though. When you catch the flow, it's hard to stop." She took Cedra's hand, and they rushed back to the car.

"I am so proud of you. I can't wait to hear you do this in the studio."

"Will you sing it with me?"

"I'd love to. You first, and then we can experiment a bit."

"Deal." Juliet put the car in gear.

†

"Ma, I can't wait for you to hear this," Cedra blurted out when they came through the front door.

"Are the rest of us chopped liver?" Wayne teased.

Cedra turned to see Wayne, Keith, and Stone already in the living room. "Sorry, guys. I didn't see you in there." Cedra pulled off her coat. "Go get your guitar," she told Juliet and shooed her upstairs.

"Oh my, this sounds exciting." Ma wiped her hands on her apron.

"Juliet finished her song," Cedra announced. "All by herself. I can't wait to hear her sing it."

"That's fantastic news," Ma replied as she walked to the living room and took a seat. "I heard the new song no less than three times today. Have ya'll heard it yet?"

"Yes, we heard it this afternoon," Cedra said. "It was awesome."

Ma nodded. "Yes, it was. Did you enjoy the Walk of Fame?"

"Yes, that was fantastic, too." Cedra asked, "What are you guys working on?"

"We thought we'd do Garth's 'Low Places,'" Wayne said. "I think we've got it sounding pretty decent."

"Let's hear it," Cedra replied as Juliet returned.

"No, I think we need to hear Juliet's first, so you can calm down a bit," Wayne teased.

"I'm sorry, guys. I'm just so excited. I challenged her to write the title track of our next album, and she's done a great job. All I gave her was the title, and she's written it by herself."

Juliet picked up her guitar. "Let me correct that. You gave me some thought prompts, and they really helped."

"Okay, I'll own that, but the lyrics are all yours," Cedra stated.

"What's the title?" Keith asked.

"'Midnight in Nashville.' She is making us stick to this wild notion that each of us writes at least one song for this album. I hope you will like what I've written, so I can say my part is done." Juliet chuckled.

"Oh, honey, you're just beginning," Cedra teased.

Juliet looked at the guys. "This is just a rough draft, so all feedback is welcome. I'm not sold on the music either, but this is what I've got started."

Ma's foot tapped along to the music as Juliet played, and the boys smiled as they listened carefully to the lyrics. Juliet finished the song and waited.

"I'm so freaking jealous," Keith told Juliet. "You make me want to tear my one verse up and start over."

"Trust me, I started over several times on this one," Juliet said.

"That's really good," Stone praised.

Wayne nodded. "Love the lyrics, and I think there's a lot we can do with the music."

"That's where I really need your help," Juliet told Wayne. "You and Keith both have better ears for the music than I do."

"Can we hear it again?" Stone asked.

"Sure," Juliet repeated the song.

Wayne gasped. "It needs Cedra's keyboard and maybe a bit of bass guitar from Keith. Especially the honky-tonk sections."

"We can play with it when we get back to the studio tomorrow," Keith suggested. "I like it."

"I do, too," Ma agreed. "Great job, Juliet."

"What do you think of Cedra singing it with me, and we all sing the chorus?" Juliet asked.

"We can do it several different ways and let Bud decide," Wayne said.

"Okay, let's hear 'Low Places,'" Cedra replied.

"Y'all got that one down pat. I didn't know you could go that low, Wayne," Juliet teased.

"I surprise myself sometimes." Wayne laughed. "What other covers do we want to do?"

"I've got an idea if Keith will sing the song," Cedra stated. "I'd like to work Juliet's harmonica into our music, and I think the perfect song for that is 'Ol Red.' What do you think, Keith?"

"Hell yes, I can do some Blake." Keith grinned.

"Hey, her harmonica may be good for 'Midnight,' too," Wayne said. "Maybe a bit of harmonica for a lead-in and to end the song. I can use the drum pad in the studio for 'Ol Red,' as well."

"I have one more request," Cedra told them. "I need some bass, a slide, and some drums for 'Fire Away.' I want to cover that with Juliet."

Juliet looked at Stone. "I know you've been itching to play a slide."

"Yeah, I have. I was thinking of doing 'Traveler,'" Stone replied.

"That would have been our second choice," Juliet admitted.

The timer on the stove rang out. "Y'all have about twenty minutes before dinner is ready." Ma returned to the kitchen wearing a huge smile. Damn, she loved these kids.

†

"Can you download the music for the new covers?" Wayne asked Juliet.

Juliet nodded. "I'll print out copies for everyone in the morning."

"If we can cut all four tomorrow, it would be a fantastic day," Cedra replied. "We'd only need songs from Keith and Wayne. Then Stone and I can pick out five more for the rest of the album. I'm working on something new, too. How about you?" she asked Stone.

"I've got one bouncing around up here." Stone tapped his temple. "The rest we can pull out of our backlist."

Keith bumped shoulders with Juliet. "Can I get your help with my song, miss songwriter?"

"Why, sir, I'd be delighted," Juliet responded with a laugh. "Do you have a title in mind?"

"'Redneck Paradise,'" Keith replied. "A pure honky-tonk song."

"That sounds like fun. Count me in. I'll channel my inner redneck tonight," Juliet teased.

"Hey, can I get some love here? I need help, too," Wayne exclaimed. "I don't have a title yet, but I've got some ideas."

316

"Why don't the three of us sit down at work tomorrow when it's slow and start putting your ideas to work?" Stone suggested.

Wayne beamed. "I'd like that."

"Sounds like a plan," Cedra agreed.

†

Juliet stood to walk into the kitchen, and she noticed movement outside. "Y'all aren't going to believe this. It's snowing?"

"What?" Keith nearly tripped over a guitar case rushing through the living room to the front door.

Cedra joined them at the door while Stone and Wayne looked out the front windows.

Keith grabbed his coat and rushed outside.

Cedra handed Juliet her coat with a laugh. "I swear he's going on twelve sometimes."

"Let the boy have his excitement," Ma called out. "Don't stay out long."

"We won't," Cedra said and followed Juliet outside.

Stone and Wayne followed her outside. "Look at the size of those flakes." Stone was in awe as they watched large flakes spiraling down.

"I bet you don't see these in Florida," Wayne teased.

"Our snow consists of tiny little flakes that rarely last minutes once they reach the ground." Stone then laughed at Keith, trying to catch one in his mouth.

"It's beautiful," Cedra remarked as a flake landed in Juliet's hair. "I wonder if it will stick?"

"It's cold enough," Wayne responded. "It's good we got that wood stacked and covered."

"Yeah, it is," Stone agreed. "I think I'll go lay some wood in the fireplace and fill the rack. Just in case."

"Hang on, bro, I'll help you," Wayne replied.

"It's sticking on the vehicles, so maybe we will get some accumulation," Juliet stated. "Too bad you have to work tomorrow. It would be a beautiful day to go to the Bluffs."

"I know it's not the same, but we could go after dinner," Cedra replied. "It's not far."

Juliet smiled. "Let's see if it's still snowing and decide then. I bet we will have a few snow days this year."

†

Keith ate more quickly than usual and even skipped dessert to rush outside. He was disappointed to find that the snow had nearly stopped and there was no accumulation. After walking back inside, he plopped down in his chair. "I reckon I'll have dessert after all. It looks like the snow has passed through."

"I'm sure that won't be the last we see of it this year," Ma told him. "These old bones tell me there is plenty more coming."

Keith grinned up at Ma. "You're not old."

†

318

Juliet looked at the guys. "Will you help me with music tonight?"

"Sure, go get your harmonica," Wayne suggested.

Juliet raced up the stairs. "Thanks, guys," Cedra said.

"I think your keyboards, some drums, and guitar will suit that song," Wayne told her. "I really do like the thought of starting it off and ending it with a harmonica, though."

"You may think me nuts, but when I read these lyrics, I see her dressed in black, a guitar on her back walking down the middle of Lower Broadway at midnight." Cedra looked up when Juliet finished coming down the stairs.

"Do you really?" Juliet asked.

Ma smiled. "It's quite a visual."

"It would make a great video," Keith replied. "Some flashes of being on stage at a honky-tonk, recording in the studio, maybe falling snow or a bolt of lightning at the end."

"That's quite a stretch." Stone grinned.

"Actually, it's not in today's digital age. Just about anything can be dubbed," Keith told them.

"A visit to Johnny Cash's star to leave a rose and then walk away into the dark playing the harmonica," Juliet suggested.

Ma sat down next to Cedra. "You all are simply amazing. You take an idea and run with it so well."

"If they like the song, I think we should pitch the video idea," Cedra stated. "With the bars closing early, what better time than to try to film Lower Broadway at midnight or later?"

"That is a good point," Juliet agreed. "What a great way to introduce the new album too." She smiled. "First things, first. The music."

Cedra looked at Juliet. "We think you should start it off with your harmonica and maybe end it repeating the same tune."

Wayne nodded. "Something filled with melancholy or loneliness. The harmonica is the perfect instrument for that."

"Something like this?" Juliet closed her eyes and lifted the harmonica to her mouth. She played for about thirty seconds before opening her eyes.

"Just like that." Wayne smiled. "At the end of it, we can join in with keyboards and strings as you begin to sing. Cedra will sing with you, right? We can all join in for the chorus."

"That sounds as good a place to start as any. Maybe some drums, too?" Juliet asked Wayne.

"Yeah, that works. Let's run through it with the harmonica, strings, and lyrics tonight," Wayne suggested.

"Let me run back upstairs and print a few more copies then," Juliet replied and made a beeline for the stairs.

"I think we should knock out the four covers tomorrow and then spend some time on 'Midnight' since we have access to the instruments," Cedra suggested.

Stone nodded. "I agree. Bud can help us fine-tune it too."

"I think you should pitch the video proposal to Carrie, too," Keith encouraged them. "I really like your ideas."

"I agree with Keith." Ma nodded. "I haven't seen many music videos, but that sounds like it would be really cool." Ma took a sip of coffee as Juliet returned and passed out copies.

"Why don't you play through the harmonica and then pick up your guitar and play through how you imagine it sounding. It should be easy enough for us to pick up on it, and when you think we have it, you can start with lyrics. We'll add the chorus," Wayne suggested.

Juliet nodded, brought the instrument to her mouth, and began to play. She shortened it a bit and then began strumming her guitar. Keith and Cedra were the first to join in playing, followed by Wayne and Stone. Juliet looked at Cedra, and they started singing.

Ma tapped her foot to the beat of the music and watched them perform. She smiled at them. "For the first time, that sounded pretty good," Ma admitted. "Can you let the harmonica fade out?"

"I sure can, Ma," Juliet replied. "You up for a couple more runs at it before we call it a night?"

"Heck yeah," Keith exclaimed.

After two more attempts, Ma nodded her head. "That last one is good. I can't wait to hear it with full instruments."

"Come with us," Juliet said.

"You know I could be a bit sneaky." Ma grinned. "I'm sure Carrie will be there watching, and maybe I could ever so gently drop the story of the video image you guys imagine as you perform."

Cedra burst out laughing. "Ma, you are so devious, but I love it. Plant the seed, and maybe Carrie will bite and propose it herself."

"I'd bet you all Happy Meals at McDonald's, she would," Ma teased.

"Happy Meals, Ma? I'd have to have at least two Big Macs," Keith declared.

"I better change that to White Castle then. Maybe I could afford to feed you there." Ma grinned.

"I haven't been there in ages," Wayne replied.

"She pitches a video, and we'll buy you all the tiny burgers you can eat," Juliet told Ma.

Cedra looked at Juliet. "I think we've got the four covers down, so we could spend an hour or two if needed on 'Midnight' and get some advice from Bud."

"Honestly, I don't think it will even take that long. We know where we want to go with the music and the lyrics are good. We just need the equipment," Stone stated. "I bet three runs."

"I think we'll have it in two," Keith challenged him.

Cedra grinned. "I'll take four just to be the rebel."

"Thanks for all your help tonight, guys. I'm excited I've written a whole song and one that will be the title of our next album."

Stone placed a hand on Juliet's shoulder. "You have done well."

He looked at Keith and Stone. "Now we get these other two motivated," he teased.

"It'll come," Cedra promised.

"I think I'm calling it a night," Ma replied.

"We're right behind ya, Ma." Cedra looked at Juliet. "Do you think you can sleep, or do you need to wind down some?"

Juliet raised her harmonica. "I think I'll play around a bit first. I'm not one hundred percent on the sound yet."

"I'll keep you company and maybe work on my song a bit," Keith said.

"Go get it," Juliet told him.

"Love you." Cedra kissed Juliet and made her way upstairs.

†

Cedra was sound asleep when Juliet crept into the bedroom and snuggled into her. Cedra turned toward her but didn't wake. Juliet's smile filled her face as she dreamed of walking down the middle of Lower Broadway at midnight.

†

"We'll see you this afternoon, Ma," Cedra told her as they grabbed their coffees and headed out.

"Be safe," Ma called after them.

"I'm glad you're driving today, Wayne," Stone replied. "It looks kind of slippery out there."

Wayne nodded. "We'll take it slow. We left in plenty of time."

Stone turned to Cedra in the back seat. "Did Juliet sleep at all last night?"

"She was sounds asleep when I left. I have no idea when she came to bed," Cedra replied.

"I heard them come up a little before midnight," Wayne reported. "Keith can't be quiet to save his soul."

†

When they pulled up at the café, Cedra smiled. "I hope today goes by quick. I can't wait to get into the studio today."

"Me, too," Stone agreed.

"The sooner we get started," Wayne said as he pulled the door open, "the sooner we can go have some fun."

†

"Are you ready yet, Keith?" Juliet called up the stairs.

"Almost. Two more minutes," Keith called back.

Juliet smiled at Ma. "I'm going to get the car warming up. It's still cold out, so wrap up."

"I will." Ma began wrapping a scarf around her neck.

†

Wayne pulled in behind them when they reached the studio. "That was great timing," Ma remarked.

"Yes, it was," Juliet agreed. "Keith, grab your cases, and I'll get mine."

"Hey, guys," Ma said as Cedra, Stone, and Wayne emerged from the truck.

"Hey, Ma. Are you ready to put your devious plan to the test?" Cedra teased.

Ma chuckled. "I've been practicing all morning. Tiny burgers, here I come."

Cedra tossed an arm around Ma's shoulders. "You will have all you can eat, either way."

†

"Hey guys," Bud said as they entered the studio. "Everyone doing well today? Hey, Ma. Did you come to watch today?"

"Yes, is it okay if I hang out in the break room?" Ma asked.

"Sure is. I think Carrie and maybe Felecia will be in soon."

†

Ma walked through the studio and entered the break room. Bud had turned the monitor on for her to see and hear the band as they set up. She was amazed at how relaxed they had all become from the first time she had seen them perform. She smiled as Juliet looked at Keith.

"'Ol Red?'"

Keith nodded back to her as they began playing.

Cedra played guitar and watched Bud's face light up when Juliet played her harmonica.

"You all never stop amazing me. I had no idea you played the harmonica," Bud said to Juliet.

"Just wait until you hear our last song today." Juliet beamed back at him.

Bud nodded. "Let's do one more run at that one."

†

When Bud was satisfied with the second run, Juliet looked at Cedra. "Ready?"

"I'm always ready to sing with you," Cedra answered.

They performed "Fire Away" flawlessly.

Bud grinned at them from the booth. "Damn, that was good."

†

The door to the break room opened, and Carrie walked inside with another woman. "Hey, Ma," Carrie said. "Felecia, this is the one and only Ma Bentley," Carrie introduced them.

"Nice to meet you."

"Likewise. Those kids love you and talk about you all the time," Felecia said.

Ma felt her cheeks get warm as she blushed. She pointed to the monitor. "They are cooking already. They've already got two tracks done."

"What? So fast?" Carrie said. "What have they done?"

"Keith did 'Ol Red' and the gals did 'Fire Away,'" Ma replied. "They want to knock the four covers out to work on something new," Ma told them. *Might as well start now.* "Juliet has written the title track for the next album, but they need some of the instruments here to develop the music."

"Did you just say Juliet wrote a song?" Carrie asked.

"Yes. Stone and Cedra have challenged the others to write one song for the next album," Ma explained.

Felecia smiled. "I love the sound of another album so soon. What are they naming it?"

"*Midnight in Nashville,*" Ma answered. "Juliet wrote the title song in less than two days."

"That's impressive," Carrie said.

"Cedra told the band when she first read the lyrics, she could visualize Juliet dressed in black, with a guitar slung over her shoulder walking down Lower Broadway at midnight. The images spun off from there. There are flashes of playing on a honky-tonk stage, here in the studio, and placing a rose on Johnny Cash's star at the Walk of Fame. It was exciting just listening to them. Keith suggested it would make the perfect video. I can't wait until you hear the song.

They needed the keyboards and drum pad to finalize the music, but they hope Bud will coach them on the music."

Stone was finishing the first run of 'Traveler,' but neither Felecia nor Carrie heard a note. Ma smiled as she could visualize the gears churning in their heads. *Seed planted.*

†

"Let's do another run of that before we move on, and we can take a quick break," Bud told them.

Juliet nodded to Bud. "You heard the man."

"I think there are donuts in the break room, Keith," Bud teased.

"Now we're talking." Keith chuckled. "I'll be there in a minute."

†

Carrie, Felecia, and Ma were chatting when the group entered.

"Y'all have been busy this afternoon," Carrie said as Cedra grabbed water for her and Juliet.

"Thirsty, Ma?" Juliet asked. "I can pour you a cup of coffee."

"That would be great."

"They've got three covers cut and one more before they have something new to show us," Bud told Carrie with a smile.

Juliet looked at Bud. "We need some of the instruments in the studio we don't have at home, and we need your keen ear to help us get the sound right."

Cedra smiled at Juliet. "Juliet wrote the title track for the next album."

Bud's eyebrow shot up, and he grinned at Juliet. "You are just full of surprises today. First, the harmonica, and now you've written a song?"

"In less than two days," Stone said.

"What's it called? You said title track?" Bud asked.

"'Midnight in Nashville,'" Juliet replied. "Cedra came up with the title, and I wrote the lyrics."

"That's impressive as hell," Bud said. "I can't wait. One more cover and we can work on it?"

"Yes, please," Juliet replied.

"Ma, can I share with Bud what you told us?" Felecia asked.

"There's more?" Bud asked. "Hit me."

"When they were discussing the lyrics, Cedra told them she could visualize Juliet dressed in black walking down Lower Broadway at midnight. With flashes of singing on stage at a honky-tonk, here in the studio, and placing a rose on Cash's star at the Walk of Fame."

"Not my forte at all, but it sounds like a good foundation for a music video idea," Bud said.

"With the bars closing early these days, it would be the perfect time to record downtown at night," Felecia said. She looked at Carrie. "You think Mark would go for that?"

The group looked at the speaker and waited for a few seconds to see if Mark was listening. They heard a chuckle. "I'm two steps ahead of you already. I heard Ma's original version, and I made a call to our top video guy. He'll be here tomorrow to discuss the project."

Carrie pumped her fist in the air. "I can't think of a better way to introduce a new album, boss."

"I agree completely," Mark said. "Get back to work on the last cover as soon as you've listened to the tracks you've recorded. I want to hear this new song myself."

Juliet shot a panicked look at Cedra. Cedra calmly nodded. "We got this," she replied.

"Damn straight we do," Wayne said.

"Headphones on then, guys." Bud hit play. When they finished, he looked at them. "Everyone satisfied we have three good covers?"

Everyone nodded. Bud grinned. "Hit the restroom, and let's get cranking. You've got me dying to hear this new song."

Keith grabbed another donut on their way to the restrooms. "Man, don't you ever get enough sugar?" Wayne teased.

"No such thing." Keith popped the last bite in his mouth.

†

The boys would perform "Low Places" by themselves, so Juliet took a seat next to Cedra to watch. "I can't believe

Mark is coming to watch. We're not ready for that," Juliet said.

"Relax. It may take a few runs, but we have the best producer working for us. Bud will tell us exactly what is needed."

Wayne gave his best performance yet of "Low Places" as Cedra, and Juliet watched. Bud's voice came over the speaker. "Honestly, I can't find anything wrong with that version. Good job, Wayne."

"Thanks, Bud," Wayne said, and high-fived Keith and Stone.

"Okay, so tell me what we need for the next song?"

Juliet turned toward him. "I'll lead in and end the song with some harmonica. Stone and Keith will join me, Cedra on keyboards, and Wayne on the drum pad when I play my guitar. We only had guitars and the harmonica to practice on last night, so we needed to run through it with all the instruments. Cedra will join me on vocals, and we'll all do the chorus."

"I'm ready when you are."

†

Mark rushed into the room, just in time to hear Juliet talking to Bud. "Hello, Ma. Exciting, isn't it?"

"Yes, it is, Mark. This is really good."

They watched Juliet take a deep breath and look to make sure everyone was ready. She hung the guitar over her shoulder, pulled out her harmonica, and began to play.

"Whoa, that's haunting," Carrie said.

The band joined in, and Cedra joined Juliet on the lyrics. When they reached the chorus, Keith, Wayne, and Stone joined them.

At the end of the song, Juliet's harmonica faded away softly.

They all turned expectantly toward the booth to find Bud tapping his forehead in thought. He smiled as he looked up. "Great song, Juliet. Let's try the music a bit differently, though."

He looked at Keith. "Banjo?" Then he looked at Stone. "Fiddle?"

"We can give it a shot," Juliet said.

"The drums were perfect, Wayne. Don't change anything," Bud praised. "I loved the harmonica, Juliet. That was genius."

"Different, too, from what we started with," Cedra teased.

"Keith and I tweaked it a bit last night after y'all went to bed," Juliet explained.

"I like it even better," Cedra replied.

†

"That was good, but it's missing something," Mark replied. "It's time for Bud to work his magic."

"For a first time playing it, they did great," Carrie remarked.

They listened to Bud's suggestions and waited for the band to begin playing.

†

Ma could sense the shift in energy with the addition of the banjo and fiddle. The instrument change added additional layers to the sound, and Ma could tell the band could feel and hear it, too, as their smiles grew between verses and the chorus.

†

"Much better. Come, let's have a listen. Something still seems off," Bud remarked.

"That second run sounded better," Cedra replied. "What do you think we're missing?"

Juliet shrugged. "No clue."

"Any ideas, guys?" Cedra asked.

They all shook their heads. "The only thing I can think of is dropping the keyboards and adding your guitar to Juliet's," Wayne suggested.

"Hey, Bud," Juliet called out.

Bud turned back toward them. "Yes? Do you have an idea?" he asked Juliet.

333

"One more run? This time, no keyboards. Cedra back on her guitar with mine," Juliet suggested.

"I'm game," Bud said. He returned to his seat and put his headphones back on.

"Ready to kick it?" Juliet asked.

"Hell, yeah," Keith said.

Bud's head was bobbing to the music as he listened closely. When Juliet ended the song, she looked up.

"Let's go listen," Bud announced.

They entered the break room, and Bud handed Mark a set of earphones.

"Hey, guys," Mark said. "I loved the song."

"Thanks, Mark," Juliet replied.

"Let's listen to all three, but I like the last run the best, I think," Bud reported.

The group listened to all three cuts and ruled out the first one right away. "I have a suggestion," Bud said. "Let me burn a couple copies. Y'all take one, I'll take one, and we can dissect it and tweak some tomorrow. We are so far ahead of the production schedule we have plenty of time to get this perfect. This song deserves it, Juliet. Well done."

"Thanks," Juliet replied.

"I love the song. Your lyrics are fantastic," Mark praised.

"I agree," Felecia said. "I love the idea of each one of you writing a song for the album."

"I think Mark has something he wants to share with you, too," Carrie added.

"I do," Mark grinned. "I love your ideas for a video. Todd Cotton and Carrie will be meeting with you tomorrow to discuss developing a video as an introduction to the new album."

"Even more reason to get the music spot on," Juliet replied.

"I have no doubt, we will," Bud replied. "I just want to sleep on it and want you all to let me know if you hear something we're missing. You know your music the best." He stood. "I'll be right back."

"Both songs are kicking ass on the radio," Mark said.

"'Six Strings,' is now number two most downloaded, and I think the 'Wedding Song' will break the top twenty this week. That bodes well for an excellent full album release next week."

"That sounds fantastic," Cedra exclaimed. "Thank you all so much."

"Thank you all for bringing us such great music. I'll check in on you tomorrow and see how the video project is progressing. Have a great night."

"Thanks, Mark, you too," Carrie said.

"Wow," Stone declared.

"Yeah, I think we're all a bit shell shocked at how things are progressing," Cedra agreed.

"Your hard work is paying off," Felecia said. "I can see so much growth in y'all in the short time I've known you. Everyone is creating such a unique sound, and now you're all writing. Incredible." She smiled and shook her head.

Juliet looked at Ma. "We'll go pack up while we're waiting on Bud. We have tiny burgers to eat." She shot a wink at Ma.

"Yes, we do. I'm suddenly feeling hungry." Ma grinned.

"We can get us loaded up if you want to wait here for Bud," Wayne suggested.

Juliet tossed Wayne her keys. "Thanks."

†

Bud walked back into the room with CDs. He looked at Juliet as he handed one to her. "I'm very proud of you. We will make this a great song together, so relax. We are very close."

"Thanks, Bud," Juliet replied. "We appreciate all your help. We'll listen to it tonight and hopefully come up with a suggestion or two tomorrow."

Cedra stood. "Ready, Ma?"

"It was great to see you all again," Ma said. "Let's go, ladies."

"See you tomorrow." Carrie nodded.

"Goodnight," Cedra answered.

†

Cedra and Keith swapped rides. Cedra laughed as she climbed into the back seat and patted Ma's shoulder. "I wonder if any of them realize just how bad you just played them?"

336

"Doesn't matter. It got the job done." Ma grinned. "Let's eat."

"Okay, Keith," Juliet teased Ma and followed the boys down the drive.

CHAPTER FIFTEEN

"Let's drop the fiddle this time and bring the banjo back," Bud suggested.

The group made the instrument changes and played through "Midnight" again.

"I think that's the one. It's almost time to meet with Todd, so meet me in the break room."

"I think he's right. That one sounded good to me," Juliet said.

Cedra placed her guitar on the stand. "I liked it too. Let's go hit the bathroom and take a listen."

†

When Juliet and Cedra entered the break room, a young man sat next to Felecia. Mark introduced Todd Cotton to the group.

"Good evening, guys. Felecia and Carrie have given me some of the ideas of what you visualize. I'd like to hear the song again and then hear the thoughts directly from you."

"I really like the last run," Bud replied. "Let's take a listen."

They all put on headphones and listened to the song.

"I don't know about y'all, but I loved it," Todd said.

Carrie and Bud both nodded. "That's the 'Midnight' we needed to cut," Bud stated. "Are we in agreement?"

"Absolutely," Juliet agreed.

"Okay, I'm going to burn some copies. See you tomorrow after work for a few more covers and catching up on the intros?" Bud asked.

"We'll be here. Thanks for all your help, Bud," Cedra replied.

"My pleasure. As always." Bud grinned. "Have fun with Todd."

†

Todd smiled at them. "I'm excited to hear your thoughts, so who wants to take the lead?"

All heads turned to Cedra. "It was your idea," Juliet revealed.

"First, let me explain something," Cedra told Todd. "When I read or write lyrics, I put a voice or voices to the music and sometimes images to the song. When I read through 'Midnight' for the first time, I visualized Juliet. She's walking down Lower Broadway late at night, the neon signs still ablaze. Static images of her performing on stage at a honky-tonk and us in the studio are mixed in as she's singing. I haven't mentioned this to the others yet, but since we will be introducing *Midnight in Nashville,* our second album with this song and video, I think we need to add some other shots." Cedra looked at Juliet and the boys.

"Like what?" Juliet asked.

"Something with Ma in it and maybe a shot of us jamming on her front porch, where this all began," Cedra said. "Maybe a shot at the Redbird to give Lisa Marie thanks for giving us her stage to get us a jump start as a band?"

"I like the heck out of that," Todd replied. "Maybe I'll just give you a camera. You seem to have it all planned out," he teased.

Everyone laughed. "Um, no. We are musicians and writers," Cedra reminded him.

"Very creative ones too," Todd added.

"One more thing. I want to place a rose on Cash's star before I walk away and end the song with the harmonica," Juliet said.

"Nice touch," Todd remarked. "Why Johnny Cash?"

Juliet smiled. "I don't know of any musician who doesn't appreciate his story. The hard times and determination to sing his brand of country has always inspired me," Juliet answered.

"That's good enough for me," Todd answered. "Do you have still shots?"

"I've got a couple from the Redbird," Carrie responded. "On my phone, though, so I don't know if the quality is good enough."

"We can take a look," Todd replied.

"If not, it's no problem. Stone, Wayne, and I still work at the Redbird, and I'm sure Lisa Marie would let us take as many shots as you want."

Todd's eyebrow shot up. "You all work there?"

"I used to tend bar. Until Corona virus," Wayne said, "but Lisa Marie took me right in when I got laid off."

"When can you get started with some shots there and a brief video clip of y'all playing in the studio? We can do still shots at Ma's. We can also video you leaving the rose. That should be easy, so start thinking of some poses," Todd informed them.

"How would you handle walking down the middle of Lower Broadway?" Felecia asked. "We don't want anyone run over," she teased.

Todd smiled at Felecia. "I can record Juliet walking anywhere and simply dub it in. I'd like to do some research to see if we could do it live, though. That's always the best." He looked at Juliet. "If I can get some permits to shoot and have traffic blocked off, are you good for the middle of the night? Maybe two or three in the morning?"

"Just name the place and time, and I'll be there," Juliet replied. The smile on her face warmed Cedra's heart. It felt good to see Juliet so excited about the song she had created and the video it was leading into.

Todd nodded. "Okay, I think we have a good idea of where we want to go. No offense, Carrie, but I need better resolution than a phone camera can provide."

"No offense taken. Do you want to ask Lisa Marie if we can use her stage?" she asked Cedra.

"That will be a no-brainer."

"Same with the studio shots, and I presume Ma will be okay with using your home for some?" Carrie asked.

"We may have to drag her into some shots, but I think she's such an important part of us that we need to include her."

"Y'all are making this too easy. I love it when an artist knows exactly what they want to produce. It makes my job cake," Todd said.

"Did someone mention cake?" Keith asked.

Carrie and the others broke into laughter.

Cedra looked at Todd. "Keith is our sugar hound. Don't make the mistake of getting between him and anything sweet."

"Got it." Todd chuckled. "So, bring donuts or cupcakes as reinforcement," he teased.

Keith smiled. "I love this man."

"Okay, so let me get started on some research. Let's plan to meet back Friday if that's good for everyone?" Todd asked.

"That works for us. We'll get permission from Lisa Marie and Ma and think up some poses," Cedra said.

"You're recording some covers tomorrow, right?"

"Yes, we'll be here from three to eight tomorrow," Juliet said.

"Excellent. I may sneak in and get some stills and a video clip then."

"Do we need to dress up?" Stone asked. "We'll be coming straight from work."

"Nope, whatever you normally feel comfortable recording in. Juliet will need to dress in black like you envisioned for the video and maybe a shot at a honky-tonk. Do you have any you've performed at that will let us in for a quick shot?"

"Wild Bill's," Wayne replied. "With the limited hours and capacity, I think we could get a day shot in, and they would appreciate the promotion."

"I'll make the arrangements for that," Carrie volunteered.

Felecia chuckled. "I get the easy job," she said.

"What's that?" Cedra asked.

"All I have to do is play the hell out of the video once it's done," Felecia answered. "I can't wait to see a finished product. It sounds as incredible as the song."

†

"Let's do this," Todd stated and stood to leave.

"Thanks, Todd," Juliet replied before he left the room.

Todd smiled back at her. "I'm looking forward to it."

"We'll let you talk to Bud about Todd coming into the studio," Juliet told Carrie.

Carrie laughed. "Ha! I don't think he'll have a problem as long as it's quick, especially for y'all. He's taken a shining to you all."

Juliet smiled. "Let's pack up and head home, guys. We'll see you tomorrow."

Bud walked into the studio as they were packing up to give them several copies of "Midnight." He smiled at Juliet. "You did a great job performing the song today. I'm proud of it, and you all should be, too."

"Most definitely," Cedra replied. "We've got more covers ready for tomorrow."

"I'll see you then." Bud smiled and left the studio.

†

Cedra rode home with Juliet. She inserted the CD into the player, and they listened to the song several times. They ended up singing along at the top of their lungs as they pulled into Ma's drive. Cedra looked over at Juliet. "Are you going to pitch the photo shoot to Ma?"

"Might as well ask as soon as we get home. I don't see Ma saying no, though. It may take all of us to convince her to join us for some shots."

†

"Is that fried pork chops I smell?" Cedra asked.

Ma looked up from the stove. "Yes, with rice and gravy. I cooked some greens and cornbread too."

"That's what I'm talking about," Juliet exclaimed as the boys filed into the kitchen. "How much longer?"

"Five minutes on the cornbread."

"Can you sit with us for a minute? We have something to ask you," Juliet requested.

"Sure," Ma said and dried her hands on her apron. "Everything okay?"

"Couldn't be better," Cedra answered.

"We met with Todd Cotton today to discuss the video idea, and we need your permission for something," Juliet explained. "We want to do a photo shoot here. We want some shots with us jamming on the front porch since that's where we started, and we want a couple of photos with you in them."

"Me?"

"Yes, you are critical to us, and we consider you a part of the band. If it hadn't been for your support and encouragement, some of us might have already packed it in and headed home."

Ma ran her hand through her hair as she did when nervous. "Well, I'll have to go get my hair done and maybe a new outfit," Ma said nervously.

"We all just need to wear what we do every day," Cedra answered. "If you want to get your hair done, I'll take you. I could use a trim."

"Alright with me, I guess," Ma answered.

"I promise we will make this as painless as we can," Juliet teased.

†

The timer for the cornbread sounded, and Ma rose to take it from the oven. "Will someone start pouring drinks"?" she asked while removing two skillets of cornbread from the oven.

"I've got it," Juliet replied.

"Grab the vinegar and pepper juice out of the fridge also," Ma requested.

Cedra stood to help Ma. Ma handed her two plates of cornbread and dipped out the greens. Cedra placed the plates on the table and returned for bowls of greens and rice. Ma followed her to the table with the gravy.

†

After feasting, the group moved into the living room to write more introductions for the songs. Cedra walked back into the kitchen, and she overheard Ma bragging to Patsy about her being in a music video. When she returned to the room, her coffee cup still empty, Juliet cocked her head.

"I thought you were getting coffee."

"I was. I heard Ma on the phone before I got there talking to Patsy. She was bragging about being in a music video. I didn't want to interrupt that conversation."

"It will be time to take a break soon anyhow. I'm about ready for some buttermilk pie."

†

The next night they recorded "Craving You," "Standing Outside the Fire," "Ring of Fire," and "The Thunder Rolls."

As promised, Todd came into the studio and shot dozens of photos as Juliet and Cedra sang "Craving You," and shot video of "Standing Outside the Fire."

"These all came out nice. Do you want me to call Felecia for some intros?" Bud asked.

"If you're ready," Cedra said.

The intros with Felecia went well, and they were excited to get home.

"Let's take a recording break tomorrow, so y'all can focus on the video and maybe have an early start to the weekend. Do you want to shoot for some studio time?"

"How about Saturday and we take off Sunday?" Juliet said.

"I can work with that. One more week and we'll break for the holidays. Be sure to bring Hank by to see me while he's in town, Cedra."

"Sure will." Cedra grinned.

†

347

"I think we should all totally veg out tonight. We've already had a productive week," Cedra suggested as they finished dinner.

"You won't get a complaint from me," Wayne replied. "A hot shower, and I'm off to bed."

"That sounds like a good plan for all of us. You've all had some long days and nights," Ma said.

Juliet nodded. "We're working on the video tomorrow and off Friday night. We'll record more covers and maybe a new song on Saturday and be off Sunday."

"That's good that you're taking some breaks. When are you heading home, Stone?" Ma asked.

"I'm heading out after work on Tuesday. I'll drive halfway and park for the night if I get tired," Stone answered.

"Dude, you know you'll drive the whole way," Wayne teased.

"Probably so." Stone grinned. "I can't wait to see my girls."

"I bet Lisa Marie will shoo you out the door early, so you can get on the road," Cedra said.

"We better finish your shopping Sunday then," Juliet reminded him.

"Would you go with me? I have all the sizes you needed."

"I'd love to," Juliet agreed.

"Pick up some wrapping paper, and we can wrap them for you, too, so they will be a total surprise," Cedra suggested.

"Thank you. My wrapping skills are horrific," Stone replied.

"No problem. I actually enjoy wrapping."

"Is anyone else planning to go home? I know Hank is coming up," Stone asked.

"Not me. My family is right here," Juliet replied.

"Me either," Keith answered. "I thought about it, but I need to get as much work in as I can."

"Ditto to that," Wayne replied. "I want to hold onto as much of the advance as possible."

"I appreciate y'all picking up the extra shifts while I'm at home," Stone told Cedra and Wayne.

"Not a problem, bro," Wayne said.

Cedra smiled. "You can return the favor when Juliet and I go visit Dad one day."

"When it warms up enough to go to the beach. I've only seen the Gulf once," Juliet replied. "A spring break in high school that I don't remember very well."

"We can make that happen. Goodnight, all," Cedra told them.

†

The following morning, Cedra approached Lisa Marie with the video idea.

349

"Like I would ever tell y'all no?" Lisa Marie said. "Take whatever you need here. It's a good advertisement for the café too."

"That it is," Wayne said.

Cedra caught Lisa Marie by herself later that morning. "Stone is heading home after work Tuesday. Could you boot him out early so he can get on the road?"

"I already planned to do that. After eleven, we should be able to handle things well."

"Thanks. I know Stone's excited and will drive all the way through."

†

When they rolled into the studio later that day, Todd and Felecia were waiting for them in the break room. Carrie saw them enter and joined them.

"We've got permission from Ma and Lisa Marie for photo shoots," Cedra reported.

"That's great news," Todd said. "The shots from the studio came out great. I'll come in Friday since you aren't recording today. I'm waiting on a call back about the permit, but I think it's a go."

"Stone is heading home on Tuesday," Juliet replied. "Can we get the photos at the Redbird and Ma's done before then?"

"That's not a problem. Carrie is still working on Wild Bill's. If we could shoot there Sunday morning, would that

350

be a problem? We could do the Redbird, too, and have all the shots done."

"We're off Sunday, so that shouldn't be an issue. Monday may be cutting it close," Juliet said.

"I'll keep after Wild Bill's then," Carrie replied.

"I was thinking about letting the opening harmonica music lead into the video and start the walking scene once the music and lyrics start. End it with Juliet placing the rose and then a shot from behind her walking away playing the harmonica to finish the song."

"I like the sound of that," Felecia stated. "What's the run time on the song?"

"Four minutes and fifteen seconds. Fantastic length for a video," Todd reported.

"I know this may sound crazy, but when we were first dreaming this up, we joked about snowflakes or a bolt of lightning at the end," Wayne told them. "Would that be hard to dub in?"

"Let me play with that," Todd said. "The lightning as Juliet walks away would be easy. Snowflakes may be a bit trickier, especially at night, but I'll give it a shot."

"Thanks. It was just an idea."

"I like it. Especially the lightning. I can already see the sky glowing with spider lightning. I think it's a great idea."

"I guess I'd better get Ma to schedule a salon appointment," Cedra teased. She looked at Todd. "That was her only requirement that we allow her to get her hair done."

"That sounds like Ma." Carrie chuckled.

"She's pretty excited about a photo shoot," Cedra added.

"Unless you all have other ideas, let's call it a day then," Todd replied. "Great job, guys. I'll see you Sunday. I'll call you with details."

†

"That's rare," Juliet said as they stepped outside.

Cedra looked at her. "What is?"

"That we are leaving here before dark," Juliet teased.

"I'd better call Ma to have her get a hair appointment set."

"If she can get one tomorrow before three, I'll take her."

"Got it." Cedra dialed Ma's phone.

CHAPTER SIXTEEN

Bud and Todd met them in the studio on Friday. Todd was setting up the last of the lighting he'd need to take the shots. "Are you guys ready to get started?" Bud asked.

"Yes, sir," Cedra replied.

"Just act as you normally would and don't pay any attention to me in the studio," Todd instructed.

"What are you starting with today?" Bud asked.

"A little Keith Urban," Cedra replied. "Juliet's going to do 'God Whispered Your Name.'"

Bud smiled. "I love that song. Let's nail it."

✝

Juliet gave the nod, and they began to play. Juliet did an excellent job on the lyrics. Todd's camera whirled with action as he took dozens of shots and video.

"What's next?" Bud asked.

"'Life is a Highway,'" Juliet answered.

"I love the songs you've chosen today," Todd replied. "Great for individual and group shots."

Bud shook his head. "Let's run through that one again. A bit more energy this time." Bud was pleased with the second run. "Are you good to keep going?"

Cedra nodded. "Stone is doing 'Broken Road,' next, then we have a bit of a throwback for you."

Bud cocked his head. "That sounds interesting."

Todd sat on a stool to listen and take more shots as Stone sang.

"Good job, Stone," Bud praised. "One more before we break? You seem to be on a roll."

The band exchanged several instruments and began playing. Cedra watched the smile grow on Bud's face when he recognized "The Chains" by Fleetwood Mac. Juliet and Wayne nailed the first run as Keith, Stone, and Cedra added the chorus. Keith was excellent on the bass solo runs and his face beamed with pride.

"Wow," Todd exclaimed when they finished. "I had forgotten how great that song was."

"Great job, guys. Come take a listen," Bud requested.

Carrie waited for them in the break room. "I've got good news," she reported. "We can do Wild Bill's at ten tomorrow morning."

"We are scheduled to record tomorrow," Juliet replied.

Bud chuckled. "Get your video shots done. We are way ahead of where I imagined we could be at this point. That way, you can have Sunday off to rest and plan."

"That sounds great. Maybe we can come back next week with some new songs," Cedra replied.

"I can work on the video and maybe have an early Christmas present for y'all," Todd stated.

"That would be awesome," Juliet answered.

"Maybe you can carve out a still for the cover, too," Cedra suggested.

"I'll keep that in mind," Todd said. "Will you clear the shoots with the Redbird and Ma for tomorrow after we finish at Wild Bill's?"

"That shouldn't be a problem. Ma got her hair done today." Juliet grinned.

"Ready to take a listen to what you did today?" Bud asked.

All four tracks came out really good. Cedra looked at Bud. "Can we use covers on the second album, or should we stick to our original music?"

Bud gestured to Carrie. "Do you want to answer that?"

"I'd be inclined to say stick with all original songs, but the way you've performed some of these covers, I'd say you've earned the privilege to record a couple. No more than three, though."

"What if we added them as extra tracks?" Bud suggested. "Twelve original songs and three covers."

"I think that would work. I really like the sound of several of the covers we've done," Cedra agreed.

"Which ones?" Bud asked.

"'Fire Away,' 'Low Places,' and 'The Chain,'" Cedra replied.

"I think I'd add 'God Whispered Your Name,' to that list," Bud said. "Sixteen tracks are legit." Bud looked around the table. "What do the rest of you think about the idea?"

"The more music, the better," Stone stated.

"Agreed," Juliet said.

Bud nodded to Carrie. "I'm good with it."

"Me, too," Carrie agreed.

Bud looked at Stone. "Since you are leaving on Tuesday, we need to concentrate on any songs you will be the lead vocals on for Monday."

"We can do that."

"I would like to fine-tune the new album over the holidays if we can get everything recorded," Bud replied.

"A new album and another video." Juliet whistled. "That would be great."

"If we are in agreement, let's call it a day. I'll see you back in the studio Monday afternoon. Good luck with your photo shoots, and have a great weekend."

"Thanks, Bud," Cedra replied.

"I guess we'll see you at Wild Bill's at ten. Then we can hit the Redbird and wrap it up at Ma's," Juliet said.

"I'll call Lisa Marie on the way home. I'm sure she won't have a problem," Cedra replied.

Cedra turned to Juliet as they drove home. "Have you given any thought to poses at Ma's?"

"To be honest, no. Do you have some ideas?"

Cedra grinned. "You should know I do. I think we all need to sit in a circle like we do when we jam on the front porch. I also think we need to sit on the front steps with Ma in between you and I. Wayne and Keith below us, and Stone sitting in front on the bottom since he's the tallest."

"Maybe a shot in the kitchen too."

"How do you feel about using some of the covers on the album? I should have discussed it with the rest of you first. We can always change it if we decide not to use them."

"I don't have a problem with it at all. I like the idea. The songs show a wide range of what we can do and who we are as a group. It also gives a bonus product for the people who buy the whole album."

"That is a thought. Sometimes, I just blurt ideas out without thinking."

"You have done very well for the band so far. You have a quick and creative mind." Juliet smiled at her. "Nothing to be sorry for. We are blessed to have you thinking for us."

†

Ma was tickled about the shoot being Saturday. "Do you think Todd would stay for lunch?"

"If he gets a smell of your cooking, how could he resist?" Wayne asked.

"That's a good point," Stone agreed. "Didn't you suggest we get a shot around the kitchen table? More realistic if it's filled with Ma's great cooking."

"A late lunch then?" Ma looked at Cedra. "Fried chicken, rice, gravy, corn, and collards?"

"Is it Saturday yet?" Keith asked.

†

After they finished cleaning the kitchen, Cedra excused herself to shower. Juliet grinned once Cedra was upstairs. "I need your help," she said to Keith and Wayne.

"What's up?" Wayne asked.

"Stone and Cedra have to work Sunday, but there's a song I want to record for her and for the album. Another cover," Juliet answered.

"Are you being devious?" Ma teased.

"Yes, ma'am, I am, but I need some backup." Juliet looked at Keith. "I want to record 'Perfect' for Cedra, and if it's good enough, add it to the covers on the album."

"We'll make it good enough. That's a great song, and it fits you two perfectly," Wayne remarked.

"Ha! I see what you did there," Juliet replied.

Ma looked at them. "I don't think I know that song."

"I got this," Keith pulled out his phone and played it for Ma.

Ma smiled. "That is a pretty song."

"Bud is on board and said he'd meet us in the studio Sunday while she's at work. Is eight okay?" Juliet asked.

"Eight will be perfect." Wayne laughed.

"You are on a roll tonight, bro." Keith laughed.

"Cookies tonight?" Ma inquired.

"That would be perfect," Keith said.

"Do I need to print the song out for you?" Juliet smiled.

"That would be great. Maybe we can sneak in some practice on the music," Wayne said.

Juliet nodded. "Sounds good. I'll go do that now and let Cedra know we have cookies baking." She looked at Stone. "Saturday is going to be busy. Why don't we plan on finishing up your Christmas shopping tomorrow when y'all get home from work?"

"That would be perfect," Stone answered with a grin. "Sorry, I couldn't resist."

Juliet smiled and shook her head. "I wouldn't expect anything less of y'all. I'll be back in a few."

†

Juliet printed three copies of "Perfect" while Cedra was in the shower and rushed them downstairs when she heard the water cut off. Then she walked back upstairs to wait on Cedra. "We have cookies tonight," she said when Cedra walked into the room. "Ma and the boys are working on

359

them. I also suggested to Stone that we finish his Christmas shopping after work tomorrow since Saturday is going to be so busy."

Cedra was towel drying her hair. "That's a great idea." She smiled at Juliet. "We need to give some thought to shopping, too. I've got no clue what to buy anyone."

"I've got an idea for the guys. Will you split gift certificates for them to go get those new Stetsons they've been dreaming of for weeks?"

"That's perfect. What about Ma?"

"How about a Smart television for her bedroom? That TV she has is probably as old as we are." Juliet chuckled. "Doesn't have to be huge. Maybe forty-two inches or so with a wall mount. I'm sure we could talk Hank into installing it for her with the boys' help."

"Dad?"

"A satellite radio system for his truck and home. That way, Hank can listen to us easier."

Cedra smiled. "Perfect." She sat in Juliet's lap. "And for you, my love?"

"I have everything I could ever possibly want sitting in my lap right now."

"While that is a good answer, it simply will not do. Maybe I'll get you one of those fancy irons," Cedra suggested.

"Ma's iron is good. I'll see if I can come up with something," Juliet promised. "What about you? What would you like?"

"I need some new songbooks and pens. I'm using the laptop more, but it's still satisfying to scribble the words."

Juliet nodded. "I can understand that." Juliet nuzzled into Cedra's neck. "Let's go scarf down some cookies with the guys and come back to snuggle."

"Let me throw some sweats on first. Go on and get us some milk poured and I'll be right there."

†

Stone and Juliet were laughing as they came out of the boot shop. "That was so much fun shopping for Destiny. It almost makes me wish for a little one to shop for."

"Really?" Stone said.

"Almost. I think I'll be satisfied spoiling Destiny for a while." Juliet smiled.

"Those little Cinch jeans you bought her are too cute," Cedra told Juliet.

"The matching ball cap you got her will look great," Juliet replied. "Stone will have to send us some pics at Christmas."

"I can't tell y'all how much I appreciate your help. I would have been lost on my own," Stone admitted.

"Sarah will look good in her new outfits, too," Juliet said.

"One more stop for wrapping paper, name tags, and tape, and you will be good to go," Cedra promised.

"You're on your own there," Juliet warned. "I can handle handing you tape strips, but I can't wrap."

"Just keep me company. Stone can make out the tags, and he'll be ready to roll." Cedra smiled.

"I've worked up an appetite," Juliet stated.

"Any idea what Ma has planned for supper?" Cedra asked.

"Mexican night. Tacos, burritos, chips, and salsa, the last I heard," Juliet replied. "The meat she was cooking when I left smelled delicious."

"Now I'm hungry," Stone exclaimed. "Only one more stop, you said?"

"We'll make it a quick one," Juliet promised.

"I'll drop y'all at the front door and circle to make it faster," Cedra told them as she pulled into the shopping lot. "Mask up," she reminded them.

"Be back soon," Juliet promised as she stepped out of the truck.

†

When they arrived home, Ma had ironed outfits for each of them. "I've got to keep y'all looking respectable for your photo shoots."

"Thanks, Ma. That saved me from doing some ironing tonight," Cedra replied.

†

Saturday morning, Ma wrapped them all in towels before feeding them French toast and bacon for breakfast.

"Let me know when you're on your way back home so I can freshen up a bit. I'll have lunch ready if you want to eat before we start taking photos."

"I'll give you a call when we wrap up at the café," Juliet promised.

†

Todd and Carrie waited for them at Wild Bill's. "The manager is on his way," Carrie reported.

"I'll snap some shots of the building while we wait," Todd said. "Oh, Juliet. We are set for Lower Broadway for Tuesday night. One o'clock, but it could be worse."

"One is fine with me," Juliet replied.

"Me, too," Cedra answered. "I can watch, and you can drop me off for work. I'll even treat you to breakfast if we have time."

"You better come home, eat, and go to bed if you're going," Juliet suggested. "We can't have you face-planting in a bowl of grits at work," she teased.

"I will," Cedra promised. "I don't want to miss a thing."

"I've got a red rose with me if you want to knock out the Walk of Fame shot today, too, while the boys get set up at the café," Todd asked.

"We can pack up here and meet you at the Redbird to speed things up," Wayne suggested.

"That works for me," Todd replied.

"I hope you don't have plans for lunch," Cedra told Todd and Carrie. "Ma is putting on a spread for us."

"I'll never pass on a home-cooked meal," Todd said.

"Me either, and I hear Ma's cooking is epic," Carrie added.

"You won't leave hungry. That's for sure," Juliet promised.

†

A few minutes later, the manager opened the side door for them. "Good morning. I'm happy that you all chose Wild Bill's for your video. Just let me know what you need. Otherwise, I'll stay out of your way."

Todd explained what shots he would take and a short video clip. "If you can get the stage lights warmed up, we won't keep you long."

†

"'Backwoods Boogie?'" Juliet asked.

"That sounds good. Maybe the two of y'all can do 'Fire Away' at the Redbird," Wayne suggested.

"Works for me. Todd, let us know when you're ready."

"Locked and loaded, so hit it when you're ready. I'm going to get the video clip first."

They all pulled out their Ray-Bans, and Juliet nodded. "Let's rip."

"Backwoods Boogie" never sounded better as they played one of their favorite honky-tonk tunes. The energy was high, and their blood was pumping when they finished the song. "That was perfect. I've got what I need here. Meet you at the Redbird?"

Wayne nodded. "We got this."

Juliet reached for Cedra's hand. After a quick thanks to the manager, they walked out to the parking lot. "I'll follow you," Cedra told Todd and Carrie.

Cedra entwined her fingers with Juliet's. "That went well."

"Painless." Juliet grinned back at her.

The Walk of Fame was vacant when they started taking candid shots, but a crowd had begun to form when they finished. Carrie took the opportunity to introduce Cedra and Juliet and explain to the group they were shooting a video for a new album. The crowd clapped, and several shouted, "We love your music."

"Thanks," Juliet called back to them, and they waved as they started back toward their vehicles.

A young girl of about ten called to them and stopped them for autographs. Todd was quick to capture the shot of them giving their first autographs. "We'll meet you at the Redbird. It won't hurt to get the parents' consent to use the girl's image in the video," Carrie explained.

Cedra nodded, and they climbed into her truck. "Do you realize we just signed our first autographs?"

"We were lucky Todd was here and caught it with his camera. We will have to ask for an enlarged copy." Juliet smiled. "That was exciting."

"Yes, it was," Cedra agreed, and turned back toward the Redbird.

†

The guys had everything set when they got to the Redbird. Lisa Marie watched as they performed "Fire Away." When she was sure Todd was finished filming, she clapped. "That was awesome. You two sound so good together."

"We've been practicing," Juliet replied with a wink at Lisa Marie. "Thanks for allowing us to use your stage."

"It's great for business. I feel fortunate to have you all here at any time."

"We really gelled here that night," Cedra admitted. "If you hadn't given us that opportunity, we would not be standing here together."

"Thank you. I don't believe that for a moment. You guys are destined to be great." Lisa Marie turned and hugged Cedra.

"See you in the morning, boss," Cedra stated as they finished packing up and prepared to go to Ma's.

"Yes, you will." Lisa Marie smiled.

†

When they entered Ma's house, the air was filled with aromas of food. Todd sighed. "I have died and gone to heaven."

366

Ma reached out her hand and introduced herself to Todd. "Hey, Carrie. I hope you all brought appetites. Have a seat, and I'll bring the last of the food."

Carrie's eyes grew wide as she looked at the table. "There's more?"

"Just cornbread and the greens," Ma answered with a chuckle. "Would you girls pour us up some drinks?" Ma asked Cedra and Juliet.

"Sure thing, Ma," Juliet replied. "Sweet tea good for everyone?"

"That sounds perfect," Todd answered. "Where would you like us to sit?"

Ma pointed to two chairs, and the boys took their usual seats. "Go ahead and start serving yourselves." Ma pulled two skillets of cornbread from the oven.

"I may need a nap after this meal," Todd declared. "Before everyone begins eating, may I get a photograph of y'all sitting around the table?"

"That's no problem," Juliet said as she sat glasses of tea on the table.

"I've got the greens if you will bring the cornbread," Cedra told Ma and began dishing up fresh greens in a serving bowl.

"Ma, would you and the girls mind, standing behind the guys?" Todd asked.

"Not at all." She placed the platters on the table and stood behind Wayne. Cedra and Juliet stood to either side of her. Carrie moved back from the table to stand beside Todd.

"All smiles," Todd instructed and took several shots before placing his camera on the foyer table. "Those will work fine. Thank you."

Ma and Cedra sat at opposite ends of the table, and Juliet sat beside Todd. "Dig in."

†

Once everyone was finished eating, Ma smiled at the group. "If Cedra and Juliet help, we'll clear the table while the boys set up the instruments on the porch. After the photos are done, we'll have some buttermilk pie and coffee or milk."

"I have just one question," Todd stated. "Who's going to drive me home after dessert? Ma, that was an excellent meal. Thank you."

"I'll help in the kitchen while the guys get set up," Carrie offered.

Ma nodded. "You can hand me dishes while the girls put up the leftovers."

†

Ma wiped her hands on the apron, turned the coffee pot on, and joined the others on the porch. Todd took several photographs of the band jamming and looked at Cedra. "What's next?"

"I thought we'd sit on the front steps with Ma, Juliet, and I on the top, Wayne and Keith next, then Stone on the bottom since he's the tallest."

"Wait a second." Ma removed her apron.

"That sounds good to me." Todd snapped several shots. "How about giving Ma a kiss on the cheek?"

Juliet and Cedra leaned into Ma and kissed her cheeks.

"That's perfect," Todd said.

"May I get copies of those?" Ma asked.

"You can have copies of whatever you'd like. I'll print them out, so you can choose the ones you like, and I'll have them blown up for you. That's the least I can do for that wonderful meal."

"That's not necessary, but thank you."

"I'll send them home with Cedra Monday, and y'all can decide which ones you'd like to have enlarged," Todd replied.

Ma looked at the boys. "Put the instruments away, and we'll have dessert."

Juliet looked at her friends. "Milk for you boys?"

"Yes, please," Stone answered.

Juliet looked at Todd and Carrie. "Coffee, milk, or something else?"

"Coffee is fine," Carrie replied, and Todd nodded in agreement as he packed his camera gear.

†

After Todd and Carrie left, Juliet looked around the table. "This has been an intense day." She grinned. "After the downtown filming, Todd will have everything he needs to put the video together."

369

"I can't wait to see it," Wayne said.

"Will you shoot me a copy if it's done before I get back?" Stone asked.

"Sure will," Cedra replied.

"That was a great meal today, Ma," Juliet praised. "I think we need to warm up leftovers for dinner?"

Ma nodded. "Between today's meal and the taco meat leftover from last night, I think we'll have plenty to choose from, and it will give us more room in the refrigerator. Dinner around seven?"

"That sounds great," Juliet agreed.

"What do y'all have planned for the rest of the afternoon?"

"I'm working with the guys on their songs," Stone replied.

"I need to select more original songs to work on for Monday," Cedra replied. "Maybe we can practice some tomorrow?"

"I may take a crack at starting a new song," Juliet stated. "Not for this album, but maybe for the next."

"I like the sound of that," Ma replied. "I'm going to nap for a bit. I'll see you all later."

"How many songs do I need to select?" Stone asked.

"Two will be good I think," Cedra answered.

"No problem. I'll pick two out tonight, so we can work on those tomorrow too."

Cedra looked at Juliet. "Will you go up and grab my songbook and the laptop? Let's sit around the table, and maybe we can all pitch in to help these guys finish their songs."

"I've got bad news to break to Keith, so maybe your offer of help would be a good thing tonight," Stone reported.

"Bad news?" Keith groaned. "What?"

"Hank Jr. already has a song named 'Redneck Paradise,'" Stone replied.

"I knew it was too good to be available. Back to the drawing board."

"We can come up with a new title. It's not the end of the world," Juliet told Keith.

"So says the woman that has already written her smash song," Keith teased.

"I'll be right back, and we can listen to what you've got already," Juliet replied and walked upstairs.

When she returned, she handed Cedra her songbook. Cedra smiled at Keith. "Don't worry. I'm going to be listening. Then we can hear what Wayne has and get busy."

The group listened to the lyrics Keith had written. "Let me ask you something," Cedra said to Keith. "When you think of this song, where does it take you?"

Keith smiled. "Back to high school. We would meet up in someone's cornfield or down by the river to party every Friday or Saturday night. There was usually a bonfire and a jar of shine being passed around. Sitting around on tailgates as rock or country music played from someone's truck or boom box. Couples dancing or necking, but no one would go too far. We all had dreams that we knew would be destroyed if we weren't careful. Most of us wanted out of our little town."

"And the others?" Cedra asked.

"Hearts set on their high school sweethearts, a white picket fence, and settling down to raise some kids and work the ground."

Cedra nodded. "Now write these down. What are the emotions you associate with those memories? How did you feel on those Friday and Saturday nights?"

"Invincible, happy, excited, love, anxiety, fearful, and eager." Keith scribbled down the words.

"Now, take the first word, invincible, wasn't it? What about those nights made you feel that way?" Cedra smiled. "Write it down without saying it out loud." She turned to Wayne. "Ask yourself the same things and do the same exercise."

Cedra turned back to her book and started flipping through pages as she selected a few more songs to record. Stone was searching his book while Juliet was tapping away on the computer. She leaned over to Cedra. "Want some coffee?"

"Sure," Cedra whispered back with a grin.

†

Cedra gazed over the top of her book, watching Keith's intense concentration as he scribbled notes. She glanced over at Stone, who smiled and nodded to her, and she shot him a wink. Wayne was also writing, his head bobbing as if he heard the music in his head as he visualized the lyrics. Juliet's movement near the coffee pot drew her attention, and she was dancing as she waited for the coffee to brew. Maybe she was dreaming up lyrics of her own.

†

Juliet poured mugs. "Anyone else want coffee?"

"I'll take one," Stone replied.

Wayne looked up. "Me, too, please."

Keith looked up long enough to shake his head. "No thanks. I'm wired up enough already."

Juliet brought four mugs to the table and settled in next to Cedra. "Which ones did you pick?"

"Thirty-two and seventeen for starters. That's the first one of mine you sang. We can't forget that."

"That's a great song and easy to play and sing," Juliet agreed. "Are they on here already?"

Cedra nodded. "Yeah, they are. Print out forty and fifty-one, too, please. Enough copies for everyone."

"Have you picked out yours yet, Stone?" Juliet asked.

"Yeah. I'll go grab my laptop and email the songs to you, and you can print those as well, please," Stone answered.

"Sounds good to me," Juliet replied as she began searching Cedra's songs and sent them to the printer. "Dang, out of paper. I'll be right back."

Stone emailed the songs and Juliet resumed printing.

Cedra watched Keith. He seemed to be stuck. "Are you ready to share with us what you've got so far?"

"Yeah, I'm kinda dead in the water," Keith answered.

"Go ahead, let's hear your thoughts."

Keith began to read his notes.

Invincible – feeling on top of the world dancing around the fire, not a worry in the world.

Happy – surrounded by friends laughing and passing a jar of shine, sitting on tail gates watching the moon and stars.

Excited – friends engaged to marry after graduation, singing along with a song and it felt so right.

Love – ready for a band on her left hand, a white picket fence.

Anxiety – becoming a dad or chasing dreams out of the small-town world.

Fearful – not being enough for family or fame.

Eager – to work the ground our families have held for generations or to venture away from the security we've known for years.

Keith stopped reading and looked up to find Cedra smiling at him. "What?"

"Read them silently to yourself." Cedra instructed.

Keith's eyes grew wide. He looked up at Cedra. "I've got the bones for lyrics, don't I?"

Cedra nodded. "Yes, you do. Congratulations."

"Clean them up, decide on a title, music and you have your song," Juliet said.

†

Cedra looked at Wayne. "I have to ask. Were you playing the music in your head as you were writing? I noticed your head was bobbing like there was a tune playing up there."

Wayne laughed. "Yeah, I was."

"Do you remember the tune?" Juliet asked.

"That's the easy part," Wayne answered.

"Go get your guitar," Cedra told him. When Wayne returned, he looked at her. "Play the music in your head."

Wayne played through the song.

"Play it again and let me see your notes, please," Cedra requested.

Keith picked up his pen and wrote for several seconds. He waited for Wayne to finish playing.

"What about 'Small Town Universe?'" Keith asked.

"I like it," Stone agreed.

"I do, too. It's the universe you grew up in before you expanded your wings to fly away," Cedra stated.

"One step down, two to go," Juliet praised.

Cedra walked Wayne through the same exercise they had done with Keith. Wayne's eyes were sparkling when he looked at Cedra. "You make this seem so easy."

"You made it easy. The music is in your head. You just need some tips on how to draw it out." Cedra smiled to him.

"I really like how you did that," Stone replied. "I'm going to try that with my writing."

"That's basically how I started writing. Mom and Dad would prompt me to write down ideas and then they grew from there," Cedra told her friends.

Juliet went upstairs to retrieve the songs she had printed and passed them out to the others. Ma came downstairs from her nap. "Have you all moved at all since I left?" Ma teased.

"Some of us have," Juliet replied. She looked at the clock. "Is it time to start warming up dinner?"

"Yes, I thought I'd get started on leftovers. Y'all keep doing what you're doing. It looks like you're being productive."

"Cedra is teaching us how to write," Keith told Ma.

"You couldn't ask for a better teacher." Ma slipped her apron over her head.

"Why don't you and Stone work with Keith on cleaning up his lyrics, and Wayne and I will go into the living room and work on his?" Cedra suggested to Juliet.

"That sounds good," Juliet answered.

"It will take me a half an hour or so for dinner."

"That should give us a good start," Cedra said. She nodded to Wayne. "Let's go."

†

Cedra looked up when she heard Ma tell Juliet, Keith, and Stone to clear the table and set it for dinner. She looked at Wayne. "You've done really good so far. Do you think you can finish this on your own?"

"I'll do my best to knock it out before we go back into the studio. I know we're all anxious to get the new album cut. Thank you for all your help."

Cedra smiled at him. "You're doing all the hard work. Do you have a title yet?"

Wayne nodded. "I have an idea." He smiled. "'Missed Opportunity.'"

"What is her name?"

"Haley. My high school sweetheart. I came to Nashville, she went off to college, and now she's getting married."

"Your first love?"

"First and only," Wayne answered. "I hoped she would wait for me, but our lives went in different directions."

Cedra placed a hand on his arm. "There will be another. Be patient."

Wayne nodded. "When the time is right, I know I'll meet the one meant for me."

"That's right. Come on, let's get ready to grub."

CHAPTER SEVENTEEN

Juliet waited until she heard Stone and Cedra leave for work before showering and going downstairs. She listened to the shower running in the boys' area and smiled as she started down the stairs.

"Okay, what's going on?" Ma asked when Juliet entered the kitchen. "You're up and dressed. Wayne and Keith are scurrying around upstairs, too. Something I don't know about?"

"Remember, the boys and I are going into the studio this morning to record a surprise cover song for Cedra. Bud has promised he will sneak it into the new album for me."

"That explains it nicely," Ma said. "I reckon I'd better start cooking some breakfast then. What time are you due at the studio?"

"At eight. We can eat cereal."

"Nonsense, there's plenty of time for a hot meal. Hand me a couple of those ham steaks in the fridge, please. How about those with some eggs and toast?"

"Sounds perfect." Juliet chuckled and pulled out two steaks and a carton of eggs. "Can we have some dippers?"

"Fried, over easy, coming up." Ma placed the steaks in a frying pan. "Is the new album coming along well?"

Juliet had started setting the table. "Yes, we hope to have the rest of the original tracks recorded tomorrow. Then Bud will work his magic while we finish the video. There's a good possibility the rough cuts of both will be done before Friday."

"Will you all take a break after that?"

"The studio is closed the entire week of Christmas, and I think the café is closing for a few days as well. You may get sick of seeing us," Juliet teased.

Wayne was first down the stairs. "I was hoping you were cooking breakfast. I'm hungry. What can I help with?"

"Pour some drinks for everyone. I'll get started on the eggs, and Juliet can make the toast. Keith will rush in just as food starts hitting the table." Ma chuckled.

"He does have a good sense about his arrival times."

Ma cut the steaks into smaller portions and cracked the first two eggs. "Dippers okay with you?" she asked Wayne.

"They're perfect."

Ma and Juliet started laughing.

"I take it you told Ma about our secret mission this morning?" Wayne asked Juliet.

"Yes, I had to remind her why all of us were awake. We should have plenty of time for breakfast and to work on your songs a bit more before we have to leave."

"I think I'm getting close. I shouldn't have any problem finishing today."

"No pressure, but yours and Keith's are the only ones we're waiting on."

"Right. No pressure there." Wayne smiled.

"We want to finish the last tracks in the studio tomorrow before Stone leaves."

"I think we can do it if we work hard. We could cut the first song of Cedra's you sang today, too, if you want to knock it out."

"That's not a bad idea," Ma agreed. "It would also give you some cover for being in the studio today without her if Cedra gets wind of it."

"That's right." Wayne smiled. "Brilliant as always, Ma."

"Bring me your plate, Wayne," Ma said as Keith came rushing down the stairs. She slid two eggs on his plate and Juliet added toast.

"Right on time," Ma told Keith. "Are fried eggs good?"

"Perfect."

Ma shook her head. "I don't know if I'll ever not laugh when I hear that word again," she told Juliet.

"It'll be hard," Juliet admitted. "At least until the album comes out." She reached for Keith's plate. "Save ham for Ma and me," she warned Keith.

"I'll cook more if you're still hungry," Ma told him.

"This should be good for a while, Ma."

Ma cooked eggs for herself and Juliet and sat down at the table.

"Go grab your songs when you finish so we can work on them until it's time to leave for the studio," Juliet told Wayne and Keith.

Juliet was still sopping up the egg yolk with her toast when the boys returned. She took a sip of coffee. "Who wants to read first?"

"I will." Keith started reading his lyrics.

"Read the line about the gold band again." Juliet popped the last bite of toast in her mouth. "Why don't you add a gold band on her left hand?"

Keith reread it and nodded. "That does sound better. Anything else?"

"I think it's good. What about y'all?" Juliet asked Ma and Wayne.

"Reread the chorus again, please. It's missing something," Wayne requested. He bobbed his head as Keith read the lines.

"Running fast or staying firm in our small-town, small-town universe," Ma suggested.

Three heads spun to look at Ma, who was rinsing dishes.

"That's it," Juliet declared.

"I like it," Keith cried out. "Ma, you're a genius."

"Hardly, but I do have two good ears." Ma chuckled without turning around.

"Your turn, Wayne," Juliet instructed.

Wayne read through his song and looked up to see Juliet smiling at him. "Damn, bro, I wouldn't change a thing," Keith told him.

"I wouldn't either. That's really good, Wayne," Juliet replied.

Wayne looked at Ma, who had joined them at the table. She smiled. "Exactly what they said. I wouldn't change a thing. Good job, guys."

"Do you need us for anything today, Ma?" Juliet asked.

"Not a thing I can think of. You want to practice Wayne's and Keith's songs, don't you?"

"We might as well since we have time. Bud can help us with the music, too. As long as we're back here by two, no one's the wiser."

"If you manage to cut those four, there are only three left, correct? One of Cedra's and two from Stone?" Ma asked. "I would think you could knock that out easy on Monday."

"I think so, too, Ma. Grab your gear, guys. The banjo, too," she yelled to Keith. "I think that would sound great in your song." Juliet looked at Wayne. "Can you sing while playing the drum pad?"

"Ha! With my eyes closed."

"Let's roll then and see if Bud is his usual early self. Who's driving today?"

"I will," Keith answered.

"Give me your keys, and I'll get your truck warming up."

Keith tossed her the keys, and she slipped outside to start his truck. She rushed back inside for her coat and guitar case. "Damn, it's cold out."

"How about some vegetable soup tonight?"

"With cornbread?" Wayne asked.

"And brownies?" Keith added.

Ma smiled and nodded. "Yes, with cornbread and brownies."

"That sounds great, Ma. Don't worry about lunch for us. We'll play as long as we can and grab something on the way home."

"That's fine. Maybe I'll take a nap."

"Go for it." Wayne pulled on his jacket.

Juliet picked up her guitar. "We'll see you later, Ma. Call if you need anything."

"I will." Ma locked the door behind them.

†

Bud smiled when he looked up to see them enter the studio. "Good morning," he called out.

"Good morning. Thanks for coming in. Do you have any time limits today? We'd like to try a few other songs," Juliet asked.

"I'm good as long as you need me." Bud smiled. "What's on the table? I know 'Perfect' is one of the songs."

"I'm also going to record the first song of Cedra's I ever performed. Wayne and Keith have finished their drafts, and we were hoping you could help us out with them."

"I'll give it my best. Get warmed up, and let me know when you're ready to start."

"Thanks, Bud." Juliet pulled her guitar out and several pages of lyrics.

Wayne took a seat at the drum pad while Juliet and Keith picked up their guitars. "We can knock this out in two runs," she teased.

"I'll take three," Keith replied.

"Nope, you're both wrong. We're going to nail it right off the bat," Wayne replied.

Bud chuckled at their playful banter. They never failed to amaze him with their dedication to production. "I'll go with Juliet," he said to himself. "Wayne could be right too, as much as Juliet wants this, though."

Bud turned the video and audio to record when Juliet nodded to him. *Never hurts to have both.*

Juliet closed her eyes when they started playing as the lyrics began to dance off her tongue. She tried to portray the love she had for Cedra in words, and her voice vibrated with emotion. "I'll be damned," Bud spoke to himself.

When the song ended, they looked up at Bud. "Wayne wins. I think that's a good take. Let's run through the next song, and we can listen and see if there is anything we need to change."

Juliet had performed the next song many times, so recording it was a breeze. "Meet me in the break room," Bud called out.

"This is going too smooth," Keith replied.

"It will give us more time to work on your songs." Juliet grinned. "Won't Cedra be surprised to hear them?"

"That would be great if we could get them down. You go first, bro. I know you've already got the music in your head."

"Sounds good to me," Wayne said.

†

Bud played the first two songs, and they agreed they sounded great. "I don't think I'd change a thing on either of them." He looked at Keith and Wayne. "So, what're we doing next, guys?"

"We decided Wayne will go next. He's got an idea for the music. Let's have him run through it on his guitar until Keith and I pick up on it, and then Wayne will go back to the drum pad to sing and add some percussion," Juliet replied.

"I'm not one hundred percent sold on anything, so any recommendations you make would be appreciated," Wayne added.

"Do you realize that if we can nail these two down, we're only three songs from finishing the new album?" Bud asked.

"Yeah, that hit us this morning," Juliet admitted. "We could be finished by Monday."

Bud nodded. "I've already finished mixing the other tracks. Can we meet to review if I can get the rest done by Thursday? The studio will be shut down all next week."

"I don't see why not."

"Good. We can start the new year off with a second album, a second video, and the *Bentley Break* program. What better Christmas present could we ask for?"

"That would be pretty awesome," Wayne admitted. "Surreal, but awesome."

"Let's get back to work then. Run through the music, and then let me know when you're ready," Bud told them.

Wayne picked up a guitar and joined Keith and Juliet. "This is what I'm thinking." He played through the music twice.

"I think I've got it," Keith replied.

"Me, too." Juliet nodded. "Let's add the drum pad and see what it sounds like."

"That's not a bad sound. Are you ready to put some words to it?" Bud asked Wayne.

"Yes," Wayne answered.

When they started playing, Wayne began to add lyrics. "Stop," he called out after the first verse. "It's dragging. Let's speed it up a bit."

Juliet glanced over at Bud, who nodded in agreement.

"Ready when you are," Keith instructed.

The added tempo was an improvement, and Wayne's vocals were flawless.

"Let's add a run with Keith and Juliet coming in on the chorus," Bud suggested. "Slow the tempo just a bit, but not back to the original."

†

Juliet felt her foot tapping to the music as they played. She looked back at Wayne, who was singing with his eyes closed, and she could feel the longing in his words as he sang. Whoever the woman was in his song, she must have been someone special to him. Juliet made a note to ask him sometime when they were alone. Juliet looked up at Bud and swore he wiped a tear from his cheek when Wayne stopped singing.

"Can we take one more run at it?" Wayne asked.

"We'll do as many as you want," Juliet stated. "Do we need to change anything?"

Wayne shook his head. "You don't, but I need to soften the lyrics a bit in a few spots. The music is tight."

They performed the song again, and Wayne smiled. "Can we have a listen to that one, Bud?"

"You know the drill."

"I'll be right back." Keith peeled off to use the restroom.

Juliet smiled at Wayne. "I think we're going to like the last cut."

"I think so, too."

Keith returned and grabbed a bottle of water before sitting at the table.

"Are we ready?" Bud asked.

Wayne nodded, and they listened to the song twice.

"You've done a great job, Wayne. That's a beautiful song. Are you happy with this track?"

Wayne smiled at Bud and nodded. "Yeah, I am. What about you guys?"

"I think 'Missed Opportunity' will become a popular song," Juliet replied. "It's easy to sing along to, and the music is catchy."

"That brings us to your song." Bud looked at Keith. "Before we get started, could y'all eat some pizza today?"

"We can always eat pizza," Wayne replied. "Do you want me to order some?"

"No, I'll get one of the staff to order. I'll be right back, and we can talk about Keith's song next."

"Dude, you rocked that song," Keith told Wayne.

"I am pleased with the way it came out," Wayne agreed, and his face beamed with a smile.

"I think this exercise has been good for all of us. I think we've realized that songwriting is something all three of us can do," Juliet admitted. "We had this mental barrier that Cedra and Stone helped us tear down."

"I have to admit it was mostly Cedra," Keith stated. "She made it so easy by helping us visualize the song."

Wayne nodded. "I agree. Stone is a good writer, but he doesn't hold a candle to Cedra when it comes to teaching others."

Bud returned and sat beside Keith. "Tell us about your song."

"It's called 'Small Town Universe.'" He smiled. "I went back to my high school days and what my group of friends and I used to do on Friday and Saturday nights in the country. I think we've decided some banjo and drums will be good for the music."

Bud looked at him. "Why don't you sing the song first without music, and we can slowly begin adding instruments."

"That's as good a plan as any," Keith agreed. "Are we ready?"

"Let's do it, man," Wayne said.

Keith sang the song and watched the smiles grow on Wayne and Juliet's faces.

"I love this, even without music," Juliet declared. She turned to Bud. "Where do we start with the music?"

"Start with Keith's banjo, and when you feel like you know where the music is going, add your guitar. Wayne, you can jump in on the drum pad when you feel the rhythm."

"All three of us on the chorus?" Keith asked.

"We can try it both ways, but I like how y'all sound together."

"Okay, Keith, it's on you," Juliet replied. "Play it through once, and I'll try to pick up on the second run." Juliet closed her eyes to listen to the sound of Keith's banjo. Juliet played with him on the second run-through, and Wayne added percussion.

"Wayne, join them with your guitar. I'm not convinced it needs percussion," Bud voiced.

Wayne picked up his guitar and positioned a microphone in front of him. "Ready when you are," he told Keith.

"That was much better. Come take a listen."

The pizza delivery arrived when they entered the break room. "That was great timing," Bud teased.

They opened the three pizza boxes, and Keith started laughing. The box he opened held a dessert pizza. "Apple pie pizza. My favorite. Thanks, Bud."

Bud teased him, "You still have to share, but I know how you love your sweets. Do you want to eat and listen or eat first?"

"I think it's safest to do both," Juliet said. "I can hear Keith's stomach growling from here."

They listened to the last cut, and all agreed that it was better with just the strings. "Are we good with that, or is there something else you want to try?"

Keith beamed. "I'm pleased with it."

"Me too. You all have done well today. Do you want to listen to all four as we eat?"

"That would be perfect." Juliet grinned.

When the four tracks were finished, Bud looked at the group. "How do you want to play this? Do we wait until the end of the day Monday to spring it on Cedra and Stone?"

"I vote yes," Juliet replied. "After we've cut the last three, play these for them and tell them it's a wrap."

"I agree." Wayne nodded.

Keith swallowed quickly. "Me too. I think they will be surprised."

"I think they will be very impressed by your efforts. I am so excited the three of y'all have begun writing. I see a great deal of promise in your skills as writers I wasn't expecting."

Wayne smiled. "We can all thank Cedra for that. She's done a great job teaching us to believe in our writing ability.

She gave us all prompts and assignments, but the lyrics are almost exclusively of our own design. After all the stress we've gone through, she made us realize how fun it could actually be."

Bud smiled. "It's never simple to write a great song, but I admit you have a great teacher. She's got fantastic writing ability."

"Yes, she does," Juliet replied. "I think we'll all take a more active role in writing moving forward."

Wayne glanced at the clock. "It's time for us to get packed up and home before they get off work."

"Thanks again for working with us today, Bud," Juliet said.

"I'll be here any time you all need me," Bud promised. "Keith, will you take the leftover pizza home?"

"I sure will. I can't guarantee it will make it there, though."

Juliet held out her hand. "Give me the keys. You two can eat, and I'll drive." She combined the last few pizza slices in one box while the guys packed up their instruments. Bud tossed the empty boxes in the trash.

"Y'all did really well today, and I'm very proud of what y'all have written. I do hope you will continue to write. I've never seen so much talent in one group before."

"Thank you, Bud. That means the world coming from you. We appreciate all that you have taught us, and I think we have a better understanding of the sound we are trying to create than ever before."

Ali Spooner

"You've got a good ear for the music, and your vocals are powerful and sultry at the same time," Bud told her. "I hope you never lose that quality."

"Me too, Bud. Me too. I guess we'll see you tomorrow afternoon."

"Yes, ma'am, you will. Have a great evening."

"Thanks, Bud."

Juliet left the break room and opened the truck for the boys. She handed Keith the pizza box and climbed behind the wheel. "Let's go home, guys."

†

Ma was waiting for them in the kitchen when they entered. "I'll take it things went well by the smiles on your faces."

"We got all four tracks cut, Ma. They sound pretty danged good, too," Wayne bragged.

Ma smiled at Juliet. "Are you going to be able to keep this a secret?"

"I only have to last one day. When we finish the last three songs tomorrow, Bud is going to play the four we did today as a surprise."

"That's good. I think you can make it until tomorrow," Ma teased.

"Me, too. I think I'll stretch out for a quick nap before Cedra and Stone make it home."

"Relax and enjoy the rest of the day. Y'all have worked hard. I'll have dinner ready at about six. The soup has been cooking, so all I need to do is the cornbread and brownies."

"I can make those," Keith offered. "I know how to thanks to you."

"I'll certainly accept that offer, young man. The kitchen is all yours," she told Keith.

†

Keith was sitting at the table when Cedra and Stone arrived home. "You've got something smelling good," Cedra remarked.

"I'm cooking brownies for tonight," Keith answered.

"Where is everyone?" Stone asked. "It's quiet in here."

"Everyone is taking a nap," Keith replied. "Except me. I decided to try out my new baking skills."

"Well, you certainly have it smelling good. What's Ma fixing for dinner?" Cedra asked.

"She's got vegetable soup cooking and will make some cornbread to go with it," Keith answered.

"That sounds good. I think I'll try to get a nap in, too." Cedra hung her coat by the door.

"That does sound pretty good. Today was a long day," Stone replied.

"Ma told me dinner would be at six," Keith replied as Cedra headed up the stairs.

†

Cedra crept into the room to find Juliet sleeping soundly. She was curled up on her side, and her face looked peaceful. *Like an angel. Yes, my angel.* Cedra walked into the bathroom to change into sweats and a T-shirt. She gently climbed onto the bed and wrapped her body around Juliet, burying her face in Juliet's hair. She could smell the scent from the coconut shampoo she had used. Juliet must have sensed her arrival and reached for her hand to pull her closer to her body without waking. Cedra closed her eyes and breathed in the scent of her lover as lyrics started dancing through her brain.

†

Ma smiled at the two pans of brownies cooling on the counter. She was even more impressed that neither pan had been touched. She was sure it took mighty restraint on Keith's part to prevent sampling. She pulled down a bowl and began mixing cornbread.

†

Cedra heard Ma's footsteps on the stairs, disentangled herself from Juliet, and slipped on her house shoes to go downstairs. Ma was at the counter mixing cornbread batter when she entered. "Hey, Ma. Do you need some help?"

"You can set the table and check the tea to see if we need to make more. Did you get a nap in too?"

"Yes, I did. It was a busy shift today for a Sunday," Cedra replied. She opened the refrigerator and decided to make more tea. She pulled tea bags from the pantry and put a pot of water on the stove to boil. "Will you drink some coffee with me?"

"I'd love a cup," Ma answered as she poured the batter into two preheated cast iron skillets.

Cedra started the coffee pot and set the table while she waited for the water to boil, then dropped the tea bags in to steep. "It turned out sunny after being so cold this morning," she stated as she poured them a cup of coffee.

"I was glad to stay inside today."

"Did y'all have a good day?"

"Yeah, we did. I relaxed, did some Christmas shopping on the internet, and the others worked on their music, I think."

Cedra smiled. "Look at you, shopping on the internet," Cedra teased.

"Hey, I'm learning from you youngins."

"Nothing wrong with that." Cedra grinned.

"Is Hank still planning to arrive Tuesday?"

"Yes, ma'am, he is. I can't wait. Speaking of which, I have some packages being delivered this week. I'll pick up some more wrapping paper. Is there anything else we need?"

"I can't think of anything. I will ask Keith and Juliet to pick out a tree for us tomorrow. It's been a while since I've had one."

"Juliet will love that. They are both like kids excited for Christmas. Do you have lights and decorations?" Cedra asked.

"Yeah, but they are old. I'll ask Juliet to pick up a few strands of lights while they are out."

"I think I need to start waking them up for dinner," Cedra said as she poured sugar into a pitcher and mixed the freshly brewed tea.

"I'm up," Juliet called from halfway down the stairs. "You want me to wake the boys?"

"Yes, please."

"I'll go knock on Stone's door," Ma said.

†

Juliet entered the kitchen and kissed Cedra. "My nice heater left me," she teased.

"I wasn't sure if you knew I was napping with you or not," Cedra replied. "You were sleeping so peacefully."

"I can always tell when you enter or leave the bed, even if I'm sound asleep. His brownies turned out nicely."

"Yes, they did," Cedra agreed.

"I've got an assignment for you and Keith tomorrow," Ma spoke as Keith entered the kitchen.

"What's that, Ma?" Keith asked.

"I want the two of y'all to go pick out a Christmas tree for us and buy some lights to go on it. I have everything else."

"Heck yeah," Keith cried out. "How big can we go?"

"It'll go in the living room, so six, seven feet at the biggest."

"We have a mission," Juliet told Keith. "I've seen some nice ones on a lot at the edge of town."

"We'll go right after breakfast."

"You have studio time tomorrow night, right?"

Cedra nodded. "I hope we can come close to finishing the album. We don't have much left."

"I'll plan on a pot roast for dinner tomorrow night, then. I'll cook it in the crock pot, and it will be hot when y'all make it home."

"That sounds perfect, Ma," Juliet said with a wink.

Ma looked at Juliet. "I'll need to plan an early dinner Tuesday since you will need to get some sleep before you go to town tomorrow night to shoot the video."

"Would you mind if I go with you?" Keith asked.

"Not at all," Juliet replied. "We'll grab some breakfast and drop Cedra at work afterward. She can ride home with Wayne. Stone's leaving from work to go home, right?"

"Yeah, Lisa Marie is booting him out about eleven, I think," Cedra replied.

"Good. That should enable Stone to make it home Tuesday night," Ma stated.

†

"Are you up for some writing tonight?" Cedra asked Juliet after dinner.

"Yeah, I think I've got a new idea." Juliet smiled.

397

"I think we're good on tomorrow's music. Then we'll just have Keith and Wayne's songs to cut, and we will be done. Do you guys need help?"

"Nope, I think we've got this," Wayne answered. "We'll get Stone to help us with the music while y'all go up and write."

†

"Do you want the laptop?" Juliet asked.

"No, go ahead. You seem to do better using it. I've got my trusty songbook." She held up her book.

"You do need some new ones. Not many pages left in that one."

"I may have to resort to post-it notes soon," Cedra teased.

"Naw, I think Santa will bring you some for Christmas. You've been a very good girl this year." Juliet leaned in to kiss Cedra.

"Yes, I have." Cedra laughed and opened her book. She positioned pillows behind her and leaned against the wall.

Juliet opened the laptop and started making notes.

CHAPTER EIGHTEEN

"I think that's a good start to the day," Bud stated as they recorded the last of Stone's songs. "Take five and meet me in the break room for a listen."

"I am ready for a bathroom break," Cedra replied.

"Me, too." Juliet grinned. "I'm dying for a kiss."

Cedra spun around into Juliet's arms when they entered the bathroom and kissed her. "You seem to be excited today," Cedra said when the kiss ended.

Juliet smiled. "I've got the perfect woman. We're almost done with a second album, and our second video is soon to be done. That's plenty for me to be excited about."

"That's a great look for you, too. I don't think you've stopped smiling since we walked in."

"You make me incredibly happy. Now go pee so we can get back to work," Juliet teased.

†

Carrie, Felecia, and Todd were waiting in the break room when they entered. Todd handed Cedra an envelope. "Here are the prints we took Saturday. I promised Ma I'd send them home with you for some enlargements."

"Can we get some extras? I'd like to do some for Christmas presents," Cedra asked.

"Just let me know which ones and the sizes. I'll do the prints, and you can frame and wrap them," Todd replied.

"Thanks, Todd."

"Are you all set for tomorrow night?" Todd asked Juliet.

"All pressed and ready to go." Juliet smiled.

"I'm looking forward to it. The more I think about it, I love the idea," Todd told her. "We've got some great shots to dub in, and I've found the perfect lightning strike for the end."

"That sounds exciting," Carrie replied.

"I can't wait to see it," Felecia added.

When Keith made it to the table, Bud asked, "Are we ready to listen to some tracks?"

"Let's do it, so we can get back to work," Cedra said.

Bud looked at Juliet and smiled.

When the three songs finished playing, Bud addressed the group. "Do we need any changes?"

"I think they sound perfect," Cedra replied.

Keith and Wayne snickered at the end of the table, and Cedra looked at them with a confused look.

"In that case, I have something else I want you to hear."

"Okay, Bud," Cedra replied.

Carrie, Felecia, and Todd seemed as confused as Cedra.

Cedra's head spun to look at Juliet as the music began playing. "'Perfect.' Really? That's a great track," Cedra exclaimed.

"I wanted to do that one for you."

"Now I know why the knuckleheads were chuckling," Cedra teased Wayne and Keith.

"Wait, there's more," Bud replied.

He played the first song of Cedra's that Juliet sang at the Iron Horse. "That sounds better every time you sing it," Cedra told Juliet.

"Wait," Bud grinned.

"There's more?"

"Get a good grip on your seats for these next two," Bud warned. He nodded to Wayne. "You want to do the intro?"

Wayne smiled at Cedra. "I finished 'Missed Opportunity,'" he told her.

Cedra couldn't hold back her excitement during the song, and a tear slipped down her cheek. "That's beautiful, Wayne. You did great."

"With your help," Wayne replied.

"Never to be outdone. Go for it, Keith," Bud instructed.

"You, too?"

"Ladies and gentlemen, please allow me to introduce you to 'Small Town Universe,'" Keith announced.

"Oh my God. Those are both great. When did you record those?" Cedra asked when the song was finished.

"Bud met us yesterday and helped us with the music. We wanted to surprise you." Wayne said. "Originally, it was Juliet's idea to record 'Perfect,' but we decided to knock out our songs and another of yours so we could finish the tracks for the album today."

"What a great surprise," Carrie replied.

"I am so proud of all three of y'all," Cedra told them. "You did a great job with the songs."

"Well, we did have a great teacher," Keith stated.

"Very impressive, guys," Felecia added.

"This dream just keeps getting better and better," Carrie exclaimed. "Please don't wake me."

"Congratulations," Mark's voice came over the intercom. "You've cut your second album in record time. Juliet, Wayne, and Keith, I'm extremely proud of the efforts you've made in writing a song for this album. It makes it even more special."

"Thanks, Mark," Juliet answered. "We wanted to take a more active role in the whole process."

"Mission accomplished. Great job, guys."

"I only have today's three tracks to mix," Bud replied. "Can we meet Thursday to finalize the tracks?"

"Whoa, I need to get started on a cover," Todd stated. "We'll use a still from the video, but I'll need the lyrics."

"I'll bring them on a jump drive to you tomorrow, or I can email them to you?" Juliet suggested.

"Email is fine."

Cedra turned to Juliet. "You guys are so sneaky. I love it, though."

"We're done!" Keith cried out.

"On to the next," Wayne declared.

"I hope you will continue to produce with the quality of the first two," Carrie said.

"I have no reason to believe they won't," Bud replied. "They are hitting their stride as writers and performers. I couldn't be prouder."

"You've been a tremendous help, Bud," Cedra stated.

"I had the easy job." Bud smiled back at her. "Get out of here and go celebrate."

"Yes, boss," Juliet teased.

"I'll see you tomorrow night," Todd told them.

"Yes, you will."

"Felecia and I will see you Thursday when you come in for the final cut listen," Carrie informed them. "Great job."

"Let's pack up and head home, guys," Cedra suggested.

"I'm riding with Cedra," Juliet announced.

"Okay, we're stopping off to buy beer," Keith said. "We need a toast."

"Sounds good to me," Cedra replied.

†

Juliet climbed in beside Cedra. "I have to admit, you did well, keeping this a secret. I had no clue. Did Stone know?" Cedra asked.

"Nope, he only knew about 'Perfect.' The rest we did on our own. Ma was the only other person to know besides Bud."

"You did a beautiful job on 'Perfect.' I was impressed."

"I think of you every time I hear that song."

"Will you sing it for me again tonight?"

"I'd love to. Ma hasn't heard it or the boys' songs. Would you mind if we played them for her? I can always give you a private performance upstairs later."

"Both sound perfect." Cedra broke out laughing.

"Maybe Ma will join us for a toast, and we can hear them then?" Juliet suggested.

†

They carried their instruments inside and set them in the living room. "That's a beautiful tree," Cedra stated as Ma was adding decorations.

"It's the first one I've had in years. Keith and Juliet did a great job picking the perfect tree. Oh, you had some packages come in today. Both of you. I put them on your desks."

"Goody," Cedra replied.

"Where are the boys?"

"They're making a beer run. We need to celebrate tonight, Ma. We finished *Midnight in Nashville* today," Juliet told Ma.

"That's fantastic news. I wondered why you were home so early."

"The secret mission they went on Sunday allowed us to finish today," Cedra stated. "It was a beautiful surprise."

"They were very proud of their accomplishments. I can't wait to hear their songs."

"I'm sure the boys and I will give you a mini-concert tonight," Juliet promised.

"I'm going to check my packages," Cedra said. "I'll be right back."

"I love you." Juliet kissed her as she walked by.

†

Later, after they had gone upstairs for the evening, Juliet picked up her guitar and sat at the desk and sang "Perfect" for Cedra as promised. "You have the perfect voice for that song. No pun intended. It really sounds great."

"Thanks, Baby Girl." Juliet smiled.

"Now go put up that guitar and show me some love," Cedra instructed.

†

Once they could catch their breath, Cedra looked at Juliet. The candle flames were dancing in her dark eyes. "Now that was perfect."

"I'd have to agree with you, my love." Juliet took Cedra in her arms. "Things are just so perfect for us right now. Does it seem scary to you sometimes?"

405

"Not scary, but I don't think things will always seem so effortless for us. We need to continue having as much fun as we can playing together. I bet life gets more stressful once we hit the road."

"Only time will tell. I think we've got a huge advantage over a lot of new bands by having at least two full albums out before we hit the road."

Cedra nuzzled her neck. "That's true, and at least two videos recorded. Are you excited about tomorrow night?"

Juliet's hand stroked down Cedra's bare arm. "Very excited. I'm glad you and Keith are going with me. Especially since Hank arrives tomorrow."

"I'm sure Ma will keep him entertained. I think she plans to do some gift wrapping tomorrow night after dinner. Dad won't be much help, but he can keep her company."

"I hope you get some sleep tomorrow. I worry that you won't have much sleep," Juliet said.

"I'll be fine. I'll be so excited that work will fly by and only one more day before the café closes for the holidays."

"I'll take the photos back to Todd and see if he can print the ones you want for gifts while I wait. He promised it wouldn't take long."

"I'd like to pick up frames for them too. I want to give several to Ma and Lisa Marie. Dad, too. I want the photo of our first autographs to hang up in here."

"Do you have a preference of color for the frames? I can pick them up tomorrow, too," Juliet suggested.

"Why don't we stick with black? It goes with everything," Cedra replied. "I'll leave you some money on the desk in the morning."

"We can split the cost."

"Deal." Cedra snuggled deeper into Juliet. "Goodnight, my love."

"Goodnight, Baby Girl."

†

Cedra hugged Stone. "Be safe and let us know you've made it home. Tell the family hello for us."

"I will," Stone promised. "Y'all have a great Christmas, and I'll see you soon."

"Not so fast, young man," Lisa Marie said. "She hugged him and handed him an envelope. "Merry Christmas. Open it on Christmas, please."

"Be safe, bro." Wayne shook Stone's hand, and hugged him. "Have fun with the family."

"I plan to. I'm outta here." He grinned.

†

"Are you going back to Chattanooga for Christmas?" Cedra asked Lisa Marie between customers.

"Yeah, I had so much fun at Thanksgiving, I thought I'd go back. I'll leave Friday and come back the day after Christmas."

"What's Nashville going to do without the café for five days?" Wayne teased.

"I'm sure Nashville will survive just fine. I want to close early on Thursday too. I know you've got a big meeting to review the next album. I'm so danged excited for y'all."

"We do the recording for the video tonight. Well, actually tomorrow morning," Cedra corrected.

"I'll get you out early tomorrow then. I know you'll be going to watch," Lisa Marie told Cedra.

"Yes, I am. I should be fine. I'll probably be too excited to sleep anyhow. Juliet modeled her outfit for me last night. Damn, she looks great in black."

"Juliet would look good in a paper sack," Lisa Marie teased. "Y'all are such a cute couple. When do they expect to release 'Midnight?'"

"The plan is to start releasing a single every few weeks like they did with 'Six Strings,'" Cedra replied.

"Remember to grab me a couple of copies before they start disappearing, please," Lisa Marie requested.

"You are always on the top of our list."

"Thank you. What time is Hank coming in today?"

"He should be here by four or so. I've already asked Juliet to bring him by for a visit tomorrow."

"Thanks. I'd hate to miss Hank."

"He'll be here until after New Year's Day."

"Good, I'll see him a couple times then."

"Yes, ma'am, you will. If you don't have plans for New Year's Eve, why don't you join us? You can stay in Stone's room."

"I may just do that. It looks like we're done for the day, so why don't you two head out, and I'll see you tomorrow?"

"Thanks, boss." Cedra clocked out.

†

"Juliet asked me to send you upstairs when you got home," Ma said as Cedra walked into the house. "I think she's on another secret mission. She came in with several bags and went straight upstairs."

"I better go see what she's into."

"Have you heard anything from Hank?"

"He'll be here around four."

"I would have suggested a nap, but I think Juliet's got other plans for you," Ma added with a chuckle.

"Sounds like it." Cedra hung her jacket and headed upstairs.

†

Juliet looked up when Cedra entered. "Welcome home, Baby Girl," Juliet said and pointed to the spread of photographs she had framed and displayed on their bed. Then she turned and pointed to their autograph photo now proudly hanging over the desk. "Is that spot okay with you?"

"It's perfect. You've been busy. Those look great."

409

"I thought we could box them up and wrap them before Hank gets here so we'd have some gifts wrapped under the tree. Unless you're tired and need a nap."

"Nope, I'm good." Cedra picked up a roll of paper, scissors, and tape then spread it out on the floor. "Hand me the ones we want for Ma first. Did you get enough boxes?"

"I got one for every frame."

"Good job. I'll start on those, and you can make out the tags."

"Dammit."

"Don't worry, Ma's got plenty. Go down and ask her for some."

"I'll be right back." Juliet rushed out of the room.

†

Keith pulled out a pan of brownies when Juliet walked into the kitchen to ask Ma for tags. "Damn, those smell good. You're turning into a regular baker."

"I thought I could give Ma a break. I'm making cookies, too."

"Good job. Ma, can I get some present tags from you? Cedra told me you have some. I forgot to buy some today."

"Yeah, I've got a bunch." Ma retrieved several sheets for Juliet.

"Thanks, Ma." Juliet kissed her on the cheek before bolting out of the kitchen.

"You're welcome," Ma called after her. "I guess that explains her secrecy this afternoon. She needed help wrapping gifts."

"You're still helping us tonight, right?" Keith asked.

"I sure am."

†

Juliet and Cedra wrapped presents until Hank arrived. Juliet carried a stack of boxes and placed them under the tree. "I have some to go under the tree, too. Wayne, Keith, will you help me?" Hank asked.

"Sure thing." Keith jumped up and met Hank and Wayne at the door.

Cedra came down and met them when they returned. "Hey, Dad." She kissed him on the cheek. "I'm so glad you made it safe."

"Me too, Baby Girl," Hank answered as he handed Juliet a stack of boxes for the tree. "Ma says she's putting me to work tonight, while you two get some sleep before you have to go shoot the video. That's so exciting."

"Will you and Ma join us Thursday to review the album and video?" Juliet asked.

Hank looked at Ma. "What do you think?"

"Hell yes. We can do dinner afterward to celebrate if we can find anything open."

"Or, I can barbecue some chicken if you'll make some sides," Hank suggested.

"That sounds even better," Ma replied. "Macaroni and cheese, beans and slaw good for you?"

"That sounds good to me, Ma," Keith said. "I'll grate the cabbage for you if you want."

"You are becoming so domesticated, Keith," Hank teased. "It's good for a young man to have some kitchen skills."

"Ma says I'm a work in progress, but I'm doing well." Keith puffed out his chest.

"He's become quite the baker," Ma praised. "I'm thinking of teaching him to make biscuits tomorrow."

"Why not tonight, Ma? You always make biscuits to go with the pot roast."

"You're on. Go wash your hands, and we'll get started, so these girls can eat and get some sleep. Take Hank's bag up when you go, please."

"Got it, Ma."

"Can I get you a cup of coffee, Hank?" Ma asked.

"That sounds good." Hank took off his coat. "I hope you don't mind, Ma, but I invited Lisa Marie to join us for New Year's Eve. I don't know if she'll come or not, but she can use Stone's room."

"That's fine with me. Patsy may join us, too, but she can bunk with me."

†

After dinner, Cedra and Juliet went upstairs to get some sleep. Cedra was ready to snuggle into Juliet, and she hoped she wouldn't be too excited to sleep. They'd get up at midnight and meet Keith at a quarter to one. At that time, traffic would be light, and they wouldn't have to wait long once they arrived.

†

Ma, Hank, and the boys wrapped some presents around the kitchen table.

"Your biscuits turned out great, bro," Wayne praised.

"I think with Ma's supervision a few more times, I should be able to do them on my own," Keith replied.

"I'll be glad to help you practice. Can you teach Keith to make your sausage gravy, too, Ma?" Wayne asked.

"That could be arranged."

"I need to get in on those lessons," Hank teased. "I can't make a decent gravy to save my life."

"You probably just overthink it. I'm sure we'll have a chance for lessons while you're here."

"Are you going to try to sleep?" Ma asked Keith.

Keith shook his head. "Naw, I'm good. I'll nap when we get home in the morning after dropping Cedra off at work."

†

Keith was sitting in the living room watching television when Cedra and Juliet came downstairs. "Damn, girl, you look good in black," Keith stated, a bit too loud.

413

"Shhh, you're going to wake up the house," Juliet teased.

"I've got the truck warmed up if you're ready."

"Did you sleep at all?" Cedra asked.

"Naw, I'll nap when we get home. Umm, Juliet, are you forgetting something?"

"Shit yeah. Hang on." Juliet climbed the stairs to get her guitar and harmonica.

"Thanks for catching that," Cedra stated. "That would have been embarrassing."

"No problem."

"Great catch." Juliet returned with her instruments.

Keith grinned. "Ready to roll?"

"I think so." Juliet pulled her coat on.

†

Todd was waiting on them when they arrived. "Hey guys," he said when they stepped out of the truck. "We're just waiting on the police to finish blocking off the road, and we can get started. I want to get two takes before they send us on our way."

He started to walk away and turned back to Juliet. "You look damned good in black." He grinned.

"See, I told you," Keith replied.

They followed Todd to his truck. He introduced his wife, Stella. "She will drive while I film from the tailgate as you come down the street."

"Hey, guys. Todd raves about you all, and I love your music."

"Thanks," Cedra replied. "Todd's been great to work with."

"He's a pretty good guy. I think I'll keep him around for a bit," Stella teased.

"Thanks, baby. Do you want to ride on the tailgate with me?" Todd asked Cedra and Keith.

"We'd love to," Cedra replied.

"I promise to be quiet," Keith stated.

Todd laughed. "Can he do it for five minutes?" he asked Cedra.

"It may be tough, but I have faith in him."

"When we get to the end of the video, I want you to jump in with Stella," he told Juliet. "She'll keep the heat cranked up for you."

"Thanks. It's a bit chilly."

"Did you bring a coat to wear until we start shooting?" Todd asked.

"Yeah, it's in the truck."

"I'll grab it for you." Keith jogged back to the truck.

"I want you to stroll leisurely down the center of the street until you reach the yellow X I taped as a marker for you. Then pull out your harmonica and start playing. It doesn't matter what you play. I can dub over it, but play the ending if you want. I never get tired of hearing it," Todd told her.

"Facial expression?"

"Thoughtful or a smile. Your choice. That I can't dub." He chuckled.

"Thoughtful," Cedra suggested. "If it doesn't feel right, a smile on the second take."

"Good suggestion," Todd agreed.

"Okay, Juliet, hop inside and get warm. Tell Stella she can drive us to the starting spot we discussed. You two, hop on the tailgate with me."

Stella drove them up the center of Lower Broadway and then made a U-turn. "Good luck," she told Juliet.

"Thanks." Juliet took off her coat to lay it on the seat.

"Okay, put your case over your shoulder," Todd instructed. "Got your harmonica?"

Juliet positioned the case across her back. "Right here," she said as she lifted her hand to show him the instrument.

"Ready?"

"All set." Juliet took a deep breath.

"Okay, on three, start walking," Todd instructed. He sat on the tailgate between Cedra and Keith. He steadied the camera on a trolley in front of him. "That looks good. One, two, three."

Juliet looked up at the camera and started strolling down the center of Lower Broadway.

✝

Cedra's heart pounded with excitement as she watched Juliet. Damn, she was sexy as she walked down the neon-clad street. The expression on her face was perfect, the pensive look of someone deep in thought. She saw the X appear from under the truck and watched Juliet lift the harmonica to her mouth to begin playing. She played the ending to the song, and as she played the last note, the roar of a jet engine filled the air. Juliet never missed a beat as she continued to walk.

"Damn, I didn't consider UPS flights coming in from Louisville," Todd said. "I think we are okay, and she had just finished playing. I can dub out the jet."

"That was totally unexpected," Juliet stated as she caught up with the truck.

"I forgot about checking the UPS schedules, but I think we are okay. You had finished playing before it roared in. Give Keith your case and hop in to warm up as we go back down the street."

When they stopped at the starting point, the female police officer shrugged. "I can stop road traffic, but I can't control the skies," she joked.

"That's true. I think we're okay, though," Todd called back to her.

"You've got plenty of time left for several more takes," the officer informed them.

Todd gave her a thumbs-up. He hopped off the tailgate and walked to the truck's passenger side. Juliet rolled the window down. "You did great. The pacing was perfect. I want to shoot two more if you're good with that."

"As many as it takes to get what you need." Juliet smiled.

"Are you warm?"

"Stella has me toasty. Are you ready?"

"Yes, when you are."

He walked back to the tailgate and took his position while Keith handed Juliet her guitar case. Keith returned, and Todd started recording. "One, two, three," he called out.

They made it to the end of that run without jet noise. "That was good. Do you want to try one with a smile? Not a toothy smile, something sultry. Like you do when you look at Cedra," he teased.

"I'll just keep my eyes on her until it's time to start playing," Juliet shot back to him.

"Works for me. Do you need to warm up?"

"I'm good."

"Hop in, and let's get back to the starting point."

When they reached the start line, Todd stated, "This should be interesting."

"What?"

Todd lifted his hand and pointed behind her. "We've got some fog rolling in. It might make a great backdrop. Ready?"

Juliet smiled. "All set."

"One, two, three," Todd called out.

Juliet locked eyes with Cedra and gave her the look Todd hoped for. Todd was beaming when she finished playing and caught up to the truck. "Holy shit, that looked good. Hop in the truck, and we will drive back to the start point to let the police know we are done," Todd instructed.

Todd walked over to talk with the police officer and thank her for blocking off the road.

"No problem. I love the Bentleys," the officer replied.

"Give me your information, and I'll make sure you get a copy of the new album we shot this video for." Todd took down her information.

"That's awesome," the officer replied. "Thank you."

"Thank you." He put the camera in a case and loaded the trolley into the back of the truck. "Do y'all have time for breakfast?"

"Yeah, we planned on getting some before dropping Cedra off at work," Juliet replied.

"The Redbird, right?" Todd asked. "What time do you have to be there?"

"Five," Cedra answered.

"We've got plenty of time then." Todd grinned. "Follow us."

Keith had started the truck, and Juliet warmed up quickly. He followed Stella to an all-night breakfast place and pulled in beside them.

Juliet smiled when she saw him pull out his camera case. Todd saw her smile. "You want a look?"

"Hell, yes," Juliet answered.

"I was hoping you would." Todd grinned.

They were taken to a large booth big enough Todd could place the case beside him and pull out the camera. They ordered while he cued up the video. He took a sip of coffee and pressed play. They watched all three takes while they waited on the food to arrive.

"Okay, so which one did you like the best?" Todd asked.

"I'm neutral here, but that last one is damn hot," Stella chimed in.

They broke out in laughter. "I agree with you, honey. That fog in the distance accented the shot, and that look you were giving Cedra sizzled."

"I don't think any of us disagree with you," Cedra replied. "They were all good, but the last one was perfect."

"I'll go ahead and mock up all three for Thursday's meeting, but I think three is the winner." Todd packed away the camera as the waitress started delivering food. "Damn, this looks good."

"May we get two large glasses of apple juice?" Juliet asked the waitress.

"No problem. More coffee, too?"

"Yes, please. Keep it coming." Todd answered.

"Thanks for ruining your sleep tonight to make this video," Juliet said.

"Girl, he's been dying to make this video since you started talking about it," Stella replied. "He'll have it mocked up by the end of the day."

"Well, thank you for coming out in the middle of the night."

"I enjoyed meeting y'all and being a part of this. I'll be asleep as soon as my head hits the pillow," Stella replied with a smile.

"Me too," Keith admitted.

"I'll stay up with Ma and nap when Cedra gets home from work."

"That's sweet," Stella said. "I think she loves you just a bit."

"Maybe just a bit." Cedra smiled. "I had a thought when you were recording the last take."

"What's that, Baby Girl?"

"When we do get to hit the road, I'm buying you a black fedora to go with that outfit."

"Will you make an exception and wear one, too?"

"For you, yes, I would."

"Uh oh, we're starting to approach the mushy zone," Keith teased.

"Hush," Cedra, Juliet, and Stella cried out in unison.

"You heard the ladies, Keith," Todd warned.

"Uh-hm." Keith filled his mouth with pancakes, and smiled.

The waitress brought them the check, and Todd took it. Cedra was about to complain when he shook his head. "Compliments of Big Machine. Mark told me to make sure you were well fed."

"That was a great breakfast," Keith stated. "Thank you. We'll thank Mark when we see him again."

"He'll be there, Thursday. He's extremely excited to see the video and hear the new album."

"We are, too. We're bringing Ma and Cedra's dad, Hank, with us," Juliet replied.

"That's a good plan. Have you given Ma the photos you had printed for her yet?" Todd asked.

"Nope, they are under the Christmas tree, though," Juliet stated.

"That's what y'all were sneaking around about?" Keith asked.

"Yeah, I can't wrap to save my life, so I had to wait on Cedra," Juliet admitted.

"They turned out really nice," Cedra said. "When you pick out a still from tonight for the cover, will you go ahead and print me out a copy?"

"It would be a pleasure. I may do a couple different ones for you."

"That works. I reckon we'd better go so I can get to work. Thanks for everything," Cedra replied. "It was great meeting you, Stella."

"Same here. Maybe after the holidays, we can have y'all over for a cookout if it's warm enough. He cooks a great steak."

"Count us in," Keith promised. "Ready, ladies?"

†

Keith pulled up to the front door, and Juliet stepped out of the truck to open the door for Cedra. She pulled her into a hug and kissed her. "Thank you for going with me. I hope you have a good day. I can't wait to wrap my arms around you for a nap."

"Me, too. Love you."

"I love you, too."

Lisa Marie opened the door for Cedra. "Damn, don't you look sexy," she told Juliet and winked.

"Thanks. See you later." Juliet climbed in beside Keith.

CHAPTER NINETEEN

Ma rode with Cedra and Juliet while Hank went with the guys to the studio. "I am so excited to see how things turned out," Juliet said.

"We will know here shortly," Ma replied.

"Yes, we will," Cedra answered.

Mark, Carrie, Bud, and Felecia waited for them in the break room. All of them were wearing smiles, so Cedra thought that was a good thing. They settled in around the table, and Mark called out to Todd. "Everyone is here, Todd. Please join us."

The door opened, and Todd stepped inside carrying two objects. The first was a large picture frame and the second a bag. When he turned the picture toward them, Cedra let out a gasp. Todd had blown up a still to use for the cover, and at the bottom were the title and the band name.

"Dear Lord above, that's one sexy cover," Ma praised.

Juliet remained speechless as she stared at the photograph.

Cedra could only nod in agreement with Ma's assessment. "Hell, I'd buy the album just for the cover," Keith declared.

"That's really beautiful," Wayne replied.

"Ladies?" Todd asked.

"All I can say is, wow," Juliet exclaimed.

Cedra regained her power of speech. "That's mine, right?"

Todd broke out laughing. "Yes, Stella framed it for you, and she also sent you these." Todd handed the bag to Cedra.

Cedra opened the bag and smiled as she pulled out two black fedoras.

"I love them," Juliet said. She put one on her head right away. "Fits perfect." She placed the other hat on Cedra's head. "It looks good on you too."

"Please send our thanks to Stella." Cedra grinned as she adjusted the hat.

Bud nodded. "My only regret is that we didn't think of this before we shot the video, but given everyone's reaction to the photo, I don't think they were needed." He smiled. "Other copies are coming, but none this size. This was special for y'all."

"Thank you, Todd," Cedra replied and hugged his neck. She couldn't help but stare at the photo. "Damn, you look great."

"It was a difficult decision on which still to use, but I think this was the best," Todd shared.

Cedra placed it carefully on the table before her.

"That was a well-received cover reveal, Todd. Do you want to share the video with us, and we'll move on to the album?" Mark asked.

"I thought you'd never ask." Todd grinned.

"Finally," Carrie teased. "He hasn't let any of us see it yet," she complained.

Todd picked up the remote and hit play. The fog behind them on the last shot muted the brightness of street lights and added to the ambiance of the video. They watched in stunned silence as the song played and the photo's flashed throughout the video. When Juliet played the final note on the harmonica, the sky lit with a bolt of spider lightning illuminating the downtown skyline.

Cedra actually jumped in her seat when the bolt flashed. Mark led the applause. "Very well done, guys."

Felecia grinned. "I can't wait to start streaming that."

Bud looked at Juliet. "Well done," he told her.

"That came out fantastic," Cedra praised Todd. "Better than I ever dreamed it would."

"It was all your idea. I just put it together," Todd reminded her. "No recommendations for a change then?" he asked.

"Not a one," Carrie replied.

"Take it away then, Bud," Todd said and took a seat beside Keith.

"As impressive as the video turned out, I hope you will be as pleased with the album. We ended up with seventeen tracks, including the covers we added," Bud explained. "Headphones, please everyone."

†

The entire album ended up a few minutes beyond an hour in length. Faces were filled with smiles, laughter, and a few tears as the songs played. Juliet's "Perfect" cover once more brought Cedra and Felecia to tears. When Wayne's music played last, everyone removed the headphones.

"Is it good enough for *Midnight in Nashville?*" Bud asked.

"Damn straight it is," Keith announced.

"Are we all in agreement?" Bud asked.

"I believe we are, Bud," Mark answered.

"Good, I've already burned a few copies for the band. Todd burned the video for you as well," Bud stated as he started passing out copies to everyone, including Ma and Hank. "Carrie will deliver a copy to the Redbird and Wild Bill's in appreciation for the use of their venues."

Juliet asked the burning question. "So, what's next?"

"Some much-needed break time for you all," Mark replied. "You've worked hard to create two albums, videos, and music for the *Bentley Break* show."

"I plan to begin your first segment of the show on January fifth," Felecia informed them. "It's not required, but I would love for you to be here to listen to the first show."

"We will definitely be here," Juliet promised. "Just let us know what time."

"I will keep you informed," Felecia replied.

"I have been very impressed with the new writing skills you, Keith, and Wayne have demonstrated, and I hope you will use this break time to write some new material," Bud said to answer Juliet. "It's been a pleasure working with you all, and I hope we can get back into the studio after the New Year."

"We will be ready," Cedra assured him. "I think we are starting to hit our stride."

"I hope you will all have great holidays and an even better start to the new year," Mark stated as he stood.

Todd handed Cedra a large envelope. "Here are some extra copies of the cover shot."

Cedra hugged Todd and Bud before clutching the photo and envelope to her chest. "Thank you all so much. For everything," Cedra told them.

After sharing their goodbyes, the crew walked out to the trucks. "What a great day," Juliet said.

"The album and video turned out amazing," Hank replied. "I am very proud of you all for doing such a wonderful job."

"Congratulations," Ma stated. "Are y'all ready to go home and celebrate?"

428

†

"I think a cold beer is in order," Wayne agreed. "Then we can finally sink our teeth in that chicken you've been tantalizing us with all day."

"That sounds like a great plan to me," Hank replied. "Do we need to make a beer run?"

"Naw, we've still got plenty at home," Keith answered.

"Ma, could I ask you to ride with the boys?" Juliet asked. "There's a side trip we need to make. We won't be too long."

"Not a problem." Ma smiled, and Hank opened the door for her.

†

Cedra placed her cover photo and envelope on the back seat and climbed behind the wheel. "The Bluffs?" she asked.

"Yes, ma'am. If you please."

"I do." Cedra smiled and started the truck.

†

"I think you and Bud deserve a raise," Mark said as they watched the two trucks leave the lot.

"I certainly won't complain," Carrie replied.

"Me either, but it was indeed a pleasure working with them. The Bentleys have such a promising future," Bud stated.

"Yes, they do," Mark agreed. "I'm heading home. I hope you both will have a wonderful Christmas."

"You too, boss," Carrie responded.

When Mark left, Carrie turned and hugged Bud. "You did a fantastic job with them."

"You brought me a dream group to work with. Go find us more like them," Bud teased.

"I'm not sure there are any other groups like them, but I'll sure keep looking," Carrie said. "Merry Christmas."

"You, too, Carrie."

†

"What are the girls up to?" Hank asked Ma.

"They have found a secluded spot on a bluff that overlooks Nashville. They often go there to celebrate important events together," Ma explained. "It's on the way home, so they won't be far behind us."

†

Cedra pulled into the overlook. "I would like us to have a home with this view one day."

"Maybe we will. I want to thank you for making my every dream come true. Seeing the video today and listening to our second album was unbelievable. I never would have dreamed this could be possible six months ago."

"We all worked hard to make it happen."

"Yes, but you have always been the backbone. The writer and creative thinker that has propelled us forward."

Cedra leaned toward Juliet, intent to kiss her, and laughed when the brims of their hats struck together. They pulled them off and shared a passionate kiss.

Cedra sighed and leaned back in her seat when the kiss ended. "What now, Ms. Tucker?" she asked.

"We do exactly as the boss suggested. We recharge our batteries and continue to write as many new songs as possible. Maybe the new year will bring good news regarding touring or playing some local gigs."

"We will be prepared when that day finally comes," Cedra promised.

"I have no doubt in that or in us. You know what?"

"What?"

"I've got the name of the title song for the next album and our first tour." Juliet smiled.

"Really? Lay it on me."

"'Out and Loud.' I've already got the lyrics dancing around up here." Juliet tapped her temple. "When we get to tour, I think it would be awesome to pair up with other out gay artists. Maybe tap into some of the bigger Pride Festivals."

"I love it. Especially that you're already planning our first tour." Cedra smiled. "Are you ready to go home, my sexy video star?"

"I'll go anywhere with you, my love."

OUT AND LOUD PREVIEW

Out and Loud

Songwriters Series Book 3

Prologue

The Bentleys, a new country band formed in Nashville, have completed the final review of their second album, *Midnight in Nashville*, and their second music video. The Covid-19 pandemic has halted all live performances and tour dates, so the group has taken advantage of additional studio time to record the new album. Stone Watson, one of the group's writers has returned home to Florida to spend the Christmas holidays with his wife and daughter while the rest of the group celebrates at Ma Bentley's boarding house with Hank Tyler, Cedra's dad.

Chapter One

Cedra, Juliet, and Hank sat around the kitchen table while Ma taught Keith how to make oatmeal and chocolate chip cookies.

"My mom used this recipe off the Quaker box for years. I could hardly wait until they came out of the oven," Keith told them as he stirred in the chocolate chips.

"I bet you burned your mouth on them several times," Juliet teased.

"Don't you know it?" Keith answered. "Where'd Wayne get off to?"

"I think he may be upstairs working on a song," Cedra replied. "I saw his head bobbing while we ate dinner. That usually means he's got music in his head."

"I think it's great that you all have committed to writing," Hank said. "You did great on your songs for *Midnight*."

Juliet placed her hand on Cedra's shoulder. "I think we all have Cedra to thank for that. She was relentless in insisting we could all write."

"Thankfully so," Ma agreed. "Look what it produced."

Cedra nodded. "I agree. This album is even better than the first."

"You think so?" Juliet asked.

"Maybe not better, but a different sound," Cedra added.

"I think it's the confidence factor," Hank replied. "With the first album done, you all seem much more confident now that you know that you have a great sound together."

"I think that is spot on," Ma replied. "You aren't tentative or afraid to try something different. You understand the sound you are looking to create, and it comes more naturally." Ma glanced over at Keith. "You done mixing?"

"Yes, ma'am." He grinned. "My arms are aching."

Ma handed him a spoon and pointed to the cookie sheet. "Get to spooning. Three to a row, and we'll put the first batch in to bake." She tore off a sheet of wax paper and spread it on the counter.

"Put them there to cool off?" Keith asked.

Ma nodded. "Yes, sir, that's the plan. Can you keep from burning yourself while they cool?"

"I think so, Ma." Keith grinned.

He had just set the timer when Wayne came rushing downstairs. "It's snowing," he cried out.

Keith rushed to the door with him to look outside. "It's sticking, too," Keith hollered. Keith looked at the stove and then at the front door.

"Go ahead," Ma said. "I'll keep the cookies going."

Keith hung his head.

"Go!" Ma repeated. "I've got this."

Keith rushed over and kissed her cheek. "Thanks, Ma." He looked at Juliet and Cedra. "You coming?"

Cedra looked at Juliet. "Let's go. We'll be back, Ma."

"You two go ahead. Hank and I'll stay in where it's nice and warm," Ma teased.

Cedra handed Juliet her coat. "Be back soon."

"Stay warm," Hank called after them. He chuckled and looked at Ma. "What are the chances for a white Christmas?"

Ma cocked her head. "Well, it's Christmas Eve, it's snowing, and if it sticks, I'd say the odds are good."

"We had a white Christmas once, but Cedra was only two or three. I doubt she even remembers."

They heard the laughter from outside. Ma looked at Hank. "Go ahead and join them. I've got this handled."

"You sure?" Hank asked.

"Go for it. Just don't break anything," Ma teased.

†

Hank pulled his coat on and walked out onto the porch. Cedra was bent over, laughing as Keith tried to scoop enough snow for a snowball. It had been a long time since Cedra had been so happy. He looked around for Wayne, who was sneaking around the vehicles gathering snow. Juliet and Cedra were so busy watching Keith they had lost track of Wayne. Hank watched as Wayne molded the snow into a ball and let it fly just as Cedra bent over, and it hit Juliet on her arm. The surprise on Juliet's face made Hank laugh.

"You are so in for it now," Juliet yelled and grabbed Cedra's hand as they raced for the cover of her truck. Juliet and Cedra scooped handfuls of snow and formed balls as they stalked Wayne and Keith. They had reached the back of Wayne's truck when Keith and Wayne popped up and launched. Cedra ducked out of the path, but Juliet took both shots before they raced after the boys.

†

Hank remained safely on the porch leaning against a pillar as the snowball war ensued. It was difficult to determine who was having the most fun, but when Cedra's hands became cold, she stuck them around Juliet's neck.

"Damn, that's cold." Juliet laughed.

"I'm going in to get warmed up and put my gloves on," Cedra stated and dashed through a rain of snowballs as she ran for the porch.

"Duck." She heard Juliet cry out, but it was too late. An errant throw caught Hank right in the chest as he was watching Cedra.

"Now you've gone and done it," Hank declared as he wiped the snow from his chest and raced out to join Team Juliet.

"Come on, Dad, let's get them," Juliet called as Cedra disappeared into the house.

†

Cedra wiped her feet off on the rug. "It's gotten cold out there," she told Ma as she entered the kitchen.

"Did you abandon Juliet?" Ma asked.

"Naw, Dad teamed up with her. My hands are freezing, but I don't want to ruin my gloves."

Ma nodded toward the foyer. "Look in the bottom drawer of the foyer table. There should be some gloves that will fit you and Juliet. The boys are on their own."

"Thanks, Ma. You okay in here?" Cedra asked.

The timer went off, and Ma pulled one pan out and slipped another inside. "I'll put on a fresh pot of coffee, and we can have warm cookies when y'all come inside."

"That sounds good," Cedra said as she slipped her hands inside the gloves. "Thanks, Ma."

"Be careful," Ma warned as Cedra returned outside.

Cedra rejoined Juliet and Hank, and the added advantage had the boys running for cover. Keith called a truce and started jogging toward the porch when they all tired. When Keith's boot hit the frozen sidewalk, his feet shot out, and he landed in the snow-covered grass.

"Well, damn. At least I had a soft landing." Keith reached up to take Wayne's hand. "I don't reckon I need to tell you to be careful," he said as he wiped himself off.

"That was fun," Hank declared as he pushed the front door open and pulled off his coat.

"Yeah, it was, Dad. You're a great shot."

"I can attest to that," Wayne reported. "He got me in the head twice."

"I probably shouldn't admit I was aiming for his chest then," Hank replied and broke out laughing.

"Does anyone want hot chocolate?" Ma called from the kitchen.

"Sounds great, Ma," Keith replied.

"That does sound good," Cedra agreed. "What can I do to help, Ma?"

"Grab a bag of marshmallows from the pantry. I've already got the hot chocolate on the stove. There's fresh coffee, Hank."

"Are you ready for a cup, Ma?" Hank asked.

"Yeah, that would be great." Ma handed him her mug.

Cedra looked at Juliet. "Coffee or hot chocolate?"

"Hot chocolate," Juliet answered. "The cookies look good."

"Go ahead and plate some up, please," Ma told her. "There's more coming out soon."

Wayne took a sip of the hot chocolate. "I had forgotten how good this is from scratch. I'm so used to the packaged type."

"It is delicious, Ma. Thank you," Juliet said.

Ma smiled. "I hope it will help get y'all warmed up after being outside. Is it still snowing?"

"Huge flakes, Ma. They are so pretty as they come spiraling down," Keith answered.

"Hopefully, it will continue, and we'll have a white Christmas tomorrow." Ma pulled out another sheet of cookies.

"I'll get the next pan ready, Ma. Sit and relax for a minute," Keith told her.

Ma handed him the potholder. "I won't argue with you. Just don't get burned."

Keith smiled. "I'll be careful, Ma."

Juliet smiled. "Is it my imagination, or is that pile of presents growing?" She pointed at the tree. "That tree sure looks good with the light and decorations."

"It is a beautiful tree," Hank replied. "It reminds me of when we'd go out and cut our own when you were growing up," he told Cedra.

"I don't think we ever got one that pretty, though." She chuckled. "I'll admit it was a lot of fun hunting it down."

Wayne looked at Cedra. "I worked at a Christmas tree farm one summer in high school. I didn't think I would ever finish shaping trees so they would grow to perfection like that."

"We never had a big tree like this one," Juliet replied. "Ours always looked like the Charlie Brown tree." She chuckled.

"I love the smell of a fresh tree," Ma admitted. "Those artificial trees just don't do it for me, and that fake canned smell is horrid."

"I'll agree with ya on that," Hank stated. "I mentioned getting an artificial tree one year, and I thought Cedra and her mom were going to toss me out of the house until I promised we'd get a real one."

"I remember that, and yes, you almost did get tossed. That was our last real Christmas," Cedra said, then ducked her head to hide the tears suddenly filling her eyes.

"We will always have a real tree then. Next year, maybe two if Ma will let us put one on the front porch," Juliet replied.

"We can get a bunch of lights on sale after Christmas and light up the front porch, too," Keith suggested.

Ma smiled at the thought that the group planned to be with her next Christmas. "Why don't we get one to plant in the front yard this spring?"

"Can we, Ma? I'll dig the hole," Wayne promised. "Maybe if I go home for a visit, I'll stop by the farm and get one already established."

"That would be great," Ma agreed.

Juliet laughed. "Look at us planning for next Christmas, and we haven't made it through this one."

Cedra looked at Ma. "I hope this is one of many we spend here."

"Me, too. This house hasn't seen this much joy in years," Ma replied.

"Is there anything we need to prep for tomorrow?" Hank asked.

"Not tonight," Ma replied. "Kitchen Keith is going to make biscuits, and I'll make some gravy for breakfast. We need to know if we eat before or after gifts?"

"Let's eat before," Wayne suggested. "Then we can open gifts."

"I've got a lot of the sides prepped already," Ma said. "You can peel and slice potatoes after the gifts," she told Hank. "Cedra and Juliet already have desserts made, and I can pop the ham into the oven first thing and still have room for biscuits."

Keith pulled out a final pan of cookies, sliding them off the pan to cool.

"You've gotten very handy in the kitchen," Hank praised.

"Ma's a good teacher."

"Yes, she is," Juliet agreed. "I've learned how to make buttermilk pies and caramel cake this week. I hope you like them."

"I'm sure they will be delicious, and no crumb will go uneaten," Cedra stated.

Juliet looked out the window and saw that it was still snowing. "Do y'all want to get another cup of something hot, and sit on the porch to watch it snow before it's time to head to bed?"

"That sounds nice," Hank replied. "Will you join us for a bit, Ma?"

"I'd like to. Pour us more coffee while I get my coat and scarf," Ma requested and passed Hank her mug.

"I'm going to wash these pans, and I'll be out," Keith told them.

"I'll get them later," Cedra replied.

"My mess, my cleanup." Keith smiled. "It won't take me long."

"There's enough hot chocolate for three more," Juliet reported as she began refilling mugs.

"I'll swap over to coffee," Wayne offered.

Cedra handed Juliet her coat, and the group walked onto the porch and sat in chairs or the swing. Juliet placed her arm around Cedra's shoulder and pulled her close as they began to move.

"It's sticking well," Hank pointed out.

"If it goes like this all night, we could have several inches," Ma suggested.

"It's cold enough," Hank replied, then sipped his coffee. "I'm glad I don't have to drive in this."

Cedra smiled at her dad. "I'm glad none of us have to go anywhere for a couple of days at least."

"We'll have to make a milk run in a few days," Wayne teased. "I've got four-wheel drive and the most experience driving in snow, so I'll go. Just let me know if there's anything else we'll need, Ma."

"I'll go with ya," Hank offered.

Keith stepped onto the porch. "Where are we going?"

Ma rocked in her chair. "Wayne and Hank were discussing a milk run in a day or so."

"Do you think the snow will last long?" Keith asked.

Ma saw the shine of excitement in Keith's eyes. "I hope so. It sure is beautiful."

"I'd love to bundle up tomorrow and build a snowman," Keith told them.

"I've never seen that much snow," Cedra admitted. "It looks like so much fun."

"We'll bundle up after we open gifts and come out to play," Juliet promised.

"That will be fun." Cedra smiled and leaned into Juliet.

"Too bad Stone isn't here," Wayne replied.

"I bet he calls tomorrow," Ma stated.

Cedra smiled. "I'm sure he's having a blast with his family. Destiny is old enough to enjoy Christmas now."

"Speaking of family. I'm going to call it a night and call home," Wayne said.

"Me, too," Keith added. "I don't want to wait and forget tomorrow. I hope everyone's gifts made it on time."

"Are you going to call home?" Cedra asked Juliet.

Juliet nodded. "I'll wait until the morning. The folks are probably already in bed tonight."

"That's right. Your family is an hour ahead of us," Cedra replied.

"Merry Christmas, guys," Hank called out as Wayne and Keith walked into the house.

"You, too," Keith replied. "Make sure I'm up, please, Ma."

"I will. Sleep well," Ma answered.

Ma stood and collected mugs. "I think I'll wash these and head up to bed, too."

"I'll help you," Hank volunteered, and took Juliet and Cedra's mugs. "I'll see y'all in the morning."

"We won't be out much longer," Cedra answered. "Love you."

"I love you, too," Hank replied. He winked at Juliet. "Both of you."

"Love you, too, Dad," Juliet replied.

†

"I'm coming, Ma. Hold the door," Hank requested and followed her into the kitchen.

Ma set the empty mugs in the sink and turned for the ones Hank carried. "It warms my heart to see you interact with Juliet the way you do."

"I get the impression her family isn't close," Hank stated.

"Nor are they supportive of her lifestyle," Ma replied. "She doesn't speak of them often."

"Anyone who can make my Baby Girl as happy as she does deserve my love and admiration," Hank replied. "It pains me to think that parents can be so shallow."

"Me, too, but it happens all too often. You couldn't ask for two better young ladies, in my opinion. They are so different, but complement each other beautifully." Ma grinned. She opened the door to the dishwasher and began rinsing mugs and handing them to Hank.

Hank loaded them inside the machine and watched Ma start it. "I'm looking forward to biscuits and gravy in the morning."

"That should hold us until lunch."

"I'll see you in the morning for some coffee then," Hank answered and left the kitchen.

"Goodnight." She wiped down the counter and turned off the light.

†

445

"It's so beautiful out here," Juliet said as she stared into the night.

"There's just enough light to help you see the snow coming down. I'm glad the wind has died down some. It was wicked cold earlier."

Juliet leaned in to kiss her cheek. "Still plenty cold to keep the snow falling. I'm looking forward to making a snowman with you tomorrow."

"Me, too. Another first for us."

"Maybe one year we will go where there are feet of snow for Christmas," Juliet suggested.

"Snow or no snow, I don't care as long as I'm with you. I love you so much," Cedra replied as she looked into Juliet's eyes.

Juliet closed the distance between them and kissed Cedra passionately. She felt Cedra shiver. "Are you ready to go get warm?"

"I'm ready to be naked in your arms." Cedra grinned.

"That ought to get us warm," Juliet replied with a soft laugh. She stood and reached for Cedra.

Juliet's tender caresses turned into passionate strokes as she lay next to Cedra. Her kiss deepened to muffle the moans elicited from Cedra as her climax arrived. Cedra thrust her hips, pressing Juliet's fingers deeper inside her. She could feel her inner muscles squeezing as her world began to spin.

Cedra's body relaxed, and Juliet answered with a softer kiss. "That was intense," Juliet whispered.

"I can attest to that." Cedra was working hard to suppress a giggle. She pulled Juliet's head down for another kiss.

†

Juliet felt Cedra's hand gliding down her body and quickly captured it in hers as she broke the kiss. "I can't be quiet like you, and I don't want to wake up Hank," Juliet replied to Cedra's pout. "I'm good for now. I just wanted to give you an early Christmas present. Merry Christmas, Baby Girl," Juliet whispered. "Our first of many, I hope."

"Me, too." Cedra snuggled into Juliet. "I love you," she whispered.

"I love you, too." Juliet felt the smile grow on her face as she wrapped Cedra in her arms.

Release date March 2023

ABOUT THE AUTHOR

Ali Spooner lives in beautiful northwest Florida with several fur babies. Ali's writing began as a hobby, and with the assistance of the Affinity Rainbow Publishing team has advanced her love of storytelling to a new level.

Ali's characters are primarily everyday people, from cowgirls to psychics. Ali also has created a few supernatural characters in her paranormal series. Several of her twenty-plus books have been Amazon-rated number one choices and always include a happily ever after. Ali's hobbies include photography, reading, travel, college sports, and spending time with family and friends.

OTHER AFFINITY BOOKS

Compound Interest by Annette Mori

The kick-ass women in The Organization are back and they have their sights set on a few new recruits. Not everyone is jumping for joy at the choices, considering subterfuge is front and center in the games the new recruits have been playing.

Dani is supposed to get her happily ever after, but she's not sure what's real anymore including Candy's feelings for her. When a new enemy takes Candy captive, Dani vows to uncover the truth by insisting on going on the mission to save her. Candy is not what she seems, and that presents a new set of complications for Dani and her feelings.

The Organization continues to have challenges when those damn book magicians and book witches keep popping back in to warn them of new catastrophes on the horizon. She doesn't have time for their warnings, until their enemies intersect once again to keep them working together.

From award-winning author, Annette Mori, find out what happens in this final chapter of the combined Asset Management/Book Addict series.

Six Strings and a Dream by Ali Spooner

Cedra Tyler's dream of becoming a songwriter in Nashville was put on hold due to her mother's failing health. When the time came for Cedra to start her journey, she left her home in south Alabama with a heavy heart.

Arriving at Ma Bentley's boarding house, meeting her housemates, also fledgling musicians, she feels the warmth she was missing since leaving home.

Her housemates realize Cedra's talent as a song writer and begin to gel as a group. The pain and loss she had experienced added a layer of emotion and longing in her lyrics unusual for someone of her age.

They form a band, The Bentley's, named after Ma who is much more than a landlord to them all. Cedra falls for bandmate Juliet, and that inspires her creativity even more. Will The Bentley's achieve their dream of making it big in Music City? Has Cedra found her forever in the arms of Juliet?

Trouble in Paradise-Trophy Wives Club book 4 – Ali Spooner & Annette Mori

The gang from the Trophy Wives Club is back. This time they're taking their fun to a new and exciting location. The club's future is looking bright, and as a thank you, Lindy rewards the crew with an all-expenses paid trip to paradise over the holidays. Soon after arriving on the island, an attractive stranger catches the eye of more than one person in their tight-knit group, but Lindy is especially intrigued.

Could Angel Dubois, the owner of an all-woman financial planning company be the answer to Lindy's crushing feelings of loneliness? Along with fun in the sun, the gang navigates treacherous waters to ring in the New Year.

Georgetown Glen by Annette Mori

Lucy Manetti is positively euphoric over her recent purchase of an old ghost town. Unfortunately, she failed to consult with her wife, Bea, before buying the abandoned village. Predictably, Bea is not as enamored with transforming the ghost town into a sapphic retirement community, but Bea's love for her wife trumps her displeasure over Lucy's impulsiveness. The mature couple hires Fiona, an expert at restoring old houses, and Saville, a certified electrician, to bring the ghost town back to its glory days.

According to the adorable real estate agent who recommended the pair, Fiona and Saville have *history*. Lucy detects a spark between the two young women and decides, against the advice of her wife, to play matchmaker, bringing her beautiful niece into the mix. As the ragtag team begins their work on the old saloon, they discover a lot more than they bargained for, including ghosts, long-buried secrets, an abused golden retriever, and maybe even love.

Artist Free Zone by Annette Mori

Melissa just moved to a conservative part of Washington State. A move designed to set her and her longtime partner up for early retirement. But best laid plans go awry when her partner, Colette decides, out of the blue, their relationship isn't working for her. The only thing left to do is sob all over her beloved kitties. Vowing never to get involved, ever again, with another artist.

451

Colette is torn up about hurting Melissa. She hasn't been entirely honest about her reasons for leaving and that tears her up even further. She keeps calling to make sure Melissa is okay. Life is exciting and wonderful for her because she's met her soulmate and plans on moving to Alaska. But will Karma exact its revenge?

This is a raw and honest portrayal of love lost and love found again.

Not to mention the soothing influence of a beloved feline.

Finding her Heart by Samantha Hicks
Ellis Davis's self-imposed isolation is blown apart when a new neighbour moves in next door. Having spent the last five years working from home, shutting herself away from the world she once knew. The last thing Ellis wants, or needs, is the woman next door challenging her beliefs about herself and bringing out feelings Ellis has never experienced before.

Melissa Cole moves into her new home as a recently divorced woman, raising her young son as a single parent with the help of her parents. Melissa is instantly intrigued by her mysterious neighbour next door.

Forever Home by Ali Spooner
Nat, Marissa and Maggie survived their first winter by the ocean. Spring brings new growth, friends and unwelcome visitors to the homestead. Find out how Nat and Marissa's tiny community deal with the hazards and rewards before them, as their homestead continues to grow and prosper. Expect romance, adventure, danger, good fortune, and the odd meal or two, in this sequel to The Bee Charmer.

Disconnected by Annette Mori

Vanna has always felt like something was off with her parents, leaving her feeling oddly disconnected. She decides to move across the country and establish a new and independent life after college. On the way to her new position in Flagstaff, Arizona, Vanna meets out and proud Trey, who loves to flirt.

Trey has never forgotten the beautiful young woman she met briefly and is determined to ensure their paths cross again. Thousands of miles from home, Vanna finds out more about herself, but not her feeling of being disconnected from her parents. Will Vanna ever form the connection she desperately seeks? Does Trey's determination work out?

Darcy Comes Home by Jen Silver

After twenty-five years Darcy and Angie meet again and from the faintly flickering embers of their forbidden teenage love, a flame erupts. Family complications arise including a reluctant engagement, secret surrogacy, and a persistent ex-wife.

Villagers in Professor Darcy Belsfield's childhood home of Sycamore Haven remember her being sent away to a Christian conversion camp in Canada when her father discovered her making love to her school friend, Angie.

Angie has never married but she does have a past and some unenthusiastic plans for the future. Will the differences in their lives doom the chance of Darcy and Angie discovering if they can build a future together?

Affinity
Rainbow Publications

eBooks, Print, Free eBooks

Visit our website for more publications available online.

www.affinityrainbowpublications.com

Published by Affinity Rainbow Publications
A Division of Affinity eBook Press NZ LTD
Canterbury, New Zealand

Registered Company 2517228